Dance, Gladys, Dance

CASSIE STOCKS

Dance,
Gladys,
Dance

NEWEST PRESS

Library and Archives Canada Cataloguing in Publication
Stocks, Cassie, 1966–
Dance, Gladys, dance / Cassie Stocks.

Also issued in electronic format.
ISBN 978-1-897126-76-9

I. Title.

PS8637.T618D35 2012   C813'.6   C2011-906882-6

Editor for the Board: Anne Nothof
Cover and interior design: Natalie Olsen, Kisscut Design
Vintage crocheted doily © Elzbieta Sekowska / Shutterstock.com
Author photo: Terry Gasior

NeWest Press acknowledges the financial support of the Alberta Multimedia Development Fund and the Edmonton Arts Council for our publishing program. We further acknowledge the financial support of the Government of Canada through the Canada Book Fund (CBF) for our publishing activities. We acknowledge the support of the Canada Council for the Arts which last year invested $24.3 million in writing and publishing throughout Canada.

#201, 8540–109 Street
Edmonton, Alberta T6G 1E6
780.432.9427
www.newestpress.com

NEWEST PRESS

No bison were harmed in the making of this book.

printed and bound in Canada   1 2 3 4 5 13 12

*To all those who came before
and all those who will come after.*

She Needs The Room To Bake

I had no point of navigation but I was hell-bent on finding my way to Ordinary. I didn't know what I hoped to find on that voyage or, God forbid, at the end of it, but I knew there was nothing but bilge rats and bullshit on the course I'd been following.

I still awoke at night as if in midthought. That copy of Emerson's *Essays* . . . did Norman keep it? I'd be compelled to run downstairs to the storage room and root through the boxes I brought back from Kentucky with me. First, though, I had to rouse Ginny to find the key. Ginny tolerated these wakings only twice, and then, griping about delusional roommates, she had a copy of the key made and hung it by the condo's front door.

It's a physical deficiency you feel in the middle of the night after a breakup. *Oh shit*, you lie there thinking. *It's not the books or the brassieres — I've left my thighs in his spare closet.*

Along with my ex, Norman, and possibly some missing-in-action body parts, I'd abandoned my creative spirit in Kentucky too, left it disintegrating underneath a tree beside the Barren River (symbolically enough), buried alongside the last paintings I swore I would ever do.

Ginny had left the newspaper on the kitchen table folded open to the employment section, alongside a conspicuously placed red pen. I sat down at the table and wriggled in the chair. Ginny's condo is the Shrine to Design: titanium white walls, ebony floors, leather furniture, and none of the clocks had numbers. I could never tell what time it was, not that I had anything to be late for. The two kitchen chairs were Bertoia Wire Chairs, sans cushions. The wire frame was incredibly uncomfortable and my butt would be dented like a reverse waffle when I stood up. If the other items in the room and I were featured in a certain *Sesame Street* game, I'd be one of the things that's not like the others.

I unfolded the paper and turned past the help-wanted ads to the furniture-for-sale column. I'd be getting my own place again, someday. It didn't cost anything to look and I wanted to feast my eyes on the cost of a nice flat-bottomed kitchen chair.

Underneath the AMAZING queen mattress & box, cost over $1100, sell $495, there it was:

> BEAUTIFUL old phonograph for sale. 78 record player.
> Excellent condition. Gladys doesn't dance anymore.
> She needs the room to bake. Bring offer. Ph. 254-9885.

Now there was a woman grown earnest about life. It must be a joke. I picked up the portable phone and dialed the number. I didn't need a phonograph. (Who does, really?) I wanted to see Gladys. I imagined a woman wearing a flowered housedress, her arms covered in flour, polkaing and shaking the floor while cookies turned black in the oven. But now Gladys had abandoned dancing and turned serious about her baking, perhaps trying for a blue ribbon at the neighbourhood fair. I wanted to look at this woman, to see if she looked broken. I wanted to see how she managed to give it up.

"Hello." An old man's voice spoke on the other end of the line. Gladys was probably busy baking pies.

"Hi. I was calling about your ad in the paper."

"You're an early riser; that's good. I had people call at noon sounding like they just got out of bed. I didn't even let them see it. Do you like to read?"

"Uh, yes." What did that have to do with a record player? Perhaps Gladys had been driven to baking by her insane husband.

"Listen, could I come to see it?"

"Certainly. How about ten o'clock?"

I wrote the address down with the red pen, hung up the phone, and went back to flipping through the newspaper. It had been only two weeks since I returned to Winnipeg and moved in with Ginny, but she made it seem like I'd been lying about for months — decades even. I first met Ginny at the Paraskeva College of Art three years ago. She was excelling in Commercial Art. I was dropping out of Fine Art. I randomly circled help wanted ads and made big noises with the pages. See, Ginny? *Flip.* I'm trying to restart my life. *Flip. Flip.* Look at me go.

I'd returned to Manitoba to live as I believed a normal person lived. No more Frieda Zweig the Artist. Abstract depictment in exchange for appropriate deportment. Who was I going to be? I was more inclined towards inertia than upward mobility and didn't like most people enough to devote my life to helping others less fortunate than myself. I'd work somewhere, I thought, watch TV in the evenings, and become wholly involved in the lives of non-existent people. I'd develop my own life of quiet desperation, as Emerson's buddy Thoreau suggested the mass of men (and, presumably, women) led.

Ginny walked into the kitchen in her pyjamas. I too wore my PJs — a black Rolling Stones concert T-shirt and a pair of men's long-underwear bottoms. Classic sleepwear. Ginny wore a peacock-blue satin slip and matching robe. The *other* kind of classic sleepwear. Immense yellow Velcro rollers clung to the sides of her head. We looked at each other silently for a moment; neither of us was the dreaded Happy in the Morning species of human. She smelled like cucumber face cream and vanilla fabric softener.

"You should get a haircut today," she said. "You're a wreck."

"Good morning to you too. A wreck, huh? Plane wreck or bus wreck?" I circled another arbitrary ad.

"You know what they say — dress for success." She poured herself a coffee from the completely intimidating automatic espresso machine, which, thankfully, she pre-programmed to perk at 7:45 each morning, and sat down at the table. "Your appearance indicates the level of work you're qualified for."

I eyed her head. "This from a 1950s alien queen? Where are you going to work? The mothership?"

"Volume," she said. "The rollers lift the hair at the roots and give you volume. You can borrow them if you like."

"I'm applying at a pancake house today. My chances would be better with flat, greasy hair, don't you think?"

Ginny and I are oranges and apples, or peaches and broccoli. Hint: I'm the one that's green and fibrous. She's California classic, with bouncy blonde hair, blue eyes, a skinny little nose, and what they used to call bee-stung lips. Her lips get that way from collagen injections, which is slightly easier than sticking your face in a beehive, which I'm about as likely to do. My nose is bigger, my lips are smaller, and my eyes are brown like mud. However, Ginny envies my dimples, two craters in the middle of my cheeks that explode however slightly I smile. She can have them. They make people think I'm far friendlier than I am.

"I could make you a hair appointment with Angelico." Ginny added three drops of skim milk to her coffee and stirred, clinking the spoon against the sides of her mug.

"Last time he made me look like a brunette Dolly Parton, only missing the boobs. I prefer the long lank look." I added two sloshes of cream and three spoonfuls of sugar to my mug. I feel the same way about unsweetened espresso as I do about progressive jazz — it's hopelessly unsophisticated not to like it, but no matter how I try, I can't get my ears, or my tastebuds, around it.

"Oh, please, that was years ago. Big hair was back."

"Back from where? Hell?" I shook my head. "I'm not going."
Who knew what hairstyle had emerged from the underworld
by now?

She eyed my sleepwear with a slight pursing of her lips.
"Are you going for interviews today? Do you want to borrow
something to wear? I have a super new ecru linen suit that
would fit you."

"No — thanks," I said. "Isn't ecru a large bird? Never mind,
that's an emu."

Ginny's body type is champagne-advertisement model. All
her artificially created bumps, or lack thereof, are in the right
places. I, on the other hand, resemble an advertisement for a
nature program — *The Amazing Life of a Walking Stick Bug*. I
was born the way I am. My mother often told, probably still
tells, but in Florida, so I don't have to hear it as often, thank
god, the story of how a four-year-old cousin, upon seeing me
for the first time after my difficult birth, demanded they name
me Arrow because I was long, skinny, and had a pointed head.
My head rounded out after a few weeks but the long and skinny
remains. Ginny's swanky apparel hangs on me like I'm a scare-
broccoli. I'm also prone to spilling drinks and dripping ketchup
and I can't afford to dry clean Ginny's clothes.

She shrugged. "I've got to get ready for work. Three accounts
to close. Maybe my team will actually bring their brains today
instead of leaving them in their sock drawers or whatever the
hell they did with them yesterday." She wafted away down the
hallway to the bathroom to play with her pots of beauty voo-
doo or to sneak a peak at the *Cosmo* magazines she hid, like
pornography, underneath her perfectly rolled white towels.

Ginny called from the bathroom: "I have extra art supplies
from work in the guestroom closet if you want to paint anything."

"I told you I'm not painting anymore," I shouted back. "I'm
exchanging artistry for drudgery."

"You," yelled Ginny, "are completely asinine."

Gee, thanks. Strike four on the confidence-o-meter at only eight-something-or-other in the morning.

Ginny stopped at the table and had the last swallow of her coffee before she left. The 1950s Alien Queen had been replaced by an immaculate Corporate Chatty Cathy — a dolly dressed in Ralph Lauren career wear for the Downtown Offices. Pull her string and she'll say things like, "Let's have a meeting," "I'll have a venti skim cappuccino," and "Where the hell is my report?"

"What happened to your work?" I asked. In college, in Industrial Sculpture 207, Ginny discovered an aptitude for metalwork, creating sinuous forms of brushed aluminum. One of them stood on a white pedestal in the corner of her living room.

"I don't have time anymore, the job keeps me going twelve hours a day," she said. "But you have ten times more talent than any of the schmucks in the art department at work. I know what happened with Professor Gimlet in college and you've been having trouble with your work, but. . ."

I tapped the pen on the table. "It has nothing to do with Gimlet and I'm not having *trouble* with my work at all. I no longer have any work. Period." I began to turn the pages of the paper again. "Have a good day at work with the schmucks."

After Ginny left I took a piece of paper and made a list:

Five Steps to an Ordinary Life
1. Get a real job.
2. Stop seeing the world as a series of potential paintings.
3. Learn how to talk about the weather.
4. Do the things that normal people do.
5. Figure out what normal people actually do.

Then I got my waffle butt out of the chair, got dressed, and went outside, the piece of paper with Baking Gladys' address safely in the front pocket of my jeans. It was the sort of rainy

May afternoon that would make anyone with less ambition than Ginny want to lie in bed all day reading trashy novels, but I was inspired: Gladys would be the beginning of my normal people research.

The streets outside seemed washed of colour, a cityscape of black, white, and greys. There was a bright spot of colour on the bus, the yellow raincoat of the young girl seated across from me. A tiny violin case sat beside her, one end on the floor, the other resting against her knees. I settled into my seat and assumed the bus-riding countenance, slightly unfocused eyes, and an upright chin: I see nothing, but I know where I'm going.

I thought back to my not-terribly-illustrious musical career. I was six years old and couldn't wait to start music lessons. My piano teacher was a formidable woman with black hair and a very straight back. She was a thousand years old and, it seemed, constantly pissed off at me. She hit my fingers with a ruler if I looked down at them while playing. *Thwack.* I tried to learn, but fear froze my mind. I'd lose track of my fingers on the keyboard and stop in the middle of a piece, too afraid to look down. She would sit beside me and shake her head, ruler in hand. One day, when my mother pulled up to the house, I, in the back seat of our blue Pinto, clutching my Leila Fletcher Beginner's Piano Book (Who was Leila anyhow? God, I hated her), burst into tears and refused to go in.

But little suburban girls must take classes and, after my piano failure, the empty spot in my life marked "extra-curricular activities" or "cultural edification" was filled with tap dancing classes. I approached my hours at Ms. Telford's Academy of Dance with initial enthusiasm. Within a week, because I could never remember to keep my arms in a straight horizontal line as I turned in circles on the rehearsal floor, Ms. Telford threaded a broomstick through the sleeves of my cherished pink leotard. I practised with my arms hanging off a broomstick for the next month of classes. Frieda, the crucified tap dancer.

Dance, Gladys, Dance

For recitals and competitions, they removed the broomstick, and I was transformed into a stiff mannequin in a short sequined dress with circles of rouge on its cheeks. Smile. Smile. Show your teeth. Keep your head up. Shuffle-Ball-Change. Whose idea of art were those rigid little dollies? I never placed in a competition and my mother grew tired of sponging stinko nervous vomit off my shiny dresses. No more tapping for me.

I wanted so badly to dance, to make music, but though I tried and cried with frustration, I could not follow what they were teaching me. I could not make the leap between the lessons I took and what I felt inside.

In time, I came to believe I was hopeless and just too damn stupid to learn what they were teaching me.

The bus stopped a block away from Morning Street. I stood and gave the little girl with the violin a smile. "Good luck," I said. She turned away. Well-trained — don't talk to strangers. I got off the bus, pulled up the hood of my sweatshirt, and walked through the drizzle looking at the houses. Judging from the size of most of the homes, the district had once been genteel, but no more. The sidewalks were cracked and littered, the houses, for the most part, unkempt. Porches sagged, and many of the windows were boarded up.

The address I took from my pocket led me to 1228 Morning Street, the only house besides the house next door that looked as though it had been painted in the last twenty years. 1228 was set back farther from the street than the other houses. The outside was painted Post-it Note yellow with white trim, and there was a big wraparound porch with large wooden columns.

On the neighbouring porch, an old lady sat in a rocking chair with a motionless white cat on her lap. I smiled at her, but she didn't turn her head. She was so still, such a picture of aged contentment, white-haired and wrinkly, that I thought she might be made of papier-mâché and been placed there as an art installation. I wondered that the day's dampness didn't bother her, cause her edges to curl and warp. I climbed the steps of 1228 and rang the bell, still looking over at the old lady. I was thinking of shouting at her when the door opened.

"Hi, I'm Frieda. I called about your ad."

"Hello." The man at the front door appeared to be in his eighties. He wore a slightly wrinkled white button-up shirt and practical canvas pants held up by a pair of frayed purple paisley suspenders. His hand, when I shook it, was soft. He's a retired lawyer, I thought. No, professor. No, accountant.

The woman next door leaned forward in her chair. The cat gave a cranky meow. "Good afternoon," she yelled to the man.

"Good afternoon, Miss Kesstle," he said, inclining his head slightly.

The lady looked right past me. Snotty old thing.

"Will you be over for dinner on Sunday?" she shouted.

"Of course, wouldn't miss it," he said.

She leaned back in her chair and he gestured me through the door.

"Miss Kesstle is getting almost as deaf as Beethoven," he said as he closed the door behind us.

"But can she play the piano?"

"No, but Beethoven can," he said.

"So they say." Did the old fellow think this was news?

"It's the cat." He took my jacket and hung it on a hook, ignoring the water that dropped on the wooden floor. "Beethoven is the cat. White male cats with blue eyes are always deafer than doorknobs."

I smiled at the man. "And he plays piano, this cat?"

"He doesn't exactly play it. Just walks across the keys. Can't hear the noise he's making. Do you like experimental music? I don't care for it myself."

"Ah, I can't really say. I just moved back from Kentucky."

"Oh, yes, Kentucky," he said nodding as though that completely explained my out-of-touch musical tastes. "So, did you want to see it?" He gestured down the hallway in front of us.

"Yes, absolutely." I followed behind him, looking for Gladys in the rooms we passed.

He led me through a shabbily comfortable living room filled with overflowing bookcases, two velvet couches (one burgundy, the other blue), and a big old black vinyl recliner next to the fireplace with a side table stacked with newspapers. We went through the kitchen, in which there was, disappointingly, no Gladys. I sniffed the air but couldn't discern any lingering scent of cinnamon buns or chocolate cake.

Past the kitchen, we went up two flights of stairs in the back of the house. Framed black-and-white portrait photos covered the walls. I recognized one subject as the woman next door sitting on her porch. The picture made her look gentle and a little sad somehow.

"Someone's quite the photographer," I said.

"Thank you. I teach at the Downtown Art Centre. Are you interested in photography?"

"No. I used to paint, though."

He was getting a little out of breath by the time we reached the top of the stairs, where I could see a bedroom with sloping ceilings, hardwood floors, and two large windows, one of which threw a leaf-dappled shadow in the centre of the floor. There was an old cast iron bed, a green desk, a wooden dresser with a round mirror, a plush rocker covered in burgundy, Early Victorian Whorehouse upholstery, and several other odd bits of furniture, including, in one corner, a phonograph.

"Does it work?" I asked, walking over to it.

"What?"

He seemed quite normal for a deranged person. "The record player."

"Ah, the euphonious apparatus. Yes, quite well, if I remember correctly. I was going to move most of this stuff out, but I could leave it here. That is, if we decide we're compatible."

Nuts. "I'll give you, uh, twenty dollars," I said.

"I believe the ad said two hundred."

"Two hundred! You must be joking."

"I thought it was quite reasonable. Two hundred a month and —"

"A month? Who'd buy a phonograph for a month?"

"I haven't looked at that thing for years," he said. His eyebrows squinched up. "The *room* is for rent."

"But what about Gladys?"

"Who?"

"Gladys. She doesn't dance, she needs the room to bake."

He raised his eyebrows. "There is no Gladys here."

"You didn't put an ad in the paper for a phonograph for sale?"

"No."

"Oh, shit. Sorry. Shoot. I thought I called a phone number for someone with a 78 record player for sale. I don't really want a record player, of course, but Gladys. . . Maybe the paper got the numbers wrong or I misdialed." I'd pissed away half the day for nothing. I leaned my head against the wall.

"I'm sorry, dear, there must have been some kind of mix-up. Listen, you don't look swell." He patted my shoulder.

"Mister, I don't feel swell."

A Taciturn Old Dame

Not only had I not found a job, or even looked for one; apparently I couldn't even use a telephone correctly. Telemarketing was out as a career choice.

"Come downstairs and sit for a minute — you look like you could use a drink of something," said the old man.

In the kitchen, he took two glasses from the cupboard, left the room for a minute, and then came back and busied himself at the counter. I sat at the table, unable to believe Gladys would not appear and begin kneading bread, her feet planted solidly on the floor.

The old cupboards had been painted white. A brightly striped plastic tablecloth covered the table. A calendar with a picture of Butchart Gardens hung on the wall, the squares surprisingly filled in with notes and appointments. He had more places to go in a week than I'd been in three months. Under the calendar was a small antique telephone table. All of the furniture was antique. When the old fellow died and his relatives had a garage sale, people would snatch this stuff up. I wouldn't mind some of it myself.

"They make a lot of cigarettes in Kentucky," he said from the counter.

"I don't know about that," I said, "but they sure smoke a lot of them there."

I waited for him to bring a glass of weak lemonade, or a cup of tea brewed from a twice-used tea bag. He approached the table with two tall iced glasses.

"Here, a glass of Glornic always perks me up."

"Glornic?" It sounded like an old person's tonic; I'd probably spend the evening on the toilet.

"Gin, tonic, lemon, and a touch of grenadine. My wife Shirley used to drink it in the summertime."

He sat at the table and smiled. His round face creased like the craquelure on an antique portrait.

I lifted the glass. "Thank you."

"So," he asked, "why did you leave Kentucky?"

"Messy breakup, all that, you know how it is."

"I've never had a breakup, but I have read about them. Doctor Zhivago. Madame Bovary."

Never had a messy breakup? Good God, what had this man been doing with his life?

"What are you doing now?" he asked.

"Nothing. Staying at a friend's house, driving her insane with my slothfulness. I need to find a job, but I can't seem to bring myself to do it."

"You should try and find work that's fulfilling," he said.

Everyone's a career counsellor. "Listen, Mr. . . . ."

"Hausselman."

"Mr. Hausselman, did you ever read Emerson's *Essays*? The bit that goes, 'Your genuine action will explain itself and will explain your other genuine actions. Your conformity will explain nothing.'"

"I may have." He waved the pitcher at me.

I nodded and held out my glass. "Well, what if you're not good at anything? Or what if it turned out that you were lousy at the only thing you ever wanted to do? Can working at 7-Eleven be a Genuine Action?" I swallowed my drink.

"I suppose any work, if you approach it properly, could be

a genuine action. I think that part comes from the inside."

I sighed, picked up the pitcher, and refilled my glass. Everyone said things that sounded good but were impossible to put into practice. I leaned back in my chair and looked up at the ceiling medallion in the kitchen, what a great old house. I leaned back farther to see if there was a medallion in the hallway too. Someone was standing in the hall. The chair tipped completely over. I was on the floor. Oh, shit. He'll think I'm drunk. *I* think I am drunk. I probably should have eaten something today.

"Don't worry, it's alright," he said as he helped me up. "They don't make chairs like they used to."

"This is a very old chair, Mr. . . ." I took his hand and he turned the chair back upright. I stood and looked down the hallway. There was no one there.

"Hausselman," he said. "Even in the old days, they didn't make chairs like they used to. Here, sit back down."

I sat. "Cavemen used to sit on rocks," I said.

"Or on the ground perhaps." He went back around to his chair and sat.

"I wish I were a cavewoman," I said.

"Frieda, listen, regarding rent and your Genuine Action Problem."

"To Ralph the Rebel." I raised my glass. It was empty.

"Cheers," said Mr. Hausselman. "I have a problem too: laughed-overs."

"Laughed-overs?"

"Leftovers."

"Oh, right. Horrible things. Get green. Use up all your Tupperware. Hate 'em."

"So why don't you move in here? Perhaps in return for helping me use up my laughed-overs, I could work out a reduction in rent until you get back on your feet."

"Where would I stay?"

"The attic room I put in the paper. I've been advertising it for a few weeks, but the people so far seem a bit. . . dubious. Miss Kesstle thinks some psychopath will stab me in my sleep, but there are still nice, normal people in the world. Well, look at you, just between paths, hardly psychotic at all. It sounds like you could use a new place to stay."

He wasn't kidding. "Why are you renting the room?" I asked.

"Since my wife Shirley died, it's been too quiet in this house." He paused for a moment. "I thought by renting out a room for a reasonable price, I could help someone else out and have some company too."

I studied him. Becoming the kept woman of an eighty-year-old man with purple suspenders who thought I'd service his sexual needs in return for eating two-day-old shepherd's pie was *not* in my plan for an ordinary life.

"I'm a woman, right?"

"A cavewoman."

"No, I'm a nineties woman."

"Good for you," he said.

"I mean, we'd be *friends*, right?"

"Hopefully, yes."

"I mean *just friends*," I said.

"Well, it would be difficult to be friends and enemies at the same time, wouldn't it?" Mr. Hausselman frowned.

This was ridiculous. He obviously had no idea what I was talking about.

"Okay, there's one thing I need to know. Do you subscribe to *Cosmo* magazine?"

"No."

"All right then. I'll let you know tomorrow."

Back at Ginny's, I hung my damp hoodie on the back of a kitchen chair and went straight for the newspaper. I went through the classifieds looking for the phonograph ad. Page by page, then row by row, and ad by ad. When I realized I was looking at the Pets Give Away column, I gave up. It was as if the advertisement had never existed. But how could that be? Maybe Ginny came home for lunch and took a section of the paper back to the office at LG with her.

I was waiting by the door when Ginny came in after work. "Did you come home for lunch today?" I asked.

"No, why?" She slipped off her leather boots and wiped them with the cloth she kept in a basket in the entryway.

"I'm missing a section of the newspaper, I think."

"How did your day go? Find anything?"

"No. Well, yes. I found a place to stay. Maybe."

"Is something the matter with you?" Ginny looked up from where she was lining up her boots with the others in inspection file on the closet mat.

"I'm fine," I said, resisting the mad urge to reach over and whack the first boot to see if the others would topple like dominoes. "A little woozy from the Globnics — no, Glornics."

"The what? I thought you were going to find a job before you found a new apartment. I said you could stay here."

I leaned against the wall and twisted my hair around my fingers. "I had a few drinks with the man whose place I'm moving into, I think. But, I wasn't looking for a place; I went for a record player. I ended up there by mistake. He seems nice, though, kind of grandpa-like, and the room's only two hundred bucks a month. I'd be okay for awhile before my money runs out. I still have time to find work."

She hung up her coat, straightened the lapels, and swung the closet doors closed. "Frieda, why don't you do something sensible for once? You know how you are about living with people. You don't even know this man. He could be an axe murderer."

"No, *I'm* supposed to be the axe murderer. You should meet his neighbour, Miss Kesstle. The two of you would get along just fine."

Dance, Gladys, Dance

"What?" Ginny held up her hand. "Okay, Frieda, never mind. Do as you like. If you want to move in with some stranger, go ahead." She walked into the kitchen. I heard her sigh, then she walked back past me with my hoodie dangling from her hand like a rat she'd picked up by the tail.

"It was wet when I came in," I said. "And yes, I do want to."

"What?" She hung my jacket up, pushed her coats away from either side of it, and closed the closet door. "If you took better care of your clothes, they'd last longer."

"I buy my clothes already wrecked, so I don't have to worry."

"You're not still shopping second-hand, are you?" She wrinkled her nose. "I thought you'd outgrow that."

"Yes, I am and yes I do," I said.

"Do what?"

"I do want to move in with some stranger. Thanks for putting me up. I'll start packing tonight."

Ginny sighed a lot as I packed and ran boxes up and down the stairs but was overall less annoying than I thought she'd be — a debt of gratitude I owed to her discovering the personal ads.

"I thought they were all losers, but a woman in the accounting department is getting married next week to a lawyer she met through the personals," she said.

I was happy, not only that Ginny left me alone to go out on her whirlwind of dates, but that someone could actually find what they were looking for in the classifieds.

Later that week, I moved in with Mr. Hausselman. I didn't bring much — my CD player, my clothes, my books, and the art supplies Ginny had given me — but I left them boxed in the corner of my new bedroom. I thought I'd donate them to the Downtown Art Centre where Mr. Hausselman volunteered. Everything else I left in the storage room at Ginny's condo. If this didn't work out, I didn't want to have to pack it all again.

Mr. Hausselman made supper the first night. Breaded pork chops, creamed peas, and rice. It smelled delicious. It smelled like home. I sat at the table, hooked my feet over the rungs of the wooden chair, and tried remembering the terminology I'd memorized for number three on the Ordinary Life List: learn how to talk about the weather. Air mass, Altocumulus, Atmospheric Pressure. I wasn't prepared for a sit-down-together dinner. I'd envisioned myself eating pizza alone in my room most nights. I forked a mouthful of food in. "My mom used to cook pork chops like this," I said.

Mr. H. passed the rice. "It's one of my very limited repertoire of dishes. Are your parents in Manitoba?"

I swallowed. It was so nice to eat something I could pronounce. Not spanakopita or bruschetta primavera but pork chop. Pork. Chop. "No, they're in Florida."

"Snowbirds?"

"They migrated permanently about four years ago. My dad had an equipment dealership in Kindersley, Saskatchewan and a farm he'd inherited from Grandpa. He sold the land to an oil company and they retired and moved away." Well, there went half of my conversational topics in one fell swoop.

"Do you keep in touch with them?" he asked.

"At holidays sometimes, but that's about all. Mom sends pretty regular letters about which of her friends' daughters have become nurses, or teachers, or who had a wonderful wedding, or a gorgeous baby. Pass the butter, please. Why are careers, babies, and weddings the only measures of success?"

"Most parents want the best for their children; sometimes they just don't know what that is." He handed me the dish.

Real butter. I was in heaven. "Thanks. But can you imagine some mother out for lunch with her friends saying, 'My daughter is growing spiritually at an incredible rate,' or 'Suzy is really doing some soul-searching lately, we're very proud of her'?"

Dance, Gladys, Dance

He tilted his head. "Some parents probably wish their children did more soul-searching. However, I think, right now, you need to do what you need to do. Don't worry about other people."

"Thanks. And how much do you charge for your counseling services?"

"Free — but I can't be held responsible for any irrational happiness," he said.

"Heck of a deal."

I offered to buy the phonograph, but Mr. Hausselman refused. I travelled around the city on the bus and bought 78 records at second-hand shops: Sarah Vaughan, Eartha Kitt, Edith Piaf, and Billie Holiday.

One night, the left speaker gave a small sigh and quit. I didn't attempt to see if it could be fixed. The music sounded as though it came from far away and I preferred it that way.

It was a slow, quiet world at Mr. Hausselman's: no ringing cellphones, loud music, dishwashers, blenders, hair dryers, or air conditioners. We seemed to click, Mr. H. (as I took to calling him) and I. We both liked our space and enjoyed each other's company.

Mr. H. worked for a zillion charities and went to the Downtown Art Centre to teach photography or help out nearly every day. I spent my days wandering about the house, watching the patterns of light and shadows on the walls, reading, or taking long walks or bus rides to nowhere. I developed such a peaceable melancholy that I had no energy to look for work. I wrote my parents and asked for a "loan" to get me through a month so I could enjoy the quiet. Mr. H.'s house was, I thought, the perfect place to begin my new, ordinary life.

I lay on my bed one afternoon trying to envision myself as the woman in the conventional life, the woman with no desire to create. Where before I'd been struck dumb and motionless by a beautiful patch of sky, a swirl of water going down a drain, or the arch of an eyebrow, I would become blind to it all. I'd simply stop looking for beauty to capture and stop being captured by beauty. I'd find another way to get along. Ginny could teach me about shoe shopping.

Anyhow, why, why bother with such a fucking feeble pursuit? Why use up so much for the return of so little? And why offer up what's been sweated over and take the risk of having it disregarded, or rejected? No wonder so many artists are insane — you'd have to be crazy to keep doing it. Sanity ho! I'd find my way back. What did I have to lose besides a few glimpses of beauty in an otherwise ordinary world?

I rolled onto my side and tried to ignore the colossal emptiness expanding in my chest.

"Are you all right?"

"I am swell." I answered, then realized I hadn't asked myself the question.

I turned my head. In the old burgundy plush rocking chair sat an elderly woman I'd never met before. Her grey hair looked as though it had been chopped with a razor and hung in untidy chunks around her face. Her eyes were an almost scary bright blue; her cheekbones were high and handsome. She crossed her arms over her bosom, which was enveloped in a high-necked, long white dress with a blue and white polka-dotted apron over top. I could see bare toes peeking out from underneath the hem.

"Hullo," I said and sat up. I was not, at first, concerned with how this woman had come to be in my rocking chair, but with the fact that she'd interrupted my indefinite grieving. She smiled, nodded, and continued rocking.

Seeing as this taciturn old dame with dubious fashion sense

was in no hurry to introduce herself or explain her presence, I said, "I'm Frieda; this is my bedroom."

She looked around the room. "It's nice."

"Pardon me?"

"It's a nice room."

"Well, I'm glad you like it. If you don't mind me asking, what are you doing here?"

"I'm rocking." She gave a little more emphasis to her next push-off. "See? Rocking."

"And you are?"

"Gladys. I thought I'd give you a little time to settle in."

"Who?" An image of the classified ad that had led me to Mr. H.'s house flashed in my mind. *Gladys doesn't dance anymore. She needs the room to bake.*

"Gladys," she repeated.

"*The* Gladys?"

She raised her eyebrows a little and continued rocking.

"You can't be the Gladys, you're not baking. . . or dancing."

"No, right now I'm rocking."

"Oh," I said. I closed my eyes, but I could still hear the squeaking of the chair. This was bad. I'd advanced from frustrated artist and college dropout to *insane* frustrated artist and college dropout. What to say? "Are you a ghost?" "How did you get here?" "Are you a flashback from those three hits of acid I did on the side of a mountain in Northern BC?" "Can you walk through walls?" But what came out of my mouth was, "Do you still dance?"

She frowned and vanished. The chair still rocked slightly but she was gone. I gasped, stood, went to go downstairs, then sat back down. What would I say? Did you see a spirit from the great beyond go by? And if Gladys was a ghost, why visit me? What might she have to tell me? How to make a perfect pie crust? The steps to the foxtrot? How not to dress? I already had Ginny for that. Perhaps I'd nodded off in bed without realizing it and had just now woken up. It sounded as good as anything I could concoct on the spot. I was absolutely *not* going to add insanity to my list of flaws.

Mr. H. called up the stairs. "Time to go for supper, Frieda."

"Be right down." I shook my head, combed my hair, and took a last look around the room to make sure I was awake. Business as usual. I opened the wardrobe and looked inside. No one there. I put the copy of *Crochet Magic* magazine I bought as bribery for Miss Kesstle into my bag, started down the stairs, then came back into the room, got on my hands and knees, and peeked underneath the bed. Nothing but dust. Right. Here we go then, I told myself, it was just a nice nap. I wouldn't say anything about Gladys. Telling other people your dreams really should be the eighth mortal sin: pride, envy, anger, sloth, covetousness, gluttony, lust, and behaving as though the dream you had last night was the new Hollywood blockbuster.

Mr. H. waited by the door with his suit on. We walked out on the porch and he closed the door behind us.

"You should lock it," I said. "This neighbourhood isn't as safe as it used to be."

"I haven't locked this door in twenty years," he said. "I'm not about to start now."

"You'll be sorry if someone breaks in and makes off with all three sets of your encyclopedias."

"Big demand for them on the black market?" Mr. H. smiled and took my arm as we walked down the steps.

"Sure, haven't you heard? There's something in the ink of encyclopedias produced before 1959 that gets you stoned."

"Smoke the pages, do they?" He started up the steps to Miss Kesstle's.

"It's the new drug of choice."

The door to 1226 was locked, chained, and alarmed. A salesperson had gone through the neighbourhood last month and, as Mr. Hausselman put it, scared the bejeebers out of Miss Kesstle.

Dance, Gladys, Dance

She had the works installed: the Peace of Mind System Model 848 with all the bells and whistles. The alarm was so sensitive that Beethoven constantly set it off going in and out through his cat door. Miss Kesstle slept right through the noise and Mr. H. had to ask her for a spare key so he could go in on a regular basis and reset the system in the middle of the night.

Miss Kesstle hadn't been too happy about my addition to Sunday dinners, but as I hadn't killed Mr. H. in his sleep yet, she'd warmed to me a little. Her house gave me the creeps. It was like the cavern of a very talented and bored spider. Every available surface was covered in elaborate doilies. Surfaces impractical for doilies were swathed in plastic.

Mr. H. pushed his chair back after dinner. "That was truly egg salad, Miss Kesstle," he said.

I followed Miss Kesstle into the kitchen to help with the dishes. There were crocheted fruit baskets, potholders, and lacy curtains hung at the window above the sink. Even the dishcloth in my hand was crocheted. We waited for the sink to fill. Beethoven circled around her legs, purring and leaving white hairs poking out of her support hose like old man's whiskers. I leaned down to pet him. He hissed silently at me. I stuck my tongue out at him and straightened. "Nice cat."

"He's an angel," said Miss Kesstle. "It's sad, isn't it?"

"What's that?"

"Mr. Hausselman's brain problem. I saw a documentary about it on the educational channel."

"His what?" I wondered if she'd been smoking the pages of her encyclopedias.

"I'm not saying he's insane. It must be an organic problem. That's what the program said. It's a physical thing. Organic. . . orgasmic? No, organic. You know."

I was going through extreme facial movements to keep myself from laughing — I bit my cheeks, wrinkled my nose, and grimaced.

"Do you have gas?" she asked. "I have Pepto-Bismol if you need some."

"No, thanks. I'm fine."

"I think that's why his son never calls or visits him." She put the glasses in the sink.

"His son? Mr. Hausselman has kids?"

"Just the one. Whitman. Strange name. Did you want to wash or dry? Mr. Hausselman probably meant to say Winston and it came out wrong. He's a big muckety-muck in the movies in L.A."

Whitman. If I knew Mr. H., his son was probably named after his favourite poet, Mr. Walt Whitman. It was odd; in all our conversations he'd never mentioned a son. "I'll dry."

"I can't imagine how he manages at the deli," said Miss Kesstle.

"Who? At the deli. . ."

"You have to say what you want at the deli. Like tonight. Mr. Hausselman said supper was egg salad, but it wasn't; it was potato salad."

"He meant *excellent*," I said.

"Exactly. His brain confuses words. He calls everything by the wrong names."

I decided not to try to explain further. I agreed, "It's a tragedy. But he does manage quite well."

"I admire him greatly," she said and carried out dessert, blueberry pie, which Mr. H. later declared "arm-raising" (i.e., amazing). Miss Kesstle gave me a meaningful glance and politely agreed with him.

After we got home, I said good night to Mr. H. and cautiously entered my room. There was no one there.

Heavy

When I was growing up, my family had stacks of yellow *National Geographics* in a bookshelf in the family room. I butchered them for elementary school reports, gluing photos of Mayan artefacts on loose-leaf pages, next to my pencilled words. When I was nine, looking for pictures of Spain for a social studies report, I came across a photo of Pablo Picasso's painting of Dora Maar. She was like nothing I'd ever seen. I sat on the green linoleum floor (which my mother referred to as battleship linoleum because it lasts forever — as if that was a good thing), held the magazine open in my lap, and stared at the photo. I had no idea who Picasso was, but I knew that painting, that style, those colours, in my bones. Dora's face was wrong; it was orange, with stripes of green and white. Her nose tilted over to one side, her eyes were too big, and her ear was a piece of macaroni. Shapes of colour formed her clothes: purple, black, blue, and the background just two flat panels of orange. She was as ugly as heck, but she was powerful. She looked like I felt.

I began to make drawings of people's faces from my mother's *Chatelaine* magazines. I tried to draw what I felt from them instead of their outside appearance, as I thought Picasso had done with Dora Maar. Not so easy using women from shampoo ads. I had a little tin box with circles of watercolour paint and I tried to paint the portraits in colours like Picasso's, but I couldn't get them bright enough. The loose-leaf paper would begin to disintegrate, leaving rolled-up bits of pulp stuck to my brush.

My mom mentioned my interest in art to our next-door neighbour, Mrs. Hernd, during coffee one day, and Mrs. Hernd invited me over to her house to paint with her. Mrs. Hernd was not at all my idea of a painter. Her grey-brown hair was frizzed up from the Toni perms my mom gave her at our kitchen table and she wore giant velour caftans everywhere, even out to the grocery store. She was even older than my mother was (not to mention rounder and plainer). She had a painting studio in her upstairs spare bedroom between the main bedroom and the bathroom. It had been her daughter's bedroom before she moved away. The easels and paintings seemed out of place with the ruffled purple curtains on the window and the beige shag carpet covered with thick plastic runners.

Mrs. Hernd taught me how to clean my brushes, how to be patient and not muddy an area by overworking it before it dried, and how to thin the paints and not use up great gobs of the supplies she had to ask her husband for money to buy — a husband who smoked cigars, but complained ad nauseam about the smell of the turpentine and oil paints. Mrs. Hernd and I would stand side by side in the little room and paint in silence, our hair flying in the breeze of the fan she kept running to cut down the smell. Mrs. Hernd's favourite subjects were old buildings on the verge of collapse. I didn't quite get it. "To each her own," she would say, looking at the flamboyantly coloured faces I produced.

I did family portraits, my mother and father with green hair and blue faces. My mother had them framed and hung them in the laundry room.

The more I painted, the more I wanted to paint. The more I learned, the more I wanted to learn. My mind filled with pictures, ideas, and plans for my next great works.

While I was painting, I was growing up — not perfectly, but

inevitably. Painting gave me someone to be, an identity, bonus enough during my turbulent teen years, but I wanted more. Mrs. Hernd was lovely, but the thought of ending up like her sent me to the depths of teenage despond. I grew, I graduated from high school, and I waited for my big chance.

It came when the local tavern booked the Bang Howdy Band for a week. The Bang Howdy Band traveled in a former school bus painted a chalky shade of blue with half the seats taken out to make room for the gear. They churned out covers of seventies hits and, one night, between sets, following a rousing rendition of "Smoke on the Water," I hooked up with the blond bass player, Geordie Davies.

Four nights into their booking, Geordie and I lay naked in the single bed in the Motel 88. I was wrapped in a scratchy grey blanket. Geordie lay uncovered beside me, smoking a cigarette and looking up at the ceiling.

"Band pulls out tomorrow," he said.

"Oh? Where're you off to?" I asked. I gently stroked his stomach, dipping my fingers in and out of the well of his belly button.

"Edmonton. Do you want to come?" He continued staring at the ceiling.

"No thanks," I said. "I think I just did."

He laughed and rolled over facing me. "I'd miss this," he said. He reached his arms around me and grabbed my ass with both hands.

It was so romantic I nearly died.

I didn't tell my parents of my plans until the day I was going, frightened they might convince me to change my mind. Geordie parked the band bus in the driveway. My red plaid suitcase of clothes and my paintbox sat packed and waiting on the floor beside my bed.

Mom and Dad sat at the kitchen table. I took Geordie in and

Dance, Gladys, Dance

he awkwardly shook hands with them. I told them that I was leaving, gave them Geordie's phone number in Vancouver, and explained that we wouldn't be there because the band was on tour.

My mother looked confused, torn between freaking out and not wanting to freak out in front of this long-haired man she might have to call her son-in-law.

"Well," said my father. "You're an adult now, aren't you?"

I nodded. I hadn't expected this quietness. I'd been counting on scenes and arguments like the three of us had been having for the last four years. I was counting on that anger to expel me from the house. I went to the bedroom to get my things. When I walked back into the kitchen, my mother was still sitting at the table, staring at the window above the sink. Her hands were wrapped around her coffee cup and I could see her fingers turning white and red with pressure.

This was freedom. This was the great escape. I felt my chest collapsing. "I'll call you when we get to the next booking."

She didn't even turn to look at me. I picked up my things and walked down the hallway. My dad stood on the front steps. Geordie was in the driveway moving things around in the bus.

"If we said you couldn't go, would you stay?" asked my father at the door.

I shook my head. He pressed some money into my hand and then grasped me in a half-hug and patted my back too hard.

"Even artists have to eat, Frieda," he said and turned away. I wasn't worried about money. I'd soon be a famous artist, sending Mom and Dad away on tropical vacations with the proceeds from my New York shows. Edmonton was a long way from New York and also in the wrong direction, but it was out. That was the first step, no matter the geographical point of the compass.

I turned to wave at my father, but he'd already gone back inside and closed the door.

"Heavy," said Geordie, as we backed down the driveway.

Now, here I sat, years later, at the desk in Mr. H.'s study with a pile of T-4s, scraps of calendars, and pink slips in front of me, working on my résumé — expanding and renaming jobs. I decided on "Retail Consultant" for the year I'd spent in Kentucky. Norman's mother, Lady March, and I had done a lot of shopping together, so I used her name as a reference. If a potential employer did call, they'd be so confused by the aura, star sign, and past life information Lady March would give them they'd never notice if she didn't mention me as an employee.

The study was in the back of the house off the kitchen. The desk was a massive old oak teacher's desk; built-in shelves held teetering stacks of books and a small stereo on which Mr. H. listened to symphonies while he wrote diatribes to the newspaper about the government's lack of social conscience. There was also an armchair that matched the blue velvet couch in the living room but had a large hole in the seat. Topography maps in all textures and stunning jewel-tone colours covered the walls. Modern art with no effort at all.

The maps dated back to Mr. H.'s job as a photogeologist with the provincial government, which he informed me involved analyzing aerial or orbital photographs for lithologic geological features. Whatever that meant. He'd retired at sixty-five. Thirty-five years at the same job.

The old wooden office chair swiveled, rocked, and creaked wonderfully. I took a break and spun around for awhile, imagining I was that writer, Dorothy Parker, whose book Mr. H. had lent me.

If I should labor through daylight and dark,
Consecrate, valorous, serious, true,
Then on the world I may blazon my mark;
And what if I don't, and what if I do?

And what if I don't, and what if I do?

"I hear they have a dance called the two-step now."

I went cold. Gladys, the ghost woman, or whatever the hell she was, sat in the armchair between the bookshelves. She wore the same floor-length plain white dress, but this time a blue silk scarf was wrapped around her head like a turban. Without her weird haircut showing, she looked almost normal — a beautiful old lady who dressed like it was the 1900s. Her hands were folded in her lap and she was smiling. I looked away and began to clean up the papers on the desk, shuffling them into manila folders. I was *not* going to interact with madness.

"Can you do it? Couldn't be hard. Only two steps and all. Can you hear me? Hellooo?" she said.

"Don't talk to me. I don't want you to speak to me. You're freaking me out." I gathered my folders and stood.

"Freaking out. That sounds bad," she said.

"It is. Trust me." I hesitated behind the desk, the papers held against my chest. I wanted to leave but didn't want to walk past her. What if she grabbed me?

"Why don't you trust me?" she said.

I could think of a thousand reasons, beginning with the fact that trusting hallucinations was never a good idea. "All right. What do you want?"

"I have a story to tell you and then there's something you need to do."

"You want me to do something?"

She nodded.

"Well, get in line, lady," I said. "You and everyone else. What is it?"

"Let's start with the story."

"Will you tell me and then leave?"

"Certainly." She settled deeper into the blue velvet chair. I wondered for a second if she'd emerged from the hole in the seat and perhaps might sink away back down into it. She remained where she was.

"All right, then. . . shoot," I said.

"Shoot? I don't have a gun. They're dangerous, you know."

If I was going schizo and she was some fractured aspect of my personality, parts of me were definitely thick.

"Are you a ghost?"

"I'm not the tooth fairy, if that's what you thought." She reached up and adjusted her turban.

"Fine, just tell me the damn story."

"Now you're being rude," she said. "Perhaps I'll start another time when you're not so cross."

"I am not *cross*. I'm losing my ever-freaking-loving mind. Shit." Too much. Assembling the résumé from hell that showed the world what a screw-up I'd been my whole life and now some ghost or demented vision telling me I had to *do something* and calling me rude. Everything welled up from the pit of my stomach into my throat, and, to my surprise, I began to cry.

"There, that's what you need to do. Have a good cry. You'll feel better. I'll come back later." She disappeared.

I dropped the folders, kicked over the metal garbage can beside the desk, collapsed into the office chair (causing it to give an alarming squeak), put my head on the desk, and wailed. I cried for what felt like an hour, pausing only to swear. Then I stopped, stood, and began to pick up the garbage I had kicked over.

"Frieda, I'm home. Come see what I bought." Mr. H.'s voice boomed through the house.

I threw the last crumpled piece of paper back in the garbage can, wiped my nose on the sleeve of my sweatshirt, and went into the kitchen. On the table sat four cardboard flats of blooming flowers. Petunias, I thought, a mixture of red, white, pink, and peach. Mr. H. stood by the table wearing his usual white shirt, canvas pants, and suspenders, but he had on big green rubber boots with yellow laces up the front.

Dance, Gladys, Dance

"They're nice," I said, fingering a leaf. "What are you going to do with them?"

"Are you all right? You look a little peaked," he said.

"I'm fine. Working on my résumé gave me a bit of a headache. Cool boots, by the way. Are you allowed to wear them in the house?"

"I'm going to plant," he said. "Come outside. I have a trowel with your name on it."

"I don't think so. I'm kinda beat."

"Come on. A little dirt up your nose will make you feel better. Shirley always had the yard looking so nice. I'd like to get it going again." He picked up two of the flats and started out. I picked up the other two and followed him, too exhausted to protest.

"Watch your step," he said, as we went down the front porch stairs into the yard. "The board on the bottom is loose."

At some point, he'd cleared and spaded the flowerbeds. I hadn't even noticed.

"Haven't you planted since Shirley died?"

"I tried the year after, but I put in some sort of purple flower that damn near took over the entire yard. I had to dig it out after it crossed the fence and got into Miss Kesstle's roses." He looked around and lowered his voice. "She threatened to call the Noxious Weed Police on me."

It did feel good to be outside digging in the dirt. My knees pressed into the grass. I took one tiny plant after the other, dug a hole, and placed it in the ground. Mr. H. came along behind me with an old metal watering can. The rich, heavy smell of the wet earth was soothing.

It was getting dark when we finished. Mr. H. gathered up the tools and the little plastic pots. I followed him to the garden shed; it had been a chicken coop once, the ancient boards a soft weathered grey. Mr. H. spent a lot of time working on the shed, propping it up, and trying to keep it intact.

I stood outside and listened to the sounds of the evening city, a radio playing a French station, children in the park down the street. Then I heard a strange sound, from right behind me. Clapping. The sound of one person clapping — one person clapping, not one hand. There was nothing Buddhist about it. I glanced around, but no Gladys. There was no reason for the sound to be so frightening; after all, it wasn't frantic screaming or a chainsaw roaring. Still, a shudder ran from my lower spine all the way up to my neck. Then, as suddenly as it started, it stopped. Mr. H. emerged from the shed.

"Do you believe in ghosts?" I asked.

"Ghosts? I don't know." You could trust Mr. H. to take any topic of conversation in stride. "I always assumed Shirley would come back and see me if she could. She never has, but I hear her voice inside my head sometimes."

"Saying what?"

"Things like 'Are you sure an electric egg poacher is really practical?'" He put the rest of the tools inside the shed. "You can store some of your things in here if you like. There's an old Chevy in the back shed you can use if you need to drive anywhere. I haven't used it in a few years, but I keep the insurance going on it just in case."

"Thanks." We walked side by side back to the house. The streetlights had come on, and long dark shadows appeared on the lawn.

"Miss Kesstle told me you have a son."

"I do," he said softly. "Whitman. He lives in Los Angeles."

I turned toward Mr. H. and wanted to paint him as he looked at that moment, his face blue twilight, his hair silver, with a background of leaves and shadows. I shook my head, trying to clear it like a mental Etch A Sketch. I didn't want any pictures forming on that screen.

"You see him much?"

"No. We're not close. Shirley and I were older when we had

Dance, Gladys, Dance

him. We were selfish. Or I was. I didn't want to share her with anyone."

"But you loved him when you had him?" I could see moths fluttering around the front porch light as we turned the corner of the house.

"I thought I did. Not enough, I suppose. I was wrapped up in Shirley, and work, and my pictures. . . I've been trying to make it up to him for years. I'd like to be closer to him but. . ."

"But?"

"But you can't always get what you want," he said.

"The Stones made out pretty well, though."

"Ah yes, to be igneous and ignorant of it. The stones have it easy."

I smiled in the darkness.

"He didn't come to see Shirley before she. . . went. I called him, but perhaps I wasn't clear about how bad things were. He came to the funeral, but without Shirley there as a bridge between us, things just got worse and more awkward."

As we walked into the kitchen, he put his hand on my shoulder. "How about you? Are you sure you're all right? Do you want to have a cup of tea and talk awhile? My crossword puzzle can wait."

"Not right now — I have some things to figure out first." Like how quickly and for how long I'd be locked away if I told anyone about my ghostly hallucinations.

"Good night," I said as I climbed the stairs to my room. "I'll be job hunting again tomorrow."

He folded the newspaper open. "Good for you. 'Night. Don't let the head-thugs fight."

The Dominant Oblique Direction

I believed my bright and shining future had begun when I was eighteen and Geordie backed the band bus down my parents' driveway. Travelling with a rock band wasn't a show in a New York art gallery, but it was metaphysically closer to it than a day shift at donut shop, or so it seemed at the time. To celebrate my new life on the road, I did a series of dead rock star paintings with psychedelic celestial backgrounds.

The other band members had obviously never heard of groupies. They thought my travelling with them cramped their style; old ladies should be left at home. The drummer took to walking out of any room I walked into. Drummers are, of course, notoriously over-sensitive. I painted all the cooks from the hotel restaurants with fried egg eyes. I would have been the Yoko Ono of the Bang Howdy Band if Geordie had chosen me instead of his bandmates, which he didn't. We broke up after a year somewhere in northern BC. The bus ride back to Saskatchewan took forty-six hours.

I got a cheap apartment in Saskatoon where I waitressed and let my hair grow long. My parents left Kindersley and moved to Florida. I think they hung around for awhile, hoping for a wedding before they left, but after seven years of a different fellow every Easter, Thanksgiving, and Christmas dinner, they gave up and went.

CHAPTER FOUR

Seven years may seem a long time, but it passed like nothing; time flies when you're doing sweet fuck all. I lived in a strange sort of non-space during those years. I was intelligent and knew it vaguely, but it didn't seem to matter. There seemed nowhere to go with it, nothing to do with the ideas that drifted around in my head. I could not imagine myself as either nurse or doctor. I could not imagine myself as wife or mother. I could not imagine myself as anything except an artist and I had no idea how to get there.

I paid the rent on time most months by working a series of jobs: a waitress here, a clerk there, a dead end everywhere. I set up easels in spare corners and worked throughout the craziness of fellow drifters and the demented situations that too much partying and too many unstable personalities bring. Painting kept me going. It was the one thread that never changed in the crazy quilt of my life. Even when I had no idea where I was (and there were days like that), I knew where my latest painting was. When I didn't know who loved me, I knew what I loved: my art. The painting kept me steady, gave me something to hold onto, a purpose in life besides the next big party. Still, I was far from the fame and fortune I'd imagined before I left home. I worked my ass off, but was I even an Artist? How did you know and what gave you the right to declare yourself one? Was twenty-four old enough? Of course, Basquiat had already painted all his great works and died by his late twenties. Now *that* was a depressing thought. Or maybe a certain amount of money had to be earned from your art before you became credible. I looked up galleries in the Yellow Pages and gathered up a few of what I thought were my best paintings.

I had to take the bus, so I chose three small paintings that I wrapped and placed in my backpack.

The gallery had a large front of glass. On the entrance in gold script were the words *Felinchi's Gallery*. I pushed open the door and wandered around looking at the paintings on the walls. It was so quiet you could have heard a nose-hair drop. I wondered if I'd chosen the wrong gallery. If it were always this empty, I'd never sell anything. Massive modernist paintings, in frames of ornate gold or simple black, filled the walls. I stood in front of a huge impressionistic painting of an old woman on a park bench. It made me want to weep and tear at my hair, it was so good. The woman, her face, her clothes, her bags, and the bench were solid, sombre shades of grey and burnt umber. The park, the people, the world behind her swirled in a kaleidoscope of colour. The expression on the woman's face was not exactly sadness. I couldn't find the word for it at the time, but a few years later, I'd be able to place it as resignation. I moved closer to read the artist's name on the small typed card on the wall when I heard the click-clack of high heels on the floor behind me. I didn't see the name, but I did read the price — $8,525.00. Holy shit. I turned. A woman in her thirties stood with one hand on her hip. She wore a slim black skirt, a quilted black vest, and a white turtleneck. Her blonde hair was up in a bun with what looked like red chopsticks sticking out of it.

"Can I help you?"

"I was wondering if. . ." I took the knapsack off my back.

"Sorry, but I'll have to ask you to check your bag. Theft, you know."

"Oh no. I brought you some paintings to look at." I gestured at the walls. The knapsack banged against my knees.

"Did you have an appointment?"

"No." I eyed the door, ready to bolt, but then she'd probably think I had stolen something and call the cops.

"It's normally done by appointment only, of course. But let's have a quick look."

Thank God. I followed her to a small room behind a counter at the back. She gestured to a table in the centre of the room.

As I unwrapped a painting, I realized the towels I'd used as coverings looked pretty grotty. One was spotted with purplish stains from when I'd briefly dyed my hair black, and all of them had holes and strings hanging off the edges. Note to self: Buy new towels to wrap paintings in.

She took the first one I uncovered and held it up. It was Jimmy Wong from the fried egg eye cook series. I'd painted him sitting formally, his hands folded in his lap, wearing a cerulean blue mandarin jacket. The background was Chinese red wallpaper with a repeating pattern of blue and white sauce-pans and dragons.

"Hmmm," she said and looked at me. I tried to appear as artistic as possible while holding my breath. She was slightly pleased, I thought. I heard the front door open and footsteps cross the gallery. A portly man in a black suit entered the room. The lady put the painting down. The man nodded at her and she nodded back.

When she looked back at me her eyes held something different. "And your training?"

"My training?" I imagined myself doing push-ups on the floor in front of my easel.

"Do you have any formal art training?"

"No. But I've been working really hard." I started to unwrap another painting; "This is of a woman who lived in an apartment beside me. I think it's one of my best."

The man by the door cleared his throat. "The people from McKinley Design will be here in. . ." He looked at his watch. ". . .three minutes."

The lady stood. "Well, thank you for bringing these in, but I'm afraid they don't quite meet the. . ." She glanced at the man. ". . .standards we have at Felinchi's." She walked out of the room and the man in the suit followed her.

I packed the paintings back up and walked through the gallery. The man and woman stood in front of a large painting. The woman held a clipboard and wrote down what the man said. As I went out the door, one of the backpack straps caught on the door handle. My hands shook and I couldn't get the strap untangled. I was afraid I'd dump the contents. There were tampons, safety pins, and linty mints rolling around in the bottom of it. I'd die if it all went scattering across the white gallery floor. The lady turned and walked over to me. She unhooked the backpack strap and whispered in my ear. "Your paintings are good. Go to school. Don't give up." Then she walked back over to the man.

I exited, took a deep breath, caught the bus to the library, and researched art schools. Over the next week, I prepared a portfolio, crossed my fingers, took a lot more deep breaths, and, at the grand old age of twenty-five, applied to the Paraskeva College of Art in Winnipeg, Manitoba.

The day I got the acceptance letter in the mail, I whoo-hooed until my voice was hoarse, broke up with my current boyfriend, and began packing.

I moved into a dorm room on campus and, on the first day, wrote in big black letters on the inside cover of my binder, *Paintings have a life of their own that derives from the painter's soul. — Vinnie Van Gogh.* The campus of Paraskeva wasn't large, but I still found myself lost almost every day. I'd arrive in class fifteen minutes late, breathless and disheveled, trying not to meet the eyes of the cool cucumbers already in their seats. I thought art school would be a huge community of freaks like me. I wasn't prepared for the divas, the careerists, the competition, or the striving, striving, striving. I'd spent so many years with pipeliners, burnt-out musicians, and café cooks that I wasn't sure how to talk to my shiny-faced classmates. My marks were good, but I was overwhelmed by all there was to learn and my inability to absorb it all. The other students seemed to know everything already, all the names of the famous painters, all the styles, schools, and techniques. I wondered if they were *real artists.* I felt like an amateur. They all seemed poised on the edge of greatness. I teetered on the window ledge of a

Dance, Gladys, Dance

high-rise, inside of which was the life I wanted. On the walls of that room hung the paintings I desperately wanted to paint. Off the ledge was more of the same life I had been living; the same people, the same parties, the same hangovers, the same dreams one always talked about but never got any closer to.

Professor Gimlet taught Design Fundamentals 108, Thursday afternoons at one o'clock. He was older, maybe in his late forties, but he had a wonderful, wild mane of red hair that suggested deep emotion and sophisticated bohemianism. He wore jeans, impeccably cut blazers, and crisp cotton dress shirts unbuttoned low enough to show his sexy, hairy chest. He'd stride about on the platform waving his arms as he lectured. He seemed more like a conductor than an instructor and we all sat upright in our seats waiting for his hand to point to us — to take our turn in the piece he guided.

"The first principle of design, Matthew?" His arm would sweep out, point at the chosen student, and rest on him or her until the correct reply was given.

"Balance."

Gimlet would give a quick nod and then another flourish. "The other principles, Ginny?"

"Proportion. Rhythm. Emphasis. Unity." His hand would beat along with the answers, fingers opening and closing like someone making a shadow bird on a wall.

Rumours passed from behind student canvases that he'd once held a position at a prestigious American college, but had been let go for transgressions that, according to the gossip, ranged from drug use to theft to an inability to get along with his colleagues, to (notwithstanding his lovely faculty wife) sex with students. I hoped the latter was the truth.

My voice quavered when I answered the questions Professor Gimlet asked me in class. Once I spat a wad of gum right out of my mouth onto my desk as I tried to articulate the principles of two-point perspective. I didn't want to be the sour note in his orchestra of answers. I wanted him. I needed him to escape that teetering ledge I stood on. He would teach me one-on-one what I needed to know about art. I would be his protégée and his muse, inspiring him to artistic heights he'd not yet reached. We would become famous together. He would be the maestro of my next great escape.

I took to waiting beside his desk after class and asking awkward theory questions endlessly planned and rehearsed the night before. I'd stand, nod, and smile at his answers, wondering what it would be like to lie in bed beside him. Once class was over, I seemed invisible to him, another face in the shuffle of students filling and emptying the desks each week.

In my second semester, I had another class with him, Advanced Design 231. About a month after this set of classes started, Professor Gimlet finally saw me. Before I walked up to his desk, I'd unbuttoned my green plaid shirt almost to my navel (three buttons lower than he wore his) and I'd left my bra in the dresser drawer in my room. The classroom was empty. It was so quiet I thought I could hear the ticking of the big round clock way up on the wall. He shuffled papers into his briefcase.

I leaned against the desk. "Professor Gimlet? I wondered if I could ask you some questions about the dominant oblique direction you mentioned in regards to relating design elements."

He sighed slightly and lifted his head. His eyebrows rose at the sight of my bare skin. His eyes traveled up to my face and met my eyes with the same silent question I'd been asked by men in barrooms since I was eighteen. By then, at twenty-seven, I knew how to answer yes with nothing but a small smile.

"Well, Frieda," he said, his eyes travelling back down and coming to rest above my belly button. "One of the most important things an artist can do, beyond all this theory, all the elements of design, is to experience life." He looked around the classroom, up at my face again briefly, and then began to slowly run his finger up and down my arm.

I held onto my breath and the edge of the desk.

His fingers were long and his nails perfectly shaped. I'd never been with a man with hands more attractive than mine. You were lucky to find a pipeliner who still had all his fingers, never mind a manicure. "Do you think you want to experience life?" he asked.

I nodded, unable to speak. The bell for the next class rang and I jumped a little. His smile twisted at the corners as though he'd taken a bite of something slightly sour.

"I'm working on a series of drawings of Hindu gods and goddesses for a book," he said. "Do you think you'd like to pose for me?"

"I'm not Hindu." Brilliant, I thought. "Yes" might also have been a good answer.

"It's the body form I need. The faces will be modelled on ancient drawings." He circled his fingers around my wrist.

I couldn't think. Visions of Eastern gods flew around in my head. "It's not the elephant, is it? What's its name?"

"Ganesh? No, I was thinking of Durga," he said. "The goddess Durga."

When a man tells you he wants to model a goddess after your body, it's hard to resist. I didn't know then that Durga had eight arms.

The Gimlet Portraits

And so it had begun. I posed for Professor Gimlet once as Durga in a hotel room for about ten minutes with my arms raised in prayer above my head, before other, more imperative matters took over. He never had me pose for him again, at least not for any artistic purposes. We had four months of awkwardness in class, hurried phone calls, and meetings in seedy motels. The only good thing about the motel rooms we met in were the grim paintings on the walls. We made up names for them: Rigor Mortis Mountain Range, Bridge Over Putrid Waters, The Ruptured Metropolis.

For the first time in my life, I became obsessed with my appearance, terrified that one day Professor Gimlet would look up and realize I wasn't attractive enough. My bathroom came to resemble a cosmetics counter in a downtown department store. It was during this wannabe-diva phase that I cultivated a friendship with Ginny. She became my beauty advisor.

Did I imagine Gimlet would leave his wife for me? Of course I did. Did I care about her — this shadowy figure who kept him from me? Not really. I wanted what was best for him, and that was me. I'd soon be going to gallery openings and swanky parties with him. I'd join cultured society. The lovely young artist, Frieda Zweig, arrives on the arm of suave Professor Gimlet. What a beautiful couple they are.

When I did paint, it was portraits of him: Gimlet in Repose, Post-Coital Gimlet, Gimlet the Marauder. I spent hours on them. Where John William Waterhouse had placed beautiful women in flowing gowns, I put Gimlet with flowing hair in medieval tunics. I thought the paintings were incredible, filled with longing and passion, but I certainly couldn't turn them in for marks. I didn't show them to Gimlet either. I planned to show them to him as a surprise, after we moved in together — a testament to how much I cared for him. I'd have a gallery show one day: *Frieda Zweig: The Gimlet Portraits.*

I imagined both of our paintings on the walls of the mental apartment I'd decorated for the two of us, in a downtown high-rise. I had an amazing red lacquer and gold leaf cabinet already picked out from a boutique on King Street. The high-rise apartment was, of course, a precursor to the Victorian home with two studios in the back that we would move into later after we tired of life in the fast lane.

However, I, as the lovely young artist, had given up working on my own assignments for school. I'd sit at the wobbly faux-wood desk in my dorm room, full of good intentions, with sketchpad and precisely sharpened pencils in front of me. Minutes later, I'd be lying flat out on the single bed, staring up at the speckled ceiling tiles, deep in the fantasyland I'd created of my future glamourous life. My grades and attendance began to fall until I was in danger of being suspended.

I told Professor Gimlet about my academic standing one afternoon in Room 12 of the Clover Leaf Motel. We'd already made love and sat together on the edge of the bed. The hard afternoon light shone through the pilly blue polyester curtains on the window, making the skin on our naked bodies seem pale and thin. He kissed his way up my arm.

"You're failing?" He dropped my arm.

"Well, we have been rather busy." I leaned my head on his shoulder and drew circles on his thigh with my fingernail. One of a set of long red fingernails applied and painted by Ginny the night before. She insisted men found them sexy. They made me feel like some sort of mammalian digging creature, like a vole, but it seemed Ginny had been right — until now.

"Have you told your parents?"

"About us?"

"*No.* You haven't told them about us, have you? About failing?"

"I suppose I will have to eventually."

He pushed my hand away. "You can't blame this on me."

I sat straight up. "I'm *not* blaming you."

He stared at me as if he couldn't quite recognize me. "You're not pregnant, are you?" he asked.

"Where the hell did that come from?"

He ran his hands through his hair. "Are you certain you want to go to art school?"

"What?" My head was spinning.

"Maybe you could do something else — hairdressing or something. It would take the pressure off us."

"Did you just say hairdressing? In case you've forgotten, I'm an artist."

He rolled his eyes. "Oh, right — an artiste. Your marks don't reflect any particular talent." He got up from the bed and pulled on his jeans. "Maybe this wasn't such a good idea."

My carefully constructed and endlessly detailed future life exploded right in front of me. I was certain I felt fragments of martini glasses puncturing my skin.

"Don't you care about me?" What a fucking dumb thing to say.

"Frieda, Frieda," he said. He reached over and patted me on the head. I shook his hand off. Who did he think he was? Patting me on the head while I sat there, naked, still leaking his cum?

He began to gather his things, getting down on his hands and knees on the brown carpet to retrieve his socks from under the side table. "You knew what this was when it started. This isn't going to get messy. I can tell you that. I'm not giving anything up."

I felt thoroughly messy already, about to become messier, if I actually vomited like I felt like doing.

"I never asked you to give anything up." I said. I just thought he would.

He quickly put on the rest of his clothes. We were supposed to have at least three hours together this afternoon.

"Are you leaving?" I asked.

"What does it look like?"

The room seemed to be shrinking and expanding. I couldn't fathom how we'd gone from our glorious future together to "you knew what this was." It never occurred to me that I had the imagination to make the whole thing up, that he in no way felt the same way about me as I felt about him. I pulled a sheet free from the knotted tangle on the bed and wrapped it around me.

"*And* you don't think I'm an artist? You think I should be a fucking hairdresser?" My voice rose an octave with everything I said.

He sighed from the mirror by the door where he stood adjusting his shirt collar. The *Ruptured Metropolis* painting hung on the wall beside him, the high-rise buildings dripping down in black globs.

"Do you want the truth, Frieda?"

I nodded.

His mouth moved in the reflection. "Are you sure?"

"Yes, I'm sure. I'm not a child."

"Your work is competent, but not above average. I don't think you're doing Paraskeva College any favours by staying there." He came back to where I still sat on the edge of the bed. He took my face and tilted it up to his.

"You are, however, one hell of a fuck. But don't tell anyone I told you that."

He walked to the door. "I'll maybe try and call you later this week," he said. He paused for a moment, like an actor who'd forgotten his lines. His mane seemed bedraggled and limp.

In a fleeting moment of compassion, before I began to despise him forever, I realized he'd been playing a part for me as much as I'd played a role for him. I was the proverbial lovely young thing, fresh-faced and eager for the experience and he the suave pedagogue dominated by his virility. I wasn't the role I'd played and I doubted he was either. I wondered who he really was, what made him behave as he did. I wondered if I'd known him at all.

"By the way," he added, "those press-on nails make you look cheap." He closed the door softly behind him.

He didn't call. I didn't go to any classes the next week. I stayed in my room and stared at the phone, willing it to ring. I never heard from him again. I waited another week and then I moved out of the dorms and never went back to school. I didn't think I had the stamina to screw my way to above-average standing.

Gimlet was a prominent art professor from a design college and part of me believed that everything he said about my talent, or lack of it, was true. Who else was there to believe? Mrs. Hernd in her giant polyester caftans in the spare bedroom studio? She hardly seemed authoritative. Besides, Gimlet had been right about the press-on nails.

Gimlet's damning assessment of my talent rattled me. I continued painting but when I finished each piece, all I could see were flaws and inadequacies. Fair. Below average. I'd put a large black slash across each canvas and stack it in the closet. When I ran out of canvases, I whitewashed them all and began the whole process again. I didn't talk to anyone and rarely left the basement suite I'd moved into. I had a bit of money left from my student loan and I was determined I would create something worthwhile before the money ran out. I'd prove him wrong.

I didn't. The harder I tried to prove something, the worse the paintings got. I stayed up for days smoking, drinking coffee, and painting until I could barely see the canvases. Nothing. It was all shit.

Soon I no longer aspired to paint something worthwhile; I just wanted to stop wanting to paint at all, but I couldn't completely stop then. I didn't know *how* to stop. If I weren't Frieda Zweig the Painter, who would I be? What would I do? Starting with the flamboyant portraits I'd painted with Mrs. Hernd, colour had become my language of understanding, of truth. With artist's eyes, I saw the world as something I could recreate in my own colours, and, by doing so, comprehend it. Without that sight, or if I had been wrong about it, I might as well be blind. How would I know where I was?

One of the paintings I did in the basement suite after Gimlet was of the goddess Durga. I'd gone to the library and found out that she was the destroyer of all evil. I painted a picture of her spearing Gimlet from the back of the tiger she rode. It looked too weak, as though she might be helping him up with the point of her spear. I added more gore until the canvas made me feel sick to look at it and then I gave up and painted it over.

I was in that in-between place — no woman's land — feeling too tired, broke, and sad to continue working, but still unwilling (too afraid, perhaps) to wholly give up on it when I met Norman, the Sex Store King.

Wherein I Embark On Job Interviews

From Mr. H.'s house, I embarked on the next step in the ordinary life plan: find a job. Ginny convinced me to apply for jobs in the Careers section of the paper rather than the Help Wanted columns where I normally looked. "Bamboozle them," she advised me. "The force of your personality can overcome your lack of employment qualifications." She lent me "career clothes"— severe blazers with matching microscopic skirts. I agreed. I needed to look my perky best to finance my upcoming life of quiet desperation. I even bought pantyhose —"*Nylons*, said Ginny. "What century are you from?"

Right. Away I went. . .

The first interview was for an administrative support position at the head office of a clothing company in a towering downtown building. I took the mirror-walled elevator up and adjusted my beige skirt. I wore a matching blazer and a white blouse with a floppy bow at the neck. I'd refused to wear any shoes with heels higher than two inches but still I felt like I was in drag. I carried one of Ginny's leather briefcases — empty, except for my bus transfer and keys to Mr. H.'s house. The air seemed to get thinner the higher I went and by the time I reached the fourteenth floor, I could hardly breathe. The handle of the briefcase was damp with sweat. *I can do this. It's just a job. I need to eat.*

I was ushered into the office of Human Resources, a small

room exactly like fifteen others I passed on the way in. A white particleboard desk with a computer on it faced away from the window. On the wall hung a framed inspirational poster with a picture of sun shining on a snow-capped mountain peak and underneath the words, "SUCCESS. Those at the top of the mountain didn't fall there." Oh really? I was still trying to decide whether it was a joke when the Human Resources woman came in. She introduced herself as Ms. Coleville. She had curly black hair, serious black nerd glasses, and looked a few years younger than I was. She seemed pleasant and I thought I was doing well as we chatted about the weather. Calm. Cloud Bank. Cumulus. Then the actual interview began.

She flipped open a folder on her desk. "What specific goals have you established for your career?"

Oh shit. "Specific goals? Well, finding a job is certainly my first goal — and after that, not being fired from the job. Of course, getting paid in there somewhere would be nice too." I laughed.

She managed a straight-line smile. "Everyone has strengths and weaknesses as employees. What are your strong points for this position?"

"Well, I need a job. I'm a hard worker and I think I would be an asset to your company." I thought that sounded good but she didn't even write it down.

"What would you say are areas in which you're needing improvement?"

"You mean work areas?"

She nodded and looked at her watch.

"I suppose I could improve my typing skills and I could learn more about financial operations. . . or fiscal operations of various. . ." My hand flapped in the air. I put it back in my lap. "Of the economic realities of business as a whole."

She adjusted her glasses and asked, "What have you learned from your participation in extracurricular activities?"

"Extracurricular activities? Like?"

"Like volunteer work, sports, hobbies — activities outside of your working life." She waited, her pen poised above the folder.

"Right. I don't do many of those things. I, uh, planted some flowers last night, though. That was nice. The dirt smelt good. I used to paint but, well, I don't anymore."

She flipped through some papers on her desk. "What did you learn as a Retail Consultant?"

"I've never been a Retail Consultant," I said.

"It says right here on your résumé, Retail Consultant; September 1998 to February 1999."

"Oh, right. I forgot about that. It was a completely enriching experience."

"But what did you learn from it?" she asked.

I felt like we were playing some strange version of the Pong videogame from the seventies and I couldn't get my paddle to work properly. The ball just kept sailing past me.

"I learned how to. . . I learned that some people shop for clothes according to aura colour and fashion retailers aren't, uh, exploiting this area of New Age consumer thought and might want to consider arranging their stores according to aura colours. They could also maybe give away free incense."

"Free incense? Right. If you had to describe yourself in three words what would those words be?"

"Uh, dependable, punctual, no, maybe not punctual, let's see, dependable, organized and. . ." Oh, hell, what would be three good words? ". . .responsible or maybe hard-working. That's three words, right?"

She raised her eyebrows and jiggled her head. I didn't know what that meant.

"Okay, how about. . . All. Fucked. Up?"

That effectively ended that conversation.

I rode the elevator back down and didn't go to the other two interviews. Someone should have told me they'd be asking questions like that. At my other job interviews, they just asked if I had a criminal record, did I speak English, and could I work weekends.

After the Gimlet affair and dropping out of college, I answered an ad for part-time help in a retail store. I was desperate; I'd spent the remainder of my student loan and was having no luck finding work. Not being able to type, or do anything particularly useful, was proving to be a detriment. I applied for a job on the rigs, but one of the strapping young men with grease-stained hands in line ahead of me obtained that position. The retail job I applied for paid better than Orange Julius, I didn't have to wear a polyester uniform or a visor, so against my better judgment, which was dubious at best those days, I took it. The name of the store was The Wanton Warehouse: The Biggest Sex Shop in Town (which, considering most of them were the size of a phone booth, wasn't saying much). Did I have misgivings about working in a porno shop? I did. I wasn't completely without feminist sensibilities, but by that time, it was either my principles or my pride and Professor Gimlet had damaged my pride enough.

After I showed up the first day in my plaid shirt and jeans, Melinda, the manager who hired me, gave me an armload of clothes and shoes to wear, telling me to think of them as a "uniform." Well, at least there was no visor. I tottered around in stilettos for two weeks. I began by trying to familiarize myself with the merchandise, by turns horrified and hysterical.

Realistically moulded from Dallas McRoy's actual manhood, Orgasm Balls with Sturdy Retrieval Cords, and *Betty the Life Size Love Doll. With real blinking eyes.*

The mental picture of what would make poor, daft-looking Betty's eyes blink was too much. After that, I kept my eyes off the merchandise and clientele as much as possible by staring at the ceiling medallion above the register until I realized the plaster cherubs on it were anatomically correct and engaged in most un-cherubic acts with each other. After that, I just kept my eyes closed until I actually had to ring something in. Melinda planned to train me on floor sales as soon as she hired another person. I was in no hurry.

The third week after my arrival, Melinda began a flurry of cleaning and re-organizing. The owner of The Wanton Warehouse chain across the United States and Canada was touring all the locations.

"He's filthy rich," said Melinda. "There's sixty-seven of these stores. Can you imagine getting rich from selling this stuff?"

I opened the store the morning the owner was scheduled to show up. Melinda hated getting up on time to open. "Who wants a pair of edible underwear before they've had lunch? The hours at this place are stupid." She'd passed the keys off to me a week after I started.

As soon as I got in the door, the telephone rang. It was Melinda. "Frieda. Thank God. You're going to have to meet the owner today and show him around. Things got a little out of hand last night. I'm in no shape to come in at all."

"No way. Don't you dare," I said.

"You have to do this. Please. I can't lose my job. Tell him a bus hit me or something. Please."

"But I don't know anything."

"You're smart, make it up. Thanks, Frieda." She hung up.

I sat on a stool behind the till, trying to convince myself that I could not only help customers, but also handle the cigar-smoking sleazeball owner in a plaid suit who was going to show up and grill me.

The bell tinkled later in the day, and a nice-looking younger man in round, wire-rimmed glasses and an expensive suit walked in with an older lady on his arm. Okay, younger, older, no problem. I can handle this.

"Hi," I said brightly. "How are you today?"

"Fine, thank you," said the gentleman. Frankly, he didn't look the type. His brown hair was receding and his ears stuck out a little, but he was cute in a friendly sort of way. Like a boy-next-door date for high school graduation. The older lady had more pizzazz. She wore a one-piece zip-up Pucci pantsuit with swirls of green, pink, and purple on a white background. Her platinum hair was piled on top of her head in wild curls and she wore large round sunglasses.

"Can I show you anything? Uh, a sexual aid of some sort? Well, something fun, perhaps, for the two of you — role-playing or, uh, some toys. . ."

The man smiled. "I'm Norman March, the owner of the store. This is my mother, Lady March. We're here for a tour of the store."

"Of course you are. I didn't think. . . I mean, obviously you're not the type to come to a store like this. Of course, you own them. There's nothing wrong with that. Really. But this is your mother, of course. I didn't mean to imply that you were. . ." I stood up and wobbled on my stilettos over to them. "I'm Frieda Zweig. The manager, Melinda, was tragically run over by a bus this morning, so I'll show you around."

Lady March stared at me. A small smile twitched at the corners of her mouth. "Run over by a bus?" she asked.

"Yes, the driver had something, uh, in his eye. She'll be fine, though. Just a few broken bones and such. So." I took a deep breath. "You'll be wanting to see how we have things arranged. Over here are the, you know, the mechanical apparatus that women use, when they're between boyfriends. Or men perhaps as well, I think. . . . Anyway, they come in all shapes and colours and we have them arranged by uh. . ." I cast a desperate eye over the shelves. ". . .by vibrational power, perhaps." I turned away as quickly as possible. I planned on a three-and-a-half-minute speed tour, after which I'd shake his hand, he'd go away, Melinda would keep her job, and I'd quit and go and work at Orange Julius or maybe Burger Baron. They had brown uniforms.

Now what the hell was *this* section? "And over here are the leather chaps and whips and that sort of thing for those who have, uh, cowboy fantasies or have moved into the city from the country and miss their horses. Not that they loved their horses that much, I don't mean to imply that, you know — but they miss them and this reminds them of home. Home on the range. . ." I trailed off.

Both Norman and his mother started to laugh. I was at first charmed by their obvious closeness — and intrigued. Someone who could laugh like a good friend with his mother must be a decent man. Then I recalled that they were laughing at me and I returned to my original state of mortification. Lady March pushed her sunglasses to the top of her head. "That was wonderful, my dear, truly creative," she said. "You must have been a sheha in a previous life."

"A what?"

"Sheha, storyteller in Swahili. I just attended a marvelous night of legend-telling in Africa." She paused. "A smidgen of advice. Your bustier is on backwards."

"Oh, sheha. . . Swahili. . . My bustier?"

She pointed at the ridiculous red satin top I'd chosen to wear.

"Oh, the top. I wondered how to get all those laces done up in the back. I had to get the bus driver to help me this morning."

"Well," she said to Mr. March, "that explains what the driver had in his eye when he ran over the manager."

My face turned as red as the bustier. I scrambled for something, anything, to say. I suddenly didn't want to be seen as nothing but the idiot worker who couldn't even put her clothes on right, even if it was true. "I don't know if I was ever a storyteller," I said, "but I was a painter, in this life."

Lady March squinted her eyes at the air around my head. I wondered if I'd remembered to comb my hair that morning.

"I can see that there is a great deal of bright pink in your aura but it's muddied," she said. "You might want to look at trying to get that cleared."

I nodded mutely.

Mr. March said, "I'll call later." I looked at him. A bit of the barroom look was in his eyes but tempered with something softer. And then they left, giggling together again, the chimes on the door echoing their exit.

Melinda called half an hour later. "How did it go?"

"They laughed at me," I said. "I'm forever scarred by the whole thing."

I sat on the stool for the rest of the afternoon and refused to move.

Something must have impressed Norman, or Mr. March as I called him then, because when he called later in the day to reschedule his tour, he asked me out to dinner. He was probably going to fire me, but I might as well get a free dinner before he did.

Perfectly Good Except For The Fact
They No Longer Work

Mr. H. greeted me in the kitchen with a big smile. "Good morning, Frieda, the historical people are coming today." He wore a wrinkled white apron and held a feather duster in one hand and a dirty polishing rag in the other.

"The who?" I poured myself a coffee, envisioning a horde of people in medieval clothing tramping through the house.

"The people from the Winnipeg Historical Society. Remember? They called last week wanting to look at the house. That's yesterday's coffee."

"Right. I'll just zap it and then I'll help you tidy up." When the microwave dinged, I took a long swallow of lukewarm coffee.

We picked up papers from the floor and stacked books back in shelves. Mr. H. wasn't a very efficient cleaner. He'd stop to read bits from every newspaper he picked up.

"Did you know," he asked, standing in the middle of the living room, holding a paper, "that a year on Mars lasts 685 days?"

"Cleaning, not reading," I said for the fourth time, feeling like my mother.

"Right." He put the paper in a stack and pulled the feather duster from his pocket.

"Does that mean I'd only be fourteen on Mars?"

Mr. H. picked the paper back up. "I think so."

A little later, I found a piece of mud by the back door shaped like Elvis' head. I thought we should try to sell to the *Weekly World News*. Mr. H. said it might be worth more if it looked like the Virgin Mary. I thought I'd discovered a future career: discoverer (or creator) of Holy Modern Relics. With visions of the face of Jesus in bubble gum, I tried to create Mary from another hunk of mud and was disgusted when it crumbled to dust and I had to re-sweep the back entry and accidentally crushed Elvis. Somehow, we managed to get the house into a presentable state of tidiness before the society members arrived later in the morning.

Four of them trooped in, all women in their late sixties, all dressed in shades of neutrals, buff, brown, and tan — a beige brigade with overflowing file folders, clipboards, and a digital camera. They wandered around the house with much note-taking, discussing, and quibbling over how to work the camera properly. I sat on the couch, reading the entertainment section of the newspaper with my feet up on the coffee table. They reminded me a bit too much of the Art Society people from Kentucky. When they came back up from the basement, Mr. H. was carrying a small crowbar. I heard the whinging of nails from the back entry and I wandered back and stood behind them. Deconstruction is always interesting.

"There they are," said one of the ladies. They crouched on the floor, looking at a spot in the wall.

What? Hidden jewels? Was my Mr. H. about to become a wealthy man? Human remains? Had the house been the scene of a gruesome murder? I leaned forward and saw logs stacked up like a second wall.

"What are you looking at?" I asked the closest woman.

"The wall. It's from the original log home." The lady's carefully powdered face creased into a smile.

I nodded. There's no telling what'll turn a person's crank.

"We've been trying to find the home of Jack Roulston," she continued. "The east-side library was built with his money. We knew part of his house was constructed around the original log house in the early 1900s, but couldn't find it. Most of the records for this area were lost in the 1950 flood."

"Oh, well, good for you." I started to back up toward the living room, sensing a large history lesson coming on.

"You know what's odd?" said Mr. H., looking up from where he knelt holding the crowbar. "Jack Roulston's first wife was named Gladys. Remember when you came for the record player and someone named Gladys? There was a Gladys here once; you were just ninety-some years too late."

I stared at him and made a small *gack*. My mouth opened. Closed. Opened. The ladies stared at me.

Mr. H. came to my rescue. "Would you ladies like some tea?" he asked.

"No thank you," said the lady with the camera. "We have to get back to the office. Can we drop back over? We'll have to do more looking around before we draw up the papers."

"Certainly," said Mr. H. "Come anytime."

I managed a smile. "Goodbye. See you." The ladies dusted themselves off and gathered their things.

I sat down on the couch feeling both spooked and relieved. If it was true that Gladys had once lived in this house, she was likely a real ghost, which meant I wasn't going crazy, but it also meant I'd been interacting with an authentic spook.

After Mr. H. ushered the ladies out, he came and sat across from me. "Well, isn't that something, my humbling abode a historical landmark. I bought this place for next to nothing after that 1950 flood they were talking about. There was a lake in the basement and the —"

"How long did this Jack and Gladys live here? Did they say?"

"I don't think so," he said. "The two of them lived in the

Dance, Gladys, Dance

original log home and then Jack built this house. You could call the Society."

"I might do that."

Mr. H. looked at me for a moment as though he had more to say, then he stood. "I'm going to go put that board back up."

"I'll make lunch." There was leftover liver from last night, but I made macaroni and cheese. Despite our original deal, not only had I failed to help Mr. H. with his laughed-over problem, I'd compounded it. Neither of us liked to eat leftovers, and since Mr. H. grew up during the Depression and I'd been raised by old-school parents, we were both unable to throw food away until it had been left in the fridge long enough to sprout spores; only then could it be disposed of guilt-free.

Mr. H. left after lunch to go shopping and visit the library. He invited me along, but I had my own investigating to do. This is the house that Jack built. This is the rat that ate the malt that lay in the house that Jack built. This is the maiden all forlorn that milked the cow with the crumpled horn. I went upstairs to my room and sat on the bed calling, "Gladys. Gladys."

Her smiling white-haired head appeared, floating above the record player.

"Shit." I'd called her but. . .

"I thought it might be easier for you if I didn't become completely visible," she said.

"Talking to a disembodied head doesn't really help."

"Oh, sorry." The head disappeared and she materialized completely in the armchair.

Did people go looking for stuff like this to happen, searching out ghosts and spirits? I couldn't for the life of me see the appeal in it.

"You used to live in this house, didn't you?" I asked.

"I did for a time, and then I left."

"Did you move somewhere else?"

Gladys rocked for a minute. I stared at the chair moving

back and forth. In all the ghostly novels I'd read, it took immense effort for spirits to move matter and they'd be drained after making the slightest impact on the physical world, but here this ghost was rocking away like it was nothing. Gladys obviously hadn't been keeping up with contemporary literature.

"I suppose I did," she finally said, "from here to the Brandon Asylum for the Insane."

Oh great — I wasn't nuts, but my ghost was.

"How old were you?"

"Twenty."

"Were you. . . crazy?"

"I don't think so. Not before I went in, anyway." She seemed to go away again. She rocked slowly back and forth shaking her head. I looked out the window and watched the maple tree's branches move in the wind.

I decided to change the subject. "The newspaper ad said Gladys doesn't dance anymore. Were you a ballerina or something?"

I heard the back door open. Miss Kesstle called up the stairs. "Frieda? Are you home? Beethoven is up a tree and he can't get down." Gladys dematerialized.

"Frieda?"

Damn cat.

Gladys *showed up* briefly a couple of times in the three days following her telling me about the asylum. Mr. H. interrupted us twice and she disappeared before telling me any more of her story. I couldn't stop thinking about a twenty-year-old Gladys locked away. I had to keep reminding myself that there was no guarantee that Gladys hadn't been nuts before she went in. She didn't seem crazy now. . . but maybe she'd outgrown it, or become sane again when she shuffled off her mortal coil. But how on earth had she ended up in an insane asylum in the first place?

The Sex Store King

I rummaged through Mr. H.'s shed, on a quest for my blow-dryer. The shed was full of the odds and ends people collect after living in one place for a long time: toasters and coffee percolators that are still perfectly good, except for the fact that they no longer work, coffee tins full of unidentifiable metal bits, and any number of handy-dandy bits of junk. The shed smelled slightly musty, like an old suitcase left closed up in a closet for too long. I pushed aside rakes and hoes to get at the boxes I'd moved over from Ginny's after Mr. H. offered me the space.

Mr. H. had also volunteered to clear out some room for me in the china cupboards and bookshelves in the house, but I stored almost everything in the shed. I enjoyed living without most of my stuff. Besides, I couldn't picture my plastic Einstein with the bobbing head in the china cabinet next to Shirley's bone china teacup collection.

I'd thrown my things in boxes before leaving Kentucky and Norman had shipped them to Ginny's for me. I'd labeled them handily enough: Stuff, Junk, Bits, and so forth. In one of the first cartons I opened, I found my jewelry box. No great jewels there either, just one gold earring in the shape of a fish, and a small pink stone. I held the stone in the palm of my hand.

On our first dinner out, Norman, the sex store owner, took me to Drága Táplálék, a new and very expensive Hungarian restaurant. I'd imagined goulash, Wiener schnitzel, beer, and waiters in green knickers with suspenders. Or was that Germany? It didn't matter; at Drága Táplálék, there was no schnitzel in sight, and the food on the menu was as expensive as it was unpronounceable. The waiters and waitresses barely deigned to take your order and they moved stiffly in their perfectly tailored black clothes. Norman wore an expensive-looking grey suit with a white shirt and a red tie. His round wire glasses kept slipping down his nose and his face was pink and freshly shaved. Hard to believe he was a millionaire. He ordered Halaszle, Kolozsvari Toltott Kaposzta with Nockerl, and Carp Racos Pont with a Szekszárd Cabernet Sauvignon. I nodded and smiled intelligently.

After the ordering, I looked at him. "So, Mr. March?"

"Norman, please," he said. "Your tour of the store was charming. Most of the personnel I've met in my stores aren't so imaginative," he smiled, "and it was nice of you to help out Melinda."

"Are you going to fire her?"

"No."

"Are you going to fire me?"

"No, though, not to put down my businesses, I think you could be doing better for yourself."

I shrugged. "It was either the Wanton Warehouse or Orange Julius. I chose the Warehouse."

"I'll take that as a compliment."

I shrugged again. "You could. . ."

We chatted for a while and when I mentioned the ceiling medallions in the store, he asked if I'd thought of getting a proper classical medallion for my home.

"You'd be surprised how much one of those can change the look of a room," he said and poured me a glass of red wine.

"I live in a basement suite, Norman. I'd be surprised if putting up a medallion didn't bring the whole ceiling down on my head."

Norman frowned slightly. I took a bite of my Kaposzta —
or maybe it was Halaszle. Whatever, it was delicious. "You do
know what a basement suite is, don't you?"

"Certainly. Well, no, actually not," he said and took a sip of
his wine.

"Tell you what, Sex Store King." He winced at that. "Come
to my place for dinner tomorrow night and you can see one
in person."

To my surprise, he agreed. We had a nice dinner. Norman
was charming, friendly, and, best of all, he laughed at all my
jokes.

After work the next day I created a reasonable facsimile of
my mother's famous Ten Can Chili and stared around hopelessly
at the hole I lived in. What had I been thinking? I'd stopped
hearing the squeaky furnace next to the kitchen months ago, but
it now seemed deafening. My basement suite had been decorated
by the same horde of invisible interior designers who do greasy
diners and motels on the drag downtown. Lots of dark orange,
wood panelling, and unidentifiable and permanent stains.

Well, if my place was a hellhole, I was reasonably certain I
looked okay. I'd put my hair up in a bun, leaving a few pieces
falling out for the "blown by unseen winds" look, and wore a
white cotton blouse and a pair of too-tight jeans.

Norman showed up ten minutes late. "I knocked at the upstairs door by mistake. Did you know he builds motorcycles in
his living room?"

"That explains the noises I hear in the middle of the night."
I took Norman's jacket. "I thought it was a chainsaw. Come in."

"Thanks. Sorry I'm late." He looked around. "Nice place."

"Norman, don't lie, it's bad for your character. What's nice
about it?"

He inspected the room more closely, taking in the carpet
and the panelling. "Nothing. It's quite horrible, isn't it?"

"Quite. Come and sit down. Dinner is almost ready."

Dance, Gladys, Dance

"But you are stunning." He sounded so sincere I blushed.

We had dinner to the sounds of the engines upstairs and the squeaky furnace. Norman had two helpings of chili.

"So, how did you get into the sex store business?" I asked him after dinner.

"I inherited it from my father, who inherited it from his father and so on, back four generations."

"Come on. They didn't have sex stores back then," I said.

"They imported naughty trinkets for the Victorians: crystal paperweights with engravings of naked women on the bottom and pewter pipe stampers with peepholes to see drawings of a woman getting undressed for her bath. Tame stuff, but there was a large demand for it. Photographs, too, pretty much like they are today, only in sepia instead of full colour and no extreme close-ups. My father had the country's largest collection of Victorian pornography before he died. Anyway, my not-so-ancient ancestors started getting rich and we continue to get richer. But let's not talk about all that, it's boring."

"It's fascinating. I had no idea."

"He told me it was crematoriums." Norman folded and unfolded the rectangle of paper towel beside his plate.

"Pardon me?"

"While I was growing up, my father told me our money came from crematoriums we owned in England. He sent me to business school to get my master's, but wouldn't let me get involved in the company at all. He told me he wanted me to learn with a fresh mind."

"You're kidding me."

"Not at all. I thought he was embarrassed by the crematoriums, as I was. I had no desire to be associated with death as an up-and-coming young executive. It seemed sordid. Little did I know. All through college, I pretended we'd inherited a large fortune from way back and it would just be a matter of shrewd investments to keep it enlarging."

"Instead you find out you're selling gadgets for penis enlargement. When did he tell you?"

"On his deathbed, if you can believe it, just six weeks after I graduated from college."

"Like what? 'Son, I'm dying, here's the keys to the porno vault?' Sorry. It's so incredible." I leaned towards him, my elbows on the table, my face in my hands.

"Actually, it was very much like that, only he made me promise to keep the business intact. He must have known what I'd think about it, but there's pride in keeping a business going for that long — no jokes, please — and he didn't want me to sell it off. So, I promised. And here I am: Norman, the Sex Store King."

"Let's go sit on the couch. Sorry about the Sex Store King thing. I had no idea. You don't like it at all, do you?" We settled onto the sagging brown-and-red plaid couch I'd rescued from a dumpster behind a dentist's clinic. I was dying to unbutton my jeans; after two helpings of chili, I could hardly breathe. What I would have given for a pair of sweatpants. Norman wiggled around on the couch as though trying to find a comfortable spot for his butt, then gave up and leaned back.

"I despise the whole business, but I promised. . . how do you go back on a deathbed vow? Mother, on the other hand, seems oblivious to the whole thing. It's out of her universe. Speaking of whom, Mother told me your aura had a lot of potential. She also saw an image of — what was it? — an aardvark hovering around your shoulder."

"An aardvark?"

"She said it must be your totem animal."

"I thought I was just having a bad hair day. Is an aardvark good?"

"I think so. She said something about burrowing deep underground to acquire the truth." He reached into the pocket of his trousers and held out a small pink stone in the palm of his hand. "Rose quartz, for opening up the heart chakra. I'm not certain what a chakra is either. That's why I was late. She insisted I stop and get one before I came over tonight."

"That's very strange, but sweet."

"That's Mother — strange, but sweet. After my father died, she got involved with all this psychic mumbo jumbo, channelling and chanting and meditating. She means well. She believes in it and believes she can help other people. What can it hurt?" He shrugged. "Now, back to you. What did you do before starting your stunning career at the Wanton Warehouse?"

I'd been hoping we could skip this part of the conversation.

"I was at art school but I quit."

"Why?"

It was bad for your character to lie. But was I going to tell him the whole sordid story? He'd been so open and honest with me, but who wanted to date a failure? A has-been at twenty-six?

"I couldn't afford all the art supplies," I said. "I had to quit."

He looked as though I'd told him *he* had to quit. After more conversation and wine, we made love. I initiated it. I hadn't had sex for a year, not since Gimlet. Underneath all his linen and grey flannel, Norman was a surprisingly passionate man and not a sexual aid in sight.

I stayed in bed the next morning with my face buried in the pillow, not wanting him to see my face or hair. I breathed in the spicy scent of his cologne.

"I have to go to a meeting, Frieda. I'll call you later. Thank you for last night."

I could hear him kneeling beside the mattress. He tucked my hair behind my ear and kissed my cheek. I grunted. The door closed quietly behind him. Sure you'll call, buddy. You'll fly to the next town, to the next store, and sleep with the next dumb broad in the dildo aisle.

Later that day my doorbell rang. I answered the door. A deliveryman handed me a large package.

Inside the wrapping were six canvases, twelve beautiful

brushes, and a hundred-dollar gift certificate for the Paint Pot store. There was also an envelope with a note: "Dear Frieda, I fell apart in the paint aisle — too many choices. Please use the certificate to choose what you want. Thank you again for the lovely evening. Norman March." In the corner of the envelope was a small pink stone.

Norman had continued to send gifts, notes, goofy postcards, and flowers as he made his way across Canada on the tour of his stores. When he reached Vancouver, he asked me to join him there. I packed and left Winnipeg the next day. Norman the Reluctant Sex Store King: it was endearing and he was possibly serious enough to make me forget my failures.

I put the pink stone back in the jewelry box and closed the lid. After opening and rummaging through another three boxes in the depths of the shed, I formed a brilliant plan to get enough money to last another month.

I gave up the hair dryer quest, went inside, wrote a letter, then immediately walked down the block to the mailbox on the corner and dropped it in. An hour later I was having serious qualms about what I'd written. So much for independence and making my own way. Too late. A girl's gotta do what a girl's gotta do. I needed time to think. I deserved it.

Dear Norman,

I hope you will excuse my long silence. I know I promised to call or write as soon as I was settled, but I needed time to get my head together. That hasn't really happened yet. How are things in Kentucky?

I've rented a room in a big house from a nice old man named Mr. Hausselman. You'd like him. He's kind and funny and a wonderful photographer.

Please say hello to your mom from me.

By the way, it has come to my attention that some of my things are missing. Please see attached list. Hope you are well.

Sincerely yours,
Frieda

List
(1) One hair dryer
— $20.00
(2) One paisley scarf
— $25.00
(3) One Tom Waits cd Blue Valentine
— $20.00
(4) One coffee table book The Red Couch: A Portrait of America
— $40.00
(5) Two rolls of undeveloped Fuji film
— $15.00
(6) One gold earring shape of a fish
— $30.00
(7) One package Electrolux vacuum cleaner bags
— $6.00
(8) One cassette tape Count Basie One O'Clock Jump
— $10.00
(9) One paperback copy The Agony and the Ecstasy by Irving Stone
— $30.00
(10) One Swiss army knife
— $50.00
(11) One black Wonderbra
— $25.00

Total — $261.00

I would prefer you not to send the items themselves.
Thanks.

A week and a half later, I sat at the kitchen table looking at recipe books. Mr. H. and I had decided to teach ourselves how to be real cooks. Mr. H. had dubbed it Operation Starve Wreck — mouldly going where no pan has gone before. It wasn't working too well yet; dishes cowered in the fridge with little notes

taped to them: *I think it's supposed to look like this. Be careful.*
VERY SPICY. Edible (but just). Our experiments had done
nothing whatsoever for the leftover consumption. No need to
cook anything tonight; Miss Kesstle had sent leftover tuna casserole home with us after Sunday dinner yesterday, but I was
thinking about Chinese food. How hard could chicken balls be?

Mr. H. came down the front hallway with a handful of mail.
"I have advanced," he said, looking at a large white envelope
covered in stars and exclamation marks, "quite mysteriously,
to the next winning round of the *Reader's Digest* sweepstakes.
I don't know how. The last letter said it was my final chance
to lick twelve stamps and get myself into this exalted winning
circle and I threw it in the garbage unopened."

"You're just lucky, I guess."

"Humph. I snorepose so. Letter here for you. No return address. Secret Admirer?"

"Probably not anymore."

I took the envelope upstairs and sat at the little green desk
to open it. It contained a cheque from Norman for the exact
amount I asked for. No letter, not even a note. The only personal thing was Norman's small round signature in the lower
right corner of the cheque. I was chagrined, especially since
I'd found several of the items since sending the letter. I'll call
him, I thought. I'll explain I felt desperate. I'll offer to send the
money back. He probably wouldn't want me to, though. I looked
at the clock. The bank closed in twenty minutes. I'd call him
when I got back. I could always return the cash if he wanted.

I was on the way home when Miss Kesstle called to me from
her porch; Beethoven was stuck on the roof of her shed. I rescued the cat, then it was time for supper, then Keith Richards
was on *Biography*, and then it was too late to call, and then life
carried on and I never got around to calling.

I found out later that the following exchange went on behind my back:

Dear Mr. Hausselman,

We have not had the opportunity to become acquainted; however, we have a mutual friend, Ms. Frieda Zweig. I assure you, Mr. Hausselman, that my intentions toward Frieda are gentlemanly and I have only her best interests in mind.

I received a rather uncharacteristic letter from Frieda two weeks ago and I haven't been able to stop thinking about it. I'm concerned for her. I hoped you could (confidentially) let me know if she is all right.

Sincerely yours,
Norman March

Dear Norman,

Thank you for thinking of our Frieda. I wish I could tell you she's doing fine but I don't believe she is. I have heard her speak of you and she seems fond of you, otherwise I would be even more uncomfortable writing this letter than I already am. Frieda seems lonely. The only friend she has her own age is Ginny and she doesn't seem to like her very well. This would not be so worrisome if she seemed content, but I've heard her talking to herself when she thinks no one is around, not musing aloud, but having one-sided conversations. It seems odd, to say the least, as though she's invented an imaginary friend.

Perhaps you could come and see her (Frieda that is, not her imaginary friend). I feel reasonably certain she would welcome a visit.

Sincerely yours,
Mr. Edward Hausselman

W-O-M-B-A-T

"Are you avoiding me?" Ginny asked. "Have you joined a cult? I haven't heard from you in ages."

"It's only been a week — or so. I've been busy." I wrapped the phone cord through my fingers.

"Oh, did you get a job? Congratulations."

"No, I didn't get a job. I've been planting flowers, writing letters, rescuing cats, and I'm thinking of taking up crochet."

"Crochet? Really, how quaint. Come and meet me for lunch today," she said.

Everything important in Ginny's life was within three blocks of her apartment: her work, her favourite restaurants, and the most chic shoe and clothing stores. The Zone, our luncheon destination, was in the same building as Ginny's apartment. She worked just around the corner at LG International, a monstrous advertising company. LG was one of the few large corporations which hadn't bailed out of Winnipeg yet; it also had bases in Toronto, Vancouver, and New York, so I suppose it could afford to stay. Ginny was Assistant Director of Brand Strategies and was aiming for a promotion to Director of Design. She never said so, but I knew her purple-shadowed eyes were locked on the New York office.

"Okay, lunch is fine." Best to get it over with before a squad of deprogrammers showed up at Mr. H.'s door. "See you at noon."

CHAPTER NINE

I went upstairs and got dressed in men's Levi jeans and a white T-shirt. No use in setting Ginny off on a fashion lecture. Once I got downstairs, I lost my common sense. I'd recently scored a 1940s black velvet swing jacket from the second-hand store that I hadn't worn yet and I'd polished my army boots yesterday. Both the jacket and boots called out to be worn.

I checked the mail before I left. There was a letter from my mother that I put in my pocket to read on the bus.

The cross-hatched metal floor rumbled under my feet and the letter vibrated in my hand.

Dear Frieda,

I wanted to call, but it's a weekday and you know how your father is about long-distance charges. Just wondering how you're settling in and if you've found work yet. Mrs. Conroy from the condo down the street — you remember her, she's the one with that yappy little dog she insists on bringing everywhere, last week she brought it to the Sheppards' place for our Rummoli game. We're playing for nickels now and when Mr. Sheppard lost forty cents he yelled, and the damn thing peed all over the Sheppard's carpet. It was quite funny actually, though I'm glad it wasn't at our place. I hope I haven't prejudiced you against her opinion by her yapping, peeing dog because she actually has quite good business sense, she worked for Mary Kay for years and even got a pink Cadillac, anyhow, I was talking to her about you the other day she says that real estate is the way to go. It only takes twelve weeks and you can be a realtor. Some of them make excellent money. So, anyhow, just a suggestion. I did look up the number for the Manitoba Real Estate Association, it's Toll Free: 1-800-267-6019.

Your father and I miss you.
Love, Mom

I sighed, looked down at my feet, and promptly forgot all about real estate. There's something mesmerizing about freshly polished footwear. I nearly missed my stop near The Zone while admiring my shiny boots. I disembarked and walked half a block.

Ginny sat at a table waiting for me. The first words out of her mouth were, "Where did you get that jacket?"

"It's classic," I said, avoiding the "where" issue.

"You look like a monkey."

I held out my arms. "They're three-quarter-length sleeves. I could get some gloves."

"Gloves and army boots. God help me."

I shrugged. "It's a look."

"It's not a look. It's a spectacle."

The waiter brought me my hamburger, or rather, my End Zone Deluxe on a Bun, and Ginny her salad. What was the point of eating salad in a restaurant? I could eat lettuce at home and manage to tear it into small enough pieces to pick up with a fork, which is something no restaurant has ever seemed to master.

"So, it looks like I'm a shoo-in for the promotion," Ginny said. "Mr. Swanget, the president, nodded at me this morning on his way out the door." She took a bite of her salad.

"And. . ."

"And nothing. The nod is an important part of non-verbal business communication. Besides, I'm going to get it. If they lateral me again, well, they just won't. I've substantially raised the adnorm for two of our major print publications, brought in the last three major customers, *and* I developed the communications plan for GLF which significantly increased the BDI of the product and won a CASSIE. The only other person who's even in the running is Craig and he's nothing but a marketing puke, a total wombat."

"What language are you speaking Ginny? And put your fork down before you impale someone. Is a wombat Craig's totem animal?"

"W-O-M-B-A-T, Frieda, Waste Of Money, Brains, And Time. Where have you been?"

"Some other planet, I think."

Ginny put down her fork, caught the waiter, and ordered another Perrier. "So how did your interviews go?"

"Well, speaking of non-verbal business communication, the lady in my interview did this." I raised my eyebrows and jiggled my head. "What does that mean?"

"Do it again." Ginny watched closely. "It means 'You're not making any sense and you're hurting my head.'"

"Great."

"So, how are things between you and the old fellow?" Ginny asked. "Is he keeping his hands to himself?"

"Actually, no. Mr. H. and I have decided to take our relationship to an advanced level of eroticism."

"What!"

"Close your mouth, Ginny. I can see your lettuce."

"Has he changed his will?"

"I'm not concerned with that, it's purely sexual."

"You *are* weird, Frieda."

"I'm kidding. I've taken a vow of celibacy. I'm joining The Order of the Sisters of Absolute Anarchy, or maybe I'll become a realtor."

"Now that's funny," said Ginny.

"What?"

"You a realtor? Give me a break."

The waiter left our bill; Ginny looked around, then slid the unused dessert fork into the pocket of her blazer.

"What are you doing?" I asked.

"What?" She stared blankly at me.

"You just put a fork in your pocket. Are you going after Craig?"

"It's just a fork. They have hundreds of them. Let's go. I'll pay."

I said goodbye and wished her luck at work. What was up with the fork? I feared for Craig or maybe for Ginny.

I decided to walk five blocks over to the Art Centre and drop in on Mr. H. It's amazing how a city can change in the space of a few blocks. Ginny's highbrow world almost never collided with the downbeat way of life that existed just around the corner.

The Downtown Art Centre was located in an old government building from the seventies. It had been leased by the Winnipeg Society for the Arts, a group of socially responsible people who believed art and music should be available to all, regardless of race, income, or degree of social distress. Mr. H. had been teaching photography there for three years. He'd moved all of his equipment out of the house and built a darkroom in the basement of the Centre. The building radiated colour from a block away. Kids from the local school had painted murals on the outside walls, but the DayGlo daisies and misshapen superheroes in Technicolor couldn't quite camouflage the starkness of the building's former government existence. It looked like a Capitalist Suit having a bad acid trip.

I pushed open the doors. Long corridors dimly lit with fluorescent lights led off in two directions. I heard muffled singing and a piano. The hallway walls were covered with paintings and collages. I stopped in front of them. Some were very good; there was some real talent. My hands clenched and unclenched at my sides. I wandered down the hallway looking into the rooms.

A gigantic loom surrounded by smaller looms stood in the middle of the first space. A woman occupied each loom and the shuttles went back and forth in soft rhythm accompanying the murmurs of their voices. Many seemed to be immigrants, in various forms of headgear and ethnic dress. Several small children played near the door with a pile of wool scraps. They looked up without pausing as I passed.

Some of the doors were closed with handwritten signs on

them. Watercolour Painting. Tuesdays. 1–4 p.m. Candle-Making. Fridays. 7–9 p.m.

The singing grew louder. Near the end of the hall, there was a room with an old upright piano in the centre. The sign on the door read "Hootenanny Glee Club." The singers lined up in three rows beside the piano. The front row consisted of a old man in a grubby purple down-filled vest, a woman in her twenties with long blonde hair and a tiny baby in a striped snuggly strapped to her chest, an older lady in a dress and proper heels, a young man in a security guard uniform, and a young Goth girl wearing a black velvet gown with lace ruffles at the neck and sleeves. The dress ended at her knees and was met by the tops of her black combat boots. They sang "Swing Low, Sweet Chariot." It was a bit shaky, but in tune. I stood and listened. When they finished the woman on the piano turned. "Come in," she said.

"Oh. No. I was just listening."

"Are you sure? We can always use another voice."

"No, really. I'm looking for Mr. Hausselman's photography class."

"Down the next hall to your left, third door on the right. If he's not there, he's probably in the darkroom downstairs, beside the furnace room."

"Thanks." I smiled at the group. "Nice singing."

Mr. Hausselman sat at a big wooden desk at the front of the classroom, looking through a stack of photos. The rest of the desks were empty.

"Frieda! Come in, pull up a chair. I'm having a look at the photos the class turned in. What do you think of our Centre?"

"It's neat. I stopped and listened to the singing down the hall for a minute. Where'd you get all the looms and stuff?"

"Donated, or paid for by fundraising. The students have a sale of their works once a year and the proceeds go back into the foundation. The corporate and government cash funding has slowed down, but the provincial government lets us use the building for next to nothing and pays the utilities, so I guess we can't complain." He handed me a stack of pictures. "Look at these photos, there's some arm-raising work in here."

He was right; the quality was stunning and disturbing. There were photos of the interior of what looked like a crackhouse. The walls of the rooms appeared slanted as though falling down around the occupants. The photos told stories by the contents of an overflowing garbage can in the corner of a rundown kitchen, a wallet with its contents spewed out on the floor of a bathroom with cracked linoleum, a bare foot hanging over the edge of an exposed mattress.

"A sixteen-year-old girl took those. She's a sort of street kid, I think. Doesn't show up for weeks at a time. But she always seems to make her way back again. If you listened to the singers you probably saw her. She stopped in before going into singing class this afternoon. She's a spooky-looking young woman, black hair, white face."

"The Goth. She sings too?"

"Sings, paints, dances, takes photos, she does everything when she turns up. And she's good at it all. I have quite the soft spot for her."

"What's her name?"

"Girl. I don't know her last name. Some of them get skittish if I ask questions. I try to always have cookies or something for them to eat during the class. I'm not sure if they come for the class or for the Fudgee-Os."

"What's her first name?"

"That's her given name. Girl. She had a brother too. Guess what they named him."

"No way."

"Boy," said Mr. H. "I don't know what they'd have done if they had another."

"Let's not think about it," I said.

"Why don't you come and hang around some?" Mr. H. put his papers into a desk drawer. "Maybe you could help with the art classes."

"I don't think I have anything to teach anyone right now. I'm sort of still finding myself."

"Life isn't about finding yourself, Frieda. Life is about creating yourself."

"Who said that? Emerson?"

"No, good old Anonymous. Let's stop at Barney's on the way home for a cheesecake for dessert tonight." Mr. H. stood and put on his jacket.

After dinner and two pieces of raspberry chocolate cheesecake, I went upstairs to read. Mr. H. had hooked me on a Barbara Vine mystery series. I lay on the bed staring at the same page for three minutes without reading a word. I got up, wandered around the room, put a Billie Holiday 78 on the record player, then took it off; I put the Ramones in the CD player, then turned it off; I went over to the box of art supplies I'd never got around to donating. It still sat in the corner of my room. I nudged the box with my toe. I got down on my hands and knees, unpacked it, cleared the desk, set up the easel, laid out the paints and brushes, and placed a canvas on the easel. Then I sat on the chair and looked at it.

I woke up with a squalling headache. The first thing I saw when I opened my eyes was Gladys in the armchair.

"Good morning, Frieda. Are you painting?"

"Shit, Gladys, I'm sleeping. I don't really talk to people before I've had coffee, okay?"

"Well, I'm not really people. What are you painting?"

"What does it look like? It's the proverbial white cat with its eyes closed in a snowstorm. There's nothing there. I'm not painting." I sat up on the edge of the bed. "Do you think we could make appointments or something? Not that I don't enjoy you showing up anytime, anywhere."

"Sure, when's good for you?"

"I don't know. After lunch sometime, okay?"

"Okay. Good luck on the painting." She was gone.

I started to get up, then heard something behind me; I turned quickly and bashed my knee on the nightstand. "Damn."

"Oh, sorry," said Gladys, "but I was wondering, if you're not painting, why did you set up your painting supplies?"

I rubbed my knee. "Because I was temporarily delusional, but I'm better now. Is that all?"

Gladys nodded and disappeared again.

I went downstairs to put on the coffee. Mr. H. was in the study listening to some sort of booming, crashing classical music. Cymbals — first thing in the morning.

The sink was full of dishes and there wasn't a clean coffee cup. Yesterday had been my day for dishes and I hadn't done any. I put the coffee on and started washing. In minutes, my crankiness had escalated. I was particularly peeved at Mr. H.'s egg plate from breakfast. Egg cement. Piss me off. I flicked at the little yellow globs with my fingernail. I planned to look for work today, but now I had to spend all morning scrubbing someone's egg plate. All the good jobs would be gone before I finished.

The door to the study opened and Mr. H. walked out, the classical music leaking out of the study and expanding into the kitchen behind him.

"Good morning, Frieda."

"For some."

He sat at the table. "Is something wrong?"

"Yes," I said holding up the offending egg-encrusted plate

and gesturing at the sink full of dishes and withering soap bubbles. "This is wrong."

"Is it my day for dishes?"

"That's not the point. Egg cement is the point, not having the consideration to rinse dishes is the point."

"What a thing to say."

"I think it's a perfectly reasonable thing to say."

Mr. H. pulled the sugar bowl from the centre of the table towards him and then pushed it back again. "Reasonable isn't quite the word I would use. Petty might be more like it, considering I've washed some terrifying dishes from your cooking experiments."

"Experiments? Is that what you think of my cooking?"

Mr. H.'s face turned red. "That isn't what I meant at all."

"Well, maybe if you find me so petty," I said, "I should find another place to stay."

"Perhaps you should."

"Perhaps I will." I dropped the plate back in the sink and dried off my hands. "Somewhere where they don't play music with cymbals before noon." I turned to go upstairs.

"Frieda. . ." If it had been one of my boyfriends I would have ignored him, gone upstairs and packed, but this was Mr. H. I stopped and turned back.

He smiled. "I could probably refrain from playing Schönberg symphonies before noon."

"I don't want to move," I said.

"And I don't want you to. Come, sit, and have a coffee."

I sat down at the table and Mr. H. got up, got a tea towel from the drawer, dried two mugs, and poured us coffees. "Good Lord, Frieda, this isn't coffee, it's nuclear reactor fluid."

"I lost count of the scoops. It'll get us going."

"To the moon." He sat down at the table. "I haven't had a fight like that since Shirley was alive. Only then it was her being confused and me being a jerk."

"Do you think I'm a jerk?"

He added four spoons of sugar to his cup and stirred. "Sometimes you can be a little. . . sensitive."

"You mean insensitive."

"No, I mean sensitive. Like an artist is sensitive."

"I'm not an artist. I'm Frieda Zweig, Ordinary Woman."

"Yes, right. I know. But you don't seem very happy about it."

"What's there to be all joyful about? I'm entirely immature, this morning at least, and I have no purpose."

"Man's maturity: to have regained the seriousness that he had as a child at play. Friedrich Nietzsche."

"And where the hell do you get all these pithy sayings?"

"I can't take credit for those," he said. "Either Shirley said them to me, or they're from her dream book."

"Her what?"

He stood, went to the study, and brought out a large leather-bound journal. He sat in the chair closest to me and laid it on the table. "She collected things that struck her over the years."

"May I?" He nodded. The pages of the journal were filled with poems copied out, quotes, pictures, pressed leaves, and any number of the small bits of beauty and wisdom that one finds in a life and either disregards or accumulates in one way or another. Underneath a photo of a smiling, trim Mr. H. and herself in a fifties pin-up bathing suit holding hands on a beach, Shirley had written,

> *Love does not consist in gazing at each other, but in looking*
> *outward together in the same direction.*
> —Antoine de Saint-Exupéry

I closed the journal and pushed it back over to him. "Do you still miss her?"

"Every day. I used to think the pain might quit one day, but it doesn't, it gets easier, but it never disappears." He opened the book again and turned the pages.

Dance, Gladys, Dance

"Here's Whitman's footprint when he was two. I remember Shirley trying to get him to stand still after she made the print so she could wipe the ink off and he ran away. He left a trail of tiny single footprints all down the hallway. Shirley varnished over them. You can still see some parts of them." He looked down at the table. "Lord, this is terrible coffee."

"When did you last talk to Whitman?"

"Two months ago, on his thirty-third birthday. I had IGA deliver him a fruit basket. I wanted to make sure he got it."

"A *fruit* basket?"

"Sad, isn't it? I don't even know what he likes. I couldn't think of anything else. I lack imagination where Whitman is concerned."

"Why don't you invite him for a visit?" I stood to get another cup of coffee.

"He never has the time. Besides, all we do is sit and stare at each other and try to think of ways to fill up the emptiness between us. It doesn't work."

"I think it's a excellent idea. I'm here. I'm good at filling empty space."

"Yes, dear, you are." He smiled at me. "But some spaces are too big for even you to fill. Shall we join forces on those dishes? If the Historical Society ladies came, they'd be appalled at us."

After we'd finished dishes, Mr. H. went to the Art Centre. The students' show and sale was coming up at the end of the month and they had a big celebration planned. They were desperate for more funding and hoped to get the media and local dignitaries out. I declined the invitation to join him. I went upstairs and wrote another letter.

Dear Whitman Hausselman,

You don't know me, but I'm living with your father. I am writing on your father's behalf to invite you to Winnipeg for a visit. I understand that things have been awkward between you and your father for some time, but I believe it would be in both of your best interests to try to settle things between you.

You don't choose your family. They are God's gift to you, as you are to them.

Desmond Tutu. (That's from your mother's dream journal.)

Please come.

Looking forward to meeting you,
Frieda Zweig

He's A Toad

Ginny told me she'd once been asked during a high-powered interview if she was a sandwich, what sort of sandwich would she be. She'd said pastrami on multigrain bread with hot mustard and Muenster cheese. I don't know what type of sandwich I am; maybe a tofu wiener on a white bun.

I was going to get qualified for something, go, and do it. The study desk in front of me was strewn with brochures and applications for schools in Winnipeg and beyond. A lot of them were from the company that used to advertise on match covers for career diplomas by mail. I'd ordered information on all twenty-six careers. The original brochure promised a higher standard of living, a superior salary, less anxiety about the future, and satisfaction with my place in the world. Ha. Sign me up.

Gladys appeared in the chair in front of my eyes. "Aiheee." I took a deep breath. Seeing her materialize still freaked me out. Her hair hung in front of her face again. I wondered if Angelico would mind if I brought her in for a cut and set.

"If you were a sandwich, what kind would you be?" I asked.

She tilted her head. "That's the sort of conversation that'll get you locked up."

"Apparently not. That's the sort of conversation that'll get you a high-paying job. What's new?"

"Nothing. Do you think you're a sandwich?"

"Forget the sandwich. I've been thinking about this *thing* you said I have to do. Is it something that needs to be done to set your soul at rest? Do you want me to track Jack's descendants down and knock them on the head or something?"

"Not exactly. I can't tell you. You'll know."

"I know very little, Gladys. There's no guarantee I'll recognize the right thing to do at the right moment. It's a problem I have. Maybe you should find someone else. Go haunt Ginny. She'll have a spreadsheet and action plan done up for you in a jiffy."

"You'll do fine."

I shrugged. If she wanted to put her spectral trust in a tofu wiener on a white bun, who was I to argue?

"I was thinking," I said, "of becoming something."

"A sandwich?" asked Gladys. She floated over by the window now. With the bright sunlight behind her, I could see the caragana bushes through her apron and stomach. Blue polka dots floating in the branches.

"No. Could you please move away from the window? I can see right through you."

Gladys drifted away. "What are you thinking of becoming?"

I picked up a brochure. "A Master Herbalist or," I grabbed another handful of brochures, "an Aircraft Mechanic, or Floral Designer, or I could be an Applied Organizational Leader."

"What's that?" asked Gladys.

"I have no idea, but it sounds good, doesn't it?"

"Why would you want to be those things?"

"Because I need a career."

"Do you like aircraft mechanics?"

"I like flying on airplanes," I said. "People do this all the time — they just pick a career and they do it."

"Just like that?" asked Gladys.

"Just like this," I said. I picked up a form and began filling it out.

Gladys watched me for a moment. "What're you doing?"

"I'm applying to become. . ." I flipped over the form. ". . . a locksmith. In under a year, I will learn the practices of the modern locksmithing profession. Beginning. . ." I flipped the form back over. ". . . September 5th, Frieda Zweig will have embarked on the exciting career of locksmithing. Do you think I'll get to wear one of those cool leather tool belts?"

"That's crazy," said Gladys.

"It's not crazy," I said. "It's normal."

A week later, I was sitting on the front porch, enjoying the late afternoon summer sun and painting my toenails. Though I gave up almost all of my beauty improvements after Gimlet, I retained the habit of painting my toenails. The colour of them was a sort of secret code to myself. Red as a talisman, white in surrender, blue for melancholy, and purple for rebellion. Today, Zaftig Pink for, well, I wasn't sure of the symbolism yet. I'd see what the day brought. I'd moved on to the toes on my left foot when a large black limousine eased onto the street. Drug lord, I thought, coming to check on his minions. I eyed the limo with gentle envy. If I were rich, I'd never have one, but having the choice might be pleasant. I adjusted the toilet paper I had wedged between my toes; a professional pedicure would be nice occasionally too.

The limo slowed in front of the house, then stopped. It was inert for a moment, then the back door opened and a tall thin man wearing dark sunglasses emerged. He had on a black leather blazer, black turtleneck, black pants, polished black leather boots, and probably black briefs and socks underneath it all. His long hair was an out-of-the-bottle purple-black and rose straight up from his head then exploded into tiny curls, like Gino Vannelli's hair in the 1970s.

The man took a suitcase from the driver, then stood and watched the limo leave as if he'd been abandoned alone on an island to bring religion to the savages. Cannibal savages. When the car was out of sight, he turned and started up the walk towards the house.

"Oh," I said.

"Oh," said Miss Kesstle from her porch next door. I turned to look at her. She gathered up Beethoven and her crocheting and headed for her door.

I could hear her saying, "Oh. Oh dear," as she closed the door. A ball of cotton had fallen from her arms and lay on the porch floor, a strand of it leading into the house. I hoped she wasn't unraveling a tablecloth as she went.

The man did not look at her or at me. He pushed up his sunglasses and looked at the house.

Closer up and without his sunglasses, the rock star look vanished. His face had the sharp, angular lines and luminescence of an ascetic — an ascetic of technology. I could see him in a monastery of sharp planes, polished metal, and glowing screens.

I stood up. "Hello."

He didn't say anything until he reached the top of the stairs. Then he put down his suitcase and extended his hand. "Whitman Hausselman."

"Frieda." I shook his hand

"That bottom step should be fixed; the board is rotten," he said.

"Mr. H. is going to do it. Well, he mentioned it the other day. . ."

"Mr. Who?"

"Mr. Hausselman, your dad, he was —"

"Is he home?"

"No, I think he's at the Art Centre. We weren't expecting you, you didn't call. . . I know I asked you to come. . . ."

"I *came* because I'm working on a possible TV pilot, we're hoping to get some Canadian funding." He walked past me into the house.

I followed him inside. "That sounds interesting. TV — wow, uh, how was your trip?"

"Passable." He walked through the living room, into the kitchen, opened the fridge, glanced inside, then closed it.

"Can I get you something to eat?"

"No." He walked back into the hallway and back into the living room. He had the air of a person checking out a hotel room to be sure that it was up to his standards. I followed behind him, practicing my small talk, trying to be friendly.

"The summer has been hot, a high-pressure system stalled over top of Manitoba, low humidity though. . ."

"You don't say." He picked up his suitcase and started up the front stairs. "Some things never change. All anyone ever talked about when I lived here was the weather."

"Pleased to meet you too," I said to his retreating back. "Fine, thanks, and your father is well too, yes, the garden is pretty, we've been working on it, everything looks nice except the damn front step and it's not rotten, it's only loose. Thank you very much." Whitman turned to look at me.

"Well?" I said.

He shook his head and continued upstairs. I heard the door close and the bedsprings creaking. Fine, have a nap. Had I actually invited him here? Where was my head? I hurried into the kitchen to try to create some sort of dinner. I'd show him. I'd cook an amazing dinner. Why I chose to show him by attempting something I didn't know how to do, I couldn't tell you. Whitman didn't emerge from his room. Fine with me.

Two hours later, I heard the front door open, and Mr. H. walked into the kitchen. His arms were filled with books. "I stopped at the library on the way home. The new Peter Robinson mystery was finally there. Smells good in here." He lifted lids off pots and peeked in the oven. "String beans, sauce, yams, ham. What's the occasion?"

"We have company." I flew around the kitchen.

"Did you get a date?"

"No, our guest is upstairs sleeping right now."

"You did get a date!"

"No, I. . . I mean. . ." I opened the oven door. "How long do damn yams take to cook anyway?"

"It's Norman, isn't it? He's come to see you."

"Oh, Mr. H., it was none of my business, but you know how I am and I thought. . ." I stirred the sauce vigourously.

"No, it was none of *my* business, but you seemed lonely."

"*I* seemed lonely?"

The doorbell rang. We stared at one another. Mr. H. went to get the door. I turned back to the stove.

Gladys stood beside me, sniffing at the Béarnaise sauce. "This sauce is too rich. Have you made it before? My mother used to say make what you know when you're having company."

"It's not too rich. I followed the recipe." I could hear voices at the front door.

"I'd have danced with that fellow if he asked me. Mmm. Mmm."

"What fellow?" The top of my head was going to come off. I could feel it unhinging. Mr. Hausselman was coming down the hall, still talking to someone.

"The fellow upstairs with the hair. He's handsome." Gladys was disappearing.

"He's a toad."

"Who's a toad?" Mr. H. asked.

I still stared at the spot beside the stove where Gladys had been. "No one, I. Oh shit!" The beans boiled over with an explosion of steam and the lid of the pressure cooker bounced and clanged. I switched all the burners off and gave the sauce a quick stir.

"Hello, Frieda."

I froze, still facing the stove. It couldn't be. I turned.

"Norman."

A great glob of Béarnaise sauce dripped off my spoon onto the floor. Norman held out his hand and smiled.

"Excuse me," I said, turned, and walked out the back door.

The Wooden Spoon Woman

I walked three blocks, still holding the wooden spoon. When I realized I still had it, I held it up and looked at it. It seemed alien — I couldn't quite discern its function. I had a brief flash of holding up a convenience store with it. Give me all your money. They'd call me the Wooden Spoon Woman. Why hadn't I thought of a life of crime before? It would be something to do. Then I realized I'd have to sharpen the spoon somehow or it wouldn't be a very effective weapon. That seemed like entirely too much work. I threw it in the bushes.

I kept walking. This is stupid. I'm twenty-seven years old. I can't run away. Besides, I didn't bring any money, or a coat, or shoes, for that matter. Before I knew it, I stood in front of Ginny's condo building, the Trudgdain Towers. I buzzed her number. No answer. I buzzed again.

"Hello."

Thank God, she's home. "Ginny, it's me."

"Who?"

"Frieda."

"Hi, Frieda. How are you?"

"Terrible. Let me in and I'll tell you all about it."

"I'm busy right now."

"If you don't let me up, I'm going to pitch a fit in front of your building, and I'm going to scream your name while I do it. First *and* last name. Let me up."

She gave a sigh and the door buzzer sounded.

When Ginny answered the door to her apartment, she whispered, "I have company. Behave yourself."

She was slightly mussed, as was the man sitting on the couch. Candles on the table had just been blown out and still sent up weak wisps of smoke. A half-empty bottle of wine and two glasses sat on the coffee table. An artificial log still had about an hour left in the fireplace.

"Frieda, I'd like you to meet Dr. Latimer." She sat on the couch beside him.

"Jim, please." He held out his hand. I sat down and burst into tears, which immediately dissipated any coziness my arrival hadn't already disturbed.

"Oh, Ginny, you wouldn't believe it. I invited Whitman and he came today and we had an argument he's such an L.A. snob and Gladys showed up and I was trying to cook then Norman came Norman can you believe it and then the beans boiled over and Béarnaise sauce is supposed to be rich isn't it?"

Both Ginny and Jim nodded.

"God, can you believe it?"

They both smiled but were silent staring at me.

"I mean, can you?" I tried again.

Ginny sighed, turned to Jim, and smiled tightly at him. He smiled back. It was a prime example of non-verbal communication. She'd said, "Sorry darling, but she's a friend, not a close friend, but one must do these things." He'd said, "Don't worry for now, but do try and get rid of her." They turned faces rearranged back into consideration towards me.

"Kentucky Norman is here? Why?"

"I have no idea. I wrote him a while ago, but I certainly didn't invite him. And Mr. L.A. Movie Producer Whitman is Mr. H.'s son. I did invite him because I'm an idiot."

"He's a movie producer? Well, that's interesting," said Ginny.
Jim stared at my feet.

"I didn't bother to get shoes before I left, or a coat."

"You have something between your toes," he said.

I looked down at my feet and saw four very dirty pieces of toilet paper still stuck between the toes of my left foot. Shit, I'd been following Whitman around like that. God. I stared at my foot for a moment.

"Well, I'd better go. Thanks for listening to me."

Ginny followed me to the door. "Call me tomorrow and let me know how it goes. Here — wear these." She got a pair of running shoes out of the closet.

"Thanks."

"Nice to meet you, Frieda," called Jim from the living room.

"Bye." Ginny turned to go back.

Before I put the runners on, I pulled the pieces of toilet paper out from between my toes and dropped them in Jim's shiny black shoe.

I began walking home, stopping to crawl under the bushes near the house to retrieve the wooden spoon. The closer I got, the slower I walked. It had clouded over and began to drizzle lightly. Great, nothing like taking your wooden spoon out for a walk in the rain. Lights came on in the houses as I passed. Families sitting down to dinner. Why is it all homes look cozy and settled when you see into the windows at night? I could knock on a door. "Hi, I'm Frieda, would you like to adopt me? Could I help you stir anything? I brought my spoon."

I began to snort with laughter despite myself. As I went my steps grew slower and slower. When I reached the bench at the bus stop nearest to home, I sat down. I felt dampness soaking into the seat of my pants. How? How had I come to be here, sitting in the drizzle with a wooden spoon and no purpose in life? I supposed taking the wooden spoon back home was a sort of purpose, but I couldn't see it lasting long. I thought about how I expected my life would be. My life as a grownup. As a teenager, the only adults I could understand were the artists, the ones who went before, the ones whose biographies I read over and over. I believed they had somehow escaped all the day-to-day shit of life and lived as it made sense to live, with your heart and eyes wide and constantly open. I wanted to live like that. I wanted to sense every moment fully, to see everything in its immediate existence. And by seeing it, be able to paint it. I wanted to live, I suppose, like a Zen master, but I had no idea where the mountain was.

I sat and watched a puddle form in the gutter in front of me, then stood and continued my walk back to the house. When I arrived, I went around back, wedged myself behind a dripping lilac bush, and peeked in the kitchen window. Someone had attempted to begin supper; the Béarnaise sauce had been half-spooned into a dish and then abandoned, the shrivelled yams uncovered on a plate. I went around to the side of the house and peeked in the small living room window. Oh Lord, this didn't look at all cozy. Whitman and Norman sat on the couch as far apart as possible. Mr. H. was in his favourite chair next to the fireplace, a grim expression on his face. There seemed to be little conversation happening.

It was hard to believe Whitman and Norman belonged to the same species. Norman was shorter and had no edges. He was the sort of person if you looked at for too long, started to blur; there was nothing to focus on. He wasn't fat or muscled; his body was like an armature with only the first layer of clay pressed onto it, the sculpting not yet begun. I think that was one of the problems in our relationship. I couldn't get a grip on him; even in an argument, he melted away like a scoop of vanilla ice cream.

Whitman was all edges and angles like a weathervane, an animate, unembellished armature. He radiated intensity and his leg jiggled up and down as he sat.

So, what happens when you put an ectomorph, an endo-morph, and an old man in a room together? Not much, apparently. Then Norman said something, Mr. H. nodded, and Whitman laughed. Someone else said something and then they all laughed. What were they being so jovial about?

They were talking about me. I knew it. Norman was probably telling them about my backwards bustier. Whitman about the toilet paper between my toes. Mr. H. about how I had dialed the wrong phone number and ended up here.

Here. Here, standing outside of my home spying on people. Madness. I was going to go in there and face them head on. I'd walk right into the living room, sit down, and have a conversation like a normal person. I walked up the front steps, onto the porch and in the front door. I took off my shoes and walked around the corner into the living room. It immediately grew silent. They turned their faces towards me.

"Well," I said, "I see you've all met. I'm going to bed now. Goodnight."

As I walked down the hall, they resumed their conversation. Mr. H. was talking about the Art Centre and the financial troubles they were having, Norman was saying that times were tough for corporations and Whitman that the tax breaks they used to get for filming in Canada were going down in many provinces.

Fine. Great. Good, get along, fellas. Get along, little doggies. I was going to sleep. I closed the door.

"I think you should go sit with them." Gladys was in her customary chair.

"Well, I don't think so, Gladys."

"Are you taking that spoon to bed?"

The damn wooden spoon was still in my hand. I held it up and looked at it.

"The way things are going, I just might."

"Oh."

"Well, good night." I laid the spoon on the nightstand, climbed into bed with my wet clothes on, and turned out the light.

From the corner in the darkness came Gladys' voice. "Are you going to be comfortable sleeping like that?"

"I'll be fine, thank you. Good night."

"Good night."

Squeak. Squeak. Squeak.

"Gladys, what are you doing?"

"I'm rocking."

"I can hear that. Do you have to rock here?"

"The chair is here."

I sat up and turned on the light. "You're not going away, are you?"

"I thought we could have a talk."

"Sure, a nice little confab is on the top of my list right now. Fire away." I put the pillow between my back and the headboard, folded my arms, and waited. And waited.

"I thought you wanted to have a talk," I said.

"I'm thinking."

"Well, while you're thinking, how about getting going on that story of yours. Like what kind of dancer you wanted to be and all that. That was your ghostly mission, was it not?"

"Part of it. The other part is up to you."

"And what part might that be?"

"I can't tell you," she said.

"Of course not. That would be far too easy, wouldn't it?"

"I don't make the rules and don't ask me who does. Well, I grew up on a farm just outside of what wasn't Winnipeg then."

"What do you mean, it wasn't Winnipeg?"

"If you keep interrupting, I'll never get it all told."

"Right. Sorry." I pulled the pillow up behind my back and settled in.

"I mean it was the 1800s and the town was a cluster of

buildings — a hotel, a blacksmith's, that sort of thing. My parents moved to Winnipeg from Ontario, where they first settled. My father had land hunger. It was like gold fever. A lot of men from Europe got it. They kept moving to where they could get more and more land. They never stayed anywhere long enough to develop the land, they just wanted more. Twenty acres here, then a quarter section, then two sections. Owning all that land made him feel rich even though we had nothing."

"I thought you were going to tell me about dancing."

"I'm getting there. So, we ended up outside of Winnipeg and it seemed like he finally had enough land to satisfy him. We got animals — cows, chickens, pigs, and some mean old geese. He started to farm properly or as properly as a bookkeeper from Prague could. Mother used to play the violin in Prague. Maybe I inherited the music in my head from her. I never heard her play the violin that I could remember. I found the instrument in an old trunk. I'd taken it out and tried to play it, but she got angry and took it away. 'There's no time for that here,' she'd said. But the music played for me anyway."

Gladys cocked her head to the side slightly as if she listened to the music as she spoke. I wished I could hear it.

"I knew from the time I was a little girl that I wanted to dance. I'd dance for the chickens when I was supposed to be feeding them. Sometimes I'd forget to feed them. I'd wander off when I finished dancing for them, go and perform for the cows. Hungry chickens, but well-entertained. I was always in trouble for forgetting something. I danced on the way to school and on the way home. I danced taking the threshing crews out their lunches."

"That's how I felt about painting," I said. "It was like there was always a canvas in my mind. I could look at something, sketch it, try it out, and paint it all in my head. If it worked, I'd go and paint it for real. Did you take lessons?"

"When I was about fifteen, a lady moved to town and started a dancing school. Winnipeg had grown by then and it was almost like a city. We had a proper general store and even a town hall. I suppose it would have seemed laughable in a big city, but we were starved for culture out there in the little towns and farms. Almost all of our parents came from European cities where culture had been everywhere. Prairie life would scour away even their memories of polish eventually but, at that time, they still could recall it, respect it, and hunger for it. Her name was Miss Johnstone and she was lovely. Her clothes and shoes were wonderful, probably years out of date, but they seemed so stylish to us farm girls. She wasn't paid much, thank goodness, or my mother never would have let me go. I think she was paid in eggs from one family, firewood from another — she made out all right, I guess."

"What sort of dancing did she teach?" I was fully awake now, imagining a young Gladys whirling her way across the fields, leaving wild graceful tracks in the dust behind her.

"Ballroom mostly. That's why most parents let their girls go. They hoped it might help us to make a good match. Five or six of us girls would gather once a week and foxtrot with each other, trying to remember who was the gentleman and who was the lady. She also taught us bits of ballet and jigs and about everything you could imagine. She was like a fairy godmother to me. I couldn't believe anyone understood how I felt about dancing, but she did. She started giving me private lessons without charging any extra. She said I showed great promise."

"I guess you never got hung from a broomstick."

"Pardon me?"

"Nothing. I didn't make out so well in tap dancing classes. Where did the teacher come from?"

"She never said. We girls made up stories of jilted lovers and risqué pasts for her and I'm sure the adults had their own opinions. Opinions that might have stopped a lesser woman, but she convinced enough of them that it was necessary and proper that a young lady be schooled in the social graces and that ballroom dancing was the most important of those graces."

"So what happened?"

"I got married."

"Just like that? You're getting private lessons, showing great promise, and then you get married?"

"No, not just like that. Miss Johnstone wanted to take up a collection for me. She wanted to go door to door and raise money to send me to dance school down East. She told them I'd put the town on the map. My mother was certain I'd end up as a harlot all painted up and lurking in smoky lounges in the evil city of Toronto."

"Did you go?"

"No, I told you, I got married."

"Oh shit, Gladys, what do you mean you got married?"

"Married, you know, white veil, minister, rice in the face, married."

"I know what it means, but why did you do it?"

"Because he asked me, I suppose."

"That's no excuse."

"Someone's coming," said Gladys and then swept her arms out dramatically. "My hour is almost come, when I to sulphurous and tormenting flames must render up myself."

"Are you serious?"

"No. Shakespeare."

"Oh right, *Hamlet*, English 30. The ghost. That's funny." I turned my head towards the stairs; someone was coming up. "Something is rotten in the state of Denmark," I whispered.

"There is nothing either good or bad, but thinking makes it so."

"Touché."

There was a knock on the door. I got out of bed and opened the door a crack. Norman, of course. He stood there with a hopeful smile on his face.

"Ah," I said, "The devil hath power to assume a pleasing shape."

He looked confused for a moment, then smiled. "But soft! What light through yonder window breaks?

"Wrong play, Norman."

He continued, "It is the East, and Frieda is the sun!" He went down on one knee. "Arise, fair sun, and kill the envious moon, who is already sick and pale with grief that thou her maid art far more fair than she."

"Oh, for Pete's sake, get up."

He stood and dusted off his knee. He blushed. "It's amazing what you can remember. I was Romeo in a play in high school."

"You were *Romeo*?"

"Nay, good goose, bite not."

"You may be a millionaire but you're a bit of a goof."

"I'll take that as a compliment."

"You should. Now what do you want?"

"I can't remember. Can I come in?"

I turned and looked back into the bedroom. The rocking chair was empty. I opened the door.

"Are you staying here tonight?"

"Here?" Norman surveyed the bedroom.

"Not in my room, buckaroo. I mean in the house."

"Your friend Mr. Hausselman has offered me the other spare bedroom. I might take him up on it if you don't mind."

"What, the five-star Fairmount isn't worthy of you?"

"There actually aren't any five-star hotels in Winnipeg. My travel agent checked."

"Now, that's sad. All the rich people wandering the streets with their Louis Vuitton luggage and nowhere to stay."

He looked at the easel set up on the desk. "You're painting."

"I'm not. Don't bug me."

"But you. . . all that work. . ."

I held up my hand. "Stop right now or there's a four-star

hotel waiting for your reservation. Besides, I've signed up for training in a career."

"Good for you. What is it?"

"Locksmithing," I said.

He laughed. "No, really, what?"

"Really locksmithing."

He tried to get his face under control, but the only way he could stop smiling was to frown. "I didn't know you were good with tools," he said.

"I'm not. But they teach you at schools, right? So I'll *learn* how to be good with tools."

"Right," he said, "I suppose they would." He looked at me for a long moment and then said, "If it upsets you, I won't stay."

"Stay. The more the merrier. Just promise you won't bother me about my painting. Now, it's been a long strange day for me. I don't know why you're here —"

"Mr. Hausselman invited me," Norman interrupted.

Now *that* was funny. What a pair Mr. H. and I were.

"And I don't really care right now. Stay. I'll talk to you in the morning, okay?"

"All right. Thank you."

"You're welcome, for what I don't know. Good night."

"Good night." He went back down the stairs.

The next morning, the house was quiet but it felt different, probably the vibrations of Whitman and Norman sleeping somewhere in it. "Vibrations" had been one of Norman's mother's favourite terms.

Thinking of Norman, I supposed I should get up and cook breakfast for him or something. Make him breakfast? Forget it. I hadn't invited him here. I had, however, invited Whitman. Did that mean I was obliged to cook breakfast for him? By the time I decided that none of them were my responsibility and I didn't

Dance, Gladys, Dance

have to cook anything for anyone, I could smell bacon frying.

I got up and went downstairs in my slept-in clothes without combing my hair. Not only did I not have to make breakfast for any of them, I didn't have to impress them either. Nothing like starting the day with a positive attitude.

Mr. H. stood at the stove stirring a big pan of scrambled eggs. "Does your friend Norman like eggs?"

I got a cup of coffee. "I suppose so. Yeah, he does. So, Mr. H.?"

"So, Frieda? I wrote to Norman."

"I wrote to Whitman."

"Hmm. Mate minds link alike. Would you set the table?"

"Sure. I guess it's nice to know we both care."

"It is." He stirred the eggs. "Both of us overstepping the confoundaries at the same time. However, I don't want to sit around the house staring at each other all day."

"Tell you what. I'll take Whitman off your hands for the day, you do the same with Norman, and we'll meet back here for a nice civilized dinner tonight."

"You have yourself a deal. But what will we do with them?"

"Take Norman somewhere boring and historical. He'll love it."

"It's not me I'm worried about. What'll you do with Whitman?"

"I'll figure something out. Don't be worried." I poured another cup of coffee.

An Unhealthy And Disgusting Habit

I should have been worried. We made it through breakfast, all right. We ate, drank, and made, if not merry, at least civil. Whitman had on his completely black tortured-genius-who-has-become-extremely-wealthy-despite-his-difficult-life-uniform again. Norman wore a red golf shirt and khaki shorts that exposed his peaked knees. When Mr. H. and I outlined our plans for the afternoon, Norman agreed cheerfully to go to the Art Centre with Mr. H., but Whitman wasn't at all enthused about going to the "concert in the park" with me.

I took it personally.

"That's fine," I said after Norman and Mr. H. had left. "If you don't want to go with me, I understand. I'll go wind wool with Miss Kesstle. You go amuse yourself."

"I doubt Miss Kesstle has taken to spinning her own wool."

"Fine. I'll sit around and wait until Beethoven gets himself up a tree and go rescue him." We stood in the front hall. I already had my shoes on.

"I can't believe people are still getting that cat out of trees. If they left him, maybe he'd figure out how to climb down by himself." Whitman took his leather blazer off the hook.

"You're an authority on Beethoven, I suppose?"

"He was my cat once."

"*Your* cat?"

"I found him in an alley when I was skipping school and kept him in the garden shed for a few days. But he wouldn't even look at me when I called him. I didn't realize he was deaf, I thought he didn't like me. I took him over to Miss Kesstle's while she was out shopping and put him in her wool basket to see what sort of mess he'd make." He took his boots from the mat and sat on the bottom step of the staircase to put them on.

"Miss Kesstle's door is always locked."

"It wasn't back then."

I shrugged. "So you gave Beethoven to Miss Kesstle. Is this supposed to make me like you?"

He stood. "I didn't give him to her, I wanted to see what he'd do. Kittens. Wool. You know."

"All right, we've established you were a troubled child. Now, what's the problem with the concert in the park?"

"Listen, I'm interested in finding out what sort of woman my father is living with, but I've seen that concert about twelve times." The dark sunglasses went on top of his head.

"I suppose you have a better idea."

"As I matter of fact, I do. I have someone to see." He opened the door and stood waiting. "Are you coming?"

We went by bus. I'd refused using any other form of transportation, hoping to gain the upper hand on Whitman by watching him slide on shiny orange seats and grate his teeth at every stop and shudder. Whitman had acquiesced, trying, I supposed, to be a good sport. He wouldn't tell me exactly where we were going or whom we were going to see.

"So, downtown?"

"Yes, downtown," he answered, adding as the bus halted to pick up another group of people, "Are all these stops necessary? This is inhumane. We could have been there fifteen minutes ago."

"This is public transit. That means the huddled masses can get on and off where they need to. Life's a bitch, hey?"

He groaned.

"Think of it as a tour," I said. "Look out the window, relax, see the sights."

"What sights? Sidewalks? Cars?"

"People. If you look very closely, you'll see living, breathing humans." I gestured out the window.

"One of them is breathing down my neck right now," he said.

"Fine. Never mind. What's the TV show going to be about?"

"It's a sitcom pilot about a house divided into two rental suites. A bunch of punk rockers live upstairs and Jesus rents the basement."

I snorted. "No, really."

"Really. It should have an interesting dynamic. Speaking of interesting dynamics, how did you come to be living with my father?"

"Nice segue. He put an ad in the paper for a room to rent." That was true.

"What happened between you and Norman? His cash run dry?"

"Screw you."

"Just joking."

"Not funny." I said and turned to look out the window.

"My father doesn't have any money, you know."

I didn't respond. The ensuing silence was broken only by the music leaking from the headphones of the teenager in front of us. Baduh. Baduh. Ch. Ch. Ch. It sounded like a drum machine looping the same five beats over and over. It made my teeth ache. Whitman pulled the cord.

The bus shuddered to a halt and we disembarked downtown. Not the high-class, high-tech high-rise downtown but the low-down, low-profile, low-rent downtown.

"Here?"

Dance, Gladys, Dance

"Relax," said Whitman, "see the sights."

He led the way to an old hotel. A hand-lettered sign in the window read, Housekeeping Rooms. Cheap. The letters were perfectly square and neat but they angled downward at the end, as though the words were about to slide off the edge of the cardboard.

"You gotta like that when the best thing they can say about the place is that it's cheap. I wonder if any of the Louis Vuitton refugees looking for a five-star hotel ended up here?"

Whitman ignored me and walked into the lobby. Was he a heroin addict, I wondered? It would explain his pallor. But why take me along to score?

There was no one at the front desk. Johnny Cash sang from a crappy little radio on the counter. Whitman started up the stairs. There was a large, dark, may I say blood-like stain on the carpet at the bottom of the stairs. I stopped. "Listen. I don't like this place. You do what you need to do and I'll wait for you down here."

"Fine." He continued up the stairs. I looked at the empty front desk and the stain on the carpet. It appeared old, but I was no forensic expert.

"Hang on. I'm coming with you." Halfway up the stairway, there was a cardboard sign on the wall written in the same neat square letters as the one in the front window. Whitman stopped. "Check this out."

PLEASE DO NOT DEFECATE IN THE STAIRWAY.
THIS IS AN UNHEALTHY AND DISGUSTING HABIT.

"As though anyone who made a *habit* of shitting in a stairway would know what defecate means," he said and continued up the stairs.

The hallway was dark; it smelled of piss, sour alcohol, stale cigarettes, and vaguely and strangely of chrysanthemums.

Bits of noise seeped out from behind the doors we passed — an argument, television, strange laughter, and from the door we stopped in front of, the sound of an electric typewriter being pounded at a furious rate. Whitman knocked and the typing stopped. No one came to the door. Whitman knocked again. Silence.

He called, "Marilyn, it's me, Whitman."

There was a shuffling. A woman who'd seen better days opened the door, or maybe she'd never seen any better days, and that's why she looked so bad. Her hair was bleached blonde, greasy, and short. It stuck out from her head like a child's imitation of a mad scientist for a Halloween costume. She wore a pair of tight black stirrup pants and an oversized polyester blouse in a geometric print that would have made Ginny physically ill. I couldn't tell how old she was — fifty, maybe. Her face was pale and wrinkled, she wore blue eyeshadow, and her eyebrows had been drawn on halfway up her forehead. She stared at us.

"Marilyn, this is Frieda, a friend of mine."

I thought "friend" was stretching it a bit. I turned my back to Whitman and smiled at her. Marilyn walked into the tiny room. Whitman followed her, I followed Whitman, and we all walked three steps and had to stop. We'd gotten as far as we could go. The stench was overwhelming. I searched for my social graces. Pleased to meet you? No. Nice place? No. Whitman smiled at me. I thought of evil public transit plans, of rush hour, and bad-tempered drivers.

"Sit down." Marilyn gestured at the bed. I smiled, cringed, and sat. She sat down on a folding chair at a desk made out of a piece of plywood and cement blocks. On the desk was a green electric typewriter and stacks of paper. The floor was covered in clothes and food and God only knows what.

"So you're a friend of Whitman's?" I asked her. Whitman stood and stared out the window.

"I think *friend* would be overstating it some," she answered.

I smiled at her and meant it this time.

"Is the draft finished?" Whitman turned from the window apparently not bothered that no one was willing to claim him as a friend.

"What," she said, "the FedEx man not giving you proper service, you had to come in person?"

"I had some other things to attend to. Is it finished?"

"Here." She handed him a large stack of papers.

Whitman sat beside me on the bed. I moved over as far as I could. He read for a minute, flipping through the pages. I smiled up at the peeling paint on the ceiling. Be damned if I was going to make conversation about the weather again. Marilyn lit a cigarette and blew smoke through the line of my smile.

"Looks good," said Whitman. "How much?"

She blew out a mouthful of smoke. "Five hundred bucks."

"Right," he said. "Two hundred."

"I need five." Her voice was clipped and strong, but her foot began to knock against the rung of the chair.

"Three." Whitman reached for his wallet.

"Four." *Whap whap whap* went her foot.

"Three-fifty."

"Fine, you bastard."

He handed her three hundred-dollar bills and a fifty.

The rate of her foot against the chair increased dramatically as soon as the money touched her hand. Whitman motioned to me. "Let's go."

I stood. "Nice to meet you, Marilyn." She stood up and dug through the clothes on the floor. "Where are my shoes?"

"Maybe you could come for dinner while Whitman is here."

"Fucking shoes." She was halfway underneath the bed winging things out from beneath it.

Whitman grabbed my arm. "Come on." We were out in the hallway and the door was shut behind us.

"That was rude," I said.

"Rude would be keeping her from spending her money as quickly as possible."

"God, what a place. I thought some of *my* apartments were horrible."

"She likes it there." We stood on the sidewalk, blinking at the bright sunlight.

"I don't believe that."

"Don't, then." He waved at a cab that slowed to get a look at him and then pulled over.

"We're taking a bus," I protested.

"Like hell," he said and got in the cab.

I climbed in after him. I didn't have the energy for the bus at rush hour anyhow.

"1228 Morning Street," Whitman told the driver.

"Where did you meet her?"

"I took an evening course in screenwriting when I was about seventeen and she showed up once in a while. She can knock off a perfectly constructed three-act horror script, incredibly scary stuff, like most people can put on their shoes. The last one she did for me was called *The Final Address*, about a killer who'd mail his victims the street numbers of where they'd die. But she can't manage to stay sober or clean long enough to actually get them out anywhere. So, I make sure her work gets an audience, or at least a reading. She gets some cash."

"Not much cash for a script."

He shrugged. "She doesn't need more."

"And how much do you get for these scripts?"

"A bit."

"You shit, you're probably raking it in while that poor woman sits there in that hellhole and you ride around in a Cadillac."

"I don't have a Cadillac."

"Limousine, then. You know what I mean."

"You think I should go back and give her a couple thousand dollars?"

"Yes. I. Do." My throat was closing, choking off my words.

"She's addicted to every drug ever invented, Frieda. She'd be dead before morning. I'm concerned about even giving her three-fifty, but she probably has some debts to pay. She should be okay."

"Concerned? You're disgusting. If you were really concerned, you'd get her some help." We pulled up in front of the house. While Whitman paid the driver, I slammed inside. Norman and Mr. H. hadn't come home yet. Eeaghuuugh. How had Mr. H. ever produced such a monster? I began to crash around the kitchen. I'd said I would make supper again to atone for the fiasco last night. No yams. No sauces.

Whitman came into the kitchen and leaned around the corner. "Are you sleeping with him?"

"What? With who?"

"With my father."

"*No.*" I slammed the can opener down on the counter. He turned and left while I sputtered and spat in a vain attempt to say something incredibly rude to him.

I heard him go upstairs, then come back down and close the front door behind him. Good. Maybe he was taking a plane back to L.A. where he belonged.

A half an hour later, supper bubbled in a pot on top of the stove. I made mother's Ten Can Chili, put garlic bread in the oven, and vigourously tossed a salad. Norman and Mr. H. hadn't returned yet.

"I tried to tell you yesterday, always make what you know. This smells good." Gladys stood in front of the stove, leaning over the chili.

"Great. The Cooking with Gladys Show. I'm a little too upset for culinary tips right now."

"But you always are."

"I'm always what?"

"Upset. Haven't you noticed?"

"I'm not the one who hangs around giving other people advice when they ran off, got married, and stopped being promising."

"I didn't run off."

"Sat down then. Sat down, took up marriage, and gave up dancing. Excuse me." I waited for Gladys to step aside, then tasted the chili and added another shake of chili powder.

"I never gave up. Never, not once. We had to get married. Well, I suppose Jack didn't, he could have walked away from it all right, but my father demanded Jack marry me."

"Walked away from what?"

"We were found together in a compromising position. Very compromising, considering we were both half-naked in the back of a wagon. He was so handsome. I knew I was supposed to save myself, but I thought I was going away soon anyway. Jack was from one of the other farms outside of town. He had a way of looking at a girl that melted them, and I wanted to do it, to try it once. Are you going to make a salad?"

I didn't answer.

"A salad would be good, and some baking powder biscuits. I could teach you how to make them."

"The salad is in the fridge and I have garlic bread. Please finish the story, Gladys."

"They all turned against me, even Miss Johnstone the dancing instructor. She said I should have known better, that I knew what was at stake, and if I couldn't stop myself from rolling around with farm boys then I was never going to make it anyway. So there I was, married, before I hardly knew what happened. I screamed and yelled and threatened to run away, but I was too afraid. I had nothing. But I did run away later. Later, when I was braver, or maybe more desperate."

There was a knock at the back door. I looked at Gladys. "How do you always manage to do that?"

"Do what?" There was another knock. I ignored it.

"Get interrupted in the middle of a story. Do you plan it?"

"It's not my fault."

"Sure, whatever." I turned towards the door, then sprinted to it and threw it open, hoping whoever stood there would catch a glimpse of Gladys.

"Look!" I yelled and pointed to the stove where Gladys had been standing.

Miss Kesstle jumped back about a foot, then gawked at the stove, her hands over her heart. Gladys had, of course, evaporated.

"It's good you're cooking, Frieda. But you could give someone a heart attack yelling like that."

"Sorry, I was excited." Damn that Gladys and her coming and going. "Come in. Do you want a cup of tea?"

"Is he still here?" she whispered loudly.

"Whitman?" I whispered loudly back, "He's gone out."

"Good," she said, "Is Mr. Hausselman home?"

"No."

"Beethoven seems a little peaked. Could you come and look at him?"

"Where is he?"

"Under the couch. He won't come out. Maybe he's angry at me."

"I doubt it. Let's go see." I turned the burners off and followed her out.

He Looks Bad

Miss Kesstle paused at the door, then pulled a slip of paper from her apron pocket and punched in the numbers for the alarm.

"He was fine yesterday, but he's been under the couch all day today."

I got down on my hands and knees, moved aside a small bowl of water, and looked under the couch. Beethoven's eyes were open but glazed, and his fur was rough and rumpled.

"Beethoven. Kitty. Kitty." He turned his head slightly, but didn't move. Shit. There was definitely something wrong with him. I stood up. "I think he's sick. We'll have to get him out and take him to the vet's."

Her face crumpled. "I'll get ready."

"I'll see if anyone's home next door yet."

I ran back next door. Whitman was going up the front steps.

"Beethoven is sick. I'm going with Miss Kesstle to the vet's. Please tell your dad when he gets home."

"What's the matter with him?"

"I don't know, but he looks bad."

"I'll come with you." He turned back down the stairs.

"You don't have to do that."

Norman and Mr. H. traipsed down the sidewalk chatting and laughing.

"Hey, Frieda," yelled Norman.

"We had a great afternoon," said Mr. H. as they approached us. They were both smiling. Norman carried a large square package in his arms. They seemed comfortable together as if they'd known each other for years. I felt a twinge of jealousy. Mr. H. was *my* friend. Whitman stared at them too.

"I bought an amazing photograph done by a young girl," said Norman. "You should see some of the work there. Did you two enjoy yourselves?" He looked from Whitman's face to mine, his smile thinning a little.

"Of course," said Whitman and he winked at me.

What the hell? "Something in your eye?" I asked him.

"How *was* your day?" asked Mr. H.

"It was — different. Beethoven's sick. We've got to get him to the vet's. Miss Kesstle is getting ready."

Mr. H. hurried next door. The rest of us followed. Miss Kesstle stood in the middle of the living room holding a blanket; she had her sweater on inside-out.

"He's under the couch, maybe you could get him out," she said to Mr. H.

Beethoven didn't struggle at all as Mr. H. gently pulled him out.

"I'll go get the Valiant," I said already crossing the living room.

"The keys are on a hook by the back door," said Mr. H. from beside the couch.

I got the keys and went through the backyard, past the chicken coop to the single wooden garage in the back. I could barely make out the car in the dim light. The driver's door squeaked loudly as I opened it. I put the key in the ignition and turned. Click. Click. Nothing.

I went back to Miss Kesstle's. "Dead battery," I said and handed the keys to Mr. H., who pocketed them.

Whitman said, "I'll get us a car." He went into the kitchen. Norman took the blanket from Miss Kesstle.

"I'm Norman," he said, "a friend of Frieda's. Poor kitty." He wrapped the blanket around the cat and handed him to Miss Kesstle. The cat lay there in her arms, its head lolling slightly.

Miss Kesstle started to cry. "Nice to meet. . . Oh, Beethoven. We'll take you to that nice vet, the one you bit last time, he was so nice about it, you were a bad cat, weren't you?"

Mr. H. steered her out the door. Whitman waited on the lawn. "It should be here right away. I told them it was an emergency."

Miss Kesstle started carefully down the stairs, murmuring to the cat. She stopped suddenly. "Oh dear."

"What?" asked Norman. "Are you all right? Do you want me to carry him?"

"No," said Miss Kesstle, "but the vet said he had to be sedated before I brought Beethoven in again."

"Who had to be sedated?" asked Whitman. "The vet?"

"Oh, shut up," I said to him. "Beethoven isn't interested in biting anyone right now, Miss Kesstle. It'll be okay."

We stood in a little huddle waiting for the cab. But it wasn't a taxi that pulled up in front of the house; it was the big, black limo.

Miss Kesstle balked. "I'm not going in that," she said. "What will people think?"

Mr. H. took her arm again. "I'm not eggstatic about it myself. Let's just get him to the vet's."

He helped her in and climbed in beside her. I gave Whitman a withering look as I climbed in.

"What is the matter with you people," he said, following me in, "that you're all so committed to shitty forms of transportation?"

"Whitman, your language," said Norman as he climbed in nodding towards Miss Kesstle.

"My what?"

"I happen to know how you earned this limo, remember?" I said to Whitman.

Dance, Gladys, Dance

The driver looked back. "No animals please," he said.

"This is a famous cat," said Whitman. "He's worth three million. Just drive."

"There are regulations," said the driver.

Norman handed him a fifty-dollar bill. The limo pulled away.

"How did you earn this limo?" Mr. H. asked Whitman.

"By making movies, though I doubt you'd believe that. I'm your oddball son, the embarrassment."

"I'm sure that's not true," said Norman.

"Shut up, Norman," I said.

"Be nice," said Mr. H.

"I don't have to be nice to him."

"No," said Whitman, "You don't have to do anything but take advantage of an old man."

"At least I'm not a thief."

The limo careened around a corner.

"A thief?" said Mr. H. and Norman together looking at Whitman.

There was a retching noise and Beethoven threw up. Miss Kesstle started to cry.

"Oh, fuck," said the driver, looking in the rear-view mirror.

We were silent the rest of the way.

Later that night I was in the laundry room putting Beethoven's blanket in the washer. The blanket looked and smelled disgusting. Beethoven had continued to throw up for the rest of the ride and in the vet's office. Miss Kesstle had continued to cry.

"What are you doing with that blanket? Throwing it out?" Gladys hovered halfway down the stairway.

"It's a washing machine. You put the dirty clothes in, add soap, and turn it on. It adds water and swishes the clothes around and they come out clean.

"No."

"Yup. The miracles of modern technology. Washing machines and drive-thru donut shops."

"The time I wasted scrubbing Jack's drawers. What's a donut? How do you drive through it?"

"Oh, God. Scrubbing underwear and no donuts, how did people manage to get up every morning?"

I added several cups of detergent and a splash of bleach to the washer.

"Are you coming down?" I asked.

"Basements make me a little nervous. But it doesn't seem too bad down here." She floated down the rest of the stairs and watched me turn on the washing machine.

"Were you ever happy here with Jack?" I asked.

"We didn't live in this house first. We lived in a little farmhouse right here on this land. I tried to do the right thing in that little house, you know — be a good wife. I tried to learn to bake and sew, and I raised chickens. That's still the old coop in the yard. I liked the chickens but that was about it. Jack tried at first too. He'd buy me the nicest things he could afford and tried to be patient with my lack of domestic talents. On our first anniversary, I begged him to take me to a variety and dancing vaudeville show at the Palace Theatre. The theatre had just been built and they said it was one of the finest in Canada. He grumbled about the waste of money but after I begged and cried, he finally bought us two tickets. I thought I would enjoy it, but it was terrible. I sat there in the audience wearing my farmer's-wife best cotton dress and watched all of them onstage in their gorgeous costumes doing what I dreamed of doing.

"The final number on the program was a lady dancer named Olga Dobie. She wore a midnight blue beaded gown and headdress, and danced in her bare feet while two dark-skinned men played drums. She was fantastic, otherworldly. When she finished the applause went on and on. I sat with my hands in my lap unable to clap; I was frozen with envy and self-pity. Jack stood. 'There you go,' he said. 'Happy now?' The next day I got up early and went to the Grand Hotel. If the performers had stayed overnight in town, I knew they would be there. They were in the dining room, Olga sipping tea, seated between the two drummers. I went right up to the table, introduced myself, and burst into tears. Between my sobbing and the garbled story I got out about being a dancer, then getting married, I think (them being naturally dramatic types) they thought I was being held against my will by my evil husband. I went from the hotel to the bank and took out all the money I could. I told the banker that Jack and I expected a shipment of furniture from down East. I got on the train with them and I left, ran away. I suppose the troupe-master thought I couldn't do the company any harm, I was young and pretty, and I could dance. I went back to Toronto with them. I thought Jack would let me go, that he'd be happy to find himself a new proper wife. I was wrong."

"Did you get to dance in Toronto?"

Gladys smiled, the pleasure lighting up her blue eyes. "Oh, I did. It was the most wonderful thing, all of it, the aching feet, the practices, fittings, and the nights out after rehearsals. We were practicing for another tour, this one down into the States. The director told me I'd be a main dancer in no time. But within a month, I wasn't feeling too well. I threw up constantly and lived on saltines. I thought it was the excitement of dancing every night. The tour began in a week, but I was exhausted. I'd go right to bed after the performances and sleep all morning until rehearsals. I couldn't see how the rest of them did it. I was a farm girl, used to hard work and long hours and there I was, weak like a baby."

"Oh, no. Pregnant?"

Gladys nodded.

"Was it Jack's?"

"I hadn't had relations with anyone else. The troupe members were discouraged from getting together, though what went on with Olga and her drummers was common knowledge. I wrote my mother. I was scared. She told Jack. He showed up at my room about a week later. He was like ice. He only spoke to me once. He asked, 'Is it mine?' I nodded and burst into tears and he started to pack my things. I went with him. Back to the farmhouse. I didn't know what else to do. The troupe had been kind to me, but there would be no work for a pregnant dancer. Maybe if I knew how to sew or something, I could have stayed on, helped with the costumes, but I'd never learned how properly."

"Did you have your baby?"

"I did." She seemed to be wavering, like a bad television signal.

"Was it a boy or girl?"

"It was a — a boy."

"Gladys?" She flickered on and off. "Are you okay? You don't have to talk about it. It'll be all right."

She fizzled out and was gone. Poor old thing. I was supposed to be figuring out a way to give her some peace and instead I was wandering around making bad dinners and being rude to ex-boyfriends. I needed to start working on it. I tried to think like Nancy Drew. I needed clues. Or a hypothesis. Or a hunch. I searched my mind. I didn't seem to have any of them.

Norman came down the stairs, ducking at the lowest part. I edged away from him. The laundry room was small and I felt (for lack of a better euphemism) friendly and Norman's proximity made me bite my lips. Part of me wanted him to take me in his arms and kiss me. Yeah, then sweep me away across a rainswept moor. Idiot.

"So, you had fun out with Whitman?"

"Not really."

"You didn't?" He smiled. "He's quite handsome, don't you think?"

"Do you want me to fix you up with him?"

"No, thanks. Do you ever miss me, Frieda?"

"No."

"Never?"

"I don't see what there is for us to gain by this conversation."

"Honesty?" Norman hoisted himself up and sat on top of the dryer.

"I'm not sure honesty is always a bonus in conversation." I tried to edge past him and made the mistake of looking right at him. Aiheeee. The sad tadpole eyes, the ones that made me feel like either flipping him into the mud to watch him wriggle, or scooping him up and taking him home in a bucket. I quickly looked away, focusing on the row of laundry products on the shelf behind him. Shirley must have been quite the washerwoman: bluing, washing soda, stain removers, jugs of softener, and handwashing liquid. I'd only recently advanced to fabric softener sheets myself.

"What *is* bluing used for?" I asked him.

His eyes widened and then he ignored me. "I'm feeling terrible about what happened in Kentucky. It was presumptuous of me to build that studio. I thought it would make you happy. I wanted you to paint. You *should* paint."

"Who are you to tell me what I should or shouldn't do?"

"Why is it so arbitrary for you?" he asked. "Look at you with Miss Kesstle tonight and you won't give me the time of day."

"I gave you almost a year."

"It wasn't enough."

"It was for me." I squeezed past his legs and made my exit. He didn't follow. Halfway up the stairs I turned to look at him; he had his hands over his face and was shaking his head.

Mr. H. and Whitman sat at the kitchen table eating bowls of reheated chili in silence.

"This is good chili," said Mr. H. "Where's Norman?"

"Downstairs, hanging himself with the dirty laundry, I suppose." I got a fork and bowl and sat down.

I'd spent two weeks with Norman in Vancouver. Lady March had gone to Galliano Island for a spiritual retreat. Norman sublet an apartment on the bay for three weeks. The ceilings in the apartment were twelve feet high, the floors gleaming hardwood. There were two fireplaces with mantels, sleek Deco furniture in shades of grey and pale blue, and long lilac silk curtains on the ocean-view windows puddled on the floors. It was the kind of place I'd imagined myself in as a famous artist throwing cocktail parties and entertaining patrons, certainly finer than anything Professor Gimlet would ever attain. Norman and I stayed in bed almost the whole day, dressed for supper, then walked by the ocean. Norman had started an art collection after his father died, trying to make sure that something would be left behind in the March name other than Victorian nudie photos. We went to galleries together; I played art critic and advised him on his purchases.

He offered to leave me alone if I wanted to paint. I told him I was taking a break, that I needed to replenish my vessel of creativity. I didn't want to tell him that I had serious doubts about my talent. Did Real Artists have doubts? Would he want me if I were nothing but a clerk from his store? I also didn't tell him the real reason I'd left art school. I wanted him to believe that he had rescued me, that he was the first white knight whose horse I'd jumped on. I didn't want him to know that several other knights had already unceremoniously dumped me into the muck. Who wanted to rescue a soiled maiden? The life was so wonderful, the food so good, and Norman so sweet I didn't want it to end.

When Lady March returned, she stayed at a hotel a few blocks away. We met her for lunch.

"Frieda!" she said as we sat down. "I'm so glad to see you again. How is your search for the truth?"

The truth? I was living in a fairytale. "I'm not sure. How was the retreat?"

"Marvelous. We had a drumming circle and a bonfire every night on the beach — completely hedonistic. I slept in a bunk above a fascinating young man who could tell your future by the folds in your ears. What have you two been up to?"

I blushed.

Norman said, "Frieda should come back to Kentucky with us, shouldn't she, Mother? See the sights." He turned to me. "You could go riding. We have a wonderful stable of horses."

"Oh, no," I said, "I don't do horses. They're far too large and inscrutable."

"Are you sure?" asked Lady March. "We could get you some of those nice leather chaps, the ones that the city cowboys use when they miss their horses." She smiled.

I laughed. "No, thanks. I hope you noticed that I have my shirt on the right way around this time."

"I did. Where's the champagne? Here's to the Canadian invasion of Kentucky by Frieda-With-Her-Shirt-On-Right."

So, it was decided. Away I went to Kentucky.

Norman and Lady March lived in an incredible old mansion, like something from *Gone With the Wind*, grand staircases, big white columns, and perfectly green lawns. I walked around muttering *I don't know nothin' 'bout birthin' no babies, Miss Scarlett.*

Though Lady Alvena March appeared to be what I'd normally term a flake, obsessed as she was with all her new age theories, I liked her. Her first husband had been Sir Browne, a baronet in the United Kingdom. It wasn't a royal title, but one that had been conferred on some long-dead commoner ancestor of his. Lady March was quite in the dark about the whole baronet thing; all she knew was that if they'd had a son, he would have been able to carry on the title. They hadn't had a son or a daughter either; according to Alvena, Sir Browne had been unable to "do the deed." He'd died of a heart attack while skiing in St. Moritz and had left her with a title and a gazillion dollars. I wondered at her keeping the title, but apparently, the "Lady" gave her name auspicious numerology. She'd married Norman's father, Stephen March, on one of his trips to England. The porno shop occupation hadn't bothered her; she'd found it refreshing to find a man able not only to have sex, but to make money from it. The exploitation of the women hadn't occurred to her until I asked her about it one day.

"Don't they enjoy it?" she asked.

"Some might, but some are just desperate."

"For what?"

"Money, fame, drugs, or some are bullied into it."

"Which ones?"

"I don't know."

She'd had a long talk with Norman after and he'd been pissed off at me. He did, after all, have a promise to keep to his father. Mr. March died when Norman was twenty-two and left Lady March another gazillion dollars and all the businesses to Norman.

Norman took me to meet all his friends. He introduced me as "Frieda Zweig, my girlfriend, the Artist." He bought me beautiful dresses, shoes, and purses. He would mention my painting from time to time, but I made excuses ranging from being in new surroundings that I needed time to process through my artistic consciousness to having my period and being too bloated to paint.

After a few weeks, I mentioned going back to Winnipeg. I thought I should at least broach the subject in case he was secretly waiting for me to leave. We were sitting in the library, cherry panelling in glowing brown-red, leather club chairs, and an oriental carpet in scarlet and gold. There were bowls of fruit and vases of flowers on the coffee tables. The whole interior of the house was a still life painter's wet dream.

Dance, Gladys, Dance

"Why?" said Norman. He stood by the bar, pouring us drinks: afternoon sherry as usual into little sparkling glasses. Horrid-tasting stuff, like fermented saskatoon syrup, but very cool to have an afternoon sherry.

"Well," I said, "there's my dieffenbachia."

"Who's that?"

"My houseplant."

"I'll buy you a new one. Stay."

"You mean *stay*? Like move in?"

He came, sat in the club chair across from me, and handed me my sherry. "Like move in."

"What about all my stuff?"

"I'll hire movers. They'll do it all for you. Did you leave a key with anyone?"

"No, but there's one under the rock shaped like a manatee by the back door."

"There you go. It's as good as done. Cheers."

"Cheers." I lifted my glass, swallowed a small sip, and tried not to grimace.

On an afternoon trip into town, I wandered into an agricultural fair and was smitten by the careworn faces of the livestock keepers. Finally, tentatively, after a month of being in Kentucky, I started to paint again. A new style pulled at my fingers and niggled at the back of my mind, but I didn't quite have it yet. I wanted modern folk art, like the portraits of wealthy children holding their cats and dogs from the mid-1800s, crossed with the look of Warhol silkscreens. I began with a portrait of a man who kept fancy chickens, with his green tweed cap, weathered hands, and one of his fancy chickens in his lap.

It was hard. Hard to keep going, hard not to just stop again when I felt I couldn't get it, couldn't reach what I was trying to do. Norman would show up at the door and see me with my head in my hands. "You've been working too hard, let's go for a picnic." Instead of staying with it, I'd leave, go down to the river, sit on the grass, eat chicken breasts, and sip champagne in the sun.

When I wandered about, more inside the canvas than in the real world, frowning at people I didn't even really see, he'd take me shopping and I'd forget there was something else I should be thinking about.

Not two weeks after Norman first noticed I was working again, he invited the local artists' league over for tea. A troupe of ladies in floaty afternoon dresses and one man in a corduroy jacket with leather patches on the elbows showed up. They were horrifying. I couldn't think of a thing to say. I crumbled my biscuit in my desert plate as they discussed the merits of realism and denounced every artist since Rembrandt. One of them had recently been on a trip to New Mexico and the conversation turned to Georgia O'Keeffe. Now, I thought, I can participate.

"Oh, her flowers," said one.

"Her poppies." They gave a collective sigh.

I said, "Did you know that Georgia said that she hated flowers and only painted them because they were cheaper than models and didn't move?"

They looked at me. I smiled. "Did you see her cow's skull series?"

They shook their heads. "I love her attitude," I said. "I once read that she said, 'I can't live where I want to. I can't go where I want to go. I can't do what I want to. I can't even say what I want to. I decided I was a very stupid fool not to at least paint as I wanted to.' Isn't that brilliant? A very stupid fool."

"I suppose," said the man, Geoff, I think his name was, "that you're one of those feminist revisionists who wants to rewrite art history."

"No, I just thought it was a good quote. I don't even know what a feminist revisionist is. And," I said, crushing my biscuit into tiny crumbs and letting them fall from my fingers onto the table, "I don't care."

Geoff sniffed.

As they left, one of them patted me on the shoulder. "Not everything is political, you know, dear. You should just try to enjoy things as they are."

One whispered to another, as they gathered their handbags, "Someone should have told Norman before he started adding *artists* to his collection that they can be temperamental."

The next time Norman invited them, he insisted I show them some of my work. He convinced me that they would relax and be more "congenial" once I'd shown them what talent I had. I didn't feel ready to show anything yet. I was in that in-between space, reaching for something new and better but I hadn't reached it yet, and I'd left my old proficiency behind. I shouldn't have shown it. I would have been better off showing them a collection of paint-by-numbers. But I did.

The ladies were very polite, murmured about pleasing tones, and departed en masse shortly after. I was putting the canvases away when Norman went to see them out. As I came into the hallway, I heard Norman ask the matriarch of the society in a low, worried voice, "Do you think she has any talent at all?"

"Why," I said as I came into the hall, "does it matter to you what this. . . *woman*. . . thinks of my talent? Perhaps they're not qualified to judge, perhaps they should be asking me what I think of *their* paintings, or perhaps you should be sleeping with one of them." I turned and made a grand exit up the main staircase marred only by a stumble on the third step and a muttered "oh fuck."

The society never came again and no invitation arrived for me to join their club.

She Seems A Bit Lost

Norman and Mr. H. were sitting at the kitchen table drinking Glornics together. The room was silent when I entered but I could feel a half-finished conversation lingering in the air like smoke.

"Little early for drinks, isn't it, gentlemen?" I asked.

"No crime like the pleasant," said Mr. H.

Norman grinned sheepishly. "Join us?"

"No, thanks. How's Beethoven?"

"Still weak," said Mr. H. "I just brought Miss Kesstle back from the veterinarian's. They're giving him fluid shots. Once he's stable, they're going to operate. They think he swallowed something."

I moved around the kitchen, putting dishes away and opening and closing the fridge. I didn't want to talk to Norman. He looked so comfortable sitting with Mr. H. I was afraid if I were nice to him I'd start to like him again and where could that lead? He watched me move around and sat there with that hesitant smile on his face, saying nothing. I started to get angry. I hated it when he got all weak and wienery on me like this. I mean, show some balls, say something. It pissed me off to be made to feel like a person that someone had to tiptoe around. I frowned at him. He looked around as if to see what he'd done. Right.

I turned to Mr. H. "How's Miss Kesstle holding up?"

CHAPTER FOURTEEN

"Not so well; she seems a bit lost."

"I think I'll run over and see her," I said. Norman still hadn't said a word to me.

As I went down the hall to the front door, I heard Mr. H. say to Norman, "You could try the university; someone there might be interested."

Now what? I wondered if Whitman felt as out of sorts about this new friendship between Norman and Mr. H. as I did?

I rang the bell at Miss Kesstle's. After a minute, I could see her through the glass in the top half of the door, pushing buttons on the alarm panel. She pushed a few buttons then stopped and looked up at me, her face drooping like a wet dishtowel.

"2-6-3-8-1!" I yelled. At this rate, the whole neighbourhood would know the code. She pushed the buttons and I opened the door.

"Come in," she said. "I've just made tea." I followed her into the living room. She went into the kitchen and returned with a tray with two mugs and a teapot covered with a blue and yellow crocheted tea cozy with little tassels on top.

She sat in her chair and I took a corner of the couch.

"How are you doing?" I asked.

"It's so empty without him. I don't know what I'll do if he . . . doesn't get well."

"I'm sure he will."

She looked down at her lap, then picked up a ball of cotton and a scrap of crocheting from the side of the chair and started to work.

"What're you making?"

"A mess."

I took the cozy off the teapot and poured us each a cup. "This is interesting wool," I said. It felt like coloured plastic straw.

"It's the old type of Phentex from the seventies. It'll last forever. It'll cut your hands to bits trying to work with it, though." She paused. "I never could figure out where Beethoven came from. He just showed up in my wool basket one day. I wasn't sure I wanted to keep him. I never had a pet before, but when the vet told me he was deaf, I knew I'd have to look after him. Poor old thing."

I didn't tell her that Whitman had put Beethoven in her basket. Why ruin her memories? We sat in silence for awhile. A red binder lay on the coffee table, open to a lined loose-leaf page covered in tiny pencilled writing.

> Row 1: Ch 19, sc in 2nd ch from hk and in each rem ch. Ch 1, turn. (18 sc)
>
> Rnd 2: 2 Sc in each sc. Join with sl st in 1st sc of this row to form a ring. (36 sc)
>
> Rnd 3: Ch 2. Do Not Turn. Hdc in same st as joining. Ch 1.* Sk next st. 2 hdc in next st. Ch 1. Rep from * around to last ch. Sk last ch and join with a sl st in the fl only of the top of the beg ch 2. (36 hdc & 18 ch-1 sps)

It looked like another language or some sort of secret code. Maybe Miss Kesstle had an alternate life as a Russian spy. I picked up the binder. "What is this?"

"Those are my patterns for the things I make."

There were hundreds of projects, all written out in the same tiny letters. The pages at the front had yellowed with age. Asparagus Placemats — Mr. H. had a set of those — rectangular doilies with a pattern of asparagus spears on each corner, Tasselled Tea-Cozy, Blender Cover with Roses, Spiral Shoe Bag, anything and everything you could imagine.

"You mean you designed all of these things?"

She nodded.

"But that's amazing. What a pile of work." There was real artistry in that humble binder. I was flummoxed by the idea of

Dance, Gladys, Dance

the cleverness of hundreds of thousands of women I'd previously ignored, or denigrated as substandard. Who did I think designed all the items of creativity that decorated houses all over the world? The needlework fairies? Give me a ball of yarn and ask me to make you a blanket and I'd likely end up as tangled as Beethoven in a basket of wool.

"I enjoy it."

I sipped my tea while she worked. "There's something I wanted to ask you, Frieda," she said finally, putting down her knotted doily. She frowned and swallowed.

"Go ahead."

"Well," she said, "I don't know who else to ask. . ."

"Yes?" What could this be about? She was so serious and nervous.

"What is this oral sex?"

I sputtered tea all over the front of my shirt. "What?"

"You should sponge that off before it sets."

"It's okay."

"I hear about it on the radio talk shows and the television all the time and I don't know what it is."

Good lord. I took a deep breath. "Okay, there's two types. . ."

She leaned forward her eyebrows raised. Where was Dr. Ruth when you needed her? I blushed like mad.

"The man can use his mouth on a woman down there," I pointed quickly towards my crotch, "and a woman can use her mouth on a man — on his — you know, penis."

Miss Kesstle sat back and her eyebrows fell. "You mean she puts it in her mouth?"

I nodded mutely.

Miss Kesstle shook her head. "Thank you for telling me, Frieda." She picked up her doily and continued to work.

Well, what to talk about now?

"Have you always lived in this house?" I asked.

"It was my parents' house. After they died, I stayed."

"Did you ever work?"

"I was the best court stenographer in the city. Two hundred words per minute on a four voice and jury charge."

"You must have heard some fascinating things." I could see a young Miss Kesstle sitting in front of a little keyboard thingy, fingers flying as challenges and denouncements about affairs and murders swirled around the courtroom.

"It wasn't my job to be fascinated. Besides, it had nothing to do with me."

"I suppose not. So how come you never got married?"

"I was too busy. Father died when I was just a baby. Then mother got sick with cancer just after I turned nineteen and I had to take care of her and work." She put her crocheting down, leaned forward, and fussed with the things on the tea tray.

"But everyone got married back then. Didn't you want to?"

"Perhaps no one asked me," she said and then, to my horror, began to cry.

"Oh, I'm sorry," I said, "I didn't mean to — I've been thinking about marriage — with Norman here and all, and oh, shit."

"If Beethoven dies, I'll be all alone," she sobbed. "I have no husband, no children. I'll be all by myself."

I moved over, squatted by her chair, and awkwardly patted her arm. "You're not all alone. You have Mr. H., and me, and all your friends. We're your family."

"You're right," she said sniffing. "I've got no right to be so selfish; some people have no one." She wiped her face with the mess she'd crocheted. "I need to go to sleep. I'm worn out."

"Are you sure you're all right?" I stood.

"I'm fine, it's just been a long day." She stood slowly and followed me to the door.

"Sorry about the. . ."

"He's a nice man, that Norman."

"I know. Do you want to come for dinner at Mr. H.'s or do you want me to come back later and stay overnight, maybe?"

Dance, Gladys, Dance

"No thank you. I'll be fine. You go home." She closed the door behind me. I watched through the glass to make sure she got the alarm set all right and then I walked home.

Little Cardboard Pets

Mr. H.'s muffled voice came from inside the freezer: "A roast by any other name would be something to eat."

Whitman came in the back door dressed in jeans, a black T-shirt, and with his hair standing only about a half a foot off his head. He'd just put his packages down on the kitchen counter when the phone rang. He answered it. "Hello. . . Yes, she's right here. . . No, this is Whitman. . . Oh, hello. . . Tonight?"

I shook my head, no, and waved my arms, crossing them back and forth. It had to be Ginny.

Whitman looked at Norman. "Are you free tonight?"

Norman glanced up from the paper and nodded.

"Sure," said Whitman, "that would be nice. . . Seven sounds good. . . Okay. . . Good-bye." He hung up the phone and smiled at me. "That was your friend Ginny. We're going to meet her for dinner tonight. Hope that's all right."

"No, it's not all right. You saw me waving my arms. What did you think I was doing? Directing traffic? Landing aircraft?"

Whitman ignored this. "Would *you* like to go, Norman?"

"Sure," said Norman, "I'd like to meet Ginny and it would be nice to go out. Would you like to come, Mr. Hausselman?"

"No, not me," said Mr. H. He'd given up on the freezer and rummaged in the cupboard. "I'm tired out. I'll have a bowl of mushroom soup and a quiet evening." He sounded relieved.

CHAPTER FIFTEEN

"Good, it's settled then." Whitman picked up his packages and started out of the room.

"It is not settled. I'm not going." I said. Like hell I wasn't — as if I would leave the three of them alone to talk about me. I meant I wasn't going without a fight. Someone was going to have to work for it.

"Suit yourself," said Whitman and continued out of the room.

"I'd like you to come," said Norman.

"Well, I'm not going to."

"All right," he said. "I'm going to get ready." He folded the paper neatly and went upstairs.

I called Ginny. "Listen, I don't think I can make it tonight. Beethoven is sick."

"Good excuse, but — and I hate to break it to you — Beethoven is dead."

"Not yet he isn't."

"Will you please make sense for two minutes in a row?"

"It's the neighbour lady's cat. Besides, what happened to Dr. Jim?"

"He was a doctor, all right. Last night he tells me his doctorate is in Comparative Literature. His thesis was on seventeenth-century Hebrew poetry or something. God, talk about starving in a garret. Are Whitman and Norman still coming?"

"As far as I know."

"Okay then. Sorry you can't come. I have to get ready. Bye." She hung up.

What a bunch of assholes. Mr. H. opened his can of soup by the stove. I looked at him. He bit his lips and wiggled his jaw.

"Do you have gas?" I asked. "Do you need some Pepto-Bismol?"

"No, thanks." He let a large smile escape. "So, I guess you're going for dinner?"

An hour later, Norman and I were sitting in the back seat of a taxi. Whitman was up front, talking to the driver. Ginny had chosen her recurrent restaurant, The Zone. In the evening it turned into a high-class place: dim lights, large plates, small bits of artistically arranged food, and prices that made me hope Norman would forget I wasn't his girlfriend anymore.

We sat down at a small table near the back. I had to re-arrange myself twice to keep my knees from bumping against Whitman's or Norman's or maybe Ginny's. I didn't feel like knocking knees with any of them.

Ginny was animated; after a few glasses of wine she forgot to keep her face beauty-model blank and even appeared human once or twice.

"So Whitman," Ginny said, "you're in the movie business, I hear. What do you do?"

"I'm working on a TV pilot right now, but for feature films it's mainly producing. A bit of writing, script-doctoring and the like." Whitman leaned in towards Ginny.

I made a rude *pfffftt* noise.

He smiled at me. "I also seek out the work of unknown writers and try to get them some exposure."

"That's great," cooed Ginny.

Just who was she after here? Whitman or Norman? I looked at the two of them. Norman did look a little plain beside Whitman and they both had money. God, though, the woman had no taste.

Whitman turned to me. "Dad told me you're originally from Saskatchewan. I was wondering if you could clear up a mystery for me?"

"What?"

"Why does everyone from Saskatchewan have a box of Kleenex in the back window of their cars? Is it a status thing? Or just for show? I don't get it. It's not like they can fucking reach it."

I stared at him. I was about to deny it, but in my head I was thinking of all my parents' cars and the boxes of Kleenex faithfully riding around in the back window like little cardboard pets. When I'd last been to visit my parents in Florida, there had been a box in the back window of my father's new sedan. One of the first things I'd done after getting my first car was to place a box of tissue in the back window.

Norman interjected, "That's an interesting observation, Whitman, but I don't think the foul language is necessary."

Whitman glared at him. "Will you please stop telling me to watch my language? Who're you — the American Morality Police?"

Ha, that'd teach Norman to be so self-righteous.

Whitman continued, "You ever listen to the *language* in the porno films you sell, Mr. Decency?"

Norman, instead of rising to his own defence, looked as though he might cry.

"Shut up, Whitman," I said. "You don't know what you're talking about."

"So should we have appetizers?" said Ginny. "The cheese sticks are great."

"No. Point taken," Norman said to Whitman. "I reluctantly withdraw my objection."

We ordered and dinner eventually arrived. As we ate, the conversation turned to singles ads. Ginny told them about Jim's doctorate deception.

"I tried to put an ad in once," said Whitman. "I wanted it to read 'Single white male seeks blah, blah, for ambiguous relationship.' The woman taking the ad down over the phone said they couldn't print it, that bigamy was against the law. I told her to look it up in the dictionary but she hung up on me."

"*Ambiguous* relationship? What's that supposed to mean?" I asked.

"Do you know what ambiguous means?"

"Listen," I said, "I don't know what your problem is, but I can tell you there's no problems with my vocabulary."

"Well, good for you. I'd hate for you to think I was a phlyarologist."

"No one knows what that means, you jerk. You probably just made it up."

"Actually, I do," said Norman.

"Well good for you," I said.

"Should we go to the lounge for a drink?" said Ginny. "Or does anyone want dessert?"

I followed them into the noisy crowded lounge.

Ginny and Whitman sat down beside each other at one of the small wooden tables. Ginny looked rather fetching in a sheer black blouse, a red print skirt, and high heels. Between Ginny's tilted head and Whitman's hand on her arm, it was obvious that sparks were flying between the two of them. Norman and I took the other side and chatted about the Art Centre and Lady March's latest projects.

A man came over to Whitman and shook his hand. Whitman introduced him to us as Bob Reilly, an old friend of his from school. The guy was capital B- beauteous. He pulled up a chair beside Ginny and took her hand. "And who is this absolutely stunning young woman?"

"Pay no attention to her," said Whitman. "She's just a whore from my village."

"She hit my fucking face."

Norman and I were bent over Whitman. His chair had tipped over with the impact and he was lying on the ground. Ginny had walked out immediately after walloping him in the face with her Chanel handbag, which, thankfully or not, was relatively small and quilted. Beautiful Bob had immediately scuttled away.

"What do you expect, Whitman? 'A whore from my village'?" Norman helped him up.

"Just be glad she wasn't carrying her hard-shell Dolce & Gabbana bag," I said. "You'd be dead."

Whitman stood and brushed himself off. "It's a line from the movie about an Armenian drug smuggler I was working on in L.A. It just came to mind. Come to think of it, the guy who says it in the movie gets decked too. Shit."

As we sat down again I noticed the spoon that Norman had been using to stir his special coffee was missing. I looked under and around the table. Sometime between whacking Whitman and flouncing out the door, Ginny had stolen the spoon.

"What's her phone number?" asked Whitman, rubbing his jaw.

"Why? Leave her alone," I said. "She's just reached the conclusion that you're an asshole sooner than most of us."

"Just give me her number."

Whitman went to the phone by the entrance of the lounge and dialed. He spoke for a minute then turned and waved goodbye to us. We could see him heading down the hallway to the elevators.

"What an idiot," I said.

"Ginny or Whitman?" asked Norman. He finished his drink and looked around for the waitress.

"Ginny. What does she need with a jerk like that? Shit. Let's go."

"We could stay awhile." Norman smiled hopefully.

"We could, but we aren't. I want to see how Beethoven is doing."

We gathered our things and Norman stopped at the bar to pay our tab. I noticed neither Ginny nor Whitman had left money for their drinks, but who was I to judge? I headed outside, jostling my way through the perfumed and cologned yuppies to get out the front door onto the street. Some guy grabbed my ass as I passed. I flipped him the bird over my shoulder and kept moving.

Norman joined me on the sidewalk out front. "Should I call for a cab?"

"Did you ever try a singles ad?" I asked.

"No. Did you?"

I smiled. "I sorta answered one once," I said, thinking of Gladys. "But you know me, I didn't meet a suitable partner. I didn't even manage to meet someone human."

"What are you talking about?"

"Oh, you never know who you'll meet through the classifieds," I said. "It might be someone completely inhuman."

"What do you mean *inhuman*? Like an alien? You're freaking me out." Norman waved at cabs passing by.

"Ha. That's what I said."

"Do you think you might want to go and talk to someone, you know, maybe get some help?"

"Oh no. I know what happens. Before you know it, I'd be locked in some asylum. I know what they do with ladies who won't behave."

"You've completely lost me." Norman waved wildly at the street.

"Apparently not, Norman, because you're still here. As a matter of fact, you don't seem to know how to get lost."

A cab finally pulled over and I climbed in. Norman stood on the sidewalk.

"Aren't you getting in?" I asked.

"No," he said grimly, "I think I'm going to go for a walk."

I shrugged and the cab pulled away. I counted the loonies and quarters in the bottom of my purse, hoping I had enough cash to pay for the fare.

I didn't talk to Norman for the rest of the day after he'd asked the art society ladies in Kentucky about my talent, or lack of it. He was so remorseful, I forgave him by the following day, but I didn't forgive myself. Two days later, I took all my paintings and sketches and went to sit beside the river that cut through the back of Norman's property. The Barren River was small at that point in its journey, about seven feet across. There was a wooded hill on the far side, but Norman's side was flat. I sat under a tree and went through the pictures, slowly noting each flaw and errant brushstroke. After I'd made a complete catalogue of all my defects, I sat and watched the river pass me by for a while and then I gave up.

When I was young, art gave me so much, even in the wild years. It was my cornerstone, but it now seemed to cause more pain than pleasure. I was tired of always being on the outside for no apparent reason, looking through what was ultimately nothing more than pigment, oil, and cotton on plywood. Perhaps if I stopped painting, I'd be able to participate in the life that everyone seemed so comfortably engaged in.

I put my head on my knees for a moment and then went and found a soft spot in the pine needles under a fallen tree. I dug as far down as I could with my hands, buried all my pictures there, and placed a stone on top. The end. No more Frieda Zweig the Artist. I scraped the dirt out from underneath my fingernails as I walked back to the house. I would become Frieda March the Kentucky Wife.

Norman didn't mention that I'd stopped drawing and painting, probably afraid he'd upset me again. Maybe I should have left then, but I just wanted to do something right for once. I wanted to not feel like a freak. I'd try and make it work with Norman.

Three months later, Norman sent Lady March and me away to a spa for a week. When we returned limpid and glowing from our treatments, Norman said he had a surprise for me. He took my hand and led me upstairs. In what was once the "small ballroom" there was now an art studio, fully decked out with easels, canvases, and drop cloths. Perfect light shone through the vaulted windows.

"I'm hoping that you'll stay here with us, Frieda." He got down on one knee and took my hand. "Will you do me the honour of marrying me?"

I froze. I couldn't speak or move. The dream, the fairy tale was becoming real. But where was the wicked witch, the ogre, or the troll? Oh, yes, it was me. I took my hand away.

"I don't paint anymore, Norman."

"But you should. You're an artist."

"What if I wasn't? What if I was just Frieda the sales clerk? What then?"

"But you're not just a sales clerk."

"Yes I am. You don't want to see it. Listen, if I were an artist, this would be a perfect set-up. I could paint and have a patron, have my socks washed and bills paid. You'd make the perfect wife of an artist, Norman. I could be the selfish painter in the studio bellowing for my dinner. It's an artist's dream and it almost never comes the way of a woman, but I can't take it. I can't do it. I won't be the loser again. I'm missing something I need to be an artist. I've always been missing it, way, way back, that piano teacher bitch with the ruler knew it. I just haven't got — *it*."

"What is *it*?"

"I wish the hell I knew. Maybe your art society knows. I can't marry you. You don't know me. I don't know me. None of this is mine."

"It would be yours if you married me."

I'd thought I could do it. I'd planned my answer, even prac-tised the demure dip of my head as I said yes. If he'd asked me without building the studio, I likely *would* have dipped my head. But now I wasn't sure who Norman wanted to marry, Frieda

Zweig the Artist, or Frieda Zweig, me. The money did appeal to some part of me. Me who'd lived from cheque to cheque for so long. Me who'd bonded with creditors and asked about their kids when they called to see when and if I'd manage to pay my bills. All my money worries gone. Poof. All I had to do was be Frieda, the artist in the flowered dress, and say one three-letter word. But I couldn't. I'd lost myself once before coming to Kentucky and I hadn't found myself there. I'd just walked into someone else's life and taken on the role that was expected and now I was going to walk out again.

It took two weeks of tears and vomiting (by Norman), but I left. I couldn't marry him. I felt horrible, like I'd led him on, like I'd been lying the whole time, but I'd really thought I could make it work. In the end, I couldn't.

Norman came with me to the airport. It was the middle of the night, but the terminal was crowded. People bustled with purpose or walked slowly in bewilderment, stopping and looking hopelessly up at flight schedule announcements. Norman stood beside me, his face puffy from crying. He put his sunglasses on and gave me a wavering smile.

"I hope you find what it is you're looking for, Frieda."

"Thank you, Norman. I'm sorry."

"You'll write?"

I nodded. As I walked away, he muttered something.

"What?" I turned back.

"Chickenshit." He sniffed twice and walked away, his face crumpling into tears again. I stood dumbfounded for a minute, jostled by the passengers trying to get by to board the plane. Then I turned and took my flight back to Winnipeg.

When I got home from the disastrous dinner at The Zone, Mr. H. was still sitting at the kitchen table. He looked tired.

"Tough crossword?" I asked.

"Where's the rest of the crew?"

"Don't know. Don't care."

He nodded. "Beethoven died."

"Oh no. How's Miss Kesstle?"

"She's sleeping now. I just came back home."

Later that night I stared at the blank canvas on the desk. Now I knew what it was. It wasn't a white cat with its eyes closed in a snowstorm. It was "Beethoven Gone to Heaven."

Great If You Like That Sort Of Thing

I picked the ringing telephone up with a wary "Hello." There were very few people I could tolerate talking to before my morning coffee. It was Ginny, not a bearable pre-coffee person, but it was too late to hang up.

"Hi Frieda, is Whitman home yet?"

"I don't know, I just got out of bed. What do you mean home *yet?* Did he stay overnight? Tell me you didn't sleep with him."

"Don't lecture me. I just had the most horrible experience."

"You slept with Whitman, I'm not surprised."

"No, not that. He was actually very good. But this morning —"

"Don't tell me, he snuck away at dawn without even leaving a note?"

"No, we got up and had breakfast together."

"Really?" I tried to reach the coffee pot without tearing the phone out of the wall.

"He made me scrambled eggs in his underwear. It was romantic."

"Probably would have been more romantic if he'd used a frying pan."

"What?"

"Nothing. So, we've got Whitman in his underwear. That qualifies as horrible, but I don't think that's it." Ha. Got the pot. Now could I reach the coffee?

CHAPTER SIXTEEN

"I had a meeting to go to, so we got dressed, and tomorrow is garbage day. I had my recycling by the front door. . ."

I couldn't quite get to the food cupboard. "Can I call you back?"

"*No*. Listen to me. So as we're leaving, Whitman offers to help me take the bags out. Then we're down at the recycle bins in the back and there's this weird chick all vampire-like by the bins in the alley, and she takes my bag of magazines from Whitman and says, 'Thanks, saves me from digging through to get them.' So whatever, right? I mean, she looks like she could use some fashion tips even if they are from *used* magazines. . ."

Maybe if I lay down on the counter I could reach the coffee cupboard. I tried it, my butt falling into the sink. Almost. Mr. H. walked in, struggling with two large orange garbage bags that he left beside the back door. I smiled at him horizontally. He shook his head, walked to the counter, picked up the pot, and started to make the coffee. I rolled off the cupboard, blew him kisses, and turned my attention back to Ginny.

"So Whitman starts talking to her, and then we end up following her, and a few blocks away in this dirty back alley is this big box, like a refrigerator box. I think she sleeps in it. It was awful."

"I see," I said. "You've gained a social conscience and you're consumed with guilt about all the years and dollars you wasted getting manicures."

"No. I was so embarrassed. My name is all over that box."

"What?"

"She's using the front and back covers of my magazines mixed in with God only knows what, photos or something, as siding for her box."

Mr. H. handed me a coffee cup and disappeared into the study. It dawned on me what Ginny was talking about. She subscribed to those magazines; her name and address would be on the labels on the covers.

"That's hilarious."

"It's not. What if people see it? They'll think I live in a box in a back alley. It's mortifying. We have to do something."

"We?" I listened to the gurgling of the coffeepot. Ginny's dramatic tone cut into my head like brain surgery with butter knives.

"Please," said Ginny, "we have to make her move. We have to burn that box."

"Sure, then maybe she could come and live with you. What did Whitman think?"

"He seemed pretty amused by the whole thing. I told him off, came back home, and called you. You *have* to help me."

"Listen Ginny, I just got out of bed and I need to pee and have some coffee. I'll call you back, okay?"

"Hurry."

"Okay, bye." I snickered all the way to the bathroom. How frigging funny could you get? When I came out of the bathroom, Mr. H. was sitting at the table. "Hey, Mr. H." I poured myself a cup of coffee.

"Morning, Frieda. We seem to have lost some of our guests last night."

"Damn boarders, never give you notice. What's in the bags?"

"All of Miss Kesstle's crocheting. The whole knit and whangdoodle. She wants it all out of the house. She's a bit... hysterical. It was a piece of crochet cotton all wrapped up inside Beethoven that killed him."

"Oh, shit. What're you supposed to do with the crocheting?"

"She asked me to burn it. I told her I'd take it to the Art Centre instead. Someone should be able to make use of the yarn, and the doilies... well, someone will find some use for them."

"Shouldn't we save it all for her, I mean, until she feels better?"

"When she does feel better, she'll have lots to do crocheting replacements."

"I suppose. Should I go see her?"

"She's napping again. I'd leave her be for now. So what happened to our company?"

"They'll probably be back. Norman and I had a fight last night, and Ginny and Whitman kinda got together. And so it goes."

"Despairs of the heart. I'm glad I'm past all that."

"I have to go on a mission with Ginny. Is there anything you want me to pick up?"

"Maybe something for supper. Miss Kesstle doesn't feel up to making dinner. First Sunday she's missed in years. I'm off to the Art Centre. We've got a lot to do for the show next weekend. Are you coming? You could bring Ginny. The more the merrier."

"I'll ask her. See ya."

A man weeded the flowerbeds in front of Ginny's apartment building, the austere Trudgdain Towers. "Nice day," I said.

He pushed back his baseball cap and said, "Great, if you like that sort of thing."

I took it as a bad omen. It was.

Ginny was in a state. I'd like to say I was sympathetic, but I wasn't. I found the whole thing too funny for words. When we went to leave, Ginny headed down to the underground parking lot for her car.

"I thought it was just a few blocks away," I said.

"I'm not walking in that neighbourhood again."

We got into the car, drove for a few blocks, turned right, and crossed the invisible line that divides the rich and semi-wealthy from the poor and semi-hungry. The place was only about a block and a half from the Downtown Art Centre. I snickered occasionally.

"This is not amusing," said Ginny.

"Did you bring your blowtorch?" I asked. "Maybe we could have her arrested for impersonating a beauty queen."

"Shut up," said Ginny. "It's right down here."

We turned into an alley. Ginny parked the car off to the side and got out. I followed her to a spot hidden behind a parking garage wall and a large concrete column. The wind circled around in the corner, whipping up scraps of garbage and whirling the scent of rotten food and oil towards us. Sure enough, there was a large refrigerator box covered with glossy, wide-eyed, big-toothed model faces. Mixed in-between the magazine covers were black-and-white photos. I could still smell the urethane the owner had painted over top to protect the pictures.

"I think I recognize some of those photos —" I said as we got closer.

"It's dangerous," interrupted Ginny, looking over her shoulder towards the car. "Who knows who might see the address and come and rob and rape me?"

"You live on the twenty-second floor and your building has better security than the houses of parliament. Listen, though, those photos are —"

I was interrupted by the owner of the domicile emerging from the far end of the box. I was right. The girl in the wrinkled purple velvet dress standing five feet away from us was Girl, the young Goth who attended the Art Centre, the one whose photo Norman had purchased. She had piercings in her lip, nose, and eyebrow. Her long dark hair was tangled and her eyes were outlined in black kohl.

"Hi," I said. She stared at us and scratched her leg.

Ginny blurted, "You have to move. You can't have this box anymore. I'm getting rid of it."

"No you're not," said Girl, calmly still scratching her leg.

"Yes I am. Those are my magazines and I don't want them in this alley."

"You threw them out. They're mine now."

"They have my name on them, little girl."

"Your name is in every phone book and probably on lots of bathroom walls. Those all belong to you too, bitch?"

"Screw this," said Ginny. She walked over, reached out, and tore a ragged handful of covers off the box.

Girl grabbed her arm. "Get your hands off my property, you skank."

Ginny dropped the covers and pushed her back. Great, Ginny and a street kid were going to brawl in a back alley. I hurried between them. "Wait. Stop. I'm a friend of Mr. Hausselman's, from the Art Centre." Girl looked at me. "There must be a way to settle this so everyone is happy." They both looked at me. "I don't know what it is right now, but there must be." They both looked away. Ginny made another lunge towards the box. Girl growled. I stepped in front of Ginny. Office-speak. I needed the lingo. "The ramifications of this situation require special attention, correct?"

Ginny stopped. "Damn right," she said.

"All right, you go home and I'll meet you there in a few minutes."

She hesitated. "Don't worry, I'll take care of it," I said. She started to walk away.

"And don't come back, bitch!" yelled Girl at her back. Ginny got in her car, leaned out the window, and gave Girl the finger before she drove away.

Girl turned to me. "Shit, your friend there is totally over-clocked. So you know Mr. Haus, hey? That's one cool dude." She smiled.

"You're Girl, aren't you?"

"How'd you know?"

"I live with Mr. H."

She looked me up and down and smirked.

"We're *friends*," I said. "He showed me some of your work.

He thinks you're talented. A friend of mine bought one of your photos."

"No shit, hey?"

"No shit. Do you live here?"

"No. I just crash here sometimes when I'm too wasted to make it home."

"What about your parents?"

"I don't have any. They scooped me from the hospital when I was born and put me in care right away. My brother was already in the system. Mom was a heroin freak, a whore, and who knows what else. A total fuck-up, anyway." She leaned over, picked up the covers from the cement, and placed them on top of the box. "The last thing she did was make a deal with the social workers to let her name me. Girl. Cool, huh?" She dug into a pocket in the side of her dress and brought out a long cigarette butt and lighter. "I'm with a foster family now. They're okay. They don't raise any fuss and I don't cause them any hassles." She lit the butt and blew out the smoke.

"Oh." I didn't know what to say. She rattled the facts off like she was telling me what she'd had for lunch. "Do you see your brother?"

"He's dead, car crash, pissed. Mom too. OD'd in the bathroom of a downtown bar."

"Your dad?"

"Never knew him. I don't think my mom knew who he was — occupational hazard."

Okay. No more personal questions. I felt a little weak in the knees. "What if we peeled the address labels off Ginny's magazines before you put them on your box? Or maybe blacked them out?"

"Could do. I'm going to sell the box at the art show anyhow. Start a new one."

"Okay." I hesitated. "Are you hungry? Could I buy you lunch?"

"No. I've got some people to go see. If you could lend me five bucks though. . ."

"Sure," I dug through all my pockets. I had exactly $3.29. "Here." I handed it to her.

She smiled. "Some lunch that was gonna be. See ya." She tousled out her hair and wandered off down the alley, her velvet gown dragging behind her in the gravel like some sort of delinquent fairy princess. I imagined her in her long wrinkled gown in a Pre-Raphaelite painting, only instead of columns, drapery, and flowers behind her, a background of graffiti-painted cement. I stood and watched her go. Now back to Ginny.

Ginny gave me a ride back to Mr. H.'s. She parked in front of the house and turned off the engine.

"What're you doing?" I asked.

"I thought I'd come in and visit."

Norman was kneeling outside beside the front porch. The bottom step was partially dismantled, and Mr. H.'s red toolbox lay open beside him. While we stood and Ginny asked Norman inane tool questions, the limo pulled up. Whitman got out and spoke to the driver for a moment, then came up the walk.

"Hi," said Ginny. "Sorry for freaking out on you this morning."

Whitman shrugged. "What're you doing?"

"Trying to fix the step," said Norman. "The wood is too far gone though. I need some new lumber."

"Did Dad ask you to do that?"

"No. I don't get much of a chance to do this kind of thing. The caretakers do it all at home. I got a new battery for the Valiant too. It started right up."

"Aren't you the perfect son type," said Whitman. He stepped over the dismantled bottom step and proceeded into the house.

"Did you want to do something tonight?" Ginny called after him, smiling too widely.

"Possibly," he said.

"Well, I'd better go," Ginny said, but she didn't move. She jangled her keys and stared at the closed door.

A few moments later, the door opened and Mr. H. came out on the front porch. He invited Ginny to the shindig at the Art Centre on Saturday, and she said she'd be delighted to come. Now I was in trouble. I'd probably spend the whole evening trying to keep Girl and Ginny from brawling. After a final glance at the front door, Ginny left.

Norman looked up at Mr. H. "I'm going to have to get a bit of lumber for this. Is there a place close?"

"There's a hardware store about fifteen blocks east," said Mr. H., staring off into the distance as though he wasn't seeing or talking to us at all. "I just had a very bad phone call," he said. "The government is going to sell the Art Centre building. They've given the art society the first right of refusal, but we have to hold raffles to buy toilet paper, never mind a building." His usually smiling face was sombre.

"That's outrageous," said Norman, "you've made that place a success."

"Well, we have a month. Maybe a miracle will occur. However, that's not the issue right now, is it? Let's get going to the hardware store."

"I'm so sorry," I said as Mr. H. walked past me. "Damn government."

The two of them walked around back. I went inside. Whitman sat in the living room reading the paper.

"Did you and Ginny get rid of the girl in the box?" he asked.

"Problem's solved, no thanks to you."

"I thought it was hilarious," he said, chuckling.

"Actually, so did I," I said. Whitman and I shared our first real smile. "Did you hear about the Art Centre building? What a bunch of schmucks."

"There must be some way to stop them," he said. "Lawyers,

maybe, but I suppose by giving the society first right of refusal, they've covered their asses." He frowned and then turned back to his paper.

I was halfway upstairs when I remembered Miss Kesstle. I turned around and walked back down. I yelled at Whitman from the front door, "If anyone calls, I'm over at Miss Kesstle's."

Miss Kesstle answered the door in her pink flowered housecoat and led me into the living room. I gasped. The room looked shocking: the furniture was naked, the dining room table legs exposed without the large crocheted tablecloth draped over them.

"Different, isn't it?" she said sitting down in her chair.

I nodded. "Are you doing okay?"

"Not so bad. I keep expecting him to come around the corner at any minute. I put out his Friskies this morning before I remembered."

I picked up a pill bottle with something in it from the coffee table. "What's this?"

"The string they found inside him. They gave it to me so I could see that there was really something wrong with him."

Sure enough, a long piece of white crochet cotton wound around in the bottle. Eughhh. I quickly put it back down.

"I'd like to ask you a favour," said Miss Kesstle.

What now? I hoped she hadn't been listening to any more sex-help call-in shows.

"Uh huh?"

"They didn't give me Beethoven's body. Just that." She gestured toward the pill bottle. "I'd like to bury it in the backyard, but I'm not feeling strong enough to dig."

I didn't mention it would only take about two tablespoons of digging to make a hole big enough. "Sure. Did you want to get dressed first?"

"Hmmm? Oh." She looked down at her dressing gown. "I suppose I shouldn't go. . ."

"Never mind. No one's going to see us."

Miss Kesstle wrapped the pill bottle in a checked tea towel and we went out back. I took a hand trowel down from the wall of the back porch where Miss Kesstle kept her gardening tools hung in neat rows and walked into the backyard. Miss Kesstle stood beside me as I dug a small hole near her rose bushes. She placed the pill bottle in the hole and I began to cover it up. I heard something behind me. I turned; it was Whitman.

"I thought maybe you'd want to put this in. It was over in Dad's yard." He handed Miss Kesstle one of the furry fake mice she'd bought in hopes of dissuading Beethoven from eating the real ones. The mouse was pretty much decimated and disgusting, but Miss Kesstle took it. "Thank you, Whitman." She put the mouse in the hole with the pill bottle and then I covered it up. We stood in silence for a moment and then Miss Kesstle said she was going to go back in to watch *Coronation Street*. Whitman and I walked back over to Mr. H.'s together.

"That was nice of you," I said.

"Surprised?"

"Frankly, yes."

"I suppose there is some of my good-fellow father in me."

We went in the back door and Whitman went through into the living room. I was thinking vaguely about dinner and opened the fridge. Nothing jumped out at me, which was good considering the state of some of the leftovers. The yams were still in there, looking like a museum exhibit of mummified vegetables.

Dance, Gladys, Dance

Like An Angel

Whitman stood at the living room window watching Mr. H. and Norman work on the step together outside. He held the curtain back with one hand.

"You could go out and join them," I said.

He dropped the curtain like a child caught peeking out into the audience before the school Christmas concert.

"Just what is it between you and your dad?" I went and stood by the other side of the window.

Whitman shrugged. "I hardly remember him being around when I was growing up. He worked all day, then he was either in the basement darkroom or romancing Mom. I remember walking in on them snuggling all the time. He'd look at me as if I was interrupting. Did you know he wanted me to be an engineer?"

"Really?"

"Surprising, huh? When I was born, he gave up his dream of being a professional photographer for his photo-geologist job and he was determined I'd do the same. Be practical, be realistic. Maybe he resented me. He wasn't so easygoing when I was young."

"But he is now."

"I try to tell myself that, but whenever I get around him. . ." He paused. "I feel like that seven-year-old boy in the wrong place at the wrong time."

"It's not too late, you know."

"Yeah, I could go outside and the two of us could throw a baseball around for a couple of years. That might do it. Besides, I don't think he's ever forgiven me for not coming home when Mom was sick." He turned towards me. "So, what about you? What's this I hear about you being an art martyr?"

"A what?"

"An art martyr. Ginny said you gave up painting."

Thanks, Ginny. What a pal. "It has nothing to do with being a martyr. I wasn't good enough."

"Fat chance of getting good enough if you don't keep at it though, hey?" He crossed the room and sat in Mr. H.'s chair.

"Who asked you?" I said indignantly.

"Who asked *you* for family counseling? Ginny also told me that she heard that you and my father have decided to take your relationship to an advanced level of eroticism."

I closed my eyes. I'd kill Ginny the next time I saw her.

"It was a *joke*," I said and walked out of the room, through the kitchen, and out the back door. So much for my fifteen minutes of friendship with Whitman.

I walked to the back corner of the yard and around the huge oak tree near the fence. I leaned back against it, grateful for its solid strength. For once, I could understand the tree hugging impulse. It would be nice to hold onto something strong and well-rooted. Then again, does your average tree hugger ever wonder if the trees *want* to be embraced? Maybe they're invading the trees' personal space. I turned to look at the oak, and before I knew it, I had one leg up on the bottom branch and one arm grasping a higher limb. Next branch, foot wedged between two smaller branches, left foot searching blindly like an inchworm for the next support. Okay, a large knothole, shimmy my arms closer together, hoist, up one more. I looked up, there it was, about three branches higher, the perfect sitting branch. The bark under my foot slipped off the branch, my left hand lost its grip, I yelped and grabbed wildly, envisioning ambulances, fractures, head injuries, brain damage. I grasped another branch, but I was frozen. If I moved an inch, death was certain.

"What're you doing?" My eyes were closed but I could hear Gladys' voice from higher up the tree. She was likely sitting on the perfect branch. Not fair. If I died when I fell, the first thing I'd do as a spirit was bump her off that branch.

"Falling, dying, having a panic attack, I think."

"Oh. You look like you're just resting there."

I opened my eyes but couldn't look up. "No, I'm pining for the fjords."

This was ridiculous. However, it would be poetic justice if I had to call for Miss Kesstle to come and rescue me from the tree. Even Beethoven had the sense not to climb this high.

"Come on. You can make it."

Okay, I moved my right foot a few centimetres, found a bump in the trunk. One hold, I ventured a look up, another small branch just to the left. I tried to grab it, but my hand had devolved into some primordial state and refused to let go of the puny grip it had. Couldn't really say I blamed it. Okay, got it, now the right arm. If I just stretched a little more, right, one more push, ha. I sat on the branch and shimmied over a little, my heart still pounding. I was surrounded by leaves, in a bower of green. Gladys sat in the middle of the branch, her legs dangling down. She appeared to have gotten over her reception problem and seemed quite solid. Spectrally solid.

"Wow," I said, "that was fun."

"Really?"

"Not a bit."

"I planted this tree," she said, patting the branch. "It was just a little sapling, no taller than me. I had no plans on being here as it grew, but I needed to somehow celebrate my baby. I loved to climb trees when I was little. I was much better at it than you, if you don't mind me saying."

I shrugged. "Go right ahead." We sat in silence for a few moments, swinging our feet and listening to the leaves rustle. A sparrow landed on a branch just in front of us. It hopped back and forth tilting its head and then suddenly flew off. I imagined Gladys opening her arms and sailing off into the sky along with it.

"What happened after Jack brought you back?" I asked. "I mean, you don't have to tell me if you don't want to."

"Yes," she said, "I do." Gladys looked down and crossed her feet at the ankles. "Things were awkward between us, but I'd learned to keep my mouth shut and Jack just ignored me. I was a little over three months along when Jack began to sell everything. And I mean everything. He sold our cows, our good dishes, half our furniture, and even his Sunday suit. I thought he'd gone mad. He started buying up every little piece of land he could get his hands on, even scruffy little vacant lots between buildings in town. I didn't question him, but I was afraid of the speculating look in his eyes. Every time he came in the house, he'd look around, wondering if he'd missed anything, something he could turn into land. I sat there in this half-empty house, not caring. I never was house-proud. I imagined he might sell everything and I could just walk away unburdened from an empty piece of land, the house taken apart, timbers and nails sold, and all my clothing and trinkets. I would walk away with nothing but the baby still safely inside me."

"Winnipeg's one and only boom," I said. "I learned about it in Civic History class."

"Four months later he was rich," Gladys continued. "He sold all the land to speculators coming into town for sometimes a thousand times what he paid for it. A thousand times! Can you imagine? The only piece he held onto was a bit of our original land with the house on it, and right away he hired an architect and began building a new house, right over top of the old house."

"That's what the Historical Society was looking for," I said, "a log wall in this house."

"I was as big as a house myself by then," said Gladys, "and I just sat in a rocker in the yard and watched it happen. The town overflowed with people; they camped out in the woods, slept on the wooden sidewalks. It was crazy. Jack never lost that cunning look in his eyes; everything became measured in dollars and cents. I was worth about two wooden nickels. I could see it. His eyes would flick over me and then go blank — nothing of value there. He went to fancy parties and started smoking cigars. I heard he had fancy women too. I didn't care. I just wanted out. I whispered to that baby in my tummy. We'll go sweetie, as soon as you come out. We'll get a train to Toronto. Momma will dance and you'll have soft toast and eggs for breakfast in fancy restaurants every morning. Thousands of people lost everything after that, but Jack was one of the few smart ones. He bought the land for nothing, sold it for thousands, and stopped there. He held onto his money except for building his new house and replacing all our old farm belongings with fancy city ones. Others continued to buy, even at the outrageous prices, then it suddenly went bust, and the land they'd paid eight hundred dollars for was now worth two dollars. If you could get anyone to purchase it, which wasn't likely.

"We were in the city by then; it had sprung up all around us. Most of the houses weren't as nice as this one though. I never felt comfortable in it, it was too fancy and new, but I do now. It's nice, probably because the man who designed it was a nice person. He was the only one who'd talk to me. The others just walked by and tipped their hats without stopping. I'm feeling a little dizzy."

"Back then or now?"

"Now," she said.

"Don't look down," I said.

"I think I'd better go. . ." She started to fizzle again.

"Gladys," I said, before she faded completely away, "thank you for the tree." Like the Cheshire cat, her smile disappeared last.

I sat in the tree until it started to get dark. Eventually, through the leaves, I could see the light from the kitchen window come on. I leaned forward and moved the branches in front of me. Norman and Mr. H. stood in the kitchen, the scene bright against the dusk darkness of the outside of the house. I watched for signs of them preparing dinner and tried to send them psychic messages — *spaghetti, spaghetti, spaghetti* — but after a few moments, they both disappeared. I was getting hungry. If no one was going to cook anything, I'd order pizza. I waited for a few more minutes, then I turned and ventured down the tree. Slowly, slowly, if I made it up, I can make it down. When my feet touched the grass at the bottom, I let go, then turned and patted the trunk. I thought of Jack, his money paying for the library and his place in Winnipeg's history as a founding business-man. Someone should put a historic marker in front of the tree:

A young pregnant woman planted this glorious oak tree
as a small sapling in the early 1900s. She was scared and
all alone. Her name was Gladys Roulston.

But no one ever would. The slim upper branches of the oak waved and dipped silently in the breeze.

I walked through the backyard, quickly past the shed, and into the kitchen, closing the door behind me. I could hear Norman's voice coming from the study. The door stood open about two inches. I quietly walked over and listened. He spoke on the phone.

"Yes, I can have it here by then," I heard him say. "All of it, do you think, or just the Canadian items?"

Now what the hell was going on? I tiptoed away and began crashing around in the kitchen.

In a minute, Norman emerged from the study looking pleased with himself. He came into the kitchen, got the pitcher of Glornics out of the fridge and a glass out of the cupboard, and sat down at the table and poured himself a big glassful. "Where have you been?" he asked. "I thought you went out."

"No, I went up."

Norman nodded and smiled, his mind obviously still on his phone conversation.

"So, Norman, what's going on?"

"Not much. I'm arranging some things. Business, you know."

"Oh yeah, like what?"

"This and that. You have a twig in your hair. Do you want to go out for dinner?" he asked. "Mr. H. and Whitman went to the Art Centre."

Ha. Maybe my family counseling skills weren't so bad after all. I sat down at the table across from Norman. He reached across the table, pulled the twig from my hair, and placed it on the table in front of me.

"Are you moving in?" I asked.

"What would make you say that?"

"You don't show any signs of leaving," I said.

"I have some business to attend to here. I can still move into a hotel if you like."

"No, we wouldn't want you resting your head on a four-star foam chip pillow."

He smiled. "No, we wouldn't, would we? Care for a Globnic?"

"Glornic. No thanks. I'm going to order pizza, want some?"

Norman and I not only ordered pizza, he went out and got a movie. We sat together on the couch, Norman in the middle and me leaning over the far right side, covered up with one of Miss Kesstle's granny square afghans. Mr. H. called from the Centre to say that he and Whitman were going out for dinner together.

When the movie ended, I got up and stretched. "Well, to bed for me.

As I leaned over to pick up the pizza box, Norman stood and put his arms around my waist. I straightened. "Don't."

He kept his arms around me. "You were meant for me, Frieda. You have such potential and you were the only woman who didn't care at all about my money. I want us to get back together."

I could feel the heat of his hands on the small of my back. All I could come up with was, "Why?"

"Because I miss you. I miss making love to you."

"I can't do this," I said. I lifted his hands off my waist, went upstairs, put on my sleeping clothes, sat on my bed, and cried. It wasn't fair. I was lonely, but starting all that with Norman again? I just couldn't.

The day before the art show, I went to the Centre to help Mr. H. set up the chairs and prepare the exhibits. We stayed there until after supper, downing coffee and donuts for nourishment. Mr. H. was determined this would be the best show ever. He was on the phone all day with the media. They wanted as much publicity as possible, to show how successful the centre was for their upcoming battle with the government. I wanted to tell him to let it go; David and Goliath is a nice story, but back then, Goliath didn't have an army of high-priced lawyers behind him.

When we got home, I was beat. I hadn't worked that hard in months. Mr. H. went next door to check on Miss Kesstle and try to convince her to come to the show the next night. He told me he thought it would be good for her to get out. I agreed, but I doubted she'd come.

I went straight upstairs and straight to bed. No sleep, though. My head was full of caffeine bees buzzing back and forth. Shit. I sat up and turned on the light and was happy to see Gladys slowly materialize in the armchair. "I can't sleep," I said. "Tell me more. What were you doing while Jack ran around with his fancy women?"

"I was getting ready to leave," she said. "I saved every penny I could. If I asked Jack for a dollar to buy some groceries I only spent fifty cents and put the rest in the lining of the valise under my bed. I tried to sell what I could too, like the emerald brooch I'd inherited from an aunt, my only piece of real jewelry besides my wedding ring."

"I'd have sold the ring first," I said.

"I had to keep the ring or Jack would have noticed," she said. "I had to be sly about everything I sold. Jack was tight with the men in town. I always told them Jack had sent me to sell whatever it was. I didn't get much; the shops were filled with heirlooms being traded off, but I got what I could. If times hadn't been so crazy, more notice might have been taken of a pregnant woman sent to sell off her belongings, but nothing mattered then, nothing but money and land."

"It must have been crazy."

She nodded. "It was. People were running around like chickens with their heads chopped off. Did you ever see a chicken with no head?"

"I have, actually," I said. "My grandpa and grandma had chickens. I had to help catch them for butchering. I was totally traumatized. Wait. Shhh." I heard Norman's voice from the kitchen. "Norman's back."

"Are you going to say hello?"

"No, not tonight. I'll see him in the morning." I listened for a moment. The voices stopped. He'd likely gone to bed.

"I liked having chickens," Gladys said. "Jack wanted to tear the coop down; it didn't match his new elegant house. I convinced him that our chickens laid eggs superior to any he could buy in town, so he let me keep them. I sold some eggs for money too. I hid them in my shopping bag when I went out. Jack would have been mortified if he knew I was selling eggs like a common farm woman. He had an image as a gentleman to uphold now. It took awhile, but eventually I had enough for a one-way ticket. The only thing I had left worth any money was my ring and I imagined I'd take it off and throw it in Lake Ontario as soon as I arrived in Toronto."

"Atta girl, Gladys, good for you. So when did you get there? Did you have the baby first?"

She twisted her mouth and frowned. There was a knock at my door. Poof. There went Gladys. I yelled, "I'm sleeping."

Norman answered, "Are you talking in your sleep?"

"What?" I got out of bed.

"I heard you talking."

I opened the door. "I was praying."

"Praying?" Norman raised his eyebrows.

"I've decided to pray for everyone who makes me crazy. I've added you to my list just now." I stared up at the ceiling. "And God, please help Norman, I fear he's lost and can't find his way home."

"I wanted to apologize for last night," he said. "I shouldn't have put my arms around you. I'm sorry if I made you uncomfortable."

"It's okay." What was it about this guy that made me so darn forgiving? "By the way, where were you today? We could have used even your dubious handyman skills at the Art Centre."

"I was taking care of some things."

"This and that?"

"Uh-huh." He nodded.

"Right. Well, no sneaking off tomorrow. Mr. H. says all hands on deck.

"I'll be there. Frieda, are you sure you're okay? Is there anything you want to talk about?"

"I'm fine. 'Night." I closed the door behind him.

Mr. H. had us all up and going by 9 AM. We went straight to the Art Centre and worked all day. I was amused to see Whitman trying to hang pictures with a group of instructors who made him move the paintings an inch this way and a quarter-inch that way for hours at a time. I saw his eyes widen several times, but he held his tongue and even smiled at them once or twice. Norman spent most of the day on a ladder hanging streamers. I helped arrange the refreshment tables and the sculpture and crafts tables. Sometime after noon, Girl arrived with her giant box balanced on a liberated shopping cart. True to her word, Ginny's address labels had been changed, but rather than blacking them out, Girl had pasted new ones over top that read things like *Ms. Rich B — ch. Too Good To Be True Street* and *A Fashion Hound. Where the Dogs Live.* I hoped Ginny would have some sort of hangnail emergency and not make it to the show. I didn't get a chance to speak to Girl; she dropped her box off and disappeared.

The staff had decided to not say anything to the students about the possible closure, but every time you went around a corner a little cluster of people stood whispering. Their words floated around the corridors like little anxious birds. I was pissed off. They'd all worked so hard to get the Centre established and accepted into the community, and now that they had a solid base of students they were about to be closed down. It figured.

When we went back home, Mr. H. asked me to come next door with him and talk to Miss Kesstle. She answered the door in her housecoat again. Her hair was covered in a kerchief.

"I'm not sure I'm feeling up to it," she said to Mr. H. "I haven't had my hair done and I just don't think, I think I'll just —"

"Frieda could help you do your hair," said Mr. H. He smiled at me.

I could? How the hell do you *do* hair? I nodded. "Sure I could."

"Good," said Mr. H. "Come over for dinner after. We still have a couple of hours before we have to be back."

I followed Miss Kesstle into the kitchen. She put the kettle on to boil for tea and then went to get her hair things. She came back with a small wicker basket of bobby pins and such. I made the tea and she pulled a chair out from the table and sat waiting. I stood behind her and carefully combed out the knots. Her hair was so fine it was like silk. . . I had a sudden flash of Mrs. Hernd sitting at my mother's kitchen table. I realized that what I had taken for cheapness was actually perhaps some sort of womanly bonding.

"We don't have time to put curlers in," she said. "I don't know what you'll be able to do with it."

"Don't worry, darling," I said in my best Angelico accent. "We'll make you gorgeous." My first idea was to put it all in a small bun at the back of her neck, but her hair was so thin and soft it wouldn't hold the pins and the shorter pieces still fell down straight in the front of her face.

"You don't happen to have a curling iron, do you?" I asked. The last time I'd spent any time on my hair, I was a teenager and it had involved curling irons and large amounts of hairspray.

"I do," said Miss Kesstle. She got up and went into the bathroom.

"And hairspray," I called.

I could hear her rummaging around and she returned with a vintage 1970s curling iron still in the box and a giant aluminum can of hairspray from the same era. So much for the ozone layer.

"I bought it and never used it," she said.

Now we were in business. Within fifteen minutes, I had her hair done. She went to her room to change.

When she came back out, I asked if she liked it. I was pleased with myself. Who knew what other untapped talents I had?

"Oh," she said, "I didn't look. I'm sure it's fine." She patted her hair. "It feels a bit stiff though."

"It's supposed to be like that. Let's go show you off."

Next door, Whitman, Norman, and Mr. H. were already seated at the kitchen table. Whitman took one look at Miss Kesstle, quickly got up from the table, and went over to the fridge. I could see his shoulders shaking with silent laughter, as he stood with the fridge door open.

Norman managed better; he stood and took her hand. "Good evening, Miss Kesstle," he said. "I'm glad you decided to join us. You look amazing, just like Farrah Fawcett."

Mr. H. pulled out a chair for her. "Like an angel," he said.

I looked at Miss Kesstle again. Okay, maybe it was a bit dated and young for her to have large grey wings of feathered hair on either side of her little face, but I'd have liked to see any of them do better.

I went upstairs to get changed. Tonight I had a fashion goal in mind: colour coordination. I put on a black dirndl skirt and a white button-up shirt, and topped it off, or bottomed it off, with an amazing pair of black and white men's oxfords. I couldn't believe I'd found them in my size and without golf cleats. The shopping gods had smiled on me.

Foggy Mountain Breakdown

The evening air smelled warm and green like the beginning of true summer. Norman held Miss Kesstle's arm as we walked from the taxi towards the Centre. Cars were parked all up and down the street. The outside of the building glowed with spotlights carefully placed to illuminate the best of the kids' murals, leaving the most misshapen superheroes in shadows. The ladies from the looms had arrived, some in a flutter of coloured saris like butterfly wings, others in sombre solid black. They smiled, nodded, and preceded us through the door.

A five-piece bluegrass band walloped and twanged in the largest lecture room. Students and their families, neighbours, other artists, and visitors filled the main rooms and the hallways. Several reporters with cameras over their shoulders stood at the refreshment table nibbling on the free cheese. Miss Kesstle clung to Norman's arm and looked bewildered. By the time I'd gotten us glasses of warm white wine, the others arrived. Mr. H. and Whitman had picked Ginny up in the old green Valiant, which I'm sure impressed her greatly.

Ginny wore a red silk halter dress and strappy gold heels, Whitman a black suit jacket with a mandarin collar and jeans. Mr. H. greeted us.

"Great band," said Norman. He adjusted his tie and tried not to stare at Ginny's cleavage.

"It was a compromise between rap and big band," said Mr. H. He looked around the room. "Excuse me," he said, "Fever Buyer over that way." He headed towards a man looking at an abstract painting on the wall.

"Fever Buyer?" asked Miss Kesstle.

Whitman said, "One of Dad's word follies. Wealthy people who buy art to hang in their summer cabins or donate to hospitals. Cabin fever. Got a fever, go to a hospital."

Miss Kesstle nodded. "It's so sad."

"Nice shoes," said Ginny. "Going golfing?" Before I could show her they had no cleats, she took Whitman's arm and they wandered off.

The next time I saw Ginny and Whitman, they were leaning against a wall together, watching everyone, the too-cool couple at the high school dance. Ginny was still smiling, so I assumed they hadn't seen the exhibits yet, though Whitman's presence might keep her from getting too hissified over Girl's box and rude address labels. When I looked again, they were gone, either to the exhibits, or outside for some necking.

I knew in ten minutes. I was trying to decide which of the desserts at the refreshment table Miss Kesstle would like — creamy brown squares with tiny rainbow marshmallows, puffed wheat squares, butter tarts, or matrimonial squares with dates and layers of oatmeal that crumbled all over your front — when Ginny came and stood beside me. "Did you see what she did with the labels?" she asked.

"Who?" I scanned the room, as if she could be referring to anyone in the crowd.

"That vampirette freak. Pass me one of those Nanaimo bars."

"Well, she did cover your name up."

Ginny huffed.

I gathered a plateful of squares. Ginny lingered by the cutlery section with her hand resting on the pile of forks and spoons. She looked over her shoulder.

"Don't you dare," I hissed.

She took her hand off the table. "What?"

"What? What is up with you and forks? Are you making a collection? You could go to Goodwill and buy a bunch of mismatched cutlery, you know."

"I don't know what you're talking about," she said.

"Speaking of you being rotten," I said, "why did you tell Whitman that crap I said about Mr. H.'s and my relationship?"

"Because Whitman asked me if you'd ever said anything about it and that's what you told me, that you'd decided to take your relationship to an advanced level of eroticism."

"Did you tell him it was a joke?"

"I didn't know it was. Did you see where he went?"

"Ginny —"

She was gone, sashaying through the crowd.

I took the plate back to Miss Kesstle, who managed a weak smile. Norman escaped to go and look at the displays.

"Oh my," said Miss Kesstle suddenly, through a mouth full of chocolate puffed wheat. I quickly brushed off what I assumed were the offending oatmeal crumbs from my bosom. She wasn't looking at me, though; she stared over my shoulder.

I turned to see Girl making a grand entrance. She wore an astonishing full-length dress, completely fabricated of Miss Kesstle's doilies. Each formerly white crocheted circle had been dyed a different colour: vivid orange, purple, blue, yellow, red, all stitched together with silver lace. It was an Haute Crochet evening gown. On her head was the Phentex tea cozy.

She walked straight over to us. I saw with relief that she wore a black slip underneath her creation.

"I fixed the box, did you see?"

I nodded. "Girl, this is Miss Kesstle. Those were her doilies that you made into your uh. . ."

"You!" said Girl, turning to beam at Miss Kesstle. "That was the best thing ever. Too cool." She held her arms above her head like a music box ballerina and did a complete circle. "Do you like it?"

Miss Kesstle moved her head up and down, her mouth still full of puffed wheat. I watched her, hoping she wouldn't choke.

"I still have lots more," said Girl. "I'm going to make a bunch of clothes. You are a doll." She leaned over and gave Miss Kesstle a kiss on the forehead. "And you have the coolest hair."

Miss Kesstle swallowed and smiled. "Frieda did it."

"Do you want to come see my projects?" asked Girl. She took Miss Kesstle's arm, and away they went, looking like models from some incomprehensible high-fashion shoot.

I stood with my mouth hanging open for a minute and then went to look for Mr. H. to see if he needed any help. I found him and Norman in conversation with several reporters in the hallway near the stained glass display. Mr. H. escorted the reporters away to tour the facilities.

"Hey," I said to Norman, "it's going pretty good, I think."

"I can't believe it might be closed down." He hesitated and put his glass of wine down on the ledge of the display case. I stepped back and lifted my shoulders in readiness for another stealth hug attack. "My mom is coming tomorrow," he said.

"Lady March? Why?"

"I asked Mr. Hausselman. He said it was fine."

"Does nobody ask me anything anymore?" I picked up his wine and drank it.

"She's bringing me some things."

"Like what?" I put the empty glass back on the ledge.

He shrugged. "Just things."

"Fine. Great. Where's she staying? Or is she going to a retreat somewhere?"

Norman picked up his empty glass and frowned at it. "At the house. Mr. H. said I could sleep on the couch or in the study and Mom will take my room."

"This should be interesting."

We were interrupted by a loud yodel from farther down the hallway. I turned along with everyone else. I saw Whitman make a hasty exit into the men's room, leaving Ginny standing alone.

I pushed forward. In the middle of the hallway stood Whitman's not-friend Marilyn from the deadbeat hotel. She wore the florid geometric print blouse again, her stirrup pants, and one white high-heeled shoe.

"Whoooeee!" she bellowed. It sounded like the mating call of a consciously endangered species.

"God," said Ginny, "what is that?"

"A screenwriter," I said.

"Where's the party?" yelled Marilyn. Whitman stuck his head out the door of the men's room, saw Marilyn a foot away from him, and tried to duck back in, but not quickly enough.

"Hey, darling." Marilyn lunged over, grabbed him around the neck, and hauled him out.

"Get off me, Marilyn," growled Whitman.

Norman stood beside Ginny and me. "Friend of Whitman's?" he asked.

"Looks like they're very close," said Ginny as Whitman attempted to pry Marilyn's arms off his neck.

Norman approached the two of them. "Can I help you?" he asked Marilyn, smiling his widest Boy Scout smile. Marilyn released Whitman.

"Is this a party?" she asked, looking around. "It's a boring party. Do you want to dance?"

Norman was shaking his head no when Marilyn grabbed his arm and took off unevenly down the hallway towards the main room with him in tow. I followed; this would be too good to miss.

"Hitch up your suspenders and secure your hats," said the bandleader. "The next song is 'Foggy Mountain Breakdown.' Anyone with a heart condition should leave the floor now."

Dance, Gladys, Dance

The men in the band stomped their feet and played their banjoes quadruple time. Marilyn pivoted on her one high heel and swung Norman around like a cooked noodle. The other dancers gave them a wide berth and Norman's face blossomed a bright pink. Just as I thought one of them was going to fall, the band switched to a slow version of "Will the Circle Be Unbroken," and by the time they reached the first chorus of *by and by, Lord, by and by*, Marilyn was draped over Norman's shoulder, weeping. He talked to her while trying to lead her off the floor. She asked him something, he answered, and suddenly she attacked him, her arms windmilling but not connecting. She screamed, "You goddamn bastard! I suppose you think I'm one of those. Well, you motherfucker, you can dance with me but that's it, you shit."

Whitman and Ginny disappeared out the door. No sign of Girl or Miss Kesstle.

Mr. H. hurried over from across the room. "What's going on?" he asked. "People are starting to leave. Who is that? Do you know her?"

"Sort of, I met her once with —"

"Could you please get her out of here? Or the only story we'll get tonight is 'Assault at the Art Show.'"

Norman held Marilyn back with one hand and gestured at me with the other. Since when did I become Winnipeg's peacekeeping troop of one? Mr. H. walked off. I went to the refreshment table, grabbed a full bottle of wine, and went back to where Norman and Marilyn were still engaged in their strange grappling. I waved the bottle at Marilyn. "Why don't we get you back to your room and you can have a drink in peace."

"Sure, I've just got to finish with this fellow." Her rotating arms increased their speed.

"What did you say to her?" I asked Norman.

His glasses slipped down his nose and he looked ready to cry. "I told her what I did for a living," he said.

I waved the bottle at Marilyn again. "Well, if you're not coming, I guess I'll just have to go and drink this. . ."

Marilyn let go of Norman, stepped away, and shook her fist at him. "I'm not finished with you, buster," she said. "You better watch your back. Let's blow, chickie."

Dance, Gladys, Dance

A Scared-Ass Rabbit

Mr. H. reappeared with my bag and a pair of crocheted slippers from the crafts table. "Here, see if you can get her to put these on. She'll break her ankle in that shoe."

Marilyn steadied herself on my shoulder. She smelt sour, like she'd been on a six-day unwashed bender, which was likely. Mr. H. took off her shoe and put the slippers on. They were pink and purple and had two hairy little dingle balls of yarn on the top of each.

"Fuck, are those ugly," said Marilyn, unsteadily surveying her feet. "I'll never get any action wearing those."

"You can change when we get back to your place," I said, taking her shoe from Mr. H.

Marilyn looked down at my shoes and shook her head. "*You're* not going to get lucky either."

Mr. H. patted Marilyn on the back. "You'd better go, Cinderella, before you turn into a pumpkin."

"Ha," said Marilyn. "Okay."

Away we went. I saw Miss Kesstle and Girl wandering back up the hallway as we left. I waved at Miss Kesstle. "I'll be right back. Norman and Mr. H. are in there."

She smiled and waved. "Okay, Girl's going to show me around."

We made our way out of the Centre. Marilyn seemed calmly

CHAPTER NINETEEN

absorbed by the dingle balls on her slippers, but I didn't like the idea of her having a foggy mountain breakdown in a cab, so we walked. It was dark outside and the sidewalks were almost empty, but shouts and conversations drifted from the back alleys and buildings we passed. In this neighbourhood, the night's entertainments had just begun. The fresh air perked Marilyn up. She muttered for the first few blocks about goddamn pornographers and then gazed at me.

"Who are you again?"

"I'm Frieda. You met me with Whitman."

This didn't seem to impress her a lot. "Are you a movie asshole too?"

"No, I'm a painter. Well, I was but I quit."

"They got you, did they?"

"Who?" Marilyn stumbled and I caught her knobby elbow. She poked my palm with her elbow and I dropped my hand. "Potholes. Them, they, the soul-stealers."

"Uh, maybe."

Marilyn gestured around her, up at the seedy month-by-month apartments we walked by. "The rest of these losers never made a choice, you know, nobody ever wanted them. They're garbage people. I decided not to part-ic-ipate." She thumped on her chest with her forefinger. "I threw myself away before they could use me up."

I nodded, though I wasn't really getting the gist of it all. I could see the hotel just up the block. I tried to think of something to change the direction of the conversation. Pre-frontal squall line, low pressure system, prevailing wind. Warning: Here be inebriated screenwriter monsters.

"They never found me," she said. "You know why? Because they weren't looking for me. I could shit better poetry than Bukowski writes. A woman drunk is nothing but a drunk — I'm a genius — well, I was. You know that?" She glared at me, as though daring me to disbelieve her.

"No." If she took offence to something I said, I still had the wine bottle in my bag. I could bribe her with it, or, if worse came to worst, crack her over the head with it.

"You don't know anything. Do you think it doesn't get you? Miss — what was your name again?"

"Frieda. What doesn't get me?" I said, wondering how I'd come to be escorting a crazy drunk wearing dingle ball slippers down the street.

"It's about prejudice, honey. That's all."

"I don't think so. I haven't been prejudiced against." We'd reached the steps of the hotel. She allowed my hand on her arm as we went up the stairs, then pushed it off once we entered the doors. There was no one at the desk again but the little radio was on, playing off station, a mixture of voices and static. The large stain still marked the carpet and I stepped over it as best I could. I was happy to see no one had defecated on the landing tonight. Maybe the sign worked. "Do you have your key?"

She reached inside her bra and took out a key.

"Right here in the safety chest. They'll show you a few like Plath or Woolf and they'll say, there, look, there's a path. It's a path, all right — under the bushes that a scared rabbit could maybe fit through if it kept its skinny-ass little back down. The men are on the expressway, and don't you forget it while you're belly down in the bushes."

We stood at her door. She leaned against the wall and handed me the key. Mascara was smudged in dark circles under her eyes and one eyebrow had been rubbed off at some point. She looked lopsided and twenty years older than when I'd first seen her in the hallway at the Art Centre. I opened the door and turned on the light, but she made no move to go in.

She continued, "They swerve, swarve, sarve. . ."

"Save?" I ventured.

"Save? Are you an idiot? They *serve*," she enunciated carefully, "up those women."

Dance, Gladys, Dance

"What women?" I surveyed her room. It was as filthy as before and smelt like fifty-six dirty ashtrays.

"Listen, chickie. Plath. Woolf. They're telling you that's the price you'll pay." She rubbed her hand across her face, smearing her remaining eyebrow across her forehead. "You'll leave your little squalling babies some bread and milk and go and put your goddamn head in the oven and turn on the goddamn gas." She banged on the hallway wall with her fist. "You wonder if the next day will be the one that makes you put the rocks in your pockets. They tell you you're not fulfilling your true purpose, to have babies and serve the world, they'll tell you that you're self-ish and warped to want to do something as ego-tis-ti-cal as art. To want something as ne- ne- ne. . ." Her eyes swivelled up to the ceiling as though she might find the rest of her word up there.

"Needed?" I tried. This was some warped game show.

She shook her head.

"Nebulous?"

"Better. More."

"Uh, nefarious?"

"More."

"Negligent, neurotic?"

"Excellent!" She clapped her hands and tilted forward.

I caught her and propped her back up on the doorframe. "But," I ventured, sure that I was going to lose even the possibility of lovely parting gifts, "no one told me that."

"Every day the whole world tells you. In your bones, in the air. You think you know better, you still feel guilty. And, and, and. . ." Her eyes closed, then opened again. "And if you manage to do anything — you believe every fucking damning thing they say 'cause you don't believe in yourself. You're an idiot, go away, you give me a headache."

She didn't move from the door. I gingerly took her arm, led her into the room, across all the crap on the floor and onto the bed. I got her shoe out of my bag and sat it beside her. She seemed to have forgotten all about the wine. She began to droop and her words slowed like a pull string doll with damaged mechanics.

"You thought you. . . could make. . . it once, didn't you?" She looked ready to fall asleep, so I started to edge towards the door. She lifted her head slightly, her eyes narrowing as they met mine.

"What does that have to do with anything?" I was at the door.

"Nothing. . ." she mumbled, her head beginning to drop to her chest.

I put my hand on the doorknob and she suddenly sat upright, picked up the shoe I'd left sitting beside her, and threw it at me. The shoe thumped on the wall beside the light switch.

"*Everything!*" she screamed. "It has everything to do with everything."

She bent down, picked up an ashtray, and hurled it at me as I tried to get out the door.

"You stupid shit —" The ashtray shattered on the door as I closed it. There was another thud, then a crash on the door, then silence.

Things were winding down at the Centre. The bluegrass musicians were packing up their gear. In the days I traveled with the Bang Howdy Band, I would have been on my knees pulling up the duct tape that secured the wires to the stage and scrubbing off gooey balls of glue residue with my fingertips. The glamourous life of a groupie girlfriend.

A few people lingered by the refreshment table, packing up the squares and finishing off the wine. Ginny and Norman cleared empty glasses and plates off a table.

"How'd it go?" asked Norman. He balanced two plates in one hand and held a rag in the other.

Dance, Gladys, Dance

"As well as can be expected," I said. I took the plates from him. "You wipe, I'll carry." I gathered more plates and stacked them up and down each arm.

"Do you think there's still discrimination against women?" I asked Ginny as we walked down the stairs to the basement kitchen.

"Did you see Whitman leave?" she asked.

"Did you hear me?"

"He just disappeared. He didn't even say anything."

"Marilyn thinks prejudice still stops women from doing things." I opened the swinging door to the kitchen with a hip-check, then held it with my foot for Ginny to get through, still balancing my two armloads of dishes. Who said I never learned anything in my waitressing years? The second door swung back as I turned to get in and smacked me in the face.

"Shit." I did a little octopus dance to keep the plates on my arms.

"Do you think he went to see *her*?"

"Who?"

"That freakish screenwriter."

"No. I'm talking about feminism." I put the plates on the counter and rubbed my forehead. The room had the slightly dreary air of a church basement kitchen, designed purely for functionality, its drab whiteness relieved only by handwritten notes: Please Rinse Sink. Turn Off Lights Before Leaving. I thought I should add another: Please Let Art Students Loose in Here. I'd suggest it to Mr. H.

"Feminism is so old." Ginny set her stack of plates down on the counter. "Maybe he's waiting outside."

"It's a political movement, not a dance step."

"Feminism *is* passé," she said. "It's like nipple piercing. No one even talks about it anymore. I'm going outside to have a look."

"Right," I said as she left the room, "feminism is exactly like nipple piercing. I don't know why I didn't see it before."

"What?" Ginny turned.

I closed my eyes. Maybe when I opened them I'd be having a conversation with someone who was listening to me.

"Never mind," I said.

Mr. H., Norman, Miss Kesstle, and I finished tidying up the worst of the mess and Norman drove us back to the house. Ginny took a taxi home to see if Whitman was waiting in the lounge at her apartment building. Miss Kesstle sat beside me in the back seat of the Valiant. Her hairdo had started to droop, but she was cheerful and smiling. She talked non-stop about Girl all the way home. What a sweet person and how talented to make that beautiful dress out of her doilies.

We delivered Miss Kesstle next door and went inside the house. Norman went straight to bed; he had to get up at six to pick up Lady March from the airport. Mr. H. and I sat at the kitchen table and had a cup of chamomile tea. The phone rang. It was Ginny.

"Did Whitman come back there?"

"No. Why?"

"He dumped me. He was waiting outside my apartment building. He said he didn't think it was a good idea for us to see each other anymore. I think he's really attracted to me and it scared him. But where'd he go? Do you think he found somebody else?"

"That would be moving fast."

"Let me know what time he comes in. I'm going to go in case he calls."

"You're probably better off —"

"Okay, bye." Click.

"See ya," I said as I hung up the phone. I went and sat back at the table.

"Troubles in the big city?" asked Mr. H.

"Just the usual."

Mr. H. yawned, slouched forward, and stirred honey into his

cup. He still wore his tuxedo shirt and purple suspenders, but he'd taken off his tie. I took a sip of tea and grimaced. Herbal tea just doesn't do it for me. No matter how long you let it steep, it always tastes like something that hasn't quite happened yet. Still, I knew better than to caffeinate the head hamsters before bedtime.

"Can you believe Miss Kesstle and Girl hit it off?" I asked.

"It might be good for both of them," Mr. H. said.

"You figure? I can't think of one thing they have in common, besides the doilies now."

"Loneliness?" said Mr. H.

Rear Deltoid Development

Mr. H went to bed and the mechanical ticking of the electric clock above the stove seemed to fill the room. I imagined I could smell Marilyn's unwashed alcohol stink on my clothes. Could it be true I was a victim of prejudice so established I wasn't even aware of it? I put my elbows on the table and my chin in my hands. Were my struggles to become an artist magnified by my gender? Did I believe somewhere deep inside that the cost would be too great? Did it matter?

"How was the party?" Gladys sat across from me in Mr. H.'s chair, sporting a new look. She wore a long, plain white cotton nightgown. A kerchief of the same material covered her head.

I sat up and smiled. "Hey, Gladys, cup of tea?"

"No thanks, it goes right through me."

"Where've you been?" I asked.

"Why? Did you miss me?"

"I was worried about you."

"Oh," she said, "did you think I died?" She gave a little snort.

"Very funny."

"You look a little pensive," she said.

"I'm thinking about art and women."

"Don't you see anything you want to paint anymore?" Gladys asked, looking casually up at the ceiling.

"No," I said and images began to roll through my mind: Mr.

H.'s profile in the blue dusk, Girl in her ragged gown in the back alley. "I don't know. I can still feel it, maybe like the ache Mr. H. still feels for Shirley, or like I was missing an arm or my thighs." I thought back to the early days after my break-up with Norman. "But it's not as bad as bashing my head against that concrete wall of creativity."

"Really?" asked Gladys.

I looked down; sorrow and regret beat their mean little fists against my ribcage. I quickly stood to get another cup of tea and then sat down again because the pot was already on the table.

"Z-O-L-A," said Gladys.

"Pardon me?"

"Fifty-Four Down." She tapped Mr. H.'s crossword on the table. "French novelist. Zola."

"Oh, I'll tell him."

"Did you ever read Zola?"

"No."

"You should recommend L'Assommoir to that lady you took back to the hotel tonight."

"How did you see that?"

"I lurk about sometimes."

I tried to imagine solid old Gladys lurking and failed. "She's quite the piece of work, isn't she?"

Gladys shrugged. "Bad choices are made for many different reasons."

"What happened to your choice to leave Jack?" I asked. "Do you think what happened to you was because of sexism?"

"Sexism?"

I hesitated. "Women being treated badly because they're women, I suppose."

"Things are hard for people with only one leg, or for coloured people, or for almost anyone for one reason or another. The worse you're treated, the harder you have to work to be treated better. Do you think a one-legged man could dance if he wanted to, if he really wanted to?"

I nodded, "Of course, but —"

Gladys shook her head. "But nothing."

I felt like a one-legged man at an ass-kicking contest. "I don't think Marilyn is working too hard improving her situation in life."

"You have to find the courage to live as you need to. There will always be those who want you to be ordinary, those who expect you to settle down. Your body can settle, but you have to let your mind soar, you have to hold onto the courage of your artistic convictions. Like Olga Dobie — not only was she willing to live outside of 'polite society,' she *needed* to live out there. She was willing to make the sacrifices that come along with it, the loneliness and the pain of reaching, always, for something that most people will not understand, ignoring those who see the attempts, the process of reaching, as failure."

"What about you?" I asked. "How did you end up in an institution instead of wooing the Kings of Europe from the stage?"

"I had my one-way ticket and I was as big as a barn. Then Jack started to watch me."

"What do you mean, watch you?"

"I'd be in the yard cutting flowers, or in the sitting room reading, or right there at that counter"— she gestured to the kitchen counter beside us — "cutting fruit and I'd turn and he'd be standing, watching me. He made snide remarks to me about the architect, but I think even he knew there was nothing going on. He had friends over for dinner and insisted I sit with them. They all stared at me and I'd get nervous and babble, or sit silently with my head down. Once I burst into tears before the soup was even served and had to leave the room."

"Oh, Gladys."

"I took to doing as little as possible during the day. I'd sit and work on clothes for the baby. Surely no one could take offence

Dance, Gladys, Dance

with that. One night I woke up at about two in the morning. The baby was kicking and I had such heartburn I couldn't go back to sleep. I got up, wrapped a blanket around me, and went downstairs. Jack wasn't home. He was out swilling whiskey with his newfound rich pals. He'd probably show up the next afternoon, smelling of old booze and cheap perfume. I went outside. I hated it in this house by then. It had nothing to do with me. I stood out there in the chicken yard, closed my eyes, and imagined myself in New York. The stages, the lights, and the dances I'd do. I'd be the talk of the town. Maybe my stage name could be Winnipeg or Racy Roulston. Imagine Jack opening up the newspaper and seeing that. I hummed and swayed, dipping and turning, and I took a bow. The audience went wild, throwing roses at my feet. Then there was the sound of single pair of hands clapping. I opened my eyes and there was Jack. 'Very nice,' he said. After all my weeks of sitting and behaving, he finds me in my nightgown dancing in chicken crap in the middle of the night."

"I heard it," I said, and my shoulders gave an involuntary shimmy. "I heard someone clapping by the chicken coop the night Mr. H. and I planted flowers."

"I imagine that sound will echo there for years still. It was the most frightening thing I've ever heard. He stood there staring at me and then he said, 'You're planning on leaving, aren't you?' I shook my head, afraid he'd hear the lie in my voice if I answered. 'You won't be,' he said, 'I can promise you that.'"

Gladys stopped talking. We sat in silence for a moment. I tapped my finger on a sticky spot on the table. I didn't know what to say. What could I say? It had all ended years ago. We couldn't go and read Jack the riot act; he was nothing but bones in the ground.

"Ruminant," said Gladys.

"Does that mean to think?"

"No, Twenty Across. Goat. Eight letters. We had a goat once

and that's what they called it in the livestock manual, a ruminant."

"You should sit and do crosswords with Mr. H. one day, you'd have a blast."

"I can't."

"Just me, huh?"

She nodded. There was an awkward silence. I didn't know what to say. I could imagine her, young, outside in the dark yard with her big round tummy and I didn't want to imagine it. I wasn't sure I wanted to hear any more of her story. I stood and took the teapot to the sink to rinse it.

"I should probably tell you Norman's mother is coming tomorrow. She thinks she's psychic. Will that be a problem?" I placed the teapot in the draining rack and turned back to her.

Gladys grinned a little. "Shouldn't be. You get to sleep; you've had a long day. Toodle-oo." And she was gone.

"Frieda. Telephone. It's Ginny and she sounds excited. She asked me to wake you." Mr. H. yelled up the stairs. I crawled out of bed and went down. The phone receiver lay on the counter. This time I poured myself a cup of coffee before I picked it up.

"Hello."

"I got it," said Ginny in a high-pitched whisper.

"What?"

"The job, the promotion. I'm now officially Director of Design. I think Craig's crying in his cubicle."

"How to be a good winner."

"I know, isn't it great? They're taking me out to dinner tonight at The Zone. All the bigwigs. If you see Whitman, would you mind letting it drop in conversation that I got the promotion?"

"I'll try to work it in."

"Okay, I gotta go. I'll call you tonight."

I went and knocked on the door of the study. Papers and folders covered the surface of the desk. Mr. H. sat in the chair frowning.

"The art show only got one tiny write-up in one paper," he said. "All that cheese and wine for nothing. I'm trying to think up a new strategy."

"A strategy. I've heard those are good."

Mr. H. nodded. "Hope eternally springs, as they say."

I leaned against the doorframe. "Where's Norman and Lady March?"

"Apparently Lady March missed her plane at her layover. Norman sat at the airport for hours, he's a little ticked off. She said something called her to Chicago and she's staying a few days. Sounds like a handful." He smiled.

"She's that and more. You'll like her."

"If she's half as pleasant as her son, I'm sure I will."

"Humph. Well, I'm going to get dressed." I closed the door behind me.

My plan for the morning was going to work out. I don't mean that everything was likely to turn out okay. In fact, I sincerely doubted that. I mean I was going to exercise. When Ginny signed up for a gym near her apartment, she was given a free pass for one month for a friend. She told me she thought I could use some toning up. Nice change, from her trying to get me to tone down.

The gym, thankfully, was almost empty. I decided to brave the weight machines while no one was in the room to watch me make a fool of myself. I settled myself on the Body Solid Pec Dec, which promised to provide optimal pectoral and rear deltoid development. I wasn't sure what my rear deltoids were, but any development was better than none. I sat down, grasped the handles, and pulled them toward my chest. I pulled harder and succeeded only in lifting my butt off the seat and then slamming back down, which I didn't think was the desired objective. I got off and fiddled with the knobs in the back of the machine.

"What is this place?"

No way. Gladys sat sidesaddle on an exercise bike. I looked around the room. "It's a fitness centre."

"What are you doing with that machine? It looks like something from the basement of the asylum."

"I'm trying to exercise. Build muscle tone and strengthen ligaments or something."

"You could just help someone haul bales or pick rocks."

"I don't know anyone with bales that need hauling."

"Oh. Can I help you?"

"Do you know how to work one of these?"

"No."

"Then it's not too likely you can help, is it?"

Gladys smiled. I sat back down on the machine, reached for the bars, and reefed them forward; they flew together with no resistance whatsoever, with a crash.

"That doesn't look too hard," said Gladys.

I sighed, got back up, and moved the knobs again.

"Did you ever go to the Palace Theatre?" asked Gladys.

I nodded. "It's still going. I went to quite a few concerts during my art school days." I sat down and pulled the bars together again. Nice. Resistance, but not too much, I just might get the hang of this.

"What did you see at the Palace?" asked Gladys. "Do they still have vaudeville shows?"

"No, afraid not. Five. I mostly went to rock concerts. Six."

"*Rock* concerts? I can't imagine that being very entertaining. What did they do with them?"

"With what? Nine." I tried to remember not to hold my breath.

"The rocks."

"There weren't any rocks. Rock is a type of music, sorta fast and loud. Eleven."

"Why do they call it rock music?"

"I don't know, maybe because it's heavy. Twelve."

"Heavy. I see. So can we go?"

"Where?" I was beginning to wonder why I was trying to have this conversation. The backs of my arms were getting shaky.

"To the Palace Theatre. You're quivering."

"I know. Sixteen."

"Is that good for you?"

"No pain, no gain. Gotta feel the burn. Why don't you go? You're the one with supernatural powers."

"I can only go where you are."

"Eighteen. Tricky cosmic deities, so there are rules. I think Bonnie Raitt is coming in a few weeks. Would you like to go to a concert?"

"Oh no. We'd have to go alone."

"Well, I don't think. . . Twenty. Okay, that's enough of that." I dropped my arms and rubbed them. The door opened and a beefcake in shiny black shorts and sleeveless white undershirt walked in. Gladys was gone. I watched the man load a machine over in the corner with a stack of round weights and lift them once with a terrible groan. That was enough for me. I went home.

Norman called the house later in the afternoon and said he'd be gone all day. Whitman went to visit some friends across town. It was almost like old times. I puttered around and then Mr. H. and I sat down to a late dinner together. We'd all but abandoned our fancy cooking schemes and dinner was pork chops, peas, and rice. We were just finishing up the dishes when the phone rang.

I picked up. "Hello."

"It's me." Ginny again.

"Hi. I haven't seen Whitman all day, so I haven't been able to tell him anything."

"It doesn't matter. Can you come pick me up?"

"From your dinner?"

"No, the downtown police station."

Go Fork Yourself

I borrowed the Valiant and drove to the police station. I was getting rather attached to the old car. It had a marvelous big steering wheel that made me feel as though I were navigating a boat. *Ahoy there, mateys.* There was an empty parking spot right in front of the building. There was also a meter and I had no money. I decided to risk it. Who would bother to check for expired meters in front of the police station? No one would be stupid enough to park illegally there.

The station was set back from the street with concrete stairs leading up to it. I could see Ginny through the glass windows as I went up the stairs. She sat in the waiting area, looking at a magazine. I pushed open the door, sounding a buzzer. Ginny stood up. Her hair was falling out of her updo and her mascara was smudged under her eyes. *The fair maiden taken captive across the high seas.*

"What took you so long?"

"I left right away. Do you need to check out or anything?"

Ginny shrugged and threw the magazine down on the coffee table. "How would I know? I've never done this before."

I turned to the counter. The station was quiet but for the humming of the fluorescent lights. One officer stood behind the counter writing something on a clipboard. No eye patch or ratty parrot perched on his shoulder — quite ordinary looking, really.

CHAPTER TWENTY-ONE

I still was uneasy around police, though — probably leftover fear from the musician days when there was dope everywhere, or some underlying complex about authority figures that made me sure I was always guilty of something. I walked over. "I'm taking Ginny Berger home now, okay?"

"Help yourself," said the man behind the counter. "No, wait." He turned his head and yelled through an open door. "Phil, the Utensil Lady is leaving! Are the spoons still beside the coffee-pot? Okay, you're free to go." He smiled. Ha, funny policeman, pirate, purveyor of guilt.

Ginny was already waiting by the door.

"So," I asked once we were in the Valiant and en route to her apartment, "do you want to tell me what happened?"

Ginny looked out the window for a moment. I began to think she wasn't going to say anything at all, when suddenly everything came out in one big rush.

"So we're at my dinner, right? At The Zone where I've eaten nearly every day for the last two years, with all the bigwigs from the office and we've finished dinner and they're probably about to do some nice pre-dessert toasts to me and my accomplishments, when I notice that Henri, the owner, the big fat loser, is hanging around the far end of the table, so I'm ignoring him, because, whatever, right? All of a sudden these two cops show up and ask me to please empty my pockets. Well, everyone in the place is staring, so I said no, there must be a mistake. Henri comes and stands beside me and says, 'I'm tired of you alla time stealing things from my restaurant, this time I call the cops.' He called the cops on me. Can you believe it? I've spent hundreds of dollars in there and he calls the cops on me for a few lousy forks."

"What's up with you and forks?" I interjected. She ignored me and carried on, her fingernails rat-tat-tatting on the dash-board like machine guns.

"So I said, 'Forget it. I'm not emptying anything.' I went to get up and leave, and one of the cops grabbed my arm. It was a lady cop wearing those pants with the stripes that gave her hips like a rhinoceros, which I told her, and the next thing I know I'm in the backseat of the cop car. I've never been so humiliated in all of my life. I'm going to have to move. Wait, where are you going?"

"To your place."

"Haven't you been listening to me? I can't go back there."

"Where would you like to go?"

"I don't know, your place? No, forget it, Whitman's there. You didn't tell him, did you?"

"I haven't seen him."

"If he would have called, none of this would have happened." She sat back and sighed.

I signaled left to turn in the direction of Trudgdain Apartments. "You've been stealing forks for months."

"But I wouldn't have taken *this* fork if he hadn't dumped me."

"Listen, I'm taking you to your place, we'll go in the back, no one will see us. Here." I reached in front of me and got Mr. H.'s large old sunglasses off the dash. "Put these on. There's winter emergency stuff in a bag on the backseat floor. Maybe you can find a scarf to wrap around your head or something."

I parked in the visitor space in the back. Ginny leaned over the seat and rummaged around. When she sat up, she was wearing a black toque pulled low over her head. She put the sunglasses on. "Okay, let's go," she said. She opened the car door and got out.

"Now you look like you're about to rob a bank."

We made our way inside, to the elevator, and all the way to Ginny's apartment without anyone seeing us. She opened the door and we were in.

"I need a glass of wine," she said, taking off the toque and sunglasses. Her hair stood up in a static halo around her head. "You want one?"

"No thanks." I sat down on the couch and waited.

Ginny came and sat down with her glass of wine. "Thanks for coming. I didn't know who else to call. I'm beat, how about I give you a call tomorrow? Maybe we can go for a coffee or something."

"Ginny, you were just arrested."

"I wasn't *arrested*. Henri wanted to press charges, but the cops decided not to. The female cop wanted to book me but the other guy said, 'Do you actually want to bring a stolen fork charge up in front of Judge Williams?' So they just gave me a stern talking-to about shoplifting, like I was twelve or something. What a laugh."

"Ginny?"

"What?"

"What is up with the *fucking forks?*"

"Oh," she said, "I don't know. I had a bad day at the office a couple of months ago. I was having lunch at The Zone, I took a fork somehow, when I went back to the office, I felt better. So then the next week, I took another one, and then it sort of got to be like a habit, I suppose, and well, there you go. I'm not a kleptomaniac or anything."

I raised my eyebrows.

"It's a stressful job," she said. "I have a ton of responsibility."

"When will you be finished drawing the shoes?"

Ginny stared at me.

"Like Andy Warhol," I said. "He drew shoes for fashion magazines before he started doing his own art. How many years are you going to draw shoes?"

"Who are you to ask me that?"

"I never went commercial. I'm not drawing shoes."

"You're not drawing *anything*." Ginny stood. "I want to show you something."

I followed her down the hallway into the spare bedroom. She opened the closet and where my piles of boxes and clothes had been there was now a narrow white desk with an office chair pushed off to the side. On the desk was a board and on the board was a sculpture much like Ginny's steel sculptures in art school, but this one was entirely constructed of forks, spoons, and knives. To the side sat a box of untransformed utensils.

"It's great," I said. The sculpture had a wonderful though slightly jarring rhythm. The mundane transformed. The utensils were perfectly recognizable, but the mind almost refused to believe that the form could have been composed with such ordinary materials. "When did you start this?"

"After you left, the utensils were sort of piling up and you pissed me off asking about *my* work." Ginny sat on the bed. "What do you think is up with Whitman? Do you think he likes me? Has he said anything at all?"

I smote my brow. "You have more important things to think about than Whitman right now. This is brilliant," I pointed at the sculpture. "You should be selling these. But you should buy the forks."

Ginny waved her hand dismissively. "Easy for you to say, with Norman hanging on your apron strings." She stood and left the room.

I followed her down the hallway. "Norman has nothing to do with anything. If you're so unhappy at your job, why don't you get a new one instead of stealing forks?"

"At least I didn't sleep with a man to get ahead." She went into the bathroom and turned on the light. "Christ, look at my hair. Why didn't you tell me it looked like that?"

I went and stood in the doorway. "Are you talking about Gimlet? That's just mean."

"Not Gimlet, Norman." She unpinned what was left of her updo, wet a brush, and began running it through her hair.

"I didn't sleep with Norman to get ahead, you idiot."

She picked up a black hair band and put it on, pushing her hair off her face. "Well, it got you somewhere, didn't it? Excuse me." She closed the door.

Dance, Gladys, Dance

"We're way off topic here," I said through the closed door. "You work twice as hard as the rest of those fuckers in your office and it only gets you half as far. No wonder you're frustrated."

"Well, at least I'm getting somewhere," Ginny yelled. "You've never had to work at anything in your whole life."

"Whoa, Ginny."

She opened the door, now wearing her fluffy white bathrobe, then turned to the sink. I watched in fascination as she squirted some sort of foamy stuff into the palm of her hand. She rubbed her hands together, then applied the foam to her face, her fingertips moving in perfect little circular motions.

"Aren't you supposed to put that in your hair?"

"What?"

"Mousse."

"It's foaming facial cleanser. It removes dirt and makeup without stripping the natural, beneficial oils."

"Operators are standing by."

Ginny rolled her eyes. "That's exactly what I mean. I spent seventy-nine dollars on this stuff and you don't even know what it is. You do nothing to yourself and you look fucking fabulous. I spend hundreds on haircuts and clothes and I end up looking like every other career woman sitting in the piano bar, done to the nuts, tossing our hair around, and beaming our extra-white teeth. We're all hoping to meet someone half as nice and stinking filthy rich as Norman and we never do."

She turned on the taps, leaned over the sink and splashed her face with water, then reached for a white towel and dried off. "You, you meet Norman working in a sex shop wearing a cheap satin bustier *backwards*. Then what do you do? You dump him."

She took a cotton pad, opened a bottle of some blue oily looking stuff, tipped some onto the pad and began to rub her eyes. An astonishing amount of black smeared around her eyelids.

"What's *that* stuff?" I asked.

"Are you listening to me?"

"Yes, but it's just silly."

"It's not silly, it's my life." She repeated the rubbing process with fresh cotton pads until the black disappeared.

She looked fifteen years old with no makeup and her Alice in Wonderland hair band. "You look good like that," I said and gestured to her reflection in the mirror. She glared at me.

"Anyhow, look what you've done." I pointed down the hallway. "Your couch cost more than I've ever made in a year."

She walked past me. "You think I'm so ambitious. I have to work hard; some of us weren't born talented. I studied my ass off in school to get the grades I did. You never did a damn thing and got higher marks than me, and what do you do? You drop out. Oh, it makes perfect sense."

I followed her into the living room. She walked over to the coffee table, picked up her wineglass, and took a long swallow. "Maybe if you'd concentrated on improving your art instead of screwing Gimlet you'd be making money as an artist now. And you whine and mope around like the world has done you an injustice. Well, tough shit, cookie. I don't feel sorry for you anymore."

"I never asked you to feel sorry for me."

"Well that's good, because I don't."

"I'm going now," I said. I got my jacket and walked out the door. I left it open to give her a chance to apologize.

I was halfway to the elevator when Ginny called from her doorway. "Frieda, please don't say anything to Whitman about all of this."

I nodded silently and pushed the elevator button. Ginny closed her door. I was flabbergasted. I was the loser. Ginny was the winner. It never occurred to me that she might be paying a price for all that winning. I also felt a tiny wavering of hope. Maybe, despite Gimlet's pronouncement, I did have talent. If Ginny, potentate of all good taste, thought so, it just might be true.

Dance, Gladys, Dance

She Twitches Too

By the time I got back home, everyone had gone to bed. I locked the door and went upstairs. I crawled under the covers and was about to escape for a few minutes into a mystery novel when Gladys cleared her throat from the armchair. I didn't put the book down. "Yes?" I said.

"I don't want to bother you, I know it's been a long night."

"A long night is right. What I want to know is how I'm supposed to develop a normal, boring life when everyone around me is acting like a lunatic?" I put the book down on the comforter.

"Umm, I don't know," said Gladys, "but have you thought about going to the Palace Theatre yet?"

"I haven't had a chance. I have no idea how we'd get in there. I don't want to get arrested. Ginny would think I was trying to show her up."

"Oh," said Gladys.

"I'll think about it, okay, tomorrow, I promise."

"All right," she said and disappeared.

I picked the book back up.

The next morning, Whitman sat at the kitchen table eating waffles. He wore a Venetian red silk paisley housecoat with a

CHAPTER TWENTY-TWO

black undershirt showing at the collar. His curly hair stood up in fifteen different directions.

Norman and Mr. H. had gone to the Centre. According to Whitman, Norman wanted to talk with the board members about some strategies for saving the Centre. Everybody had a strategy except me. I sat at the table and quickly ate a waffle and then I stood to do the dishes. If Whitman and Norman stayed any longer, I was going to put their names on the duty roster.

Whitman had another cup of coffee while I stacked the plates in the sink. As I washed and rinsed, I had an idea. It wasn't exactly "strategy" caliber, but it might work, and I'd promised Gladys.

I sat down across from Whitman. "I need to ask you a favour. Do you know anyone who works at the Palace?"

He looked at me. "No, why?"

"I need to get in there alone at night. Maybe you could say you were scouting a location for a movie and needed to check out the light or the atmosphere. Like maybe you'd get the keys for me."

"Why do you need to get into the building at night?" He picked up his fork and tapped the tines on the table.

"I can't tell you. Well, I could tell you but you'd never believe me. I won't touch anything. I just need to get in there."

He put the fork down, took a last swallow of his coffee, stood, and put the cup in the sink. "I'll see what I can do."

"Thanks. So, how goes *Jesus and the Punk Rockers?*"

"Who? Oh, doesn't look like the pilot is going to go." He turned from the sink. "No matter, there's plenty more ideas where that one came from."

I remembered that, the endless well of creativity. The more you used, the more you were provided with. Now, I could likely throw a coin down my well and hear echoes of it clinking against bone-dry bedrock. "What happened? Did the funding fall through?"

"Yes. No. Actually, there never was a *Jesus and the Punk Rockers*. Well, there was a Jesus, maybe, and there were definitely punk rockers, in the seventies, in New York, but there was no sitcom pilot. I came to see Dad. I wanted to try to — you know."

"I do know," I said.

"Well, anyway, I'm off," he said. "I'll see what I can do about the keys."

I finished the dishes, went up to my room, and brought my mystery book into the living room to read. Whitman passed down the hallway and out the front door without looking in. I crossed my fingers. Shortly after Whitman left, the phone rang. I sighed, put the book down, and went into the kitchen to answer it. At this rate, not only was I never going to find out who did it, I'd never even find out *what* they did.

It was Ginny and she was in tears. "They fired me," she sobbed. "I had to clean out my desk and carry out the boxes in front of everyone."

"Are you at home? Do you want me to come over?"

"Yeah, but no, I'm going to have a bath and then sleep for three days." She sniffed. "Sorry I was such a bitch yesterday."

"It's going to be okay, I promise. You'll be back up and swinging in no time. Phone me later."

Whitman walked into the living room in the early afternoon. I'd read far enough into the book by then to find out what they did, and it was nasty, whoever they were. He dropped a set of keys on the coffee table.

"That was fast," I said.

"No use messing around when there's something to be done, but you owe me big," he said. "I had to take the manager for lunch and sweet-talk him until I was blue in the face. Told him all sorts of bullshit about needing to see the place alone so my artistic sensibilities wouldn't be disturbed. It was excruciating.

Dance, Gladys, Dance

I took him to The Zone and I think I saw Ginny walking into the building, but she looked like a Sophia Loren impersonator, scarf wrapped around her head and giant sunglasses on."

"That was probably her. She's gone incognito for a bit. Did you talk to her?"

"I didn't want to interrupt my shameless pandering to the manager."

"Why don't you give her a call? She's kinda going through a tough time. It would cheer her up."

He held up his hands. "I don't think I'm what Ginny's looking for. And I don't do tough times. I'm a fair-weather fellow."

I looked at the keys, bit my tongue, then scooped up the key ring, and put it in the pocket of my hoodie. "Well," I said, "at least you're honest. I know it's none of my business." I hesitated, not wanting to start another argument. God knows I'd had it up to my unplucked eyebrows with people being "helpful." "But I don't think Mr. H. blames you for not coming home when your mom was sick. If anything, he blames himself for not making sure you knew how bad things were."

Whitman stared at me then nodded his head. "Thanks."

I shrugged. "'Salright. Thanks for the keys."

At ten o'clock that evening, I told everyone I was going out on the town. Mr. H. looked dubious, Norman envious, and Whitman amused. I stood at the bus stop in the indigo evening with Gladys floating dimly beside me.

"Are you sure no one else can see you?" I asked. "I'd hate to start mass panic on the transit system."

"Just you."

The bus stopped and we boarded. I sat on the outer seat so Gladys could sit by the window. The bus was mostly empty when we started out, but as we neared our destination, it began to fill up. I stared straight ahead. Out of the corner of my eye, I could see a lady in a green lumpy sweater with a big black purse standing beside me in the aisle. I glanced up at her briefly and was met with a grumpy stare. I looked away and hummed a little.

"Would you please push over?" she said.

"Uh," I glanced at Gladys who was absorbed with the sights out the window. "I can't really."

The woman gave an exasperated sigh and heaved herself over my knees and into the "empty" seat. I got a mouthful of hairy sweater. Gladys disappeared from view.

"Ahhhh," I said, "you just sat on —"

"Your imaginary friend?"

"Where'd she go?" I said looking around the bus.

"Day pass, honey?" asked the woman. "Always take all the medication you're prescribed."

"Oh, be quiet." I stood up and turned, holding onto the bar of the seat. Gladys floated in the back of the bus beside three teenagers in dark sunglasses and baseball caps. They listened to rap on a portable CD player. Gladys bobbed up and down. I walked unsteadily down the aisle and stood beside her.

"What is this music?" she asked.

"It's rap," I said aloud.

"No shit, Sherlock," said one of the teens.

"Let's move to the front," I said to Gladys.

"I ain't moving," said the boy holding the CD player. "Are you a cop?"

"No, I'm out on a day pass." I looked at Gladys and jerked my head towards the front of the bus. She ignored me. I jerked my head again, twice.

"She twitches too," said the teen closest to me to the dread-locked white boy beside him.

"Hey!" I said to Gladys. She moved up and down in time to the music with her eyes closed. "It's almost our stop. Come on."

One of the fellows turned and scanned the empty spot I

Dance, Gladys, Dance

addressed. "You're totally in code, lady. Who the fuck you talking to?"

"Jesus," I said. "He's always wanted to take a bus ride."

"Riiiiight," he said. "Going to the grocery store to get you some tinfoil for a hat?" The other boys snickered.

I nodded and headed for the front of the bus. Gladys drifted along behind me. We disembarked on the sidewalk in front of the Palace. It was a Tuesday night and the street was mostly deserted. "You need to listen to me when we're out," I told Gladys. "You could have got me in big trouble on the bus. Whitman said the keys were for the back entrance. Let's go around here."

"I couldn't get over that music. Rap." Her head started to jerk up and down again, "I'm Gladys. I got no body. It's cruddy. I'm Gladys."

I stared at her for a second and then burst into laughter. "You go, girl."

Around the back was a large green steel door. There were two keys, one for the doorknob lock and one for a deadbolt. I opened the door onto a long hallway, dimly lit with emergency lights. I felt around the wall, but I couldn't find a switch. It was kinda spooky, but what was I worried about — I'd see a ghost?

About halfway down the hallway was a door marked "Stage Right." I opened it and we were in another hallway, this one shorter. There was a switch to the left of the door. I flicked it and a dim row of lights near the floor came on.

"Backstage lights," I whispered to Gladys.

"We used to have small oil lamps backstage in Toronto," said Gladys. "You had to be careful not to upset them when making your entrances and exits." She was whispering too.

We went down the little hallway and onto the stage. It was almost completely dark.

"I'm going to try and find some lights," I said. Gladys stood on the stage, looking out at the seats. I made my way across the stage and down the stairs into the aisle beside the orchestra pit.

Near the door, I found a panel of light switches and a large bar switch. I held my breath and flipped the large switch. The first row of stage lights came on. Gladys was nowhere to be seen.

"Gladys?" I said in a loud whisper. Empty theatres are so churchy I didn't feel I could yell. "Gladys? Where the hell did you go?"

Was it So Wrong?

There was a rustle of the curtains at the back and an elegant young woman walked out on the stage. Her dark brown hair was swept up into a loose bun at the back of her neck and large waves curled around the front of her face. She wore a long pale blue dress covered in shimmering golden beads.

I scrambled to think of a fib to explain why I was in the theatre. I could say I was Whitman's assistant and had come ahead to prepare for his arrival. The woman stopped at centre stage and put her arms out in front of her. I cleared my throat and was about to speak, wanting to catch her before she started to rehearse, when she began bobbing her head up and down. "I'm Gladys. I got no body. It's cruddy. I'm Gladys."

Gladys? Oh God. She stopped singing, began to move her hips back and forth, and swayed her shoulders. Gladys was dancing. She was young again and she was dancing. I stood in the dark aisle and tears rolled down my cheeks.

I stood there mesmerized until she finished her dance and then I walked up to the front of the stage. Gladys turned and smiled at me. "That felt marvelous," she said.

"You look amazing," I said.

"I was nice to look at back then." She looked down at herself. "It didn't last forever. Come sit." She walked over to the edge of the stage and sat, with her legs dangling over. I hesitated, feeling strangely shy. The old Gladys had been relatively easy to talk to, but this metamorphosed dazzling creature intimidated me.

"Do you want me to change back?" she asked as if reading my thoughts.

"No. I'd like you to stay this way forever. I wish you could have stayed that way." I went and sat down beside her.

"My labour pains started the next morning," she said, staring out into the empty seats. "The morning after Jack found me dancing in the chicken crap. It was a hard birth and I only saw the baby for a minute before I passed out. It was a boy. A beautiful little boy. When I woke up, there was a man I'd never seen before sitting beside my bed. 'Good afternoon, Gladys,' he said. 'I'm Dr. Wallberg.' 'Where's my baby?' I said. 'Is he all right?' I tried to sit up. 'He's fine,' the doctor said. 'Don't you worry.' And then he said, 'I understand you've been having some troubles lately.'"

"No," Gladys shook her head as she sat there.

Stop, I wanted to say, stop telling me, it hurts you, it hurts me, I don't want to hear it, but I knew I had to hear, I had to listen.

"'No,'" she repeated. "I said, 'I haven't had any troubles.' I was so scared. I knew something was wrong. 'Bring me my baby,' I said to him. 'Where is he?' He ignored me. 'We're worried about you, Gladys,' he said and patted my hand. 'We think it best that you have a little rest before you start taking care of your child.' 'I don't need a rest,' I said. I was so frightened I couldn't think straight. The doctor said, 'Sometimes a respite with professional care can work wonders. One of our nurses will be in to help you dress and then we'll go.' For a minute, I couldn't say anything. I was just frozen, then I said, 'I'm not going anywhere without my baby.' He was already leaving and a nurse in her uniform with a heavy woolen cape over top was coming in. I started to yell. 'Help me, Jack. They're taking me away. Please help.' Before the door shut behind the doctor, I saw

Jack standing in the hall. Our eyes locked briefly and again I saw my worth reflected there. Zero. None."

Tears traced down my face again.

"I fought," Gladys said without looking at me. "Don't you think I went easy, but I was weak from having the baby and they bundled me up and took me out into a carriage that waited outside. They took me to the Brandon Asylum for the Insane. I never went to Toronto, I never danced, and I never saw my baby again." She began to cry softly and rock back and forth.

I wanted to put my arms around her, but I was afraid they would go right through her and I didn't think that would comfort either of us. I waited and she began to calm down and her sobs slowed until she was just sitting and rocking.

"How long were you in the institution?"

"Seven years. I was hysterical at first, I suppose. The thought that they were going to keep me there. . . and my baby. . . I just couldn't. . . I cried and screamed and hit people. I. . . they threw me in cold tubs, strapped me down. There was a long metal cage they'd put over the bed and lock me up underneath it. Once, when they let me out, I broke all my fingers trying to dig through the walls."

She stared down at her hands, bending and straightening her fingers, then looked back up at me. I couldn't meet her eyes.

She continued quietly, "Once I spent all that anger there was nothing left. I stared at walls and lay on the floor. They carried me from place to place. I didn't speak. I went away for a long time."

"Oh, Gladys. What a waste — it's a crime."

"I started to come back," she said. "My life before. . . my memory of it began to disintegrate. Just shreds and tatters. Some things I could still remember, but those things hurt so much I didn't dare let myself think of them. There was a nurse who helped me, talked to me like I was a real person, made sure I got up and around. There was farm work for the men, but ladies weren't supposed to work. The nurse, Sarah, she let me help in the kitchen. She thought it was therapeutic. Jack would have loved that — he was always after me to cook and bake more, and there I was baking seven days a week."

"Gladys doesn't dance anymore, she needs the room to bake." She smiled. "Right."

"I'm so sorry," I said. "What can I do? Please tell me, Gladys. Tell me how I can help."

"You're helping right now," she said turning and looking at me. "No one knows. I never got to tell my story to anyone. There were so many of us in there. So many that wanted the wrong things or couldn't manage to be content. No one heard us. Who was there to listen? Was it so wrong to want to dance?"

"No," I whispered, "it wasn't wrong."

"I never gave up hope," said Gladys. "I never stopped believing I could dance. If they hadn't locked me away, I would have. Even if I'd had to stay with Jack, I'd have danced for those damn chickens every day again, just like I did when I was a girl. Do you hear me, Frieda?"

"I hear you, but what can I do? What is it you want me to do for you?"

"It's not time for some things yet," she said. "You can't have both, you know, you can't try to have the entire world love you, try to be perfect for everyone and still create."

I nodded. "That's when you end up stealing forks."

"Do you get the point of my story?"

"Yes, of course, but no, not exactly. Men are assholes?"
Gladys shook her head.

"Don't count your socks until they come out of the dryer? I never was very good at this," I said. "All those Aesop's fables in elementary school, what the hell, I never could figure out the moral until the teacher explained it to me."

Gladys smiled. "For a modern woman," she said, "you're not very bright, are you?"

"What?"

Gladys stood. "Well, we'd better get going. We don't want to miss our bus."

"I think I already missed it," I muttered and went and turned off the lights. By the time I got to the exit, Gladys was waiting there. She'd turned back into her old self, but I was never able to look at her again without seeing a glimmer of that beautiful young woman in the beaded gown. We took the nearly empty bus home in silence.

I heard laughter in the kitchen the next morning. A familiar honking laughter. Lady March. I dressed quickly and went down.

"Frieda darling," said Lady March, getting up from the table. "Come here and give me a hug. I missed you. Why didn't you write or call me, you silly goose?"

I shrugged from the middle of her embrace and smiled. Lady March wore a long red cotton dress embroidered with butterflies and flowers. Her platinum hair was in wild, soft curls partially contained by a green and purple scarf wrapped around the middle of her head and tied at the back of her neck with the tails hanging down.

"I see you've met Mr. H.," I said.

"I have indeed. He made me the most enchanting breakfast and I've been talking his ear off about the incredible things I saw in Chicago. Haven't I?" She reached over and tugged on Mr. H.'s ear.

He blushed and smiled. "My ears are at your service, m'lady."

"Don't you m'lady me. I'm just Alvena." She sat back down. "Now, Frieda, you get yourself a cup of java, sit down, and tell me everything about your life."

"There isn't much to tell," I said as I got a cup from the cupboard. "I haven't been doing much."

"Well," said Lady March, "you know what the I Ching says about waiting. The hsu brings nourishment. Perseverance carries good fortune. It furthers one to cross the great water."

I sat down at the table. "I think I'm up the great water without a paddle."

"Oh, hush," she said. "Trust that you'll be given all you need. It's an abundant universe."

I nodded. There was no use trying to dissuade Lady March. Her faith in a loving, giving universe was absolute.

"Where's Norman and Whitman?" I asked Mr. H.

"Norman had more business to attend to and Whitman is out and about somewhere," he said.

Lady March cocked her head to one side. "Is there someone else in the house?"

"No," said Mr. H., "just us."

She frowned. "I sense another here."

I looked around. Gladys stood at the bottom of the back stairs. Lady March stared right at her.

"Has your wife ever come back to see you?" Lady March asked Mr. H.

"No," he said, glancing about guiltily as though Shirley might be witnessing his enchantment with Lady March.

"I sense spirits here," said Lady March. She tilted her head up to the ceiling. "Could you give us a sign?"

Mr. H. paled. My mouth hung open. Was someone other than me finally going to see Gladys? She was no longer visible. There was a sudden bump by the back door. Mr. H. jumped in his seat.

"Hello," said Lady March. "What can we do for you?"

There was nothing for a minute and then Lady March's chair moved about three inches over so that she and Mr. H. sat thigh to thigh. Mr. H. gasped. "Cheese and Rice," he said, "what was that?"

"Oh," said Lady March, smiling at Mr. H., "isn't that interesting?"

Mr. H. nodded, his face a bright crimson.

"Can you speak?" Lady March asked the air. Nothing. We waited in silence for a moment and then she said, "I don't feel anything anymore. Whoever it was has gone."

"I've never seen anything like that before," said Mr. H. breathlessly. "Do you think it was Shirley?"

"I don't know," answered Lady March. "The spirits only reveal what they wish. Are you all right?" She patted Mr. H.'s arm.

"Oh, yes, fine." He half stood from his chair, sat down, then stood up. "I — uh — I'd better get going to the Art Centre. Do you want to come along, Frieda?"

"No thanks."

"I'll come if you'll have me," said Lady March. "Norman has told me so much about the Centre and your wonderful work there, I'd love for you to show me around."

"Of course," said Mr. H. "You'd better see it now, before it ceases to exist."

"Now, now," said Lady March, "we need to be positive and creative. I'll see what the building tells me."

Mr. H. shot me a sideways glance. I smiled and shrugged.

The two of them left. I went into the bathroom with an encyclopedia — Petard to Quadra. A polite cough sounded in the hallway.

"That you, Gladys?"

"Yes."

"Can you hang on for a minute?"

Silence.

"Gladys?"

"I miss having to go to the bathroom," she said.

"Oh." I couldn't think of anything to say to that.

"I'll wait in the living room," she said.

When I got out, Gladys was sitting in Mr. H.'s recliner chair looking pleased with herself.

"What were you doing?" I asked. "Scaring poor Mr. H. to death."

"How could I resist?" she said smiling. "They'd make an excellent couple. What are you doing today?"

"Looking for a job, I suppose."

"Well, I'll leave you to it." She vanished.

"That's it? Gladys?"

Nothing.

I sat at the kitchen table going through the classifieds. There'd been so much going on I'd conveniently neglected to look for a job. And now that I looked at the ads, I wished I could forget again. I wonder if I could drive a forklift. I closed the paper.

There was a large manila envelope on the table underneath the sugar bowl. I moved the bowl, picked up the envelope, and turned it over. No name. It could be for me. Not likely, but it could be. It wasn't sealed; I opened it and dumped out the pages. Halfway down the first page were the words *The Devil's Cry*. I turned to the second page and read the first scene of a screenplay, a very disturbing scene involving a possessed young woman, a knife, and way too much blood for me, even in black and white. I shuddered. Was this Marilyn's script? If Whitman made big money from this stuff, maybe I could too. Let's see, there could be a man with a chainsaw, no, a clown, no, been done, okay, a psychopathic, uh, forklift driver takes to the streets, impaling people on the pokey things on the front of the forklift. Of course, it would only take the police about five minutes to catch him, unless it was, uh, a super-turbo-charged forklift, a Ferrari forklift, okay, never mind.

There was a knock and the back door opened all at once. Miss Kesstle stood there looking around the kitchen. I slid the pages back into the envelope.

"Who's here now?" she asked.

"Just me," I said, looking around to see if Gladys was there and Miss Kesstle had now picked up her spiritual vibes.

"I saw a fancy woman leave with Mr. Hausselman, all dood-led up, looked like she was going to a costume party."

"That was Lady March, Norman's mom. She's staying here for a bit. You want a cup of coffee?"

"Where did they go?" She walked in and sat down at the table.

"To the Art Centre. Coffee?"

"No coffee. It gives me gas. I can't stop thinking about that young woman we met at the art show."

"Girl? How about some toast?" I asked.

"Did you know there hasn't been a decent toaster made since they started space travel? All the inventors fooling around with outer space things instead of making decent appliances. I thought I could do something for her. Help her somehow. She's too young to be out on the streets. And did you see what she did with those doilies? She's obviously very bright. Could you find her and make sure she's all right?"

"I'm feeling like my hands are kinda full already with Norman and Ginny and now Lady March is here too."

"How long is she staying?"

"Until Norman gets his this-and-that business done, I suppose."

"Humph," said Miss Kesstle. "There's been more people here in the last few weeks than Mr. Hausselman had in a year before."

"He seems to be enjoying the company," I said.

She hmphed again. "Will you try and find her, Frieda? It would set my mind at ease. Maybe you could talk to her a little. Do you think you and Mr. Hausselman will still be over for Sunday supper?"

"I'm not sure, with everyone here and —"

"Well, I suppose they could all come. No reason for Mr. Hausselman to give up his Sunday supper because of all these people coming and going."

"I'll let everyone know," I said.

Dance, Gladys, Dance

"You'll tell me if you find her?"

I nodded. Miss Kesstle went out the back door. I hated the thought of her sitting there alone in that empty house without even her crocheting to keep her company. God only knew what information she'd pick up from radio talk shows.

I called Ginny but there was no answer. She was probably already out tearing up interview rooms with snappy answers and perfectly planned career goals. Maybe I should leave her a message about the forklift job.

I decided to go out and wander, look for help wanted signs, and keep an eye open for Girl at the same time. I had an idea, not at all perfectly planned, but it might be a way to help her.

A Regular Tornado

Girl was working on a new box in the back alley near Ginny's place. This box was partially covered in flattened-out boxes from feminine hygiene products, patches of moss, and photos Girl had taken of ordinary women holding up photos of female movie stars.

"Hey Girl," I said as I wandered closer. "Neat project. What's it about?"

"Well, no one ever thinks of movie stars being on the rag. They're always so clean and pretty. So I was kinda thinking about that so. . ." She gestured at the box.

"The juxtaposition between the women we see as above us, mixed with a symbol of their basic humanity. That's great." Who said I didn't learn anything in art school?

Girl looked at me blankly. "Uh, maybe. Thanks. I sold the other box for fifty bucks. Pretty good, hey?"

She wore a pink T-shirt and a miniskirt made of Miss Kesstle's pineapple doilies, with black bicycle shorts underneath.

"Nice skirt too. Miss Kesstle says hi."

"Cool." She carried on with her cutting and pasting.

"So, there's someone I'd like you to meet," I said.

"Who?" She cocked her head and narrowed her eyes. "You found a hot stud for me? Or some sort of social work detoxifier?"

"No, this is a female artist, a screenwriter. She lives a few blocks away. She's pretty interesting. I thought we could stop in and see if she's home."

"Could do," said Girl. "I'm pretty hungry, though. Think she'll have any munchies?"

"I doubt it. How about we stop for lunch first?"

"Have any money this time?"

"Well, no, but I have a coupon for a free muffin."

"You're even sadder than me," she said. "Never mind, let's go."

I half hoped Marilyn wouldn't be home. I wasn't at all sure how this was going to go. I did hope she would try to clue Girl in on what she was doing with her life — i.e., wasting it. Or maybe Girl would see how she could end up, or maybe the prejudice thing would help Girl understand something. Actually, I didn't know what the hell to expect, but at least I could say I tried.

"Nice place," said Girl as we walked into the hotel. "What does she write scripts for, cheap porno movies? Stud A: Ohhh baby. Chick B: Oh oh oh uh uh uh." She got louder and louder as we went across the lobby.

"Take it inside the room," yelled a voice from the room behind the invariably empty front desk.

I jumped — there was actually someone back there. "Shut up," I said to Girl.

She laughed and continued whispering as we went up the stairs, "Stud B: Come on over here, honey. . ."

"Shhh." I knocked on Marilyn's door. Nothing. I knocked again. Louder.

"Open up," yelled Girl, "it's the police."

There was silence, then the sound of scrambling and flushing toilets from behind doors all up and down the hall.

"Shit," said Girl, "what a waste."

I was ready to turn around and leave when the door opened.

"What the hell is all the yelling about?" asked a very dishevelled Marilyn leaning on the doorframe.

"Hi, it's me," I said brightly.

"Who're you? The Avon lady? I don't want any."

"No, I'm Frieda. Remember? I helped you home from the art show the other night."

Marilyn squinted. "I remember getting ready to go out, then I remember walking with someone and wearing these fucking ugly slippers."

"That was me."

"Right," Marilyn nodded slowly. "You want your slippers back? I think I lost one."

"No, I brought someone to meet you. This is Girl. She's an artist, a photographer, and designer."

Girl raised her hand. "Hey."

"Hay is for horses," said Marilyn. She stood looking back and forth between the two of us. "Well, come in." She walked to the bed and threw everything off it onto the floor. "Sit down."

We made our way in and sat on the bed. Marilyn took the chair by the packing crate desk.

"Hang on," she said, standing. "If I remember, last night, I think, wait, move." She went to look under the bed and Girl and I stood up. "I thought so," she said, emerging with a half-full bottle of tequila.

"Now we're talking," said Girl.

"No we're not," I said.

"What?" said Marilyn. "It's a social drink." She unscrewed the top of the bottle, took a long swallow, and passed it to Girl.

"I brought her here for you to *talk* to," I said to Marilyn, "not to get her drunk. I want you to tell her all that stuff you told me. About female artists and inequality and the expressway."

"I don't remember," she said taking the bottle back from Girl.

"Yes you do."

"No I don't."

"Okay, fine," I said, standing. "Come on, Girl."

"No way," said Girl. She tilted her head back and compressed her lips like a toddler refusing food. When the bottle returned, she opened wide, and took another long swallow. "I'm staying here with my new friend."

"Fine. See you later." So much for that idea. I opened the door.

"I'm not interested in saving anyone," said Marilyn. "What are you, some sort of missionary?"

"Yeah," I said, "just like the Blues Brothers, only I'm on a mission from Gladys."

"Riiiight," said Marilyn. "I think you need a drink."

"I had a great-great-grandma named Gladys," said Girl, wiping her mouth and handing the bottle back to Marilyn.

I froze. "What?"

"Oh yeah, she was a nutburger."

"A what?"

"You know, a wigger, a looney-tune. She was in the nut-house."

"Well, you come by it honestly, then," said Marilyn, patting Girl on the shoulder. They both began to snicker.

"What's your last name?" I said, staring at Girl.

"Why, are you going to report me?"

"Don't tell her," said Marilyn. "That's privileged information."

"Oh, for shit's sake," I said. "I'm not going to report you. Just tell me."

"Roulston," said Girl. "Why?"

My heart stopped.

"Do you know anything else about your great-great-grand-mother, other than that she was a nutburger?"

"Yeah," said Girl, "she was also a whore."

"No, she *wasn't*," I said.

"Yes, she *was*," said Girl. "What are you on about anyway?"

"Nothing," I said. "I'm not sure what I'm supposed to do. Please come with me."

"No way," said Girl. "I'll catch up with you later."

I dug in the pockets of my jacket and came up with a pen

and the muffin coupon. "Here," I said. I wrote down my phone number on the back of the coupon and handed it to her. "Call me."

Girl nodded. "Later."

I walked out and closed the door on the two of them. All the way home I could hardly think. Girl was Gladys' great-great-granddaughter. I didn't know whether to laugh or cry. Still, what was I supposed to do? Save her? Someone better equipped than me should have been chosen for this job. Gladys a whore? Where on earth did that come from? Family histories get mixed up over the years, or maybe Jack had started the lie to ruin Gladys' reputation.

I walked and the buildings around me emptied of office workers, and traffic on the sidewalk increased. Instead of helping Girl, I end up leaving her with a crazy woman to get pissed. Great. Did I know anything about Girl? I knew what I felt at her age. Being an artist seemed the only way out of somewhere I felt I didn't belong. Somewhere Girl obviously felt she didn't fit in either. The world in front of me had seemed empty. I didn't want to be a nurse, or a teacher, or even a doctor or a lawyer. But when I told people I wanted to become an artist, they met my youthful ignorance with amusement, as if I'd said I wanted to grow up to become a fire truck. I looked at all the people walking around me. Were they happy? All I felt was confused and lonely. It had never occurred to me that others, like Girl, maybe felt the same way. But what to do with that?

There was no one home when I got back to Mr. H.'s. I went and sat on the front porch to have a think and do my toenails. I was surrounded by nail polish bottles and trying to decide on a colour when Lady March came up the walk and onto the porch. She carried shopping bags from the IGA down the street.

"Salmon and new potatoes for dinner tonight," she said.

"Sounds good. Do you like this or this?" I held up a red bottle and a bright purple.

"I'm not sure," she said, sitting on the railing across from me. "Why don't you do each toe a different colour?"

"Good idea." I watched the birds hopping on the lawn in front of the house. "Did you ever hear of stormy petrels?" I asked. Lady March shook her head.

"They're seabirds that appear in a storm. They surround ships to catch little creatures that rise to the surface when the seas are rough; when the storm is over, they disappear."

"Oh," said Lady March, "those are magpies, you know." She gestured to the black and white birds congregating on the lawn.

"I know," I said shaking a bottle of nail polish. "But I was thinking about things, people, or birds, just appearing and disappearing. I read about petrels in the encyclopedia."

"I don't know about petrels," said Lady March, "but magpies are a sign of steadfastness; they stay even through the cold winter. Perhaps your fallow period has ended and it's the time for action."

"What action?" I asked.

"Anything as long as it's movement forward," she said.

Wasn't reading encyclopedias in the bathroom action?

"Well," said Lady March, "I'm going inside to meditate on the Art Centre quandary. Want to come?"

I shook my head and away she went, her psychedelic caftan billowing around her.

I had a sudden picture of myself surrounded by a whirlwind of people: Gladys in her dancing outfit, Ginny with a handful of forks, Marilyn at her packing crate desk with a bottle held to her lips, Girl emerging from her box, Miss Kesstle holding her red binder full of crochet designs — they spun all around me and then moved off. A regular tornado of artistic women barreling down the street and I stood still, alone. Not the calm in the eye of the storm; I wasn't even a part of the storm. I was

— how the hell did that Winnie the Pooh song go? *I'm just a little black rain cloud. Pay no attention to little me.* Except that I felt more like Eeyore than Winnie the Pooh. Eeyore's slow grey voice sounded in the back of my head: "We can't all and some of us don't. That's all there is."

"Penny for your thoughts," said Norman coming out the front door.

I turned. "Inflation," I said. "Thoughts are two thousand bucks now. Where were you?"

"Took the Valiant out to get the tires rotated. I parked in the back. Take an IOU?"

"I was thinking about Eeyore from *Winnie the Pooh*," I said.

Norman sat on the chair beside me. "I think Leonard Cohen and Eeyore sound a lot alike."

"Get out."

"That same mournful tone; it's uncanny."

"I was thinking *I* sounded like Eeyore."

Norman nodded. "Maybe, just a little higher pitched." He shuffled his feet. "Why aren't you painting? I'm sorry about what happened in Kentucky. . . I should have left you alone."

"Yes, you should have."

"But don't give it all up because of me," he said.

"What an ego. I didn't quit because of you. I got tired, okay?" I picked up the bottle of white nail polish, shook it, and began painting my toenails. "I don't want to talk about it anymore."

He sat there. And sat there. I finally looked up.

"I was wondering if I ever told you that I had an imaginary friend when I was little," he said. "His name was Poginos."

"That's nice," I said.

Norman stared at me, smiling. What the hell was this about? "Did you ever have an imaginary friend?" he asked.

"No," I said.

"Oh. Are you sure?"

It dawned on me that he was trying to give me an easy way

Dance, Gladys, Dance

to talk about the imaginary person I'd supposedly been having conversations with. Norman might, just might understand, or believe me. I could tell him and make him promise not to tell anyone.

He shifted in his chair. "I was thinking that starting to paint again might be therapeutic for you."

"*Ther-a-peu-tic?*" I choked out. "Like what — fucking basket weaving? You're too much. You are too fucking much." I left my bottles of nail polish on the porch and went inside with one set of toes painted. I clumped upstairs to my bedroom, put Deep Purple on the CD player, cleaned my room, and then I cleaned it again.

At about nine that evening, Mr. H., Lady March, and I were relaxing in the living room. Lady March sat on a kitchen chair beside Mr. H. in his recliner. She held his hand in hers. "Because you're right-handed, this is your active hand. Your left hand is your passive hand; it shows your childhood. Hmmm. Your fate line forks towards the Mount of Jupiter; this shows a person with a pleasant humanitarian approach."

I perked up. "A fate line?" I went over to the recliner and held my hand out to Lady March. "What does mine show?"

She took my hand.

"Your fate line is broken."

"Broken?" Typical.

"See, it isn't a continuous line. All these breaks mean you will have a variety of life experiences —"

The phone rang. I took my spastic fate line hand away and went to answer it. It was Girl.

"Well," she said, "I was going to get a muffin, but I'm glad I didn't, 'cause I needed your phone number. Can you come and get me?"

"Where are you?"

"At the downtown police station."

Surprise, surprise.

Behind the front desk stood the same policeman who'd been on duty the night I picked up Ginny.

"You again?" he said when I walked in.

"What do you mean, me again? *I* haven't done anything. Maybe I'm running a home for chronically unstable females."

"You have to have a license for that, you know."

"Is Girl here?"

In the car, Girl filled me in on what had happened after I left her. She'd finished the tequila with Marilyn and then they went out on the town. One of them got the brilliant idea to go to some fancy downtown bar and of course they couldn't get past the front entry. Marilyn decked the hostess and the bouncer came out and grabbed Girl. Marilyn took off. They called the police, but because it wasn't Girl who hit the woman, they let her go.

I tried to talk to her as I drove her back to her foster parents' house across the city. "You'll kill yourself if you carry on this way."

Girl reached forward and turned on the radio; classical music from the CBC filled the car. "Holy time warp, Batman," she said. "Why shouldn't I?"

"Kill yourself?" I reached down and turned the radio off. "Your photos are stunning, that's why. They're like your box; those women are real women, just like you and me. You could be famous."

"Sure, and get chewed up in some celebrity-making machine." She leaned forward and opened the glove compartment. "The box is a joke. I was going to do something about shitting — like, even movie stars have to take a big dump sometimes. But I couldn't figure out how to do it." She rummaged through the compartment and pulled out a map of Canada. "Cool." She unfolded the map, closed her eyes, pointed, and then pulled the map closer to her face. "Want to go to Grimsby?"

"No. Where is it?"

"Uh, Ontario."

"No. Put that away. Okay, not famous, but you have talent, and you have the chance to do something with it. Eighty years ago, women got locked away. Did you know that? If a woman didn't agree with her husband or was inconvenient, they could just lock her up."

She mangled the map into a smaller package, put it in the glove compartment, and slammed it shut. "Is this going to be a history lesson?"

"It's your history." I banged my hand on the steering wheel.

"You're whacked."

We drove the rest of the way in silence except for Girl's muttered directions.

I parked in front of the house.

"Grimbsy would have been better than here," she said, got out, and slammed the door.

Damsel In Distress

"Did you see your boyfriend has his own little porno emporium set up in his bedroom?" asked Whitman as I walked into the kitchen late the next day, carrying five bags of groceries. "There's mail for you," he added, holding out a letter.

"He's not my boyfriend," I said. I put down my bags, took the letter, and went upstairs to see. I had visions of vibrators, leather clothing, and naked inflatable people strewn all over Norman's room. What would Mr. H. think?

Norman's room was filled with his father's collection of Victorian pornography. There were sepia-toned photographs of Victorian women and sometimes men in every imaginable pose. I found the collection oddly fascinating; it was such a contrast to how I believed people of that time behaved. I'd once heard that carrots were always diced when served for dinner in the early 1900s, the natural shape of them being too suggestive. The Victorians in these photos had moved far beyond titillating vegetables. There were some very explicit pictures, but what seemed amusing, in a horrifying sort of way, was the typical Victorian accoutrements involved in the scenes: heavy fringed draperies, ferns and classical urns, and ladies wearing large flowered hats and gloves and nothing else. Norman seemed to be organizing the collection; there were piles marked *Pre-1900 American* and so on, and, over on the desk, stacks marked *Canadian* with

CHAPTER TWENTY-FIVE

various dates. I was about to go and rifle through the stacks to see if Canadians had put their own distinctive mark on their photos — partially clad Mounties, perhaps, or women lounging on beaver pelts — when Norman walked in.

"So Norman, whatcha doing with these?"

"I can't tell you yet. It's a surprise."

"It's surprising all right."

He shrugged.

"No hints at all?" I asked.

"Nope. Mom and I are going out for dinner tonight with Mr. Hausselman. Do you want to come or are you still mad at me?"

"Just promise me you won't talk to me about painting ever again and we'll be fine. Is Whitman going?"

"He has to fly to Toronto for a few days. He's leaving at five."

The house to myself for a few precious hours. . . maybe Gladys would finally show up again. "I need to be alone for awhile. You guys go."

I went upstairs to my room and looked at the letter. Mom again. I opened it. She was happy about my decision to go back to school, someone's daughter had triplets, and she included a cheque, "to get some school clothes." I had a vision of myself in a blue plaid skirt and white knee-high socks, with a leather tool belt hanging from my hips — a look that would probably would fuel some man's fantasies, but I wouldn't want to meet him. You know you've been a bum for too long when your parents automatically send money without you even asking for it. Clothes weren't a bad idea, though. Since nothing else had turned out ordinary so far, maybe I could try looking conventional.

When I went back downstairs, Mr. H. was just hanging up the phone. Lady March sat at the kitchen table, her Tarot cards spread out in front of her.

"What's up?" I asked Mr. H.

He looked stunned and spoke slowly. "The government. They already have a deal in place with a hotel chain for the site. They're going to tear the building down and build a five-star hotel."

I looked at Norman. "A five-star hotel. It's all *your* fault."

"Frieda!" he said.

"Just kidding. Can they do that? That's underhanded."

"They own the building and the land," said Mr. H. "I suppose they can do whatever they want."

"Fehu," said Lady March loudly.

"Gesundheit," replied Mr. H. He sat down at the table.

"Fehu is the runestone I pulled this morning in regards to the Art Centre. It means possessions won or earned, earned income, luck, abundance, and financial strength in the present or near future. Don't despair yet, my dear. I have a plan."

"Would you like to tell me what your plan is, Mother?" asked Norman with a worried frown.

"Of course not," said Lady March. "That would spoil the surprise."

"Promise me you won't do anything foolish," said Norman

"Our ideas of what constitutes foolish are too far apart for me to do that. Don't worry, darling."

"Famous last words," muttered Norman.

After they left for dinner, I went upstairs to my room and sat at my desk. I opened my paint box and looked at the tubes, all those wonderful colours. I stared at the canvas, then pushed back the chair. Not going to happen.

I opened the wardrobe, checking as always for the entrance to the secret world, which, as always, wasn't there. That's all right, I was headed for another "foreign" world. I found a semi-respectable-looking pair of khaki pants and a black t-shirt. Nondescript but also non-offensive. I wanted to blend in. I took a deep breath. I was going to a mall. Not only to a mall, but to a women's retail clothing store to buy some clothes. Clothes with original price tags. Normal, respectable, new women's clothing. I was filled with dread.

It was eight o'clock and the mall was filled with last-minute shoppers. The blazing fluorescent light and canned air made my eyes water. The fountains roared, fifteen different types of music played, and everyone's conversation bounced off the concrete and glass. Courage. I picked a women's clothing store at random and walked in. All the clothes looked stiff and uncomfortable. Some sort of techno-bop played from hidden overhead speakers. A young, done-up, and impossibly perky saleslady approached me. "Hi there! Can I help you with anything?"

"Can you change the music?"

"No," she said, "we aren't allowed to. Can I help you find anything?"

"No. Yes. I need some clothes. Stylish, but not too stylish. Not like over the top. But in style now. What are women wearing these days?"

"Was it for a special occasion?" She beamed at me hopefully, though why she should care if I was having a special occasion, I couldn't fathom.

"No. Just life."

"For work?"

"No. I don't have a job. Thanks for reminding me. Just for, you know, walking around in."

"Oh. Exercise wear?"

"Not that kind of walking, just ambling around, looking at things, seeing the sights."

"Oh, vacation wear, then."

"No. I'm not going on vacation. I just want some clothes. Just clothes."

"Casual wear?"

I thought I might weep. "Sure, show me some casual wear."

I took an armful of clothes into the dressing room. As usual, the fluorescent lights made me look like some kind of she-zombie. I put on a pair of black pants and a green turtleneck. No mirrors in the room. Would the cruelty never end?

I opened the door and snuck out to peek in the multiple mirrors at the end of the change room hallway.

"Taking up espionage?"

"Bah!"

Gladys floated in 3-D in the mirrors behind me. "Why don't you try on something pretty? Show your elbows, at least."

"My elbows are one of my least attractive body parts."

"In my day, a woman could drive a man crazy with a properly displayed elbow."

"Probably without even getting implants." I went back into the change room. "I'll try something else."

"So, are you going to tell me about Girl?" I asked as I put on a miniskirt and a pink blouse.

"I don't know too much," she said from the dressing room beside me.

"It's her that I'm supposed to help though, right?"

"Well. . ."

"What do you mean, *well?*" I struggled with the zipper in the back of the skirt. No handy bus drivers around to help. "That's my mission — she's your relative and I'm supposed to get Girl off the streets and doing her art. So she doesn't end up being another lost voice like you. Right?"

"Well. . ."

"That has to be it. I don't have any other ideas." I slipped the blouse on and did up the buttons.

"Uhhh. . ."

"Okay, never mind. Did you know your descendants think you were a prostitute?"

"Pardon me?" asked a horrified voice from outside the fitting room door. I opened the door a crack. The cheery salesclerk peered in at me, her perfectly plucked eyebrows raised halfway up her forehead.

"Ha." I said, "Nothing — never mind. Just thinking out loud. What do you think of this?" I stepped out.

"Super," she enthused. "I'll get you some more."

"That's okay. . ." But she was gone.

Gladys was behind me again. "Now that looks pretty. And look at your knees. Men will be falling over in the street."

"Men don't fall over for knees, Gladys. You need to show T&A to get a reaction nowadays. It was probably that asshole Jack lying to your son."

Gladys looked away. "'T&A'? Tonsils and Armpits? Teeth and Ankles?"

"I've brought you a few more skirts and some dresses." The clerk rounded the corner with an armload. Gladys poofed away. God, I wished I had that ability.

"Thanks. That's enough, okay? I don't do this often; I'd better pace myself."

"Sure. If you need anything in a different size or colour, just holler. Okey-dokey?"

"Okey-dokey," I managed, rolling my eyes at her retreating back. I grabbed a few items and went back into the cage. Gladys appeared beside me in the cubicle.

"Try the green dress," she said.

"Shit! It's a little crowded in here. How about you wait next door?"

"Okey-dokey." She disappeared and then her voice came from the next room again. "There's more to my story, but I just. . . Did I ever tell you about the fire in the institution?"

"No. What happened?"

"I don't know if they ever figured out what or who started it. They housed the inmates in the Brandon Winter Fair Building for two years."

"That must have been — nuts. Sorry. You know, I think this dress actually might look okay."

"I missed it."

"Where did you go?" I walked out and looked in the mirrors. "With some sandals, I could actually pull this off."

"I don't want to tell you. You — you'll find out. . ."

"What do you mean, I'll find out? Tell me. Please?"

There was a polite cough behind me. I turned. The clerk gave me a wan smile.

"Well," I said, "tell me, please. Does this make my elbows look fat?"

She managed a small shake of her head and then quickly departed. Gladys didn't reappear and neither did the saleslady. I tried on the rest of the clothing in peace and actually found some to buy.

The clerk wrapped my purchases in tissue and rang them up. I couldn't believe the cost. I must have appeared shocked, because she sighed and began a recap of the prices.

"Oh, no. I'm sure you rang it up right. I just usually don't spend that much on clothes. But I don't have to dig staples out of the sleeves like the clothes from the Salvation Army, so that's worth something, right?"

She nodded and held out her hand for the money. I'd ground her cheerfulness down to nothing.

The first thing I heard when I woke up was the vacuum going. Better than cymbals, but only just. I took some of my new clothes out of the bag and put them on. I looked in the mirror. Low-rise black polyester slacks. I turned around and checked to see if my butt crack was showing. It wasn't, but it sure felt like it was. A polyester blouse covered with monstrous cadmium yellow and purple roses. I could go and lie down in the front flowerbed; maybe I would, after I found out who was vacuuming so early in the morning.

I walked down the hallway and glanced into the living room. Norman had a Walkman in the pocket of Mr. H.'s white apron and headphones on his ears. He swung the vacuum around and sang out loud, and way out of tune. He gave a little shoulder shimmy.

I walked quickly past and went upstairs to his room. The photos had been placed in plastic bags and turned over on the desk. I picked up one of the Canadian bags and opened it. They looked just like the American photos — no Mounties at all. I sat down on the bed. I went to put the photos back when I glanced again at the woman in the photo on the top of the pile. She seemed familiar. She looked like — who? Like Girl, sort of, but older. No, she looked like, no, it *was* Gladys, the young Gladys I'd seen in the theatre. Young Gladys, but no gorgeous gown, and her expression was empty of emotion. She leaned on a pedestal smelling a rose, naked but for a pair of black button-up boots. It was by far one of the tamer photos in the collection. Art photography, really. I flipped to the next picture. There was Gladys naked on a plush couch with a man — I quickly put the photos down. Beautiful Gladys. What had happened?

I went downstairs and back through the hallway. Norman saw me, turned off the vacuum, and removed the headphones. "Good morning."

I nodded, leaning in the doorway to the living room. "Where's Mr. H.?"

"Making a path through the junk in the attic. The Historical Society is coming for their final round today. Mom's gone to buy supplies for her big plan for the Art Centre. I wish I could talk her out of whatever it is, but you know Mother. You look nice."

As he spoke, Norman walked over to me, dragging the vacuum. He stopped about six inches away. "Thanks," I said. "I feel like I'm wearing plastic wrap. Hard as I find it to resist a man in an apron. . ." I arched my shoulders to the wall. "You wanna move back a bit?"

I could hear Leonard leaking out of the earphones. "I'm donating it all," said Norman. "My father's pornography collection. To the Women's Studies program at the University of Winnipeg. At first they only wanted the Canadian stuff, but then they agreed to take it all and donate the rest of it as they saw fit." He stepped closer and angled his head.

"Whoa. What are you doing?"

"I thought you'd be happy." He leaned the vacuum cleaner wand against the wall.

"I am, but what does that have to do with kissing me?"

"I'm doing it for you." He put his hands on my arms.

"No, you're doing it for you, because you think I might come back to you."

"No," he said, letting go and stepping back.

"Yes. It's like the art supplies. You bought them for me because it would be nice for *you* to have an artsy wife. You weren't thinking of me at all."

His face was rather green, pale cadmium green, with maybe a little hansa yellow mixed in. "Don't be silly," he said. "I bought them for you because you couldn't afford your own."

"Silly, huh? You know what? I lied to you. I didn't drop out of school because of the cost of the supplies. I dropped out because the instructor I was screwing told me I had no talent. You didn't see me at all. You wanted the 'pretty wifey' that paints the pretty pictures. You didn't want the struggle, you didn't want the pain, you wanted to make it all go away, but if all went away, all I'd be able to paint is pretty pictures and there's no sense in that. I was the damsel in distress and you were the white knight. It made *me* want to puke. I didn't want your saving then and I don't need it now."

"That's not true."

"What, I *do* need you save me?"

Norman shook his head. I continued, "It is true, and you know what, Mr. White Knight? If you're so concerned about disturbed damsels, why don't you think about all the women who suffer from the way you make your money? You're a hypocrite, Norman. You're Mr. Gentleman. Mr. Upper-Class-Snot and you're as much at fault as the men who exploit those women."

"I promised my father," he choked out.

"I was only following orders."

He stared at me. I could see him swallowing, his Adam's apple moving up and down. I stared back at him. Greener now, cheeks — naphthol red with a lot of white — mad pink.

"Fuck you," he finally said, walked across the living room, and slammed out the door. I'd never heard Norman use the f-word before.

I was stunned for a moment. Then I went after him, out the front door, and onto the porch. "Well, Fuck You Too. Oh. Hi."

The historical ladies stood at the foot of the porch. Norman was already halfway down the block, apron strings flapping behind him.

What Do You Need A Career For?

"Come in," I said. The ladies followed behind me at a safe distance into the house.

I called up the front stairs: "Mr. H., the hysterical — *historical* committee is here." Ha. He'd love that.

I smiled widely at them. "Sorry. Please sit. Mr. Hausselman will be right down. Excuse me." I escaped upstairs to my room.

I felt sick when I thought of Gladys' picture. A fire. The inmates housed in the Winter Pavilion. Had she escaped or been released? But what about her baby? The son she never got to see? What a mess. And I'd taken it out on Norman. That made me feel sick too. But why shouldn't I tell him what I thought of his businesses? I could, I should, but why did I have to get so damn mad to do it? Why couldn't I be calm and collected? Because nothing in my life had been calm and collected. Since the day I climbed into the truck with Geordie the bass player at eighteen, everything had been topsy-turvy. I'd gone so far off the path from suburbia and a white wedding gown I wasn't sure I was even still in the same forest. Where had that path gone? Probably grown over, choked with weeds and impassible by now. So what? I still had. . . what did I have? Not my art. That trail was pretty bunged-up too. My health? Ah, shit. After what I figured was a safe amount of time, I went downstairs. The house was empty. "Gladys?" I called. "Gladys?"

CHAPTER TWENTY-SIX

I went back upstairs to my room. Nothing. The armchair was empty. Back down to the kitchen. "Gladys? Come talk to me. Please." I went into the study, then upstairs in the main part of the house. "Gladys? I *need* to talk to you."

Back downstairs, into the kitchen, then outside to look by the shed, the old chicken coop. I was halfway across the lawn when Miss Kesstle yelled over the fence, "Did you find her?"

I stared wildly at her. "How did you know?"

"Know what?"

"That I was looking for her?"

"I asked you to, remember?" she said.

"Oh, Girl. I thought you meant. . . I picked her up from the police station."

"Oh, no!"

"She's fine. No, she's not. She's not fine. None of it is fine." I sat down in the middle of the lawn and burst into tears.

"Oh dear," I heard Miss Kesstle say. Moments later there was the click of the latch at the back gate and then she was sitting on the grass beside me. "There, there," she said, patting my shoulder. "It's okay."

"It's not fair," I sobbed. "None of it's fair. Not Ginny, or Marilyn, or Girl, or Gladys, or you, or me."

"It's all right. Is it the. . . curse?"

"A curse?" I wailed. "I'm cursed? By who?"

"No, is it your time of the *month*?" Miss Kesstle said, still patting my shoulder. "I used to get very weepy."

"I have to do something and I don't know what it is." I pulled a handful of grass out by its roots. "I can't know everything. I don't know how to do anything. How am I supposed to help? The whole world is messed up; it's too big for me." I wiped my nose on my sleeve.

Miss Kesstle dug a tissue out of her pocket. "Here, it's clean," she said. "We all just have to do what we can. God never gives us burdens bigger than our shoulders can bear."

I blew my nose.

Miss Kesstle peered at me. "You have a little. . ." She rubbed a spot under her nose. I wiped it again. She looked, then nodded. "When my mother got sick I thought I couldn't handle it, but I had to roll up my sleeves and get on with it. Just do the next right thing, I told myself. I couldn't cope with thinking of months or years of bedpans, sickness, and suffering. I did it one bedpan at a time."

"You're right. I've just got to do the next right thing. But. . ." I began to wail again. ". . . I d-d-on't know what it is."

"What's going on?"

Whitman stood above us, the sun shining through the curls on top of his head.

"I thought you were in Toronto," I sniffed.

"Turned out I didn't need to go. I arranged everything from here. Are you okay? Is something wrong with Dad?"

"He's fine."

Miss Kesstle slowly stood, leaning her hand on my shoulder. "Thanks," I said to her. "I'm feeling better."

"Sometimes a little cry does a world of good," she said and started to head back to her place. "Don't forget dinner on Sunday." She hesitated and turned back towards us. "You too, Whitman. You haven't been for dinner since you were a little boy." She kept going into her yard, talking aloud. "Hope he's learned to chew with his mouth closed."

Whitman sighed and smiled at Miss Kesstle's retreating back. "Hand up?"

I took his hand. "Thanks."

Mr. H. was mowing the front lawn with his vintage push mower when I went outside later in the evening. The blades clicked and threw out grass bits and the sharp scent of lawn juice. I sat on the porch and watched him for a while. After he finished, he

Dance, Gladys, Dance

came and sat beside me on the steps. He reached into his pocket and brought out a red hanky. It's one of things I love about him — I mean, who still uses hankies? He wiped his face, folded the hanky back into a square, and tucked it away.

"You ever think about getting a gas mower?" I asked.

"Too much to go wrong," he said. "If anything happens to this, I can fix it myself. Takes a little more effort to get the job done, but elbow grease is free."

He patted my knee. "Heard you were having a bit of a tough time earlier."

"Whitman tell you?"

Mr. H. nodded. "You want to talk about it?"

"I don't know what to say." I picked at the peeling paint on the stair railing beside me. "Did you ever read one of those sensationalistic newspapers that tell every terrible thing that's happened in every part of the world? And when you've finished, everything seems overwhelming and hopeless?"

"I don't read those papers much, but I think I know what you mean," he said.

"You feel like you should do something, but it's so big and what the hell can you do anyway?" I brushed the paint bits off the step; a sliver of wood poked into my pinky finger. "Shit!"

"What's the matter?" Mr. H. leaned over.

"Sliver," I stuck my finger in my mouth.

"Let me see."

I shook my head.

"You do whatever little bit you can, I suppose," he said. "Doesn't make it all better at once, but it makes it easier to bear. Norman tell you what he's doing?"

I took my finger out of my mouth. "Means nothing to me."

"He's doing the little bit he can, Frieda. Maybe more than a little, closing all the businesses he promised to keep."

"Doing what?"

Mr. H. squinted his eyes. "He didn't tell you that part? I've let the chat out of the gag."

"All he told me about was donating the — his father's collection."

"He's been trying to set it up for months, selling the buildings he owns for regular movie or retail stores. Don't know what he's doing with all the merchandise, but it's all going, lock, stock, and apparel."

"What's he going to do?" I thought I could feel the end of the sliver. If I were wearing press-on nails, I'd be able to grab it.

"Doesn't know yet. Become a philanthropist, maybe. People were funny about taking his money before. Hard up as they are, not many charities want to risk funding from the profits of Wanton Warehouses."

"Why didn't he tell me? Here I am bitching at him and he just lets me."

"Maybe he wanted to wait until he had it all settled." Mr. H. stood. "Coming inside for lemonade or tweezers, perhaps?"

"No. I'll get it."

I was still sitting on the stairs when Ginny pulled up to the curb. When she got out, I was happy to see she was dressed normally in a tan linen skirt, a tank top, and an embroidered jean jacket. She click-clacked up the front walk, up the first two stairs, then looked around and grimaced. I leaned over, pulled down the sleeve of my shirt, and scrubbed off the spot beside me on the step.

"Thanks." She sat down beside me. "Well," she said, "I'm soon to be the proud recipient of Hurry Up Get Off Your Ass and Find Work Insurance."

"How'd you manage that?"

"I made LG lay me off instead of firing me. Told them I had a file of names, dates, and suggestive things that had been said to me over the last two years, including some very senior employees, and if they didn't want a messy sexual harassment suit, it would be best to check the 'laid off due to lack of work' box on my pink slip."

I smiled. "What if they'd asked to see it?"

Ginny shrugged. "I'd have printed it off and given it to them. Why are you sucking on your finger?"

"Sliver. You actually kept a harassment file?"

"Of course. When one of the first things you hear from a man in your company is 'You have a nice ass, what do you need a career for?' it seems like a good idea. Let's see your finger, I'll get it out."

I shook my head. "So what now?"

"I'm going to take a break, get a haircut, see what everyone else has been doing while I've been working like a crazy woman. Maybe buy some forks and make more sculptures."

"Glad to hear the restaurant utensils of the world are safe," I said.

"Seems nutty now. But at the time it seemed pretty reasonable." She hesitated. "I'm going to see a psychologist too."

"Good for you."

"How about you, Frieda? Do you want to come and see Angelico with me? My treat? I booked a cut and colour, but if I dropped the colour, you could take the spot. I could give you the name of my psychologist too."

"When can you get an appointment?"

"Haircut or therapy?"

"Let's start with a haircut."

"Hang on — I'll call." Ginny took her cellphone from her purse, flipped it open, and dialed.

"Captain Kirk, there seems to be no life on this planet," I muttered around my finger.

Ginny hung up. "Tomorrow at nine."

"In the morning?"

She nodded. "It's best to go early and get him while he's fresh."

"Hmm," I said, "like lettuce." I squeezed my finger again; there was the end. I looked at Ginny's long nails, held out my hand, and closed my eyes.

"Hold still," she said.

"I am," I said, trying to control my involuntary twitching. "Why do you help me, Ginny? Even way back in art school, was I just so pitiful that you took me on as your project?"

"Well, it was obvious you had talent, but you seemed so wobbly with it, I thought you could use some help in the self-confidence department. That's why I helped you with the beauty stuff, not for Professor Gimlet. There we go." I opened my eyes. She held a microscopic sliver between her nails. She flicked the sliver away and wiped her finger on my shoulder. "But you were pretty pig-headed. You acted like every suggestion to improve your work was a personal attack."

"Maybe I didn't want them to ruin my style."

"Maybe they wanted to help you get better at it. So," said Ginny, she picked up her phone, and flipped the cover open and closed, open and closed, "I hate to change the subject, but is Whitman home?"

"He was earlier when I was fertilizing the lawn with my tears. Speaking of good advice, why don't you leave him alone, Ginny? I don't think he's a very good man."

"I like him." Ginny clicked the phone closed, stood, smoothed her skirt, and turned around. "Is my butt dusty?"

"No, it's fine. People also might like standing in front of speeding cement trucks," I said. "Doesn't mean it's a good idea."

"Don't you ever get lonely?" Ginny turned back around.

"I don't know. I suppose I've stopped thinking about it."

Like I've stopped thinking about art. Suddenly it seemed I'd stopped thinking about more things than I was thinking about.

Ginny went inside to look for Whitman. I sat on the steps trying to think about things. Miss Kesstle's front door opened and she called over from the porch, "Do you know where to catch bus number twenty-nine?"

"Downtown, I think. Where are you going?"

Ginny came back out. "He's not home," she said.

"I thought I might go look at the cats at the SPCA," said Miss Kesstle.

"I could drive you," said Ginny. I looked at her in surprise.

"Oh," said Miss Kesstle, "well, that would be nice. I'll go get my purse."

She was almost in the door when she turned. "You did such a nice job of doing my hair, Frieda, do you think you could come over later tonight and give me a trim?"

Visions of my childhood: Mrs Hernd, my mother, and the bad Toni perms at the kitchen table. "I don't think my talents cover haircutting." I paused. "But Ginny and I are going to the salon tomorrow." I turned to Ginny. "Do you think Angelico could take another appointment?"

"Probably," she said. "Dropping the colour should have opened up enough space." She pulled out her phone.

Ginny and Miss Kesstle took off. I went into the backyard, looked around, and slipped into the shed. I left the door open and sat on top of one of the boxes. It seemed that underneath the smells of mildew and oil I could still faintly smell the sharp ammonia scent of chicken coop.

"Gladys," I whispered, "are you here?"

And there she was, sitting on an old suitcase at the back of the shed.

"I never meant for it to happen," she said.

"I know," I said softly.

"After the fire, those of us that weren't considered dangerous were released. I don't know if they had to get Jack's permission or not, but there I was, standing on the walkway with a little cloth bag of clothes. It was so big outside, I felt like one of those wild cats that race from shelter to shelter, never staying long under the open sky." She wiggled back and forth on the suitcase; I watched the pile of boxes behind her teeter, then settle. "They gave me a ticket for a train to Winnipeg. I found my way to the station, sat on a bench for three hours, and waited for the train. So much noise, it seemed everyone was laughing and talking. I remember wondering how they could possibly have so much to talk about. I wasn't thinking yet. I was doing as I was told. Take a train to Winnipeg."

"Must have been a scary train ride," I said.

She smiled. "It wasn't too bad, actually. A nice older lady sat beside me and talked about her grandchildren for the whole trip. She had a bag of apples from her own tree and she gave me some. By the time I finished one of those apples, I realized I was free and I started to think maybe I could manage." Gladys rocked back and forth on the suitcase again. "And then I started to think about my baby."

"Did you see him?" I asked.

"I got off the train in Winnipeg. At first I thought I was in the wrong town. I didn't recognize anything. I could have got off the train in China for all I felt like I belonged there. I only had a bit of money and didn't want to waste it. I walked all the way to the house. You know what's funny? The only thing I worried about was seeing someone I knew. I hadn't looked in a mirror for years. There were none at the asylum because someone might break one and do something nasty with it. I looked in a store window, but all I could see was this shapeless coarse dress and my hair all every which way. I didn't even have a comb. I just kept walking."

"They could have at least given you a comb and something decent to wear," I said.

"When I got to the house, I stood in front for a long time. I was so scared. But I knew if I didn't go then, I never would. I walked up the steps and rang the bell. A woman I'd never seen before answered the door. She was young and pretty, her

Dance, Gladys, Dance

blonde hair all done, and she wore a beautiful lilac dress with pearl buttons. I'd never cared for clothes before, but I wanted that dress, I wanted to look as lovely as her. 'Go around back,' she said and closed the door. I stood there with my mouth hanging open and then I did as I was told. I went around back. In a moment the back door opened and she handed me a small bag. 'Here's a bit of bread and some cheese,' she said, looking over her shoulder, 'but don't come back. He doesn't like me to give food to beggars.' She started to close the door. 'You mean Jack?' I said. She opened the door and looked at me. I stood silently and waited. I saw realization dawn in her eyes. 'He told me you were crazy.' 'Maybe I am,' I said. She asked me how I got out, probably thinking I'd climbed over the fence and escaped. She looked relieved when I told her I'd been released after the fire. 'He read that, in the paper,' she said. 'He said he hoped you'd. . . gone, in the fire. That it would be more merciful.' Fear flitted across her face and she said, 'But he, we, got, Jack and I are *married*.' You can have him,' I said, 'I've come to see my baby.' She said, 'Your baby? Jack Junior? But he's seven. But you — you've never seen him.' I asked if he was there and she told me that Jack had sent him to a military school down east. 'I didn't want him to go,' she said. 'He's so young, but Jack insisted. I think it's hard for Jack to have him around.'"

"Oh, poor fucking Jack," I said. "As though she should feel sorry for him. What a twit."

"I wanted to hate her," said Gladys. "I should have hated her; she had my life, my husband, my house, and my son. But I couldn't. She wasn't the wicked stepmother; she was just a scared young woman. She reminded me of myself. I asked, 'Is he all right? Is Jack kind to him? Is he. . . is he a good boy?' And I started to cry, dry heaving that felt like it would tear my chest apart." She put her hands over her chest and pushed in. "I didn't know that sorrow was still there. I couldn't catch my breath. Over and over I heaved, sorrow coming out my mouth in great gasps. I could hear her saying, 'Oh, oh.' Then I heard a man's voice ask, 'What's going on out here?'"

"Oh no," I said.

Gladys nodded. "It was Jack. His hair was streaked with grey, but he was still dressed in a fine suit. His eyes were on fire. 'Get out,' he said, 'Get off my property or I'll call the police and have you arrested. The asylum will seem like a party compared to prison.' His wife said, 'She doesn't mean any harm.' He told her to shut up without even looking at her. He told her it was none of her business. I stared at him, so filled with hatred that my throat squeezed shut. I could see the two of us young and half-naked in the back of that wagon, feel the straw pricking my bare skin, our hands everywhere, laughing and panting. How, I wondered, had that led to this scene? Would that girl in the wagon have believed it? I turned and walked away. Jack yelled at me, 'If I hear of you trying to see him, I'll send him to Australia forever!' I kept walking, down the back path, past this chicken coop. The chickens were gone, of course; he probably chopped their heads off himself the day after I was put away. I heard a scuffle on the steps. The young woman ran up to me and handed me the bag of food. She was crying. 'I'm sorry,' she said and then turned and ran back to the house."

A horn honked at the front of Mr. H.'s house. Gladys disappeared, happy enough, I surmised, to not finish her story. I sat for a minute trying to compose myself. I wasn't sure if I felt like crying or breaking things. My dear old Gladys. Here I was free, the whole world in front of me, and I didn't want to leave the chicken coop. I got up and went around to the front of the house.

Miss Kesstle was slowly mounting her front steps. Her handbag dangled from her elbow.

"Did you get a pet?" I called.

She shook her head sadly. "There were some beautiful animals there, but none of them were quite right."

Ginny honked again. I went over to the car and leaned in the window. "No, don't get out, Ginny, it's quite all right."

"I don't want Whitman to see me with dog smell all over me. What a miserable place that is. Why didn't you tell me?"

"It never occurred to me. What's up?"

"Is he home yet?

"Not that I know of."

"Okay. Ciao, bella. See you tomorrow morning. Set your alarm."

Ginny pulled up to the curb right at 8:45. Miss Kesstle already stood on her front porch with her purse in her hands. I felt like I was going on some sort of trip, that early morning excitement when you've risen to go on a holiday, the dew still on the grass, the sun just rising, the promise of adventures in front of you. Then I remembered where we were going.

I opened the front car door for Miss Kesstle.

She whispered, "I'd rather sit in the back. She's a nice lady, but she drives like a fruitcake."

I sat up front with Ginny and craned around to speak to Miss Kesstle. "Tell Angelico exactly what you want. Don't let him do his own thing. You'll come out of there looking like Phyllis Diller."

"Pay no attention to her," said Ginny. "Christ, doesn't anyone know how to drive?" She swerved around a red Honda and honked. "Angelico's an expert."

"I was hoping to get something a little modern," said Miss Kesstle.

That Fancy Woman

Miss Kesstle was very brave. After we finished in the salon, she waited until she got back in the car and clicked her seatbelt shut before she began to whimper.

"I look like a crazy person," she said.

"No, no," I said. "Once we get home and wash the gel out, it'll be fine." I thought it probably would. It was just a layered cut, but Angelico had fluffed the front up like a cockatoo and pasted the back down to her neck.

I managed to get a trim from a trainee and Ginny was her usual perfectly coiffed self. Do hairdressers have a secret sixth sense of who's worthy of a good haircut, which people are likely to display their craft to its advantage, not tie it up in a ponytail or mess it up the following day? Seems like it to me.

We drove back down the streets towards Mr. H.'s. Miss Kesstle suddenly yelled, "Stop! Pull over!"

"Okay," said Ginny. She signalled and pulled over to the curb. "Are you going to be sick?"

"I have some Pepto-Bismol," I muttered.

Miss Kesstle opened the car door. "I saw Girl back there. We can pick her up."

"Oh no," said Ginny. "Close your door."

"She's back about a half a block," said Miss Kesstle. "Her hair was a different colour but I recognized my tea cozy."

CHAPTER TWENTY-SEVEN

"I'm not giving her a ride," said Ginny. "She's nothing but trouble."

"Come on, Ginny, relax," I said. "She's not going to hijack us."

Ginny snorted. Miss Kesstle got out and stood on the sidewalk, waving her arms like a hockey referee. Girl sauntered slowly up to the car. Sure enough, she had the tea cozy, but it wasn't on her head this time; it had been turned into a purse with large plastic handles. The ends of her hair were a brilliant pink. I got out. Ginny stayed in the car.

"Hi, Girl," said Miss Kesstle. "Can we give you a ride?"

"Wicked do," said Girl.

Miss Kesstle frowned and looked at me.

"Hairdo," I said.

"Oh, thank you. I thought it was a bit odd." Miss Kesstle put her hand to her head.

"No way, it's happening," said Girl. "You're like the hippest sixty-year-old I know."

"Seventy-nine," said Miss Kesstle.

"Wow," said Girl, "that is frigging old."

"Girl!" I said.

"I mean so old to be so cool."

"Can we give you a ride?" I asked.

Girl leaned over and looked in the car where Ginny sat staring straight ahead. "Oh, *her*. I don't think so. I've got some errands to run anyhow."

"Are you sure?" asked Miss Kesstle. "You could come for tea at my place if you like."

"Uh, maybe later," said Girl.

"Here, I'll give you my address." Miss Kesstle reached into the car and got out her purse.

"Don't do that," said Ginny turning her head and speaking loudly. "You'll wake up one morning and all your jewellery will be missing."

"Fuck off," said Girl.

Miss Kesstle wrote her address down on a piece of paper and handed it to Girl. "I'll be home all —"

"Do you have five bucks you could lend me?" asked Girl. "I'm a little short on food right now."

"Oh dear," said Miss Kesstle. She reached into her purse and got out her wallet.

"Lend? Ha," said Ginny from inside the car.

Miss Kesstle handed Girl two twenties.

"That's too much," I said.

"She can get some proper groceries."

"You are a dear," said Girl. She leaned over and gave Miss Kesstle a kiss on the forehead.

Miss Kesstle put her purse back on the seat. "Make sure you get some fruit or vegetables," she said, "and don't forget to come for tea." She got back into the car.

"At least grab a sandwich," I said, "before you blow the rest of it."

Girl smiled.

"I need to have a serious talk with you one day," I said.

"Sounds like fun," said Girl.

"I mean it. It's about your great-great-grandmother."

"Could we please go?" yelled Ginny.

I climbed back into the car and we pulled away, leaving Girl standing on the sidewalk with a puzzled look on her face.

"She's not going to buy food," said Ginny to Miss Kesstle. "She's going to buy booze or dope."

"Dope? You mean drugs? I don't think so," said Miss Kesstle. "And she's too young to buy alcohol."

Ginny snorted again.

Only Norman and Whitman were home when I got in. They sat at the dining room table. There was an almost empty pitcher of Glornics between them and the chessboard was in the centre of the table. Norman had captured three of Whitman's white pawns and Whitman had enough of Norman's black pieces to open a POW camp.

"Where's Mr. H. and Lady March?"

"God only knows," said Norman without looking up. He handed me a piece of paper from the table. It read, in Lady March's large loopy script, "Mr. H. and I won't be home tonight, duckies. Don't worry. We're up to no good. Love, L.M."

"Yikes," I said. "What kind of no good, do you think?"

"I have no idea," said Norman morosely.

"Check," said Whitman, moving his pawn.

Norman sighed. I hesitated for a moment, waiting for them to ask me to join them, or at least comment on my haircut. "Well, I'm going — see you later."

They both nodded, still staring at the board.

"Frieda! Wake up, Frieda. You have to see this." Miss Kesstle's voice drifted up the back stairs. Whaaaa? I rubbed my eyes. See what? Probably some sort of exotic warbler at the bird feeder. I put my housecoat on and went downstairs. Miss Kesstle was making tea.

"Not for me, thanks," I said. "I'll make some coffee."

"You'll need tea," she said, "after you see that." She gestured towards the table where the newspaper lay folded over.

What is it about tea-drinkers that makes them so self-righteous? Some sort of British thing, no doubt. Just close your eyes, drink some tea, and think of England.

"No," I said. "I can't look at anything without some *coffee.*"

Miss Kesstle and I sat silently at the table waiting for our prospective beverages to boil and perk. I eyed the paper but stubbornly waited until I could ease a cupful of coffee out of the pot. Once I poured a cup and took a sip, I unfolded the paper and turned it over. On the front page was a photo of a bunch of people standing on the roof of the Art Centre. What the hell? One of them was naked. The headline read: "Stormy Petrel Sit-In At Downtown Art Centre." I looked at Miss Kesstle. "Well, they're getting their publicity."

"Do you think that fancy woman had anything to do with that? Mr. H. is probably up there. He's an old man, he could get hurt. It's ridiculous." Miss Kesstle looked mighty pissed.

I read the article:

The closing of the Downtown Art Centre may be slowed by a group of protesters who have named themselves after a nearly extinct species of birds — the stormy petrel. The protesters vow they will not come down from the roof of the building until the government gives them a fair chance to save the Centre. Spokespersons for the group said that they chose the petrel because the birds appear in storms then disappear when the gale is over. There is certainly a storm brewing over the closure of the Downtown Art Centre.

The New Zealand Petrel was once considered extinct but was rediscovered in 2003. The spokesperson noted that Canadian Arts are also likely to become extinct unless the government renews its commitment to them. The Winnipeg Society of the Arts was given a token opportunity to purchase the building, only to learn that the local government already had a deal in place with the Grainer Hotel chain to build a downtown hotel. Alderman Gene Dids is quoted as saying the hotel will bring jobs and prosperity to the downtown core. The Downtown Art Centre opened eleven years ago serving a handful of students and now has classes which over one hundred attend. "The Art Centre is a vital part of the downtown community," said one of the protesters. "To close it down would be a crime and a slap in the face of art communities all across Canada."

"Wow," I said, "that's some piece, better than the four lines after the open house. It might work."

"The police will probably come and hose them all off," said Miss Kesstle. "Is that naked person Norman's mother? And why is she naked?"

"I'm not sure," I said, squinting at the photo. "I'll go and find out. Do you want to come?"

"Absolutely not." Miss Kesstle stood and poured her tea down the drain. "I don't want to get mixed up in that mess. I'm going home."

"Okay," I said. "Thanks for bringing the paper over."

She sniffed and went out the back door.

I took the bus to the Art Centre. There were large crowds both on the roof and standing around on the grass below. I picked out Mr. H. and waved wildly at him. He gestured for me to climb the ladder. I hesitated. What if we did get hosed off?

Mr. H. helped me onto the roof. "This is a whole different squall game, hey Frieda?" he said. "Come this way." In the centre of the roof was a doorway. He opened the door and we went in and sat down on the stairs. "So what do you think?"

"It's brilliant. Who came up with it?"

"Lady March. If we manage to keep the Centre open, we'll name her our patron saint."

"Is she the naked person in the photo?"

Lady March's voice drifted up from the bottom of the stairs. "Nothing like a little nudity to get the press out."

She came upstairs and I was relieved to see that she was covered up by one of her boisterous caftans. She sat on the stair beneath us. "We made the paper? What page?"

"Front page," I said.

"See?" She patted Mr. H.'s knee. "I told you it would work. Fehu!"

"Gesundheit," said Mr. H.

Lady March laughed. "You gave me the idea, Frieda. Remember when you told me about the petrels, the seabirds? I thought it was a wonderful metaphor for protesting. So, here we are, the Stormy Petrels."

I was pleased. I'd given someone a good idea. An idea that might actually work.

"I hope Norman doesn't pitch a fit when he sees the paper," Lady March said. "He nearly had a coronary when I was arrested in Washington at the anti-apartheid rallies." She stood. "Well, back to the battle lines." As she went past Mr. H., she paused and kissed the top of his bald head.

"Hmmm," I said, smiling at Mr. H.

He blushed and scuffled his feet. "I'm feeling as bright as the weather," he said.

"I'm sure you are." I stood. "Well, I'm going now, is there anything I can do for you?"

"Will you let Whitman know I'm all right? Lady March says we could be up here for a few weeks."

"Weeks? How do you think he's going to take all this?"

"Probably not well," said Mr. H., "but what can you do?"

Something For The Pain

I woke up in the middle of the night, unsure of what had disturbed my slumber. The clock read 3:52. I sat up and listened in the darkness. From downstairs I could hear Norman — he was either talking on the telephone or had discovered his own ghost to converse with. I got up, put on a housecoat, and went downstairs. The only light came from the streetlights shining through the windows just illuminating Norman in his blue flannel paisley pyjamas. He hung up the phone.

"What going on?" I whispered.

"I couldn't sleep," he said, turning to me. "I was sitting down here worrying about Mother when the phone rang. Miss Kesstle's alarm went off. She's terrified but doesn't want to phone the alarm company because they might send some stranger worse than whoever has supposedly broken in. I told her I'd come over."

The kitchen light flipped on. "Is something wrong?"

Norman and I blinked and started like burglars caught making a midnight snack. It was Whitman in his red silk robe; his legs were bare and muscular.

"Miss Kesstle's alarm," I said.

"I'm going over," said Norman.

"I'll come too," said Whitman. He walked to the back door and put on Mr. H.'s lace-up rubber boots. Norman followed him in his bedroom slippers. I slipped on my army boots.

CHAPTER TWENTY-EIGHT

"Should we bring something?" I asked and stopped at the door.

"Like what?"

"A baseball bat or something."

Norman looked around. "Umm."

"Here, I'll take this." I grabbed a metal spatula from the drying rack.

"Very fierce," said Whitman and opened the back door.

Miss Kesstle had her porch light on and was waiting inside. I could see her shadow through the window curtains. As soon as we started up the walk, she opened the door. Her head was covered in a burgundy kerchief and she wore a green velour housecoat, worn down to the nub in places.

"He's downstairs in the basement," she said.

"Who?"

She glared at me like I was an idiot. "The burglar."

"All right," said Norman, "let's go look." He hitched up his pyjama pants and started towards the basement door.

"If it is a burglar, shouldn't we call the police?" I asked as I followed behind him, gripping my spatula.

"It's probably nothing," Whitman whispered.

We went down the narrow basement stairs in single file. I turned and looked back. Miss Kesstle stood at the top clutching at the lapels of her housecoat, looking ready to slam the door if she heard or saw anything.

"The light is at the bottom, pull the string," she whispered.

The basement was dark and smelled of damp. Norman felt around and pulled the cord on a light bulb. There were boxes and suitcases, wooden shelves of canned food, a rack holding winter coats, and, curled up in the far corner, on the bare floor, was Girl. I looked around. One of the small wood-framed windows had been pushed in.

We went over to her and kneeled down. She lifted her head; her eyes wandered back and forth, then focussed on my face. I tried to smile at her. Her face was swollen and bruised, mascara and eyeliner smeared down her cheeks. I could smell alcohol, sharp and sour.

"Hey, Frieda," she said. "How's it going?"

"I'm okay," I said. "How are you?"

"Not so good."

"No, doesn't look like it." Norman reached out to her and she flinched.

"Did you get him?" yelled Miss Kesstle from the top of the stairs. "The place is surrounded, mister, so don't make any foolish moves."

"It's Girl," I called up the stairs.

"Girl?"

I turned back to Girl. She wore a miniskirt and a tube top with one of Miss Kesstle's doilies appliquéd on the front. Her arms and legs were covered with ugly violet bruises and red cuts. I felt a wave of nausea.

"Hi, Girl," said Whitman. "I'm Mr. Hausselman's son Whitman. I met you at the art show."

She nodded, pushing her sweaty hair from her face and attempting a smile.

"Do you want to come upstairs?" I asked. "Have a cup of tea, maybe, or some hot chocolate?"

"Can you get up?" Whitman asked.

"I don't know." She tried to raise herself on one elbow and fell back. "Oh fuck. Kinda dizzy. I think I'll rest here for a sec."

"I'll let Miss Kesstle know everything is all right," I said. I went up the stairs. "Let's put the kettle on," I said to Miss Kesstle. "I think she'd like some hot chocolate."

Miss Kesstle peered down the stairs. "Is she all right? Why is she in the basement? She could have come to the front door."

"Let's go to the kitchen," I said.

Once we were out of earshot, I said, "She's pretty banged up, Miss Kesstle. But don't freak out, try to keep calm. She's upset."

Dance, Gladys, Dance

Miss Kesstle stared at me for a moment without saying anything and then began to bustle around the kitchen. "She's probably hungry too, poor thing. We'll have some sandwiches." She opened the fridge door.

"Maybe just soft things," I said, thinking of the bruises on Girl's face.

Miss Kesstle looked at me again. "I have pudding. Do you think she'd like pudding, or maybe cottage cheese?"

"Pudding maybe." I could hear them slowly making their way up the stairs.

"You go," said Miss Kesstle. "I'll make the cocoa."

I walked into the living room. Whitman was helping Girl onto the couch.

"Blanket?" he asked.

I went back into the kitchen. "Do you have spare blankets somewhere?"

"Upstairs. Take one off one of the beds. I just washed them all." She put mugs on a tray.

I went upstairs. The first bedroom I went into must have been Miss Kesstle's. It had a woven coverlet and a dresser covered in little jewellery boxes. It smelled of lavender and talcum powder. In the next room, there was a patchwork quilt on the bed. I pulled it off and grabbed a pillow.

Back downstairs, Whitman was sitting in an armchair while Norman stood and fidgeted beside him. Girl reclined on the couch, staring up at the ceiling. I took the quilt over to her.

"Here," I said, "are you cold?"

She nodded. I covered her up with the blanket, lifted her head, and put the pillow underneath it. She closed her eyes.

"What should we do?" asked Norman. "We need to call someone."

"Shhh," said Whitman, "just leave it for a minute."

Norman turned to me. "Look at her, she looks awful."

I frowned at him.

"Why are we just standing here? This is an emergency." Norman's voice was rising. "We have to take her somewhere. We have to do something."

"Shut up for a minute," said Whitman.

"We should call the police right now." Norman walked towards the kitchen.

"Please don't," said Girl.

"Why don't you go home?" I said. "She's okay for a minute. Someone might call from the Art Centre."

He hesitated. "Call someone. Do something."

"That's enough," I said. "Go home." I walked him to the door. "Don't call anyone. We have to figure out what happened first."

"She looks awful," he said again.

"I know," I said. "Go home."

He left with a last reluctant look towards the living room. I went back in and sat down.

Miss Kesstle carried in a tray with steaming cups of hot chocolate and small bowls of vanilla pudding and cottage cheese. She put the tray on the coffee table.

"Hello, Girl," she said, a little too brightly. "I'm glad you came for tea."

Girl turned to her. "Sorry I broke in. . . I didn't know where to go. I had your address. I didn't want to wake you up —"

Miss Kesstle gasped at the sight of Girl's face. She went over to the couch. "Oh, you poor thing. Do you need to go to the doctor's? What happened? Who did that to you?" She sat beside Girl on the couch and gently stroked the top of her head. Girl burst into tears. Miss Kesstle kept stroking her head and murmuring, "It's all right. You're fine. You're safe now. You're safe." Tears ran down her face. I looked over at Whitman. His face was hard with anger, but his eyes were filled with tears.

I went into the bathroom, grabbed a box of tissue off the top of the toilet tank, and wet a hand towel under the tap. I had to steady myself on the sink for a moment; my knees had gone weak. Who would do that? Who *could* do that? I splashed cold water on my face, dried it and then went back into the living room and put the tissue on the coffee table. Miss Kesstle held Girl in her arms and the two of them cried together.

I sat in the armchair across from Whitman. Eventually Girl stopped crying and Miss Kesstle let her go.

I handed Miss Kesstle the damp towel and she wiped Girl's face, daubing gently at the charcoal lines on her cheeks. "You should go to the hospital," she said.

Girl's lips tightened and her eyes narrowed as though by closing her face she could keep her emotions at bay. "I'm okay, just bruises. Please, let me stay here."

"We'll see," said Miss Kesstle. "Would you like some cocoa?"

"I don't think I can right now. I don't feel so well."

"Do you want to talk about it?" asked Whitman quietly. "We should call the police and give them whatever information you have so they can find who did that to you."

"Don't call the police, please," said Girl. "Please don't. I can't deal with them right now. I can't — if my foster family finds out, I'm in trouble again. They told me no more chances, they'll report me, I'll end up in juvie."

"Where's juvie?" asked Miss Kesstle.

"Juvenile detention."

"You're not in trouble," said Miss Kesstle. "You didn't do anything wrong."

Girl burst into tears again. "I did. I just wanted to earn a few more bucks so I could score and I thought I could do it. But once I was in the car, I couldn't. I puked in his lap; he got so mad, and. . ." She pulled the quilt around her.

"Shhh. Shhh. It's okay. You're okay," said Miss Kesstle. "Why don't we get you into bed? You can stay here for tonight. Do you want me to call the family you're staying with?"

Girl shook her head.

"I'll get you a nightie and put it on the bed," said Miss Kesstle. She went upstairs.

Whitman and I helped Girl up, took her upstairs, and put her in the bedroom where I'd found the quilt. We left her alone to undress. Whitman followed Miss Kesstle back downstairs. I stood and listened at the door for a moment. I was afraid Girl might change her mind and escape out the window. There was rustling and some whimpering. I clenched my fists, then the bedsprings squeaked.

I tiptoed back down the stairs. Whitman sprawled in the armchair as if someone had knocked him down. He stared straight ahead.

Miss Kesstle picked up the tray from the table. "I don't understand," she whispered. "Who did she throw up on? Why would someone beat her up for that?"

I followed her into the kitchen. "Do you want me to stay overnight too? I could crash on the couch. Just in case she wakes up and is. . . upset."

Miss Kesstle smiled at me. "Thank you, Frieda, but I'll be all right. When I nursed Mother, she'd get very agitated in the middle of the night wanting more morphine for the pain. Did Girl say she was scoring? Was she playing sports?"

"No. Scoring is buying something like morphine on the street for other kinds of pain."

"Oh," said Miss Kesstle. "Oh dear. And the throwing up?"

I hesitated. Opened my mouth. Closed it.

"Tell me, Frieda."

"Remember when I told you about oral sex? I think Girl was trying to get some more money by doing it with a man in a car."

"What man?" Miss Kesstle stared at me.

"I doubt she knew who he was."

"With a stranger? In a car? She's just a child."

"She's young, but I don't think Girl's been a child for a very long time."

"What a horrible man." Miss Kesstle's eyes filled with tears again. "It's not right. It's just not right. She's so smart."

"I know," I said. I went back into the living room.

"Frieda, Whitman," Girl called from upstairs, "could you come up for a minute?"

Whitman followed me upstairs. Girl was lying in the old brass bed covered up with the patchwork quilt. She wore one of Miss Kesstle's flannel nighties.

"Can you imagine sewing something like this? By hand?" She held up a corner of the quilt. "It must have a thousand fucking-bitty pieces."

Whitman stood by the door. I went in and sat on the edge of the bed. Girl hesitated, then her face twisted. "I went to Marilyn's first. I could see her light on from the street. I pounded on her door and she wouldn't let me in. I thought he might still be after me. I was screaming at her to please let me in. She wouldn't fucking open the door."

"Oh, shit," said Whitman. "I can't believe it."

"I just wanted you to know your friend is a major league bitch," she said to me.

"She's not my friend, but point taken. She's messed up. I'm sorry I introduced you to her. Go to sleep now, okay? We'll talk more in the morning."

Girl laid her head down on the pillow. "I feel like Goldilocks. I've always wanted to sleep in a brass bed."

"Good night," I said.

Whitman and I went back downstairs. I went into the kitchen and said goodbye to Miss Kesstle. Whitman waited for me by the front door.

"I'd like to kill the bastard with my bare hands," he said.

"I'd like to tie him up and let Girl at him."

"We'll have to see if she'll tell us what he looks like. If she won't go to the police, at least we can give the description to the outreach workers down there so they can warn other women away from him."

"How do you know about all this stuff?" I asked.

"I've been keeping track of Marilyn for years." He put his hand on my shoulder. "You okay?"

I nodded. "Well, not really, but I'm in better shape than Girl."

"Thank God for that," he said.

When I woke up the next morning, Gladys was sitting in her arm-chair and looking out the window. Sun had already painted the walls of the room a golden yellow. I yawned, stretched, and then remembered Girl — bruises, cuts, curled up in the corner in the basement. Adrenaline surged through me. I sat up.

"I don't know what to do," I said. "You picked the wrong person." I looked up, wildly feeling as though the roof was about to fall in on me. "Girl's lost. I can't help her."

"Slow down," said Gladys. She stared steadily at me and continued to rock.

Gladys' placidity only served to increase my panic. I got up and began to do a whole lot of nothing with great urgency.

"I'm failing. I always fail. I'm sorry." I picked up a pile of dirty laundry, then threw it down again.

"You're not failing," said Gladys.

I pulled the covers up on the bed and straightened them. "Did you see her last night?" I cried.

"I did."

"Should I have told her about you? Would have that helped? Please tell me what to do. I'll do it." I pulled the covers off the bed and threw them on the floor with the laundry.

"Sit down. You did the right thing."

I looked around the room for something else useless but active to do.

"Sit!" said Gladys. I sat on the edge of the bed.

Dance, Gladys, Dance

"Telling Girl about me wouldn't have helped and it won't help her now. Go see her. She's all right."

"There's more, isn't there?"

Gladys nodded. "There's always more."

"Now, why doesn't that make me feel better?" I stood again and opened the wardrobe. No jeans. "It's like a dream. You slice the head off the monster, then, while you're busy doing the happy dance, it grows another one." Where the hell were all my clothes?

"We can't fix everything," said Gladys, "but we can make whatever little difference is possible."

I stopped. "That's what Mr. H. said: 'Do whatever little bit you can.'"

"He's right," said Gladys. "The way isn't clear, but the only way to make it clearer is for more and more of us to travel it."

I found jeans in the pile of dirty laundry underneath the blankets. "You sound like Lady March. Did you know I have a broken fate line?" I held my palm out to Gladys. "I don't even know which direction to travel in."

"I think you do," said Gladys. "Get on with your day. The world awaits."

"That," I said, "is a completely terrifying thought." Gladys vanished and I pulled on my pants.

It's My Policy

I headed straight over to Miss Kesstle's. The front door was open, so I knocked on the screen door and hollered through it.

Miss Kesstle called out to come in. The kitchen was in an uproar — pots, scatterings of flour, and lumps of dough lay everywhere. Miss Kesstle smiled. "You'll have to wait for tea, Frieda. We're in the middle of a cooking lesson."

Girl's bruises were even more horrifying in the bright light of day. Her right cheek was almost completely purple and a bandage above her eyebrow covered half her forehead. She wore a blue checked apron over top of one of Miss Kesstle's housedresses and had her hair tied back in a ponytail.

"Look at me, Frieda," she exclaimed. "We're making cinnamon buns." She held a lump of dough in one hand and a dripping spoon in the other. "I'm Martha-fucking-Stewart!"

"Girl. . ." said Miss Kesstle, trying to wipe a smear of dough off the cupboard.

"What? Oh, I'm Martha-freaking-Stewart."

"I'm sure Martha would be pleased," I said. "How are you feeling?"

"Better. Stiff, though."

"We should probably call someone this morning. . ."

"Is that the royal we?" asked Girl. "We did. Whitman stopped by already and gave us a phone number."

CHAPTER TWENTY-NINE

"Oh," I said.

"Did you know Girl can play the piano?" asked Miss Kesstle. "I woke up hearing the most beautiful song. Give me that spoon, Girl, we have to oil the dough now. I thought Beethoven had come back as a ghost with talent. But it was Girl. No one's played that piano since Mother died."

Girl smiled and dipped her head. "I was just messing around."

I watched the two of them work for a while, then excused myself. I had a mission and those bowls of flour had given me an idea. I took the Valiant and drove downtown. I parked near Marilyn's apartment, locked the doors, rolled up the windows, and took a deep breath.

This time there actually was a pile of shit on the stair landing of the hotel. It looked disturbing and oddly fascinating lying there. It's so seldom a person sees human excrement just lying around. Which is probably a good thing anyhow.

I banged on Marilyn's door. "Open up, it's Frieda." Nothing. "Open the door or I'll —" What? Blow your house down?

"I'll phone Whitman's studio and rat the both of you out." I waited. "No more three hundred bucks cash coming your way. He'll probably get fired." Silence.

I reached into my purse and pulled out my hairbrush. "I'm dialing on my cellphone right now."

The door opened. I shoved the brush back in my purse. Marilyn leaned her head against the doorframe. She wore a giant white T-shirt advertising a muffler shop. Her eyes were puffy with sleep.

"Can't you people leave me in peace? What do *you* want?"

I pushed past her. The room was dark, smelly, and stuffy, the curtains tightly drawn.

"Hey missy," she sputtered.

"Don't you missy me. I want to know why you didn't open your door for Girl last night."

"I don't get involved. It's my policy."

"Corporations have policies. *You* don't." I walked over to the window and opened the curtains.

"You think because I'm a drunk I can't have a policy? I can have a policy if I want. And that's it — I don't get involved."

"Whoa," I said, "this is about a sixteen-year-old girl who got the crap beat out of her." My voice shook. I turned to Marilyn. She closed her eyes and put her hand to the back of her neck. "Girl thought he was still after her —"

"How was I to know and what if he was?" Marilyn demanded, her arms flew out in the air. "Then I let her *and* him in, and we both end up dead? What about that? I'm worn out. I don't give a damn, okay? Just leave me alone." She kicked around the piles of clothes on the floor. "Besides, Whitman already came to give me shit."

"He did?"

"Well, he tried. But I asked him who the hell he thought he was, harassing me when he'd been ripping me off all these years. He left looking like a whipped dog."

"He did?"

"How many times are you going to say that?"

"Anyhow, *I* won't," I said.

"What?"

"I won't leave any of you alone because I'm sick and tired of this shit. I'm tired of people being worn out and hurt and not helping and not doing sweet dick all myself. Miss Kesstle took Girl in last night. An old woman who spent the last fifteen years crocheting has more balls than either of us."

"See," said Marilyn, "you don't even know what you're saying. Having *balls* means male. Courage equals being a man. Why don't we say, 'has more ovaries'? Anyhow, I'm tired." She sat down on the bed and squinted against the light. "It's not just the big stuff — rapings, beatings — it's the little shit. You're not beautiful enough, not smart enough, you're always trying to stay in your place, and I hate this fucking place."

"You mean *this* place?" I gestured at the mess on the floor. "That's not surprising."

"No, this, *this*." She swirled her hand around in the air like a mini tornado. "All this, whole, this whole male capitalist world."

"So why do you let Whitman use you?" I emptied an overflowing ashtray into a plastic shopping bag and tied the top.

"Quit messing with my stuff. I need those butts. I'm using *him*. I blow through that crap like nothing and he gives me hundreds of dollars for it."

"He probably gets thousands and all the credit." I looked around the room. "Do you have pants somewhere?"

"So? I wouldn't want my name on it anyway. I don't care. I can't do it. I haven't got what it takes to make it out there." She pointed at the window.

I gave up on my cleaning efforts and sat down on the bed beside her. "You know what, Marilyn? I said the same thing to Norman once."

"Who's Norman?"

"You danced with him at the art show." I leaned over, pulled a pair of stirrup pants from the floor, and shook the ashes off them.

"I did? Is he good-looking?"

"I said *I don't have it* and I gave up, but I *do* have it. I do. And I suspect you do too. Here." I put the pants in her lap.

Marilyn narrowed her eyes. "What are we talking about again? We have what?"

"I don't know."

"But we've got it?"

"Right. Get your pants on. We're going out to travel the way." I stood.

"I'm not going anywhere. I had a headache before you came over and it hasn't gotten any better, I can tell you that."

I reached into my purse. "I can still make that call."

Marilyn stood. I turned my back while she pulled on the

pants. She couldn't find two matching shoes. I suspect a good number of the orphan shoes one sees lying about the city in gutters and back alleys belong to Marilyn.

"How do you manage in the winter?" I asked.

"I stay in a lot," she said. She finally went and knocked on the door across the hall and, after a great deal of bargaining and haggling with an old man, traded three sturdy shopping bags for a pair of blue size twelve men's hightop runners. She had to lace them halfway up her knees to get them to stay on.

"What a fashion statement, hey?" she said.

I nodded. We went out to the Valiant. As I pulled out from the curb, Marilyn began to speak. She sat straight in the seat, her hands folded in her lap like a little girl who's been told to "sit up properly."

"I had a husband once," she said, "and a daughter. I was hitched by seventeen and had my daughter by eighteen. Do you have a smoke?

"No." Silence. "And?" I said. My hands started to tremble on the wheel, but I kept driving.

"We lived in a crappy little subsidized apartment. It had ivy wallpaper all over the walls and smelled like sour milk. In Oyama, in the Okanagan Valley. Land of peaches and scorpions."

"I've been through there on vacation," I said.

"I left when my daughter was a year old. I couldn't breathe and I was so bored I thought my brain would implode. It might have got better. I don't know — didn't stick around to find out, did I?"

"What do you mean, you left?" The traffic was thickening the closer we got to the Art Centre.

"Claude, my husband, he loved our daughter, and his family all lived in town, or around the valley. I knew they'd take good care of her. I got up early one morning and took a Greyhound. I left and started my new life; I was gonna be a big star. What a success, hey?" She threw out her arms.

All I could think of was Gladys and her baby being taken away from her. Gladys scrabbling at the cement walls of the institution trying to get back to him. Gladys saying, "Bad decisions are made for lots of reasons." I looked at Marilyn. No wonder she was always tanked or stoned; there was probably no other way to take it. "What about your daughter? Don't you want to find her? Or maybe she wants to find you?"

"Would *you* want to? Would you like to walk up the stairs in that hotel, open the door, and say, 'Oh look, there's my mom'?"

I hesitated. Marilyn snorted. "I rest my case."

"I read a bit of your script, *The Devil's Cry*," I said. "Scary stuff."

"Yeah," she said quietly. "I'm good at terror."

We pulled up near the Art Centre. I had to park in the back alley on the next block; the street was filled with cars.

"Come on," I said. Marilyn got out and we walked up the alley and onto the road in front of the centre. There was still a crowd on the ground and, from what I could see, the number of Stormy Petrels on the roof had increased.

"Holy crap," said Marilyn, looking at the top of the building. "What are those people doing on the roof?"

I laughed. "It's a sit-in to save the centre, and you're going to sit."

"Like hell I am." Marilyn crossed her arms.

I rummaged around in my bag. "Now where did I put my cellphone and the number to that studio?"

"That's blackmail," said Marilyn, "and those people up there are crazy."

I shrugged. "Suit yourself." I continued to look in my bag. If she didn't hurry up, I'd be forced to make a phone call on my hairbrush.

Marilyn began to walk forward. "What purpose is it going to serve having me sit on a roof with a bunch of nutters?"

"Sometimes any action is good as long as it's movement

forward. Besides," I said as we walked through the crowd, "you might meet some nice people."

"I hate people," muttered Marilyn. She put one blue sneak-ered foot on the ladder. "Do they at least have beer up there?"

"I doubt it," I said.

"Pot? Don't people always get stoned at sit-ins? They did in the sixties."

"The sixties are over."

"No shit," said Marilyn and she made her way up the ladder.

The asphalt on the roof felt warm even through my sneak-ers. Billy Bragg played on a portable stereo. The security guard from the choir was there. I smiled at him. "Don't tell anyone you saw me here," he said. He lifted his sunglasses. "I could lose my job."

Some of the ladies from the looms clustered around a fold-up table. On top were paper cups and a plastic cooler. An older lady in an amber and red sari leaned over to an even older woman in a black abaya, her head completely covered, and said, "Do you think they will bring the tanks soon?"

The other lady shrugged and nodded, "Likely soon, yes."

"No," I said. "Riot police, maybe, but no tanks. Not in Can-ada."

They didn't look convinced, or worried; they sat down on the ground and began to fan themselves.

I introduced Marilyn to Lady March. "Ah, Cinderella," said Mr. H., "we meet again. I see you still haven't found your glass slippers."

"See," said Marilyn, turning to me, obviously having no memory of Mr. H. giving her the crocheted slippers at the art show. "I told you — nuts."

"Hello, Marilyn," said Lady March. "You have the most in-teresting aura."

"Like how?" said Marilyn.

"A bright yellow, some grey, with a red overlay, interesting."

"Good, then," said Marilyn. "How long do I have to sit up here?"

"Until I come back to get you," I said.

"No fair, you get to go and I have to stay." Marilyn sat down to the left of a group of kids. A young woman read from a sheaf of papers: "Okay, *The Human Wave*, a screenplay by Lizzie Parker. Man at desk answers telephone —"

"That's not how you start a screenplay!" Marilyn yelled over her shoulder.

"How would you know?" asked the woman.

"Because I've written seventeen, and five of them have had treatments in Hollywood."

"No way!"

"Way," said Marilyn.

"So how do you start a screenplay?"

Marilyn turned around. "You need the time of day, the setting interior or exterior. You need to think in terms of camera angles. You know about those, right?"

The kids shook their heads.

"You want to write screenplays and you don't know about camera angles? Christ, you might as well jump off the roof right now. Where you kids been?"

"Well?" said one kid. "What are they?"

Marilyn sighed loudly as though she'd been explaining it for hours. "There's the establishing shot, long shot, medium shot, over-the-shoulder shot, close-up, and each one serves a specific purpose. You gotta think about that. Anyone got a smoke? The establishing shot is like a wide angle; like, if your story takes place on a boat, you show the boat on the ocean. How about a light? Get it?"

I wandered off to find Mr. H. again. He stood looking over the edge.

"I'm surprised Girl isn't here," he said. "This sort of thing should be right up her alley."

"She's at Miss Kesstle's baking cinnamon buns," I said. "I

think she needs some peace and quiet." I told Mr. H. and Lady March the story of finding Girl in Miss Kesstle's basement. I skipped the part about her going to Marilyn's first. Mr. H. wanted to go right down and see if Girl was okay, but I promised I'd go and check on her and let her know what was going on. Mr. H. gave me a list of supplies they needed and asked me to pick them up. I had some supplies of my own to get.

First, I went back to the house. Norman sat at the kitchen table with the newspaper open in front of him. He wore a tweed suit with a dark burgundy tie. "That's Mother, isn't it?" he said, indicating the naked woman on the front page.

"Nothing like a little nudity to get the press out," I said. I opened the bottom cupboard where the baking tins were kept. I thought I'd seen. . . I had to get on my hands and knees to reach the back of the cupboard.

"She's going to get herself in big trouble one of these days."

"So what if she does, Norman?" I backed out of the cupboard, dragging out a huge pot with handles and a lid. There had been one on the table at Miss Kesstle's this morning and my mother had used one for letting dough rise. She called it a Grosse Backschüssel. Loosely translated, "big baking bowl."

"You've been so worried about keeping up appearances and trying to be so straight to make up for the sex shops that you have no life at all."

He looked blankly at me. I stood up and set the bowl on the counter. Spoons too. I opened the drawer and got out my friend the wooden spoon and a spatula.

"Lady March's not worried what anyone thinks of her or if she's measuring up. If I were you, I'd get my ass out of that chair, make some sandwiches, and get up that ladder to see what's going on."

"I'm afraid of heights," said Norman.

I put the spoons in the bowl and turned to leave.

"It's all done," he said, "all the businesses are gone and the whole collection." He pushed his glasses up and gave me a hopeful little smile.

I turned back. "That's great. Now you'll have to start thinking about what you're going to do with the rest of your life." I took my bowl and walked out of the room.

I stopped over at Miss Kesstle's but no one was home. I could smell baked cinnamon buns from the porch. I left a note on the front door telling them where I was, that I'd come by later, and to save me a bun.

I got back to the Centre a few hours later. I went to climb the ladder and saw a bright blue hightop runner lying at the bottom.

"Marilyn left about an hour ago," said Mr. H. when I got to the top. "She wasn't looking very well, kinda shaky and pale, like she was going to throw up. I wasn't sure she was going to make it down the ladder; she lost a shoe."

"I see that," I said.

"She sure impressed the kids, though," said Mr. H. "Do you think —" he paused "— if we manage to keep the Centre going, she'd like to come and teach screenwriting?"

I shrugged. "I suppose it would depend on how stoned she was that day and the current state of her shoe collection. Do you think one of the kids could give me a hand? I have a bunch of stuff to bring up."

I sat on the roof covered in flour paste and newspaper scraps and surrounded by garbage bags full of inflated balloons, stacks of newspaper and industrial-sized bags of flour and salt.

Mr. H. came over and sat on the cement beside me. "Can I help?"

"Sure," I said. "You can tear newspaper strips. I borrowed your bowl and stuff."

"That's fine." He took a pile of papers. "Like this?"

"A little thinner," I said. "Aren't you going to ask me what I'm making?"

"I don't care," he said smiling. "I'm happy to see you making anything."

Lady March came and stood beside us. "This looks industrious."

"Bird heads," I said, crumpling paper and taping it onto a balloon in the shape of a beak. "Stormy petrel bird heads out of papier-mâché. They should be dry by late tonight. We can cut holes in them for eyes, paint them however we want, and wear them."

"Smashing," said Lady March. She sat down and took up a pile of newspapers. "Brilliant for photo ops."

Solidarity. Publicity. Protest.

STORMY PETREL SIT-IN: DAY THREE

"The reporters don't seem to be leaving," I said to Mr. H.

"I don't know if it's a slow news week, or if we're finally getting payback for all those years of wine and cheese, but either way, I'm happy."

We painted the papier-mâché bird heads in all different colours and designs. They were amazing: flowers, stars, medieval warrior birds, suns, and moons. A regular Mardi Gras of bird heads. We had them in constant production, a string of them drying as another set was being pasted together, and someone always painting. I had my own petrel head and was now officially "on the roof." You know what they say — you're either on the roof or you're off the roof. Looking through the holes of the mask at the people standing below and being up so high gave me the sense of actually being avian, and of having a purpose: to save the nest of so many artists.

Marilyn was back on the roof. "My room was too hot," she said when she climbed up the ladder. "I might as well be up here where there's a breeze." She sat in her newly claimed spot by the smokestack and waited for something exciting to happen.

As Mr. H. and I stood talking, there was some commotion down on the ground. We leaned over the edge to watch. An extra-long shiny black van with smoked windows pulled up

CHAPTER THIRTY

and began honking at the crowd to move aside so it could drive closer to the building.

"FBI," whispered one of the birds.

"You mean CSIS," said another.

"Who?"

"No, look on the side."

On the front panel of the van, in white print, was *Hassle The Man Productions*. The crowd parted, the van parked, and Whitman got out the passenger-side door. The next row of doors opened and three other men bustled out, opened the cargo doors at the back, and began hauling out cameras, lights, and cords.

Whitman talked to the men for a minute, then climbed up the ladder. Mr. H. met him at the top. "What's all this?"

"I've been wanting to do a documentary film for a long time," said Whitman. "I thought the Art Centre had all the right elements. But this," he waved his arms at the Stormy Petrels, "is brilliant. Are you interested?"

"Of course," said Mr. H. "Thank you."

"Great," said Whitman. He hung his head for a minute and I could see the seven-year-old boy inside him; then he snapped back into action. "I'm going to go back down and try and arrange some pointed interviews with the PM and the mayor."

"Look out, *w5*," said Marilyn.

Whitman turned to her. "What are you doing here?"

"What does it look like? I'm sitting in."

"Good," said Whitman. "I was hoping to find you today. Can you take notes on things as they happen, and we'll use them for the narration script when we put the film together? With your name on it and credit, of course."

"I don't know anything about documentary writing," said Marilyn.

"That's okay," Whitman said, "I don't know anything about making one. It's not so much, but I wanted to say I was sorr —"

"Yeah, yeah," said Marilyn. "Next time you come up, bring

me some paper and pens, nice inky ones. I'm not going to buy my own supplies."

Whitman climbed back down and I followed him. One of the local reporters came up to him.

"What's going on?"

Whitman cleared his throat. "Hassle The Man Productions, a Los Angeles film crew, is filming a documentary on the fight to save the Downtown Art Centre. You can call me later at this number for an interview after I've spoken to the city officials."

He handed the reporter a card, walked away, and smiled at me. "If there's one thing Canadians hate, it's Americans knowing their dirty business."

Marilyn stayed overnight that night but left before sunrise.

STORMY PETREL SIT-IN: DAY FOUR

Norman climbed up the ladder with his eyes shut, sat well in the middle of the building, and never looked down once. His face was the colour of spinach.

"I'm so glad you came," said Lady March. "I was worried about you down there all by yourself."

"Do you have complimentary barf bags for participants?" he asked.

"White light," said Lady March. "Just visualize white light in your abdomen."

"Couldn't we just buy the building?"

"That would defeat our purpose," she said.

"Which is?"

"Solidarity. Publicity. Protest."

"Right." Norman put his head in his hands.

Marilyn showed up again in the afternoon wearing one high-heeled shoe and one sneaker. She held her impromptu screenplay classes, took notes, and shouted rude things down at the two policemen now posted for crowd control.

Ginny must have heard about the documentary because she showed up at the top of the ladder, looking around for Whitman. She brought nail polish, makeup, and hair products to help the women keep up morale.

"It's hard to be righteous when you're having a bad hair day," she said.

"I've never had a problem with it," said Marilyn.

I got busy making more bird heads.

Later that afternoon, Marilyn was sitting in her regular position, leaning on the smokestack, when Girl's head appeared at the top of the ladder.

"Hey, you crazy birds," shouted Girl. "What're you all doing up here without me? Now we can have some serious protesting."

Mr. H. went over, gave her a big hug, and kissed the top of her head. He introduced her to Lady March. I stood off to the side and watched.

Marilyn stood up. Girl stared at her. "Hey," said Marilyn.

"What're you doing here?" asked Girl.

"Lending my support."

"You? Support?" Girl snorted.

"I'm sorry," said Marilyn. She wobbled over to where Girl stood. "I should have let you in. I was. . . I was scared."

"That made two of us," said Girl.

"I'm trying to stay on this roof," said Marilyn, "and you're why I'm up here."

"Me?"

"Well, first of all, *she* bloody well blackmailed me," Marilyn jerked her thumb at me. I smiled and waved at Girl. "But I've been coming back because I was hoping to see you so I could apologize. So, this is it. I'm apologizing. And I don't do it very often. But I was way wrong."

"Okay," said Girl. She gave Marilyn a punch on the shoulder. Marilyn wobbled to the left on her one flat shoe, and then over to the right on her one high-heeled shoe, and nearly went backwards over the edge before Girl grabbed her.

"Holy woman," said Girl, "you are one sorry shoe person."

"I think I'll go sit down," said Marilyn. "Are we okay?"

"Well," said Girl, "I'm not at *all* sure about you. But yeah, I'm okay."

Girl was like a loose cannon on the roof. Her bruises had started to fade and she may have made up with Marilyn, but she was mad at the rest of the world. She painted her bird head black with red skulls and crossbones. She made up chants for the kids to yell: "The arts have heart. The mayor is a fart." "Give us a nickel. Give us a buck. The mayor is a stupid fuck." She only subsided once Mr. H. convinced her it probably wasn't helping the cause so much.

Whitman was up and down the ladder, doing interviews and directing people. Ginny approached him a few times and he was polite, but didn't give her any encouragement. I was surprised she stayed on the roof, but she said it was like a holiday, and that she hoped that at least one of the newspaper photos showed her face clearly so she could embarrass her former employers. She wouldn't wear a bird head, but she did help paint them, and, true to her word, she gave facials to the women and manicures to the men.

I was sitting on the roof and tearing paper for more bird heads. We'd been getting requests from people on the ground wondering if they could buy them. Norman came up with the plan of auctioning them off on eBay if the Centre was saved.

Ginny was doing Norman's nails on the other side of the entrance doorway to the roof. I wasn't eavesdropping, really; the wind just blew their conversation in my direction.

"It's not like I was making the films," I heard Norman say.

"Of course you weren't," said Ginny. "You were just a businessman providing a service. If there was no demand, there'd be no need for supply, right?"

"Right. But it was still wrong."

"Absolutely," said Ginny. "Do you want your nails buffed?"

"It seemed more important to be successful than anything else."

"I hear you," said Ginny. "I'll just buff them lightly. What are you going to do now?"

"Find something else to succeed at, I suppose," said Norman.

"I have no doubt you will," said Ginny.

Humph. I ripped the papers in my hands.

STORMY PETREL SIT-IN: DAY FIVE

Miss Kesstle called Norman's cellphone in the morning. She wanted to bring Sunday dinner up to the roof and asked if Girl would come back to the house in the afternoon to help her. Girl agreed and wanted Marilyn to come with her. Marilyn had been on the roof overnight and all that day.

"I'm feeling pretty good," said Marilyn. "I'll stay up here today."

Miss Kesstle called again in the late afternoon to ask if Girl was still on the roof. Norman handed the phone to me. "I think she left quite a while ago," I said, "but it's hard to keep track of people up here."

"Oh dear," said Miss Kesstle. "I hope nothing has happened to her. I'll just call a cab and get the dishes — Never mind," she said, "she's here now. See you soon."

Half an hour later, Miss Kesstle and Girl brought Sunday dinner over in the taxi, fancy china and all. Girl helped her up the ladder and then made several trips to bring the dinner up.

Miss Kesstle stuck her hand out to Lady March. "I don't believe we've met. I'm Mr. Hausselman's neighbour, Miss Kesstle."

Lady March grabbed her in a big hug. "We've all met before."

"No," said Miss Kesstle, "I haven't met you before."

"Oh, yes, we all know each other from other times," said Lady March, "and everyone here on this roof, I know I've been with before."

Miss Kesstle waited until she moved away and then turned to me. "I'd know if I'd met her before. Is she afflicted? Like Mr. Hausselman?" Miss Kesstle tapped her temple. "You know."

"Oh," I nodded solemnly. "Yes she is, New Age Madness."

"I haven't heard of that," said Miss Kesstle watching Lady March walk over to Mr. H., "but maybe Mr. Hausselman and her would be good together, if they both have brain troubles."

We all had dinner and then Miss Kesstle wanted to leave. She was still darkly predicting that the riot squad would show up at any moment and blast us off the roof. I went to look for Girl to let her know that Miss Kesstle was going. I couldn't find her anywhere, nor was Marilyn at her usual spot by the smokestack. I was about to give up when I heard giggling from behind the doorway that led to the staircase. I opened the door and found Girl and Marilyn sitting together on the top step. It looked like they were performing some sort of junior-high science experiment. Girl grasped an Orange Crush pop can sideways. I could see a hole covered in tinfoil on the side of it. Marilyn held a lighter to the bottom of a spoon. "Oh, shit," she said.

"Is she in there?" Miss Kesstle stood right behind me. I turned and tried to block the doorway.

"No! She's —"

"I'm right here," said Girl, pushing past me. Her eyes were the size of Jupiter's moons and she had a big smile on her face. Marilyn followed behind her.

Dance, Gladys, Dance

"Wow," said Girl, "it's dark out here." She turned to Marilyn. "When did it get so dark?"

Marilyn furrowed her brow and tried to look serious. "Yesterday, I think," she said.

Girl started to laugh and sat down on the floor. "Yesterday. Yesterday. Yesterday. Yester. Day. What the fuck is a Yester?"

"Girl," said Miss Kesstle, "are you drunk?"

"Oh no," said Girl, "I'm just happy. Happy to be alive."

Miss Kesstle stepped closer to her, leaned over, and sniffed. "You don't smell like alcohol. It's drugs, isn't it? You're using drugs."

"Drugs," said Girl, "are using me."

"I'll have to ask you to come to my place and get your things," said Miss Kesstle. She pulled her hands in close to her chest. "I said you could only stay if you promised to not use drugs or drink anymore and you promised. Do you remember?"

"Oh no," said Girl, "but I didn't. I wasn't."

"It's not her fault," said Marilyn. "I brought it up and asked her to come and smoke it. I convinced her. I told her no one would notice and that a little bit wouldn't hurt. It's my fault."

"Maybe we should just leave this alone for now," I said.

Miss Kesstle stepped towards Marilyn. "What were you thinking? Do you want her to end up like you?"

"No," said Marilyn, "I don't. I'd apologize better, but I think I need to sit down first." She slid down the wall and sat beside Girl.

Girl patted her knee. "Wicked shit, hey?"

Marilyn suddenly pushed herself upright again. Miss Kesstle took a step back. "I'll leave," she said. "It was my fault. Could someone just help me down the ladder? I can't find my shoes *or* my wings." They both started to giggle again.

"Birds of a feather, blah, blah," said Girl.

Miss Kesstle said, "I'm going too. Girl, you need to think about what you want. I don't think you would have done this if it weren't for the influence of — *others*." She threw Marilyn a dirty look. "But you need to be able to say no."

"I know," said Girl, "but when I saw it, I just couldn't help it."

"All right," said Miss Kesstle. "We'll talk more later. I'm going now." She took a few steps, then turned. "You know you can't fly, right? Don't walk off the edge of the building."

Girl nodded. "No flying, nope."

"All right, be careful up here."

We got Miss Kesstle and Marilyn down the ladder and they went off into the night in their separate directions.

Later that night, I sat with Girl near the back of the roof. It was quiet; most everyone had gone to sleep. There was a row of petrel heads lined up on the ledge across from us. I stared up at the few stars I could see through the city air. Pigeons cooed from a ledge a storey below. Girl leaned back with her eyes closed.

"Girl?" I whispered.

"Uh huh." She opened her eyes.

"Why do you do drugs?"

"Well, *that's* a conversation opener," she said and closed her eyes again. She pulled her sleeping bag up higher. "Because it's boring."

"What's boring?"

"I don't know. Life, I suppose." A siren sounded in the city somewhere and was joined by another.

"You're killing your brain cells."

"So? What do I need them for? I mean, what am I saving them for — a rainy day?"

"You need brains to make your art," I said. "You won't know if you can make it unless you try."

"Did *you* try?"

I stared at her, flummoxed. *Had* I tried? Before I met Gimlet, I was filled with work and working hard, and then what? And then I'd decided that I couldn't do it on my own, that I needed a step up, a hand up, first from Gimlet, then from Norman, and where had that left me?

I looked at her, her long hair tangled around her face. "I did try and then I gave up," I said. "But it was giving up that stopped me, not not trying hard enough."

"I think that's a double negative," said Girl.

"You know what I mean. You can only care about what it gives you. If more comes, fine. If not, that's fine too."

Girl shrugged. "And," she said, "I like being stoned."

A Gnarled Root

"Frieda, could you go downstairs and get us more paint? There's some in a box in the cupboard beside the sink in the craft room."

"Sure." I was happy to get away for a few minutes. I loved being on the roof and with everyone on it, but I now knew never to join a commune.

I went down the stairs and pushed open the metal door leading onto the main floor. It felt like being inside a school during summer holidays. A faint smell of glue and poster paint lingered in the halls. The art hanging on the walls seemed like cave paintings, relics left from a people long since past. The bottoms of loose pages fluttered slightly as I walked by.

"I never got to be a part of a protest before. That Lady March, she would have made a good Doukhobour."

"Gladys! Where've you been?"

"It's crowded up there. I haven't been able to get you alone for a minute." She floated along beside me. I noticed that the pages on her side of the wall did not move.

"I haven't been able to get me alone for a minute either," I said.

We entered the main craft room. I kneeled on the floor and started pulling jars of paint out of the cupboard. Some were almost completely dried out and I had to open all of the jars to check.

"I wonder if these would reconstitute if we added water?"

Gladys sat on the counter beside me, her feet dangling down.

"I need to finish my story," she said, her voice dropping low. "I need to tell you what happened."

"You don't have to," I said. "I can probably imagine it. I mean, what were you supposed to do with no money and nowhere to go? What about your parents? Wouldn't they have helped you?" I twisted the top off a jar and flakes of paint fell in my lap.

"I was ashamed to go to my parents," she said. "They hadn't spoken to me since I ran away to Toronto. I thought once I had the baby they'd forgive me, but I never had the chance. I went to see a friend from school. She made a big show of being happy to see me, but she was scared. She wouldn't look me in the eye, and she kept looking over her shoulder as if I might split in two and come up behind her with an axe or something. I hadn't realized until then that I was marked by my time in the institution; I'd become the crazy woman. She wouldn't take me in, but she gave me a little money, some clothes and toiletries. I took the money and got a hotel room. I cleaned myself up and put on a dress. I'd lost a lot of weight in the asylum and the dress hung on me; I had to keep pulling the shoulders up so my bosom didn't show. I did my hair the best I could. I thought I looked pale so I put on some rouge. I'd never used it before and I guess I went overboard. I used to wonder if all the rest never would have happened if I hadn't put on all that rouge. I was still a little shaky, but I managed to get myself done up all right I thought. I went for dinner at a cheaper restaurant. I felt strange having dinner alone, but didn't know what else to do. As I was leaving, a man approached me and whispered something. I didn't hear him. He jerked his head towards the street and so I followed him, still doing as I was told. I followed him right to his hotel. He led me upstairs to his room, closed the door, smiled at me, and started to take off his pants. I turned my head and saw my reflection in the mirror of the bureau: the low bosom on the ill-fitting dress, the choppy haircut, the bright red circles on my cheeks, my face thin and desperate. Right then, something inside me just died. I imagined myself on my hands and knees screaming and screaming into the carpet but I stood very still. I watched him and I gave up — not on life, but myself. *Well then*, I thought, *it's come to this, has it? And I just did it.*"

"Oh Gladys," I said, my voice trembling. Not fair. Not fair. Not not not fair.

"I took the money and paid for another night at my hotel, not nearly so nice as his. I cried half the night in the hotel room, but I couldn't feel anything. I'd gone numb. It was like the tears came from my body, not my mind, or myself. It was just my body crying all night. And so it went."

"What about dancing? Did you try to find work as a dancer?" I asked. I'd forgotten all about the paint jars.

Gladys rocked, her hands folded over one another, her head hanging slightly down. "No," she said. "My legs would have still known how to dance, but that spark of hope or joy necessary to perform had been snuffed out. The last time I ever felt it was the night before my baby was born and I'd danced in the chicken yard. Sometimes when I walked past the theatre and saw photos of the dancers in the marquee, something inside of me would pinch and cramp terribly, and I'd have to walk away. I learned to not look, to not see."

"What about the photos of you?"

"I met some other low women in the city and one introduced me to a photographer. He told us the pictures he took were for his own pleasure; none of us believed it, but what did it matter? What was there to be afraid of, that I would be ruined? Too late for that. He used me as a model a lot. I knew how to move and pose from my dancing. Miss Johnstone, the dancing

Dance, Gladys, Dance

teacher, would have been appalled at how I used her training. I certainly hadn't worked my way up the social ladder."

"It wasn't your fault, Gladys. You know that, right? You didn't do anything wrong."

She shrugged. "Right, wrong, none of it mattered anymore. I was surviving. That's all." She paused. "I saw Jack once when I was standing on the street. He looked at me and laughed. He started to cross the street to come to me and I ran. I knew he was going to offer to pay for my services. I ran until I was nearly out of the city and then I stopped and vomited in a back alley. It's silly, but that was the only time I felt completely ashamed of what I was doing."

"Did you ever go to see your son, Jack Jr.? What happened to him?"

"He ended up with a drinking problem. He gambled away all of his father's money. I heard about it in the streets."

"You didn't ever go and see him? Not once?"

"Jack sent him to school in Australia. He had enough to contend with without having a visit from his mother the whore. Jack Sr. was hard on him, I heard. I suppose he hated the part of the boy that was mine. Maybe he saw artistic tendencies in Jack Jr. that he wanted to kill by sending him off to military school. It couldn't have been a picnic there. Jack wouldn't give him any money until he proved himself. However, Jack Jr. outsmarted him; he waited until his father died, then took all the money and spent it like a fool. He married a woman, Marion, but she left him after they had their first baby, and Jack Jr. never came home for weeks on end. Like father like son. The baby Jack Jr. and Marion had was Fredrick. Fredrick was Girl's grandfather. Fredrick never had a chance either; his mother lost heart after she left Jack Jr. It was like she had the strength to make that one stand, but then couldn't find the courage or maybe the energy to carry on. Fredrick's mother went from man to man, hoping to find someone to take care of them. Fredrick grew up and married Rosie in the 1950s. Fredrick turned out to be a religious man; he was the church musician and he held a tight rein over his wife. They were the perfect family in the perfect house and then they had Sheila. Sheila was a wild one and her mother let her do as she liked. When she was a teenager, Sheila decided she liked drugs, alcohol, boys, and — what did they call it in those years? Free passion?"

"Free love," I said.

"Love? Really? Sheila was an alcoholic by the time she was a teenager, ended up on the streets, living here and there. She carried a pair of bongo drums around with her; she'd play on street corners and dance. Going from one bad man to another, she had Boy, and then there was Girl. There, that's the family tree."

"And there was Girl." I smiled.

Gladys looked at me; her eyes still held the pain of her story.

"I might seem like a lousy Sir Galahad, but I'll get it figured out," I said. "I'm going to make it right somehow." She gazed steadily at me. I felt like I had in the career interview, like I just wasn't getting it. "Stop looking at me like that. I really will fix it." I started filling a box with the jars of paint. "I'd better get this up there before they send a search party out for me."

STORMY PETREL SIT-IN: DAY SEVEN

On the afternoon of Day Seven, a representative of the government came and told us, through a bullhorn, that the Grainger chain had agreed to build a few blocks down on a site that held another obsolete government building.

Girl and Mr. H. did a happy dance together and Lady March was about to disrobe when Norman came over, kissed her cheek, put his arm around her shoulder, and held her caftan on. I cheered until my voice was hoarse. So this was what it felt like to be on a winning team, to do something that mattered.

One of the cameramen caught Whitman and Mr. H. in tears and embracing. "Thank you," said Mr. H., patting Whitman's back. "Your mother would have been proud."

"She'd be proud of both of us," said Whitman. "You do good work. Remind me to send you a fruit basket."

Mr. H. looked stunned, then laughed. Whitman laughed too then wiped his eyes. "Get that thing off me," he said to the cameraman. "Go film someone else.

It was strange to be back at Mr. H.'s; everything seemed quiet and slow. The day after we returned, Mr. H. got a telephone call from the Historical Society letting him know that the house had been placed on their list. I decided I should have a celebratory dinner the next evening, something to mark what we'd all been through and to celebrate the saving of the Art Centre.

I decided I'd try and cook an oriental supper. There was a Chinese cookbook from the experimental cooking days; the pictures were so bright and pretty and the instructions seemed easy to follow. I decided on ginger beef, chicken with lychees, wonton soup, and rainbow fried vegetables. I called Miss Kesstle to see if she wanted to make dessert, but there was no one home. I headed off to try and find the proper ingredients for my dinner.

On the way to the bus stop, I saw Whitman on Miss Kesstle's front porch. I stood and watched him. He reached into his pocket, took something out, tore it apart, and put pieces of whatever it was all over the porch.

What the hell? When he finished, he sat down on the steps. He glanced up, saw me, and grimaced.

I walked over to him. "I'm not sure I want to know, but what are you hiding on Miss Kesstle's porch?"

"Nothing."

I raised my eyebrows and stared at him.

"Wieners," he said. "When do you think she'll be back? How long does she usually shop?"

"*Wieners?*"

He nodded. "Don't say anything, okay? I don't want her to know it was me."

"Is this a Los Angeles game? Hide the Wiener? Miss Kesstle won't be into it."

"No, it's — where the hell is that guy?" He looked at his watch and then pulled out his cellphone. Just as he was dialing, the film van drove down the street and parked in front of Miss Kesstle's.

"About time," he muttered and stood.

I was utterly baffled. The man driving the van got out, went around to the back and opened the doors, and a small, curly-haired black and white dog jumped out. A small, curly-haired black and white dog with only three legs. It jumped and ran in circles around Whitman, licking his hands. You could hardly tell it was missing a leg. Whitman took hold of the leash and led the dog over. "What do you think?"

"He's a beauty."

"She."

The dog sat in front of me, wagging its tail. I petted it and it turned its head to lick my hand. "What happened to her?"

"It belonged to a friend of a friend. A car hit it. The driver of the car took it to the vet's. They saved it, but had to amputate its leg. They tried to find the owner, but no one claimed her. My friend's friend can't keep it; turns out his kids are allergic. I thought of Miss Kesstle. It seemed like the kind of animal she'd like, and I thought it might help with her fear of robbers."

"Though she has Girl now; she's probably a fine watchdog."

"She won't stay forever," said Whitman.

"No, I suppose not. So what's your plan?"

"I thought I'd leave it on the porch and make it look like it knocked over the chair to block the stairs. I think the wieners will keep it occupied for a while. You won't tell her, will you?"

"Mum's the word," I said and started down the sidewalk again.

"Frieda," Whitman called. I turned.

"Did you invite Marilyn to your dinner? I know she screwed up, but she's been working hard on the film." He reached down, patted the puppy, and grinned at me. "And everyone deserves a second chance. Right?"

I groaned. "Okay, invite her, but if she and Miss Kesstle get into a scrap, you'll have to handle it."

I carried on my way, smiling. I took the bus to Chinatown, my shopping list in hand. The streets were packed. I ended up at a standstill on a sidewalk, hemmed in on all sides. Then I heard music, cymbals and chimes. The crowd began applauding and a Chinese dragon undulated its way down the centre of the street in front of me. It was stunning, the movement and the colours: pinks, blues, oranges, pure white, shimmering all over with gold. A crowd of children followed, waving banners. They wore every colour under the sun, embroidered, appliquéd, and shining. I stood amongst the clapping crowd, everything on the street drenched in brilliance. My eyes and mind began to work: that hot pink next to that spring green, the gold with the white, the scarlet beside the violet. My fingers tingled, and I began to cry. I wanted to play with these colours, to mix them, to dip my brushes in dioxazine violet and phthalo green. I cried and I drank it in. I felt a pat on my back. A small, ancient Chinese woman standing beside me patted my back again, smiled, and nodded her head.

"It's beautiful," I said waving my hand to the street, tears still running down my face.

She smiled again. Her face was lined with a thousand wrinkles and her eyes said she'd seen a sorrow for every one of those wrinkles. She nodded twice and lifted her chin to the street where more marchers were coming. I turned to watch, feasting on the colours. I wanted to embrace it, to eat it, to own it, to celebrate it. I wanted to paint it. When the parade ended, the crowd broke up, and I couldn't find my friend.

I wiped my face and, both gorged and yearning, carried on my way to the food stores, the shopping list still crumpled in my hand.

I chose the most authentic-looking store I could find, no English on the signs, everything in those amazing characters. I found most of the ingredients in the bins that I needed, guessing by smell and by sight, but I couldn't find any ginger root. I approached the man at the counter. "Ginger?" I said.

He shook his head and said, "Wo bu dong."

"Ginger root," I said. "Uh — *root.*" I held my hand up and twisted my fingers in an approximation of a gnarled root.

"Ah," he said, smiled, got up from his stool, and went into the back area through a faded red curtain.

Ha, I'm the queen of charades. He came back still smiling, pleased as I was with our successful pantomime. In his hand was a large bag of chickens' feet. He held them up. "Wei dao zhen hao!"

"Oh," I said. "I — oh, thank you." I nodded my head and pulled out my wallet.

When I got back, Girl and the new dog were playing in front of Miss Kesstle's house. "Look what showed up!" said Girl. She lay on the grass and the puppy scrambled all over her. "It's a wheensy weeny whupsy pupsy. Isn't she great?"

Miss Kesstle sat on the porch beaming down at them. "She's very smart," she said. "She can sit and roll over."

"Who," I asked, "Girl or the pupsy?"

"But," said Miss Kesstle, "we can't get attached to her until we make sure she isn't lost. Someone else might be looking for her."

"Oh no," said Girl. "No one is looking for this little three-legged darling. She's ours. I know it."

"I don't mind checking for you," I said. "I'll call the pound."

"That would be wonderful, Frieda, thank you. Are you all ready for your dinner tomorrow?"

"Not yet, but I will be. I think."

There was a note on the kitchen table from Mr. H. saying that they'd all gone to the Art Centre to work on the film. I was standing in the kitchen staring at the bag of chicken feet on the counter when Gladys showed up.

"Oh dear," she said. "What are you going to do with those?"

"I have no freaking idea."

"Maybe you should make chili again."

"Chicken Foot Chili?"

"No, normal chili. Everyone liked it last time."

"I'm tired of only being able to cook one thing. I want to broaden my horizons."

"All right," said Gladys, "you should do all your prep work tonight. Tomorrow will be busy enough."

So I set to work, chopping, soaking, and spicing various things. Gladys looked over my shoulder and offered advice.

"How come you're still here?" I asked.

"Pardon me?"

"Well, Girl seems happy, she's off the streets and I thought, you know, that was your goal, or my mission."

Gladys pursed her lips and shrugged. "Are you going to marinate those feet?"

"Gladys. . ."

"I can't say." She looked away.

I opened a tin of tiny corn and asked, with my back to Gladys, "How long were you a —"

"A street walker? Until I lost my looks and got too old. Then the Good Samaritans took me to a refuge. They were amazed at how well a woman off the street could bake." She smiled.

"I didn't tell them I learned it in an insane asylum. So, there I stayed until I looked like this." She tugged at a lock of her grey hair. "And I became, well, like *this* too."

"Like what?"

"Invisible. No one really saw me. I was just dumpy old grey-haired Gladys in an apron in the kitchen. No one asked how I'd ended up there, no one asked who I'd been or what I'd dreamed of doing. No one asked me anything but were the pies ready yet."

I put down the can of lychee nuts I was trying to open next. "That bites, Gladys. That bites and stinks and pisses me off and I'm. . . I'm sorry."

She shrugged. "What's done is done, there were thousands more like me. Stories a little slower maybe, not so dramatic, but it never stopped happening. Then one night I got old enough and I died in my sleep. Nothing dramatic, just put on my night-gown, went to bed, dreamed of dancing, and stopped breathing. And here we are."

"Here we are. I'm glad you came, Gladys."

She smiled. "So am I. You could try putting those chicken's feet in a soup with carrots and dumplings."

She's A Good Girl

It was the night of the party and I dressed the table in all the colours of the Chinatown parade: red, blue, yellow, and gold. I dressed myself in my latest thrift store purchase, a cocktail dress from the forties, black taffeta with a scoop neck and a full skirt. I even got some black nylons and a pair of black velvet pumps. I felt like a movie star. Look out, Vivien Leigh.

People began showing up at a little after six. Ginny came dressed to the nines holding a bottle of expensive wine.

"Ah, Pinot Gris Rangen de Thann," said Norman. "That's an excellent choice."

"Do you think so?" asked Ginny. "I wasn't sure. Could you open it for me?" She put her hand on his shoulder. Gack.

Miss Kesstle showed up alone. She said Girl was coming later, that she had some friends to meet. She told us that they'd compromised on a name for the puppy. Miss Kesstle wanted to call it Dorothea after her mother, meaning God's gift, and Girl had pushed for Siouxsie Sioux. The end result: Dorothea Sioux. I thought the name would likely cause the puppy psychological problems.

Mr. H. bustled around getting people drinks and fussing. It was cute to see him play host. Marilyn showed up three sheets or two hits to the wind. She seemed subdued enough though, and sat in Mr. H.'s armchair, nodding off. Whitman held up his hands and shrugged. "She was like that when I picked her up."

I went into the kitchen to heat up the appetizers. After three experimental egg rolls had exploded while deep-frying, I'd relented on my all-authentic home-cooked dinner and nipped out and bought a jumbo box of frozen assorted Chinese appetizers. I heated them and arranged them artfully on a platter.

No one was in the living room; they were all seated around the dining room table and holding hands.

"Nice to see everyone getting along," I said.

"We're trying to contact a ghost," said Mr. H.

"I sense a very troubled spirit here," said Lady March.

I looked around at the seven of them and shrugged. "Take your pick."

They sat in silence as Lady March called for the spirit. Whitman found the whole thing quite amusing and repeatedly knocked on the table with his knee until Mr. H. banished him into the living room. Gladys didn't show for the impromptu séance but Marilyn got the heebie jeebies anyway and made everyone stop.

"You shouldn't mess with that stuff," she said. "Next thing you know, you'll be having fucking ectoplasm issues with your walls."

I hadn't seen Gladys all day, which was odd. She'd missed multiple opportunities to comment on my cooking. The phone rang and Marilyn shrieked.

"I'll get it," I said. It was Girl. I could hardly hear her for all the traffic noise.

"Where are you?" I asked.

"Pay phone. Be right there," she said. "Missed the bus, get the next one." She hung up.

We waited until seven o'clock for Girl and then I served dinner. My ginger beef (with powdered ginger) smelled quite good. The chicken with lychees had become a combination dish of other ingredients, and the rainbow fried vegetables looked colorful and possibly edible. I'd made the chicken foot soup with dumplings and added a splash of soy sauce.

I served all the dishes at once and as luck would have it, Marilyn got the soup first. She ladled herself out a big spoonful and then spit her wine all over the table.

"What the hell?" she spluttered.

"Just pick the feet out if you don't like them," I said calmly. "The other chicken dish is a sort of Shipwreck Casserole, only with Chinese ingredients instead of hamburger."

"Chinese Shipwreck," muttered Marilyn. "What do you call those boats?"

"What are you talking about?" asked Ginny.

"I wasn't talking to you, Miss Fancy Pants," said Marilyn. "Those Chinese sailboats."

"Junks?" said Norman.

"That's it!" said Marilyn. "I think I found a piece of junk in my plate."

Whitman chuckled.

"It's quite good, Frieda," said Mr. H., struggling with his chopsticks.

Miss Kesstle fiddled with her food, looking at her watch every few minutes. "Maybe I should go home and see if she's there," she said. "She may have forgotten about the dinner."

"She probably forgot where you live," said Ginny.

Marilyn helped herself to more and more wine and became more voluble. Whitman tried to keep her occupied by telling her about the Stormy Petrel film, but her eyes kept drifting over to Norman. "Don't I know you from somewhere?" she asked him.

"I was on the roof at the protest," said Norman. "I was the green one."

"No, before that. What did you say you did for a living?" Something was obviously niggling at Marilyn's mind. I wasn't sure Norman could withstand another attack like the one at the Art Centre.

Norman put down his chopsticks and looked at me. "I'm a
— Well, I'm sort of in-between, uh —"

"He's independently wealthy," said Ginny.

"Better than being dependently wealthy, huh, Whitman?"
asked Marilyn.

Whitman nodded. Mr. H. sent a piece of chicken flying over
his shoulder.

"There's definitely a spirit here or something wrong," said
Lady March. "I'm feeling very uneasy."

"I'm feeling very queasy too," said Marilyn.

"So, Norman," said Ginny, "tell me all about Kentucky. I'd
love to come for a visit sometime."

"It's very green," said Norman. "Except when it doesn't rain,
then it's very brown."

"Sounds wonderful," said Ginny.

"Sounds wahhhnderful," mimicked Marilyn.

"Will you please shut up?" said Ginny.

Marilyn leaned over, ducked under the table with her head
covered by the tablecloth, and then she sat back up. "That's
strange," she said to Ginny, "when I was young, Barbie's knees
didn't bend. How *did* you get your legs to do that?"

"Girl is probably out getting drugs," said Miss Kesstle suddenly to Marilyn, "and it's all your fault."

"Like hell," said Marilyn. "She was getting stoned before I
met her."

"But you got her started on the roof again," said Miss Kesstle, "and that was just wicked of you."

"Okay, that's enough," Marilyn banged her chopsticks on the
table. "Girl brought the dope on the roof. I didn't. I didn't even
ask her to. I've got no will power, so I took it. And I took the
shit for it 'cause it seemed like she might have a chance if she
stayed with you, and I didn't want you to kick her out. Okay?
No more shitting on Marilyn."

"Is that true?" Miss Kesstle stared at Marilyn.

"I'd been on that roof for two fucking days straight," yelled Marilyn. "Where do you think I got the dope? Carrier pigeon?"

There goes my dinner party. "I hate to interrupt this stirring conversation," I said, "but if you'll retire to the living room, I'll clear the dishes and be right back."

Miss Kesstle helped me scrape the chicken feet into the garbage. "I was wrong about Marilyn," she said.

"Happens to the best of us," I said. "I've been wrong about a lot of people lately."

We finished the dishes and went into the living room. It was so quiet I thought I'd killed everyone with my Chicken Foot Soup. Mr. H. was in his recliner. Marilyn dozed in the middle of the couch. Norman and Whitman sat on either side of her. Lady March read a book in the other armchair and Ginny sat on the floor in front of the fireplace.

"How about charades?" I said. No one answered. "Trivial Pursuit?"

Marilyn suddenly sat upright and stared ahead at nothing. "Come over here," she yelled, "and I'll fuck you until your ears fall off."

"Sounds interesting," said Whitman.

"I'm not so sure," said Norman. He got up, moved to the other side of the room, and sat on the floor beside Ginny. Marilyn slumped back down on the couch.

"Good God," said Ginny. "Why did you invite her? She's a mess."

"She's a talented screenwriter," said Whitman.

"So?" said Ginny. "Some of us get a handle on our problems and get help. She's wallowing in hers."

Lady March looked up from her book. "To make sense out of change," she said, "one must plunge into it, move with it, and join the dance."

"Dancing?" mumbled Marilyn.

"Vanuatu," said Lady March.

"Is that like Fehu?" I asked.

"No, Vanuatu is my next destination." She held up the book: *Metaphysical Voyages for the Astrally Challenged.* "There are rumours of a legendary plant in the South Pacific islands. The scent of the blossoms is supposed to create overwhelming sensations of serenity."

Mr. H. smiled. "The flower of positive stinking."

"Exactly," said Lady March. "Be a stunning addition to floral arrangements for world leaders. You should come with me."

"Me?" said Mr. H. "Now that would be an adventure. I've never been out of Canada."

"You should go," said Whitman. "See the world."

Norman sighed. "Why don't the two of you take a cruise on a nice safe luxury liner?"

The doorbell rang. "Girl, finally," said Miss Kesstle. Mr. H. got up and went to the front door. Miss Kesstle glanced at me, then beetled over to his recliner and sat down. We waited for a minute. Mr. H. led a uniformed policeman into the room.

"Oh, shit," said Marilyn, suddenly wide awake.

"What's up?" asked Whitman.

Mr. H. shook his head. "He wants to speak to Miss Kesstle."

The policeman looked young to me, but as I got older, I realized a lot of people in positions of power appeared to be the age of flyer delivery boys. He had curly red hair and his face was sombre. He held his hat in his hands and stood, as policemen seem to, with his legs farther apart than a normal person would. I supposed it was to make them harder to knock down. I glanced at Marilyn.

Miss Kesstle stood up. I thought for a moment of making a dive for the recliner, but I'd likely lose it again anyhow when I had to go pick Girl up from the police station.

"Are you Miss Kesstle?" asked the policeman.

She nodded. "Was a Girl Roulston staying with you?" She

nodded again. "We found your name and address on a piece of paper in her pocket."

"She's a good girl," said Miss Kesstle. "She just took a wrong turn. It's been a pleasure to have her stay with me. If she's in trouble, we can work it out. Don't send her back to those foster people again, that's no place for her."

"There's no easy way to say this," said the policeman, "but I'm sorry to tell you —"

"No," said Miss Kesstle. "The war is over; people don't come and tell people things like this anymore."

The police officer looked at Mr. H. "Girl Roulston is dead."

"How?" asked Mr. H. He swayed slightly but stayed on his feet.

"She walked in front of a bus. We won't know for sure until the autopsy, but we strongly suspect alcohol and drugs were a factor."

"Why?" said Miss Kesstle. "Why would she do that?" She slid back down into her chair.

"We don't know," said the officer. "It may have been a mistake. She died immediately; there was no chance for resuscitation. Her foster parents ID'd her already. They told us that she was living with you."

Miss Kesstle stared at him. A shocked silence filled the room.

"Fuck you!" screamed Marilyn jumping up from the couch. "Fuck you! You just go away. You're wrong. Get the hell out of here."

"I'm sorry," said the policeman, stepping back from Marilyn. "If there's anything we can do —" He handed Mr. H. a card. "We may have to get back in touch with you."

Mr. H. led him out, then came back into the living room. Everything fragmented. Miss Kesstle put her head in her hands and started to wail. From the corner of my eye, I caught a glimpse of Gladys by the stairs. She was crying. I took a step towards her and she disappeared.

Mr. H. and Lady March took Miss Kesstle home. Marilyn looked around the room for someone to fight, then collapsed into sobs. Whitman led her out the door. Norman and Ginny left together. I slowly turned and went upstairs to my room.

Gladys was rocking in her chair. I sat on the bed. I felt like I was going to be sick; supper rolled in my stomach. I looked at her. "What did I do wrong? I was supposed to save her and I didn't. I told you to go haunt Ginny." My voice shook. "Tell me what I should have done." I twisted the bed cover in my fingers.

"She was the last of my line," Gladys said. "It's over."

"Oh, fuck. I — Why didn't you —"

"It was going to happen," said Gladys. She gave me a wavering smile. "You did everything you could and more. I wanted some good to come out of it."

"*What* good?" I cried. "There's nothing good happened. She's dead. That beautiful talented girl is dead. Probably doped up out of her mind and that's it. I hate this."

Gladys continued to rock. "Don't be angry. Plenty of good has come from Girl's life. You've done so much."

"I sure as hell don't see it," I said.

"You will," said Gladys and disappeared.

I sat and images of Girl formed and dissipated in my head. Girl emerging from her box in the back alley, at the party in her Haute Crochet evening gown with the tea cozy on her head, yelling from the roof from behind her skull and crossbones bird mask, and in her apron as Martha-fucking-Stewart at Miss Kesstle's, her bruised face filled with laughter. Then I could see Girl's broken body in the morgue. Her hand fallen out from underneath the white sheet, the cracked and bitten nails painted aubergine. I could see the terrible beauty of her hand, the translucence of the skin. Then (to the horror of my imagination) a drop of blood rolled down the arm and fell to the floor, the tiny splash of crimson extending until the world was covered, blanketed with the scarlet of Girl's blood, Girl's pain.

I went and sat in the chair in front of my desk, opened some tubes of paint, and squeezed colours on my fingers. Rubbing my thumb and my forefinger together, I blended dots of blue and scarlet into a muddy purple. A small wail of grief rose unbidden from my throat and escaped into the room. I stared at my hands and wept. I was still sitting like that when there was a knock at my door. I didn't answer. The door creaked open; footsteps crossed the room and stopped beside me at the desk. I looked up. Whitman. He reached out and brushed my cheek with his fingers then let his hand fall. I looked back down at my hands.

"I took Marilyn home," he said. "She fell right asleep. I — I wanted to make sure you were all right."

"Whitman," I said. He kneeled down on the floor beside me. My dress rustled as he leaned against my legs. "I was supposed to save her," I said. He took my painted hands and put them on his face. I couldn't see his face. I couldn't see anything. It was like looking through a broken kaleidoscope.

I leaned forward and put my lips on his forehead. His skin was still cool from outside. "I don't need you," I said. "I don't need you. I just want you."

"That's okay." I felt his head nod underneath my lips. "It's fine. It's all right."

The next morning the bedsheets were stained with oil paints and I was alone. I got up and sat naked on the chair in front of the desk. My fingers shook as I picked up a pencil and began to draw on the canvas. Later, I squeezed paints out on the palette. Zinc white, golden ochre, cadmium red, more white to make it paler, a little blue to neutralize in the shadows. I picked up a round brush and pressed it against my lips. Then I dipped it in the paint, and I began.

Damn Decent

The next three days passed in a doldrum of grief. Miss Kesstle began crocheting again: a blanket of multicoloured cotton to cover Girl in her coffin. She sat out on the porch half the night working on the blanket after we found out about Girl's death. Mr. H. finally made her go inside, but she wouldn't sleep. She wanted to get the blanket done before Girl's service on Wednesday.

I sat with my own work. I put my head in my hands and then I looked up and began to paint again. I growled at the canvas, I despaired, and I listened to a lot of angry music, but I stayed with it. And in the midst of feeling like I was empty, less than empty, that I was painting with my oxygen and my blood and my nerve endings, the perfect strokes came, the perfect colours, and filled me back up.

Norman had been staying with Ginny since the night of the dinner party. We seldom saw them, and when we did, they were smiling.

"I'm sorry to be so happy," whispered Ginny when they dropped in, "but I can't help it. He's talking about me moving to Kentucky."

"Don't be sorry," I said. "Happy is good, or so I've heard."

Part of me wanted to be pissed at Ginny. Wasn't there something in the Code about getting together with your best friend's ex? The other part of me, well, why waste a perfectly good millionaire?

"Are you and Whitman, you know?" she asked.

"No, we're not." We weren't. It had been a beautiful and sad night, but I couldn't even think about a relationship.

Miss Kesstle asked me to take her to the funeral home the day before the service. I'd finished the painting and I carried it downstairs from my room. Norman, Ginny, Lady March, and Mr. H. sat at the kitchen table playing Scrabble. Mr. H. was about to be beat for the first time in history by Lady March, who'd just scored 126 points for "xenomancy."

I held the painting up. Mr. H. began to clap. I smiled at him and felt the tears begin again. Norman stood. "Very nice," he said. "I like what you've done with the colours. This is a much stronger painting. You've a hold on your technique, the brush-strokes seem more confident —"

"Don't critique my painting," I said quietly.

Norman's mouth fell open. "Why not? I didn't say anything bad about it."

"Because I don't want you to," I said.

I felt like those were the six mightiest words I ever said in my life. Because. I. Don't. Want. You. To. Period. End of sentence. End of discussion. I didn't paint the picture for approval. I didn't paint it for anything but the love of painting and because there was something I needed to paint.

Norman looked as though he might cry. I walked over to him. "It's not you, Norman, it never was. You didn't tie me to that white horse. I asked you to give me something I didn't want. I needed to believe in who I am myself."

Norman nodded then looked even more confused. I opened

my mouth, then closed it. It wasn't my job to make the world understand.

"She's amazing," said Lady March.

Miss Kesstle waited on the porch with the blanket in a plastic shopping bag in her hands. She looked like a lady scarecrow with her print dress and sweater hanging off her. I held the painting up. "I did this for you. Actually, I painted it for myself, but I want you to have it." I propped the canvas up on the porch railing. It was Girl as I'd first imagined her in the back alley, a Pre-Raphaelite-style painting with a background of graffiti-painted cement, only instead of her velvet gown, Girl wore the long dress she made from Miss Kesstle's doilies. From Girl's hand, almost indistinguishable from the graffiti behind it, fell a tiny drop of blood, forever suspended between her hand and the cement.

"Thank you," said Miss Kesstle and she hugged me. We stood together like that for a moment and then she drew away, reached into the pocket of her sweater, and withdrew two Kleenexes folded neatly into squares. "Here," she said. "I brought plenty."

"Do you think we should stop and see if Marilyn wants to come with us?" she asked as I drove out the back driveway. "I thought it might be better if she came today instead of tomorrow, just in case she. . ."

"Pitches a fit?"

Miss Kesstle nodded. "Well, we can check," I said, "but she's not known for answering her door."

"What a place," said Miss Kesstle as we walked through the lobby. She stopped to read the defecation sign on the stairway, which was thankfully free of poop that day, then kept her eyes on the floor and watched where she stepped.

Amazingly enough, Marilyn answered her door. She looked like hell boiled over. Her hair was plastered against her head with sweat and her face was a bizarre combination of pallor and redness, but she wanted to come along. Miss Kesstle reached into the shopping bag and pulled out a pair of brand-new white sneakers. Marilyn took them from her and sat down on the bed, then stood up, hugged Miss Kesstle, and burst into tears.

"That was damn decent of you," Marilyn said as she laced up the shoes.

We waited in the lobby of the funeral home while a man wearing a black suit checked to see if we could go in yet. The smell of lilies was overpowering. We'd only been there a minute when Marilyn excused herself and went outside. I stood with Miss Kesstle for a little bit and then went to find Marilyn. She was hiding behind a shrub around the side of the building. I walked over to her, stepping around the red geraniums in the flowerbed.

"How dare you get stoned here?" I said, "after what happened to Girl?"

"I'm not stoned." Marilyn leaned over and heaved into the shrubbery.

"It's the flu, right?"

"I'm dope sick."

"That's what I said."

"Withdrawal," said Marilyn and she heaved again, hanging onto the corner of the building. "Three days. If you'd just kill me now, I'd be near a coffin. I'd appreciate the fucking lie-down."

"That's great," I said, patting her on the back.

Marilyn flung her arm back and pushed my hand away. "It's not great, it's terrible, horrible. I hate it. I tried to talk to her, you know. I tried to tell her to quit now, while she still could, but who's going to listen to an old dope hag like me?"

I helped Marilyn back inside. Her new white sneakers were covered in dirt and her face was as red as the geranium petals we'd scattered coming back though the flowerbed. Miss Kesstle was gone. The man in the black suit — Chester, I think — met us in the foyer.

"If you'll follow me," he said, "your companion has gone to the Reposing Room to visit with the deceased. Girl's foster father is in the Arrangement Room if you would care to meet with him first. If you wish to return later, visitation will be from noon until five o'clock this evening. The bereaved will be meeting for the memorial service tomorrow in the Daisy Chapel at two in the afternoon, followed by the graveside service, committal service, and interment at Gardens of Hope cemetery."

"That's way more services than Girl ever got when she was alive," muttered Marilyn.

We went into a small room with heavy gold drapes on three of the walls. Utterly noxious music oozed down from the ceiling. Miss Kesstle stood in the middle of the room, the plastic bag grasped in her hands, an open casket a few feet in front of her.

"We should have brought flowers," she said. "She has no flowers."

"I'll call Mr. H. and ask him to bring some," I said. "Did you ask them about the blanket?"

Miss Kesstle nodded. "The man said he'd check with the foster father."

We approached the dark wood casket together. There's nothing more Goth than lying in a coffin, but Girl wouldn't have been happy. She looked like a perfect young woman having a nap before the prom. They'd removed all of her piercings, painted her face a rosy pink, and curled her hair in ringlets. She wore a pale pink dress with ruffles around the bodice and white lace sleeves.

"She looks — beautiful," I said.

"But not like Girl," said Marilyn. "She looks way too healthy."

"It's not fair," said Miss Kesstle, "a young girl like her lying there and an old woman like me still walking around." She reached out and pushed the curls away from Girl's forehead. "You poor thing," she whispered. "Dorothea Sioux misses you very much. We all miss you very much."

We stood in silence for a moment. I couldn't think of anything to say. Death. No more screwing up for Girl, no more laughing or swearing or wild outfits. I thought of her last box sitting empty outside in the back alley, eventually breaking down in the rain, the pages peeling off and the cardboard disintegrating until it was thrown away in an unrecognizable heap in a dump somewhere.

There was a polite cough from the back of the room. Chester said, "Mr. Edwarg would prefer that the blanket not be placed in the casket. Perhaps Mrs. . . . ."

"Miss Kesstle," I said.

"Right. Miss Kesstle can leave it with us and we will arrange it on the catafalque for the service."

"Arrange it where?" said Miss Kesstle. "I made the blanket for her, to have with her; she loved my crocheting, she made all kinds of things with my doilies."

"We would place the blanket on the stand where the casket will sit during the service," he said.

"Is it possible for us to speak to Mr. Edwarg?" I asked. "Perhaps we could work something out."

Chester tipped his head to the side. "I could try."

"Please do," I said. Marilyn started to breathe heavily beside me. Either she was getting angry or was about to upchuck again. Neither seemed like a good thing.

"Let's follow him," Marilyn said. She took Miss Kesstle's arm and started after him.

I quickly bowed my head. There was a catch in my chest like a deep breath half taken. I couldn't think of a prayer, then, from elementary school assemblies, came the line, *Forgive us our trespasses as we forgive those who trespass against us*. It would have to do. I turned and followed Marilyn and Miss Kesstle.

Chester knocked on a door with a small brass plaque reading "Arrangement Room." He left the door open a bit and we went and stood by it.

"What is it?" said a man's voice. "Things are bad enough without those people showing up."

I walked past Marilyn and into the room. The half a breath of sorrow in my chest swelled into anger and burst into my throat. "What do you mean *those* people? You never looked after Girl for one minute. You just collected your cheque while she slept in a back alley half the night." I addressed a balding man in a drooping grey suit.

"Do I know you?" asked the man.

"If you don't want me to report you for foster care fraud, you'd better let them put this blanket in."

"Me?" said the man. "You were the ones giving her drugs. I should report you."

"You goddamn bonehead, deadbeat —" Marilyn began to sputter.

"Asshole," supplied Miss Kesstle. She had high pink spots on her cheeks.

"What is the matter with you people?" said Mr. Edwarg. He scrutinized us slowly, one by one, as though choosing between us in a police lineup. "We tried *everything* to get Girl to clean up. My wife told her that the door would always be open, she could come home anytime, no matter what. That we'd help her if she wanted." The man's voice trembled. "I don't know what else we could have done. She only had a few months before she was out of the system. . ."

We stood silently. "I'm so sorry," said Miss Kesstle. "We had no idea."

Dance, Gladys, Dance

Chester, having missed the change in tone completely, stepped in front of Marilyn. "Perhaps it's time you *ladies* left. The inside accoutrements have already been chosen."

"Oh yeah?" said Marilyn, "Well you can —" She grabbed my arm, bent forward, and threw up. A puddle of greenish bile formed at her feet and spread out across the floor.

"What the hell!" said Chester. He looked down and grimaced. Marilyn remained doubled over heaving.

Mr. Edwarg began to walk out. "We tried to help her too," I said. "We really did. Miss Kesstle made her the blanket. . ."

"Suit yourself," he said. "Put it with her. None of it makes any difference now." He left the room, looking drained, giving the mess on the floor a wide berth.

Miss Kesstle walked up to Chester and handed him the bag. "Please be sure it's pulled right up to her chin. Girl didn't like to sleep uncovered. I'll check tomorrow to see if you did."

Chester took the bag, still staring mutely at the vomit on the shiny marble tiles.

I helped Marilyn straighten up. Her head lolled to the side. Miss Kesstle took her other arm and we began to walk out.

"Thank you, Chester," I said, "and, for your information, we are *ladies*."

We laid Marilyn down in the backseat of the Chevrolet. She raised her head and looked around. "I haven't been horizontal in the backseat of a car since I was a teenager," she said, then seemed to fall asleep.

"What's the matter with her?" whispered Miss Kesstle.

"Withdrawal," I said. "She's probably got a ways to go yet." I signaled to turn towards Marilyn's hotel.

Miss Kesstle put her hand on my arm. "Bring her to my house," she said. "We can't leave her alone at that terrible place."

"She should be in detox or something. She could get bad."

"I've seen it," said Miss Kesstle. "They cut Mother off her morphine for awhile, afraid she'd get addicted. Why it mattered when she was dying, I'll never know. It's all right."

"I'm dying," said Marilyn. "Can I have morphine?"

"No," said Miss Kesstle and I together.

There was a groan from the backseat. "I don't know if I'm going to make it."

"That's normal," said Miss Kesstle. "None of us knows that."

I began another painting that night, leaning into the smell of the oil paints and breathing between sobs. From paint, canvas, and memory I began to recreate Gladys as she'd been in the theatre. I penciled her in the centre of the stage in her beaded dress. Her long dark hair was swept up away from her face. She was just beginning to take a bow, her feet en pointe, her arms held out behind her, and she was smiling though all the seats in front of her were empty.

As I was slipping into the exhausted sleep of grief, I heard Gladys say, "Is that me?"

"It will be."

"Thank you."

"You're welcome," I whispered and rolled over to speak towards the armchair, though it was too dark to see if she was sitting there.

"I hoped you'd do it," said Gladys. "Mission complete."

"That was it?" I asked. "Just for me to paint? But that's so easy."

"Was it?" said Gladys. "Didn't seem like it to me."

"But why me?"

"Why *not* you?"

"I decided I was a very stupid fool not to at least paint as I wanted to," I whispered to myself softly and with some trepidation. "I'm an artist." I held my breath. Athena, Greek goddess

Dance, Gladys, Dance

of the arts, did not hurl her spear at me and the Hindu arts representative, Saraswati, did not reach down with one of her four arms and el kabong me with her lute. I breathed.

"Who's the Catholic patron saint of the arts?" I asked into the darkness.

"St. Catherine of Bologna."

"Bologna? Seriously?"

"She was a baker for the convent."

"Get outta here." I tried it again, louder this time: "I'm an artist."

"I know," said Gladys matter-of- factly. "Did you buy your toolbelt?"

"My what?"

"You're supposed to start locksmithing school tomorrow."

"Oh yeah," I said, then laughed so hard I cried.

The lady on the phone from the locksmithing school was very nice about withdrawing my registration on the day school started, but informed me they'd be keeping my twenty-five-dollar deposit.

There was a thumping on the front stairs. I went to see. Whitman set his suitcase down by the door and reached to get his jacket from the hook.

"Going home?" I asked.

He put his leather jacket on, reached into the pocket, and placed his dark sunglasses on top of his head. "I have a few projects I need to get back up to speed on. I've already said goodbye to Dad. . ." He turned to face me and hesitated. His angular face softened with a smile. "Thank you, Frieda."

"You too," I said. "Don't worry about the other night. A woman has needs too, you know."

"I know. Take care of everyone."

"Pffft. Are you kidding?"

"Well, see you." He picked up his suitcase and turned to the door.

I walked over, put my hand on his arm, and gave him a quick kiss on the cheek. "Just for the record," I said, "I think Jesus and the Punk Rockers was a good idea." I watched as he went out the door and down the steps and handed his suitcase to the limo driver waiting on the sidewalk. Then he climbed in and closed the door.

I went into the Art Centre the next day to gather up more bird heads to put on eBay. We had five listed and bids were up to sixty-three dollars on one of them already. Not a fortune, but it would supply the Centre with toilet paper for a month or two. I started down the hallway. I could hear the Hootenanny Glee Club beginning a Stan Rogers song. They were rocking, the piano crashing out the chords. *Goddamn them all. I was told we'd cruise the seas for American gold. We'd fire no guns, shed no tears.* I sang along as I made my way to the back room where we'd stored the bird heads. *Now I'm a broken man on a Halifax pier, the last of Barrett's Privateers.*

I stopped at the bulletin board beside the craft room; everything had been cleared off it, but for one index card neatly pinned in the centre. I leaned in.

> Like new camera for sale. Lenses and cases.
> Girl doesn't take photographs anymore.
> She needs the time to sleep. Bring offer. Ph. 335-6743

I stopped singing, my breath caught in my chest. I looked around, half-dreading and half-hoping to see a translucent Girl slouched against the hallway wall. There was a whisper so soft I wasn't sure if it came from outside my head or inside. "You've had your turn."

I exhaled and grinned, imagining some poor git with Girl as a guardian art angel and, as a bonus, advice on the best place to get yourself pierced.

I walked out behind the Art Centre to where the Valiant was parked, a garbage bag of bird heads in each hand. Gladys stood halfway down the alley. "Hey," I called, "you'll never guess who has a posting in there." I gestured with my elbow back towards the Centre. She seemed not to hear me. "Hey!" I called again.

As I watched, her apron faded, her hair darkened, she grew straighter, slimmer, smaller, and the years dropped away, until she was transformed into a young girl in a short green gingham dress with a wide collar and black woollen stockings. It was young Gladys the farm girl. I looked behind her, expecting to see a coop filled with curious chickens, or a stall of bemused cattle, but the downtown alley remained.

I wanted to scoop her up in my arms and run off with her. I wanted to take her away from what would come in her future, to keep her young and unknowing. I took half a foolish step forward, my arms reaching out. Amidst the garbage and the graffiti, wild and sad Czech violin music began to play in the distance. Gladys listened, her head tilted to the side, then suddenly pirouetted, her arms held straight out from her shoulders. With her long dark curls swirling around her face, she danced. Her arms curved and extended, she swayed, bending from side to side, then abandoned herself to the music and turned, kicked, whirled in unschooled motions of delight. Oh, go, Gladys. Go. Dance, Gladys, dance. I laughed aloud and clapped.

The music faded and, as abruptly as she had begun, she stopped. She smiled at me, her face was smooth, but her eyes were those of old Gladys. She already knew what was to come. Raising both small hands to her lips, she blew me a kiss, and disappeared. It was the last time I ever saw her.

I picked up the bags of petrel heads and put them in the trunk of the Valiant, then climbed into the driver's seat and sat for a moment, looking through the windshield at the empty space where Gladys had been. Whirlwind. Velocity. Zenith.

I reefed the door closed, cranked the window down, and set sail.

Acknowledgements

To everyone at NeWest Press including Anne Nothof, Andrew Wilmot, Paul Matwychuk, and Natalie Olsen, it was a pleasure to work with you.

Many thanks to those that were there at the very beginning, believed in me and taught me so much about both writing and life, among them, Sharon Butala, Larry Bauer, and Gloria Sawai.

To all my teachers at MacEwan University, including Curtis Gillespie, Scot Morison, Don McMann, Jannie Edwards, and Leslie Vermeer (oh, the grammar), immeasurable thanks.

To my dear friends, the Banff 2002 *Writing with Style* Group, Terry G., Jackie Hogan, my former fellow students in the PROW program, and all the others throughout the years, much appreciation.

I am forever grateful to Mom and Dad and everyone in my large wonderful family for all your support and kindness.

Finally, and most importantly, to my son, Julian, who's heard too many times, "I'm working right now, Buddy," my thankfulness is endless.

And the music starts playing and a pretty woman in a long gown takes my elbow and steers me off the stage. . .

Cassie Stocks was born in Edmonton, Alberta. She's been a biker chick, a university student, an actress, and a rich man's gardener; she's worked as a waitress, an office clerk, an aircraft cleaner, has raised chickens, and many years ago, she was even the caretaker of a hydroponic pot factory.

In 2002, she was accepted to the Writing with Style workshop at the Banff Centre, where she received support and encouragement from Sharon Butala and the late Gloria Sawai. Upon her return to Edmonton, she quit her job at a steel fabrication plant and applied to the Grant MacEwan Bachelor of Applied Communications in Professional Writing.

Cassie currently lives in Eston, SK, with her son Julian. *Dance, Gladys, Dance* is her first novel.